George Augustus Selwyn, Edward Stanley Roscoe, Helen Clergue

## George Selwyn

His Letters and His Life

George Augustus Selwyn, Edward Stanley Roscoe, Helen Clergue

**George Selwyn**
*His Letters and His Life*

ISBN/EAN: 9783744688888

Printed in Europe, USA, Canada, Australia, Japan

Cover: Foto ©Raphael Reischuk / pixelio.de

More available books at **www.hansebooks.com**

# GEORGE SELWYN

## His Letters and his Life

EDITED BY

E. S. ROSCOE,

AND

HELEN CLERGUE

London

T. FISHER UNWIN

Paternoster Square

—

1899

# PREFACE

IN the histories and memoirs of the eighteenth century the name of George Selwyn often occurs. The letters which he received have afforded frequent and valuable material to the student of the reign of George the Third. A large number of these were published by the late Mr. Jesse in the four volumes entitled "George Selwyn and his Contemporaries." Except, however, that Selwyn was regarded as the first humourist of his time, little was known about him, for scarcely any letters which he wrote had until recently been found. But in the Fifteenth Report of the Historical Manuscript Commission there were printed, amongst a mass of other material, more than two hundred letters from his untiring pen which had been preserved at Castle Howard. No one who has had an opportunity of examining the originals can fail to recognise the skill and labour with which the Castle Howard correspondence of Selwyn— wanting in most instances the date of the year—was arranged by Mr. Kirk on behalf of the Commission.

A correspondence, however, which illustrates vividly phases of an interesting and important period of English history, appeared to be deserving of presentation to the public in a separate volume, and with the explanations necessary to make the allusions in it fully understood. A selection has therefore, in the following pages, been made from the Castle Howard letters. The aim of the editors has been to choose those which appeared most interesting and representative, and to place them in definite groups, supplementing them with such a narrative, remarks, and notes as would, without enveloping the correspondence in a quantity of extraneous material, enable the whole to present the life of Selwyn, and at the same time add another to the pictures of the age in which he lived.

The dates of the letters are those ascribed to them by Mr. Kirk.

The frequently incorrect spelling of proper names has not been altered.

The editors desire cordially to thank Lord Carlisle, not only for the permission to publish this correspondence, but for the kind assistance which he has given in other ways to the undertaking.

E. S. R.

H. C.

*November*, 1899.

# CONTENTS

## CHAPTER I.

## CHAPTER II.

### 1767–1769.

## CHAPTER III.

### 1773–1777 ; 1779 AND 1780.

## CHAPTER IV.

### 1781.

## CHAPTER V.

### 1782.

# NOTE ON ILLUSTRATIONS

Portrait of George Augustus Selwyn at the age of fifty-one :
from a pastelle by Hugh Douglas Hamilton, drawn in
1770. Hamilton, who was an Irish artist of considerable reputation, was at this time working in London.
After a long visit to Italy he returned to Dublin in
1792 and was elected a member of the Royal Hibernian
Academy. This drawing is in the possession of the
Earl of Carlisle at Castle Howard, Yorkshire . *Frontispiece*

Group of George Augustus Selwyn and Frederick, fifth
Earl of Carlisle : from a picture by Sir Joshua Reynolds,
P.R.A. The dog by the side of Selwyn is his favourite,
Râton. Selwyn is dressed in a pale brown coat and
breeches, a red vest trimmed with gold lace, and light
grey stockings ; the Earl of Carlisle in a reddish brown
coat and pale yellow vest. He wears the green ribbon
and star of the Order of the Thistle. This picture was
probably painted about the year 1770, and is in the
possession of the Earl of Carlisle at Castle Howard,
Yorkshire . . . . *Facing page* 28

## TABLE OF DATES.

1719.    Birth.

1739.    Matriculated at Hart Hall, Oxford.

1740.    Clerk of the Irons and Surveyor of Meltings at the Mint.

1742–3.    In Paris ; having gone down from Oxford for a time.

1745.    Finally left Oxford.

1747.    M.P. for Ludgershall.

1751.    Death of father and elder brother.

1754.    M.P. for Gloucester.

1755.    Paymaster of the Works.

1767.    Correspondence with fifth Earl of Carlisle commences.

1779.    Registrar of the Court of Chancery of Barbadoes.

1780.    Loses seat for Gloucester.    M.P. for Ludgershall.

1782.    Loses office of Paymaster of the Works.

1784.    Surveyor-General of Land Revenues of the Crown.

1791.    Death.

Health is the first good lent to men ;
A gentle disposition then :
Next to be rich by no bye ways ;
Lastly with friends t'enjoy our days.
                                    HERRICK.

# GEORGE SELWYN

—◦◦—

## CHAPTER I

### GEORGE SELWYN—HIS LIFE, HIS FRIENDS, AND HIS AGE

DURING the latter half of the eighteenth century no man had more friends in the select society which comprised those who were of the first importance in English politics, fashion, or sport, than George Selwyn. In one particular he was regarded as supreme and unapproachable ; he was the humourist of his time. His *bon mots* were collected and repeated with extraordinary zest. They were enjoyed by Members of Parliament at Westminster, and by fashionable ladies in the drawing-rooms of St. James's. They were told as things not to be forgotten in the letters of harassed politicians. "You must have heard all the particulars of the Duke of Northumberland's entertainment," wrote Mr. Whateley in 1768 to George Grenville, the most hard-working of ministers ; "perhaps you have not heard George Selwyn's *bon mot*."[1] But as usually happens when a man becomes known for his humour jokes were fathered on Selwyn, just as half a century later any number of witticisms were attributed to Sydney Smith which he had never uttered. It was truly remarked of Selwyn at the time of his death : "Many good things he did say, there was no doubt, and many he

[1] Grenville Correspondence, vol. ii. p. 372.

was capable of saying, but the number of good, bad, and
indifferent things attributed to him as *bon mots* for the
last thirty years of his life were sufficient to stock a
foundling hospital for wit." [1]

It is therefore not surprising that Selwyn has been
handed down to posterity as a wit. It is a dismal
reputation. Jokes collected in contemporary memoirs
fall flat after a century's keeping ; the essential of their
success is spontaneity, appropriateness, the appreciation
even of their teller, often also a knowledge among those
who hear them of the peculiarities of the persons whom
they mock. When we read one of them now, we are
almost inclined to wonder how such a reputation for
humour could be gained. Wit is of the present ; preserved for posterity it is as uninteresting as a faded
flower, nor can it recall to us memories sunny or sad.

But Selwyn was a man who while filling a conspicuous
place in the fashionable life of the age was also so intimate
with statesmen and politicians, and so thoroughly lives in
his correspondence, that in following his life we find ourselves one of that singular society which in the last half
of the eighteenth century ruled the British Empire from
St. James's Street.

Selwyn's life, though passed in a momentous age, was
uneventful, but the course of it must be traced.

George Augustus Selwyn, second son of Colonel John
Selwyn, of Matson, in Gloucestershire, and of Mary,
daughter of General Farrington, of Kent, was born on
the 11th of August, 1719. His father, aide-de-camp to
Marlborough and a friend of Sir Robert Walpole, was a
man of character and ability, well known in the courts of
the first and second Georges. Selwyn, however, probably
inherited his wit and his enjoyment of society from his
mother, who was Woman of the Bedchamber to Queen
Charlotte. Horace Walpole writes of her as " Mrs.
Selwyn, mother of the famous George, and herself of
much vivacity, and pretty."

Selwyn's elder brother died in 1751, and grief at his

[1] *Gentleman's Magazine*, 1791, p. 94.

loss seems to have hastened the death of his father, which occurred in the same year.

His sister Albinia married Thomas Townshend, second son of Charles Viscount Townshend. By this marriage the families of Selwyn and Walpole were connected.

The home of the family was at Matson, a village two and a half miles south-east of Gloucester, on the spurs of the Cotswold hills, looking over the Severn valley—once called Mattesdone. There is a good deal of obscurity as to the ownership of the manor in mediæval times, but it appears to have been in the possession of what may popularly speaking be called the family of Mattesdone. The landowner described himself by the place; " Ego Philippus de Mattesdone " are the words of an ancient document preserved among the records of the Monastery of St. Peter at Gloucester.[1]

To come to more recent times, the manor house was built in 1594 by Sir Ambrose Willoughby. From him the estate was purchased in 1597 by Jasper Selwyn, Counsellor at Law, of Stonehouse, who was the fourth in descent from John Selwyn, one of a Sussex family.

In 1751 the direct entail was broken by Colonel Selwyn, and the property was re-entailed on the descendants of his daughter, Mrs. Townshend, though it was left by will to George Selwyn for his life. On his death it devolved on Thomas, Lord Sydney, and has since remained in the possession of the Townshend family.[2] Walpole has given a description of the place in the days when he used to visit it.

"I stayed two days at George Selwyn's house, called Matson, which lies on Robin Hood's Hill; it is lofty enough for an Alp, yet it is a mountain of turf to the very top, has wood scattered all over it, springs that long to be cascades in twenty places of it, and from the summit of it beats even Sir George Lyttleton's views, by having

---

[1] "Historia et Cartularium Monasterii Sancti Petri Gloucestriæ," edited by W. Hart, vol. i. p. 100.
[2] Bigland, " History of Gloucestershire," vol. ii. p. 200.

the city of Gloucester at its foot, and the Severn widening
to the horizon. His house is small, but neat. King
Charles lay here at the siege, and the Duke of York,
with typical fury, hacked and hewed the window-shutters
of his chamber, as a memorandum of his being there.
Here is a good picture of Dudley, Earl of Leicester, in
his later age, . . . and here is the very flower pot and
counterfeit association for which Bishop Sprat is taken up,
and the Duke of Marlborough sent to the Tower. The
reservoirs on the hill supply the city. The late Mr.
Selwyn governed the borough by them, and I believe by
some wine too. . . .

"A little way from the town are the ruins of Lantony
Priory; there remains a pretty old gateway, which G.
Selwyn has begged to erect on the top of his mountain,
and it will have a charming effect" [1]

Selwyn's schooldays were passed at Eton with Gray
and Walpole. In 1739 he became an undergraduate of
Hertford College, Oxford, or Hart Hall as it was called.
It was to Hertford also that later Charles Fox went,
"a college which has in our own day been munificently
re-endowed as a training school of principles and ideas
very different from those ordinarily associated with the
name of its greatest son." Hertford was in the middle
of the eighteenth century a college where the so-called
students neither toiled at books nor at physical exercise.
They passed a short and merry time at the University,
fashioned as nearly as might be on the mode of life of a
man about town. In 1740 he was appointed to the vague-
sounding office of Clerk of the Irons and Surveyor of the
Meltings in the Mint, a sinecure which, after the manner
of the time, required no personal attention from the holder.

Even in those early days Selwyn, who went by the
sobriquet of "Bosky," had many friends—not only among
college boys, but in London society. "You must judge
by what you feel yourself," wrote Walpole to General
Conway, the soldier and statesman, on the occasion of
a severe illness from which Selwyn suffered in 1741, "of

[1] "The Letters of Horace Walpole," vol. ii. p. 354.

what I feel for Selwyn's recovery, with the addition of what I have suffered from post to post. But as I find the whole town have had the same sentiments about him (though I am sure few so strong as myself), I will not repeat what you have heard so much. I shall write to him to-night, though he knows, without my telling him, how very much I love him. To you, my dear Harry, I am infinitely obliged for the three successive letters you wrote me about him, which gave me double pleasure, as they showed your attention for me at a time that you knew I must be so unhappy, and your friendship for him." [1]

But then came an interval in Selwyn's academic career —if such it may be called—since he was certainly in Paris, much in want of money, at the end of 1742 and the beginning of 1743. It is probable that he had gone down from Oxford for some irregularity ; he ultimately was obliged to leave the University for the same reason. For though he re-entered his college in 1744 he only remained there until the following year, when he was sent down for an irreverent jest after dinner, having taken more to drink than was good for him. His friends, especially Sir Charles Hanbury Williams and some in authority at Oxford also, thought that Selwyn was harshly treated. Whether that were so or not this was the end of his University career. It was not a promising beginning of a life, and for some years he was regarded as a good-natured spendthrift. The death of his elder brother and father however in 1751 produced a sense of responsibility, but even before this date he had been endeavouring to regain his father's goodwill. " I don't yet imagine," wrote his friend, Sir William Maynard, shortly before the death of Colonel J. Selwyn, " you are quite established in his good opinion, and if his life is but spared one twelvemonth you may have an opportunity of convincing him you are in earnest in your promises of a more frugal way of life." As too often happens the son had not time in his father's lifetime to regain his good opinion. Certainly Selwyn made no

[1] Horace Walpole to H. S. Conway, Florence, March 25, 1741.

attempt to give up pleasure, though he was bent on it no doubt with a more frugal mind. He was a man of fashion and of pleasure, having his headquarters in London, paying visits now and again to great country houses as Trentham and Croome. To Bath he went as one goes now to the Riviera. In Paris too he delighted ; when in the autumn of 1762 the Duke of Bedford was in France negotiating the treaty which is known in history as the Peace of Paris, it was Selwyn who accompanied the Duchess when she joined her husband. "She sets out the day after to-morrow," wrote Walpole on September 28th, "escorted to add gravity to the Embassy by George Selwyn." After the treaty was completed on February 10th of the following year, as a memento of his visit the Duke presented Selwyn with the pen with which this unpopular document was signed.[1] Indeed in those days he was constantly in Paris, much to the regret of his friends at home—"Do come and live among your friends who love and honour you" wrote Gilly Williams to him in the autumn of 1764, but in spite of their wishes he stayed on throughout the winter in the French capital, and when his friend Carlisle went in 1778 to America as a peace commissioner Selwyn tried to console himself for his absence by a stay in Paris. "George is now, I imagine, squaring his elbows and turning out his toes in Paris," wrote Hare to Carlisle in December of that year. Neither politics nor pleasure could prevent continual and long visits to France.

The charming country estate and house which he had inherited from his father had little attraction for Selwyn, and to the end of his life, if he could not be in town, he preferred Castle Howard, or indeed any house where he would meet with congenial spirits. "This is the second day," he once wrote to Carlisle, "I am come home to dine alone, but so it is, and if it goes on so I am determined to keep a chaplain, for although I do not stand in need of much society, I do not relish being quite alone at this time of day."

[1] Bedford Correspondence, vol. iii. p. 206.

All this time he was a Member of Parliament.    There is a little village of small red cottages with thatched roofs lying among the Wiltshire downs between Savernake Forest and Andover.    It is called Ludgershall, and has a quiet out-of-the-world look.    In the eighteenth century it was a pocket borough, returning two Members to Parliament, and was the property of the Selwyn family.    The representation was as much in their hands as the trees in the adjoining fields.    In 1747 George Selwyn had found it convenient to enter the House of Commons.    In Ludgershall there were no constituents to take him to task ; to be able to go to Westminster when he wished added to the variety of life.    It kept him in touch with the politicians and statesmen of St. James's Street, and it made him a marketable quantity—his price was another sinecure, the place of Paymaster of the Works.    But this he did not receive until he had inherited the family property, which gave him a hold on the city of Gloucester.    For this city he was a Member from 1754 to 1780, when, losing his seat at the general election, he gladly returned to his former constituency.    The seat at Ludgershall was never in the nature of a true political representation, and even when Member for Gloucester Selwyn seems to have attended but little to the House of Commons.    He was one of a legion of sinecurists—a true specimen of the place-man of the age.    Possessed of some political influence, he was able to find in politics a means of increasing his income. It would be absurd to censure him because he was a sinecurist ; he was acting according to the customs of the time.    The man who in the reign of George III. had the opportunity of obtaining posts which carried with them salaries and no duties would have been regarded as Quixotic if he had thrown such opportunities away.    In this Selwyn is thoroughly representative of his time, and his frequent anxiety lest he should be deprived of his offices is indicative of an apprehension which was felt by many others.

Yet, sinecurist as he was, Selwyn often regarded his

position as a hard necessity, especially when he was driven into the country to look after his constituents. He would then heartily wish himself out of Parliament : the sorrows of a sinecurist might well be the title of some of the letters written from Matson.

Selwyn's was a life devoid of stirring incidents, and from the date at which his correspondence with Lord Carlisle begins the course of his days is indicated in his letters. It is sufficient, therefore, to state that he died at his house in Cleveland Row, St. James's, on the 25th of January, 1791, still a Member of Parliament, in the place where his life had been passed and among his innumerable friends.

In one sense his life had been solitary, for he was never married ; but an unusual love for the young which was a charming and remarkable characteristic, singularly opposed to many of his habits, had been centred on the child whom he called Mie Mie,[1] the daughter of an Italian lady, the Marchesa Fagniani, who was for some time in England with her husband. The origin of Selwyn's interest in the child is obscure, but the story of his affection is striking and unusual.

From a letter written by the Marchesa Fagniani to Selwyn in 1772 it is evident that Mie Mie, then about a year old, had been with him for some months, and in 1774 Lord Carlisle congratulates him upon the certainty of the child's remaining with him. The first mention of her in these letters occurs under date of July 23, 1774, where we have a picture of Selwyn, drawn by himself. He is sitting on his steps, the pretty, foreign-looking child in his arms, pleased at the attention she attracts. When she was four she was taken to pay visits with him ; but it is difficult at this time to know if he or the Earl of March had charge of her.

[1] Maria Fagniani (1771–1856). She was married in 1792, the year after Selwyn's death, to the Earl of Yarmouth, afterwards third Marquis of Hertford. She led a life of pleasure (1802–7), travelling on the continent with the Marshal Androche. She had three children, and died at Rue Tailbout, Paris.

Such interest in a young child naturally occasioned remark in London society, and the question of her paternity has never been clearly settled; in the gossip of the time both the Duke of Queensberry and Selwyn were said to be her father. The characters of the two men, however, and various points in their correspondence, seem to fix this relation upon the Duke of Queensberry. Selwyn's interest was that of a man who though without children had a strong and unusual affection for the young. He looked forward to the pleasure her development and education would be to him, and to the solace of her companionship in old age. She enlisted his sympathy and devotion. From the first time he saw her he wished to adopt her, and until the end of his life she was first in his thought, and all his circle approved of his little friend.

He soon made provision for her in his will, writing to Lord Carlisle July 26, 1774, that he must no longer delay in securing her future. In 1776 he placed her at school. After infinite trouble, Campden House was chosen, where every day he either saw her or received communications from the schoolmistress relative to her health, comfort, and happiness.

" Mrs. Terry presents her compliments to Mr. Selwyn; has the pleasure to assure him that dear Mademoiselle Fagniani is as well to-day as her good friend could possibly wish her to be. She is this minute engaged in a party at high romps."

" Mrs. Terry presents her best compliments to Mr. Selwyn ; is very sorry to find that he is so uneasy. The dear child's spirits *are not* depressed. She is very lively ; ate a good dinner ; and behaves just like other children. She hopes Mr. Selwyn will make no scruple of coming to-morrow morning, or staying his *hour*, or more if he likes it ; she will then talk to him about the head ; but in the meantime begs he will not suppose that the dear child suffers by his absence, or that anything is neglected ; for if Mrs. Terry thought Mr. Selwyn could suppose such a thing, she would wish to resign the charge. She begs he will come to-morrow."

Mie Mie was a disturbing element, if also a satisfaction, in Selwyn's life, for at all times overhanging present pleasure in her company was the dread of losing her. In August of 1776 the Marchesa Fagniani and her husband came to England. Selwyn had a fairly satisfactory interview, in which it was settled that the child should not leave him for a year. Before the time had expired he was exhausting every means to procure a longer delay; he even applied to the Austrian Ambassador that the Governor of Milan should use his influence with the family; but her return was insisted upon, and in August of 1777 Mie Mie left England to join her parents in Paris. The most careful and elaborate arrangements were made by Selwyn for her safety and comfort while travelling, and a list of the houses where stops were to be made given to faithful attendants.

He dreaded however the pain of parting with the child, and when the day of her departure arrived he absented himself to avoid the farewell, and his spirits and health suffered from her loss. Two months later Carlisle writes, " I never thought your attachment extraordinary. I might, for your sake, have wished it less in the degree; but what I did think extraordinary was that you would never permit what was most likely to happen ever to make its appearance in your perspective. March speaks with great tenderness and real compassion for your sufferings. Have you been at Lady Holland's? Are you in my house? Do not stay too long at Frognal; change the scene; it will do you good. Gratify every caprice of that sort, and write to me everything that comes into your head. You cannot unload your heart to any one who will receive its weight more cheerfully than I shall do."

But next year we hear of Selwyn at Milan negotiating with Mie Mie's relatives for her return. His proposals to make settlements on her met with alternate rebuffs and promises that kept him in a state of intermingled fear and hope. He was finally put off with the understanding that she should return to him in the spring ; and in October he turned homeward.

In the spring it was arranged that the Marchesa Fagniani should bring Mie Mie to Paris to be left a few weeks in a convent before Selwyn should claim her. The meeting did not take place without a last trial of patience for him. He arrived in Paris in April, expecting to find the little traveller, but he was informed that the departure from Milan had been delayed for a few days ; this was followed by the news of a change of plans, and that Selwyn must go to Lyons to meet the child, who would be conducted there by her mother—a meeting Selwyn had wished to avert. Eventually, early in May, we read the congratulations of his friends on the restoration of what had become dearest to him in the world.

During the month Selwyn spent in Paris, however, waiting for Mie Mie, who was passing the specified time in the convent, fresh difficulties were raised, and he began to doubt if he should ever bring the little girl to England. His health was seriously affected by the strain, and his friends begged him to give up a pursuit which was injuring it and taking him from them ; but Mie Mie was at last received from the convent under a vague condition that at some future time she should return to it ; a half promise which neither side expected would be fulfilled.

The Rev. Dr. Warner gives us a slight description of Mie Mie. A year had passed ; she is nine years old ; he is writing to Selwyn :—

"That freshness of complexion I should have great pleasure in beholding. It must add to her charms, and cannot diminish the character, sense, and shrewdness which distinguish her physiognomy, and which she possesses in a great degree, with a happy engrafting of a high-bred foreign air upon an English stock . . .

"But how very pleasant to me was your honest and naïve confession of the joy your heart felt at hearing her admired ! It is, indeed, most extraordinary that a certain person [1] who has great taste—would he had as much nature !—should not see her with very different eyes from what he does. I can never forget that naïve expression of Mme. de Sévigné, ' *Je ne sais comment l'on fait de ne pas aimer sa fille.*' "

But Selwyn was never quite free from the fear that she should be taken from him. In January, 1781, he writes to Lord Carlisle :—

"From Milan things are well ; at least, no menaces from thence of any sort, and I am assured, by one who is the most intimate friend of the Emperor's minister there, that he was much more likely to approve than to disapprove of Mie Mie's being with me, knowing as he does the turn and character of the mother."

The relationship from this time was more settled, and as Mie Mie grew into womanhood she became to Selwyn a delightful and affectionate companion.

Selwyn was a universal friend ; he was equally at home with politicians, *dilettanti*, and children ; he was a man of such consistent good nature, so unaffectedly kind-hearted, that every one, statesman, gambler, or schoolboy, liked to be in his company. Yet among Selwyn's many friends and acquaintances two groups are remarkable. The first was formed of men of his own age—Walpole, Edgecumbe, Gilly Williams, and Lord March comprise what may be called the Strawberry Hill group. It was at Walpole's famous villa that they liked best to meet, and it is by Reynolds that Walpole's " out-of-town party " has been handed down to us.[2] They were an odd coterie—cultivated, artificial, gossiping. None of them ever married ; to do so seemed to have been unfashionable, if not unpopular ; and when we see the results of many marriages among their friends, they were

---

[1] The Duke of Queensberry.

[2] The group of Selwyn, Edgecumbe, and Williams which was painted for Horace Walpole in 1781, and subsequently became the property of the late Lord Taunton, now belongs to his daughter, the Hon. Mrs. Edward Stanley, and is at Quantock Lodge, Bridgwater. It is a charming and interesting picture. A replica by Sir J. Reynolds, the property of Lord Cadogan, is at Chelsea House.

best, perhaps, as bachelors. They considered themselves
free to act as they pleased ; and this freedom became
notorious by the life-long dissipation of March, and by
the free living of Edgecumbe, who died at forty-five after
a life misspent at the gaming-table. That he possessed
a bright mind and ingenious wit is proved by his verses
and by the estimate of his friends. The amusing coat of
arms which the friends designed for White's Club was
painted by him, while he was one of the first to recognise
the genius of Reynolds.

The other group was of a younger generation, more
brilliant and more modern. They might not inappro-
priately be called the Fox group, since his personality
was so conspicuous among them. They talked politics
and gambled at Brooks's, they appreciated each other's
brightness, and lost their money with the indifference of
true friends. There was the gallant and charming soldier
Fitzpatrick, the schoolfellow and friend of Fox, the
sagacious and versatile but place-seeking Storer. Hare,
who, less well-born, had risen by his wit and talents to a
place among the cleverest men of the time, " the Hare
with many friends," as he was called by the Duchess of
Gordon. Frederick, Earl of Carlisle and Crawford, the
" *petit Craufurt* " of Mme. du Deffand ; and chief of
all was Charles Fox, who to Selwyn was incomprehensible. Selwyn had been his father's friend, and had
known him from childhood. He loved him and liked
his companionship ; yet his unrestrained folly at the
gambling-table and on the racecourse, his loose ideas on
money matters, and his political opinions, at times annoyed,
irritated, and puzzled him almost beyond endurance.
With the older and the younger group Selwyn was
on the same terms of intimate friendship : now pleasing
by his wit, and now helping by his kindness and common
sense.

Castle Howard was the place, outside London, which
most attracted him. It is even to-day a long way from the
metropolis, and one feels something like surprise that such
a lover of the town as Selwyn could, even to the end of

his life, undertake the tiresome journey to Yorkshire. But in the stately galleries of Vanbrugh's design he renewed his associations with France. There he was not bored by country society; in the home circle he had all the company he needed. He could look out over the rolling uplands and see the distant wolds, contented to observe and enjoy them from afar amidst the books and pictures which his host had collected. If he wanted exercise the spacious gardens were at hand, and the artificial adornment of temples and statuary pleased a taste highly cultivated after the fashion of the times.

In a drawing-room Selwyn was as welcome as in a club, and he could only be said to be out of place in his own country house, more especially at the time of an election for Gloucester. The modern love of landscape, of country life as an æsthetic pleasure, was unknown to him. Civilisation, refinement, seemed to him to be confined to London and Paris, to Bath or Tunbridge Wells. "Now *sto per partire*, and I ought in point of discretion to set out to-morrow, but I dare say 'twill be Friday evening before I'll have the courage to throw myself off the cart. But then go I must ; for on Monday our Assizes begin, and how long I shall stay the Lord knows, but I hope in God not more than ten days at farthest, for I find my aversion to that part of the world greater and more insufferable every day of my life, and indeed have no wish to be absent from home but to go to Castle Howard, which I hope that I shall not delay many days after my return from Gloucestershire " (August 2, 1774). A week later he had arrived at his home. "The weather is very fine, and Matson in as great beauty as a place can be in, but the beauties of it make very little impression upon me ; in short, there is nothing in the eccentric situation in which I am now that can afford me the least pleasure, and everything I love to see in the world is at a distance from me " (August 9, 1774).

To-day such a man as Selwyn would have had a choice collection of water colours ; he would be ashamed if he could not appreciate the tone and tenderness of an English landscape. But though a friend of Reynolds and of Romney, though he commissioned and appreciated Gainsborough, and valued the masterpieces of the past, in a word, was essentially a man of culture, yet this phase of modern refinement was utterly unknown to him.

As a politician Selwyn, as has already been said, was a sinecurist ; he never took a political interest in affairs of state, and he looked at events which have become historical from an unpolitical point of view. But though he writes of parliamentary incidents as a spectator, there is always in his letters a personal characterisation which gives them vividness and life. For his long parliamentary career brought Selwyn continually into contact with many varied personalities of several political generations. When he entered the House of Commons Henry Pelham was Prime Minister, and the elder Pitt had not yet formed that coalition with the Duke of Newcastle which enabled him to command a majority in the House of Commons and to be the greatest War Minister of the century. When Selwyn died, still a Member of Parliament, the younger Pitt was Prime Minister and the French Revolution had upset that old *régime* which Selwyn had known so well. In his time Pelham, Newcastle, Bute, Grenville, Chatham, Grafton, North, Rockingham, Shelburne, and Portland were successively heads of administrations : of some of these, and of many who served under them, Selwyn was a friend. Of the political and personal life of every one of them he had been an interested spectator. There was no man of the age who had a longer period of parliamentary observation and of personal association with the leading politicians of the time.

But this intimacy with political personages never impressed him with the importance of political office. " You will not believe it, perhaps," he once wrote to Lady Carlisle when he had been asked to meet Pitt at dinner, " but a minister of any description, though served up in his great shell of power, and all his green fat about him, is to me a dish by no means relishing, and I never knew but one in my life I could pass an hour with pleasantly, which was Lord Holland." Cabinet Ministers of the eighteenth century belonged to a single section of society, which included every one of note and every one in it knew their faults and their failings ; they were not afraid of offending constituents or of being lectured in leading articles. Thus their littleness, rather than their greatness, was apt to impress a daily observer like Selwyn, and to give to his remarks an aspect of depreciation and of pessimism.

That Selwyn was a gossip, no one knew better than himself, and he has incurred the censure of Sir George Trevelyan for repeating tittle-tattle, as he calls it, about Fox and his gambling. But posterity desires to see the real Fox, not an ideal statesman—to see a man as he lived, not only a political figure. Looking back for more than a century we may very well appreciate to the full Fox's great qualities and yet be aware of his weaknesses and his vices, in which he showed the strength of a passionate and virile character in contact with certain characteristics of the society of the age. Instead, therefore, of blaming Selwyn for repeating to correspondents the minor incidents of the time, we ought to be thankful to him for enabling us to picture so many of the leading personages of that day as they were. If we look to a period before or after that of Selwyn, we see an immortal gossip in Pepys, and in Greville another who will be read after the works of eminent historians have been put on upper shelves as out of date. The detailing of the minor facts of life without malice and with absolute truth enables posterity to form a sound judgment on a past age.

Among the amusements of the society in which Selwyn delighted was one which now seems both morbid and cruel —that of attending the execution of those condemned to capital punishment. Even to his friends and immediate successors, no less than to those who have written of him, the fact that a man so full of kindness, who took pleasure in the innocent companionship of children, could with positive eagerness witness the hanging of a thief at Tyburn, has been a cause of surprise.

When one is conversant with the history of the time the astonishment is ridiculous. The sight of a man on the gallows no more disturbed the serenity of the most good-natured of men at the end of the eighteenth century than do the dying flutters of a partridge the susceptibilities of the most cultured of modern sportsmen. Selwyn was ever trying to get as much amusement out of life as possible, and he would have been acting contrary to all the ideas of the fashionable society of his age if he had sat at home when a criminal was to die. It was said of Boswell, just as it was of Selwyn, that he was passionately fond of attending executions. We need not therefore be surprised that Selwyn did as others of his time. Gilly Williams was a kind and good-natured man, yet we find him writing to Selwyn :—

" Harrington's porter was condemned yesterday. Cadogan and I have already bespoken places at the Braziers, and I hope Parson Digby will come time enough to be of the party. I presume we shall have your honour's company, if your stomach is not too squeamish for a single serving."

Another friend, Henry St. John, begins a letter to Selwyn by telling how he and his brother went to see an execution. " We had a full of view of Mr. Waistcott as he went to the gallows with a white cockade in his hat." Not to be wanting in the ordinary courtesies of the time, Selwyn's correspondent presently remarks, as one nowadays would do of a day's grouse-shooting : " I hope you have had good sport at the Place de Grève, to make up for losing the sight of so notorious a villain as Lady Harrington's porter. *Mais laisons la ce discours triste*, and let us talk of the living and lively world." Selwyn made his world brighter by his wit and pleasantries, and the sight of an execution did not depress his spirits. " With his strange and dismal turn," wrote Walpole, " he has infinite fun and humour in him." [1] And the author

[1] Letters, vol. ii. p. 315.

3

of a social satire blunted his thrusts at Selwyn by a long
explanatory note which concludes with the remark that
" George is a humane man." [1]

It was Selwyn's fate—and in every generation we find
some one of whom the same may be said—to have his
characteristics or foibles exaggerated. It occurred to him
in regard to witticisms and the sight of executions ; he
did not complain of this, for he knew it would be useless,
but he disliked to be regarded as an habitual jester or as
possessing an unnatural taste for horrors. [2]

But another and more widespread habit is often
referred to in his letters. The gambling which Selwyn
disapproved, but indulged in for years, is constantly
alluded to in his correspondence. The hold which this
vice had upon nearly every one who regarded himself
as belonging to the best society of London has never
been more clearly and vividly depicted than in Selwyn's
letters. It was the protest—always varying, always
taking new forms, but always present—against the
monotony of life. Fortunes were nightly lost at
Brooks's and White's, and substantial sums were gambled
away by ladies of position and of fashion in the most
exclusive drawing-rooms in order to kill time. Selwyn
himself was a sagacious and careful man ; but he was nevertheless a moderate gambler ; he always perceived the folly
of it ; and yet, for a great many years, he was constantly
risking part of by no means a large fortune. The green
table was the Stock Exchange and turf of the time, men
and women frequented the clubs and drawing-rooms where
the excitement of gambling could be enjoyed as they now
flock to the race-course or telegraph to their brokers

---

[1] " The Diaboliad," p. 18. See post pp. 114, 115.

[2] " George, as soon as the King had spoken to him, withdrew and
went away, the King then knighted the ambitious squire. The King
afterwards expressed his astonishment to the groom-in-waiting that Mr.
Selwyn should not stay to see the ceremony, observing that it looked
so like an execution that he took it for granted Mr. Selwyn would
have stayed to see it. George heard of the joke, but did not like it :
he is, on that subject, still very sore " (" Journals and Correspondence
of Lord Auckland," vol. ii. p. 210).

in Throgmorton Street.   The nobleman now enjoys his
pleasure side by side with the publican, and his example
is followed by his servants on the course.   Gambling in
Selwyn's time was more select—a small society governed
England and gambled in St. James's Street, while in more
democratic days peers, members, and constituents pursue
the same excitement together on the race-course or in the
City.   Great as were the sums which were lost at commerce, hazard, or faro, they were less than the training-
stable, the betting-ring, and the stock-jobber now consume;
and the same influences which have destroyed the Whig
oligarchy and the King's friends have changed and en-
larged the manner and the habit of gambling in England.

Of Selwyn the humourist it would be easy to collect
pages of witticisms.   Walpole's letters alone contain
dozens of them, and there is not a memoir of the
eighteenth century in which is not to be found one of
" George's " jokes.   Though often happy, as when seeing
Mr. Ponsonby, the Speaker of the Irish Parliament,
parting freely with bank-notes at Newmarket, he remarked, " How easily the Speaker passes the money
bills," or, as when Lord Foley crossed the Channel to
avoid his creditors, he drily observed that it was " a
passover not much relished by the Jews," yet their
repetition now is tiresome.

Manner and appearance assisted his wit, an impassive
countenance hid his humour so that his sallies surprised
by their unexpectedness.   He knew how to appropriate
opportunity, and saw the humour of a situation.   A
reputation for wit is thus gained not only by what is
said, but by the mere indication of the ridiculous.   This it
is impossible to reproduce, and the celebrity of Selwyn
as a wit must be allowed to rest on the opinion of his
contemporaries.

" Je suis bien éloignée," wrote Madame du Deffand, in
1767, who, of those who knew him, has left us the most
finished portrait, " de croire M. Selwyn stupide, mais il
est souvent dans les espaces imaginaires.   Rien ne le
frappe ni le réveille que le ridicule, mais il l'attrape en

volant ; il a de la grâce et de la finesse dans ce qu'il dit mais il ne sais pas causer de suite ; il est distrait, indifférent ; il s'ennuiérait souvent sans une très bonne recette qu'il à contre l'ennui, c'est de s'endormir quand il veut. C'est un talent que je lui envie bien ; si je l'avais, j'en ferais grand usage. Il est malin sans être mechant ; il est officieux, poli ; hors son milord March, il n'aime rien : on ne saurait former aucune liaison avec lui, mais on est bien aise de l'encontrer, d'être avec lui dans le même chambre, quoi qu' on n'ait rien a lui dire." [1]

There is a popular idea that in the eighteenth century England and France were essentially hostile nations, immemorial enemies, yet at no time had there been more sympathy between two sections of society than there existed between the governing and fashionable men and women of Paris and London ; in literature, art, and dress they held the same opinions. Englishmen braved the Channel and underwent the fatigue and trouble of the two land journeys with cheerfulness in order to enjoy the society of St. Germain. They were received not as strange travellers, but as valued friends.

Of this francophile feeling of the eighteenth century Selwyn was the most remarkable example. He was as much at home in the salon of Mme. du Deffand, or at one of President Henault's famous little dinners, as in the drawing-room of Holland House or the card-room at Brooks's. He introduced Walpole and Crawford to French society, adding to the social and literary connection between Paris and London during a time when political ties were broken. He was a favourite, too, with the French Queen.[2]   Under date of February 10, 1764, the Earl of March writes to him from Fontainebleau : "The Queen asked Madame de Mirepoix—*si elle n'avoit pas beaucoup entendu medire de Monsieur Selwyn et elle ? Elle a repondu, oui, beaucoup, Madame. J'en suis bien aise, dit la Reine.*"

[1] "Correspondance complète de Mme. du Deffand," vol. i. p. 87.
[2] Maria Leschitinskey, daughter of Stanislaus, King of Poland, and Queen of Louis XV.

The correspondence of Mme. du Deffand contains frequent allusions to the intimacy between the first English and French society of the period.   David Hume, Lord Ossory, Lady Hervey, Lord March, the Duke of York,[1] and other well-known English names, are mingled with Rousseau, Voltaire, d'Alembert, and the Duc and Duchesse de Choiseul.   This oddly assorted company moves in the world of M. de Maurepas and of the Duc d'Aiguillon, and is seen in the charming salons of Mme. Geoffrin and Mme. d'Épinay ; the beauty of Lady Pembroke is commented on, the charm of Lady Sarah Bunbury analysed, Lady Grenville eulogised.

There is an irresistible fascination in the study of the men and women of the eighteenth century of France and England ; they, their manners and customs, have disappeared for ever, but Gainsborough's gracious women, Sir Joshua Reynolds's charming types, and Romney's sensitive heads, have in England immortalised the reign of beauty of this period ; in France the elegance and grace of the time are shown in the canvases of Greuze, Vanloo, and Fragonard, in the cupids and doves and garlands which adorned the interiors of Mme. de Pompadour.

It was a time of great intellectual development and progress in both countries.   It was the epoch of the salons, of the philosophers and encyclopædists, of a brilliant society whose decadence was hidden in a garb of seductive gaiety, its egotism and materialism in a magnificent apparelling of wit and learning.   Literary standing in France at once gave the *entrée* to society of the highest rank and to circles the most exclusive.   David Hume, whose reputation as philosopher and historian, had been already established there, was received with enthusiasm when he accompanied Lord Hertford to Paris as Secretary of Embassy, though his manner, dress, and speech were awkward and uncouth ; but his good-humoured simplicity was accepted and appreciated as was

[1] Edward, Duke of York (1739–1767), brother of George III., visited Paris the summer of 1767, on his way to Italy, where he died Sept. 17th.

his learning.   He had begun in England a correspondence with the Comtesse de Boufflers, he was made welcome too in the salons of Mme. Geoffrin and of Mlle. de Lespinasse, and he soon became intimate with d'Alembert and Turgot.   His reception was no less cordial at court, where the children of the Dauphin met him, prepared with polite little speeches about his works.   He had such admiration for Rousseau that he brought him to England, assisting him there in spite of Horace Walpole's ill-natured jest on the flight of the susceptible French philosopher.

During Burke's visit to Paris in 1773 he was often present at Mme. du Deffand's supper parties, who said that although he spoke French with difficulty he was most agreeable ; here and at other salons he met the encyclopædists and obtained the insight into French morals and philosophy which, in his case, strengthened conservative principles.

When "Clarissa Harlowe" appeared in Paris, the book created a sensation and was more talked of there than in England.   Diderot compared Richardson, as the father of the English novel, to Homer, father of epic poetry. In England men of letters were far less recognised in society.   Walpole remarked, "You know in England we read their works, but seldom or never take notice of authors.   We think them sufficiently paid if their books sell, and of course leave them in their colleges and obscurity, by which means we are not troubled with their vanity and impatience."   But Walpole overdrew the picture, for though literature did not hold the place in London that it did in Paris, yet wit was never more appreciated, and learning added to the equipment of the first of the fine gentlemen of the time.   Of this unique state of society and of international friendliness Selwyn and his friends were the products.   We cannot too clearly realise them as types which can never recur.

The secret of Selwyn's charm lies in the contrasts of his character ; his versatility and cosmopolitan sympathies attract us now as they attracted in his lifetime men very different in habits, pursuits, and mind.

The first Lord Holland, Horace Walpole, the Duke of Queensberry, each a type of the society of the eighteenth century ; the unscrupulous politician, the cultivated amateur and man of letters, the sportsman with half the opera dancers in London in his pay—of all he was the closest friend.  The most intimate of them, the Duke of Queensberry, led an extravagant and a dissipated life, in contrast with which Selwyn's was homely and simple. He could leave the gambling table of the club to play with Mie Mie or a schoolboy from Eton ; while his friends were crippled by dice and cards and became seekers after political places by which they might live, he was prudent in his play and neither ruined himself nor others.

He had a self-control and a sound sense, which were not common in his generation ; we see them in the tranquil, contemplative eyes of Reynolds's portraits, ready in a moment to gleam with humour.  By reason of his unfailing good-nature, he was always at the service of a friend.  Himself without ambition, he watched men, not possessed of his tact and ability, rise to positions which he had never the least desire to fill.  In an age of great political bitterness and the strongest personal antagonism he continued the tranquil tenor of his way, amused and amusing, hardly ever put out except by the illness or the misfortune of a friend.  "George Selwyn died this day se'night," wrote his friend Storer to Lord Auckland ; "a more good-natured man or a more pleasant one never, I believe, existed.  The loss is not only a private one to his friends, but really a public one to society in general." [1] Gaiety of temperament and sound sense, a quick wit and a kind heart, sincerity and love of society, culture without pedantry, a capacity to enjoy the world in each stage of life : these are seldom found united in one individual as they were in George Selwyn, and he is thus for us perhaps the pleasantest personality of English society in the eighteenth century.

[1] "Journal and Correspondence of Lord Auckland," vol. ii. p. 383.

# CHAPTER II

## 1767–1769

### THE CORRESPONDENCE COMMENCES

Frederick, fifth Earl of Carlisle—Lady Sarah Bunbury—The Duke of
Grafton—Carlisle, Charles Fox, and the Hollands abroad—
Current events—Card-playing—A dinner at Crawford's—Lady
Bolingbroke—Almack's—The Duke of Bedford—Lord Clive—
The Nabobs—Corporation of Oxford sell the representation of
the borough—Madame du Deffand—Publication of Horace
Walpole's " Historic Doubts on Richard the Third " —Newmarket
—London Society—Gambling at the Clubs—A post promised to
Selwyn—Elections—A purchase of wine—Vauxhall.

IN the chapter which contains the earliest of Selwyn's
letters to Frederick, Earl of Carlisle,[1] something must
be said of the correspondence itself. It was begun in
1767, and most of the letters which Selwyn wrote to Lord
and Lady Carlisle from that date to his death have been
preserved at Castle Howard. The collection is in
many respects unique. It records a great number of
facts, many no doubt small and in themselves unim-
portant, which, however, in the aggregate form a lifelike

---

[1] FREDERICK, FIFTH EARL OF CARLISLE.

1748. Born.
1769. Married Lady Caroline, daughter of Lord Gower.
1777. Treasurer of Household.
1778. Commissioner to America.
1779. Lord of Trade and Plantations.
1780. Lord Lieutenant of Ireland.
1782. Lord Steward.
1783. Lord Privy Seal.
1825. Died.

picture of English society in the eighteenth century. The letters are written in the bright and unaffected manner which Madame de Sévigné, whose style Selwyn so much admired, had introduced in France. Filled with human interest and easily expressed, they differ materially from Walpole's letters in that they are characterised by a greater simplicity, and a less egotistical tone. They show a keener interest in his correspondent. There is in them a delightful frankness, an unconventional freshness. Walpole's correspondence, invaluable as it is, always bears traces of the preparation which we know that it received. But Selwyn, with a light touch, wrote the thoughts and impressions of the moment, never for effect. Walpole was often thinking of posterity, Selwyn always of his friends, who were numberless and who were in their time frequently his correspondents. How numerous Selwyn's letters must have been we know from the number to him which have been published; but with the exception of those which have fortunately been preserved at Castle Howard, his appear to have perished.

The frequent French interpolations with which his letters are interspersed now strike us as affectations. They were, however, a fashion of the day; nor should we forget that Selwyn spent so much of his life in Paris that the language came to him as easily as his own.

In 1767 Selwyn and Carlisle had not long been friends. "Don't lead your new favourite Carlisle into a scrape," wrote Gilly Williams to Selwyn in the previous year. The words were written without serious intent, but they are noticeable because they are so opposite to the whole course of the rising friendship. The relations of the two men were remarkable.

It has been well said of Selwyn by a statesman of to-day that he was a good friend, a fact never better exemplified than in his friendship with Carlisle. In his affairs he took a greater interest than would be expected of the nearest of relatives, and with this he united a singularly warm and open-hearted affection not only for Carlisle but for his family. It lasted to the day of his death. There was between them, as Pitt said of his relations with Wilberforce, a tie of affection and friendship—simple and ingenuous and unbreakable.

The nobleman who has been referred to simply as Lord Carlisle had many of the qualities that mark a leader of men. He did not attain, however, to the eminence as a statesman, man of letters, or in society which had once been expected of him.

He succeeded to the earldom when ten years of age, following a father who had shown no disposition for any activities beyond those of a respectable country gentleman. His grandfather, Charles, third Earl of Carlisle, had, however, filled an important place in his day. His local influence in the North was great, and he was a man of sufficient capacity and ambition to become a personage of some position in politics and at court.

There was never a time in English history when the possession of an ancient name and wide estates gave greater opportunities for taking a large share in public affairs than when the fifth Earl attained his majority. It was natural, therefore, that a young man who was recognised by his friends as above the average should be regarded as a person of unusual political promise.

In 1775 an offer was made to him of the sinecure post of Lord of the Bedchamber. He declined it, on the openly declared ground that the position of an official at Court was such as "damps all views of ambition which might arise from that quarter." But in 1778 there came an opportunity of satisfying his public spirit and ambition by crossing the Atlantic as a peace commissioner to America.

It is a curious historical fact that this mission appears to have been partially, if not entirely, originated by Carlisle himself. The story of its inception and the outlines of its progress are told by Carlisle in a letter preserved at Castle Howard, which he addressed to his friend and former tutor, Mr. Ekins. It is doubtful if the King ever really hoped or intended that Carlisle's mission should have a successful issue. It ended, as history has told, in absolute failure.    Carlisle returned home with the barren honour of good intentions.

The trying work which he had undertaken entitled Carlisle, however, to posts of importance at home, and he subsequently filled the high office of Lord-Lieutenant of Ireland, under the administration of Lord North.    When on the resignation of Lord Shelburne, in the year 1783 the memorable and short-lived coalition between Fox and North was formed, Carlisle became one of the Cabinet as Lord Privy Seal.    With the fall of the Ministry on Fox's India Bill in the same year, Carlisle's official life ended.    No public man who attains to Cabinet rank can be regarded as a failure, and it may be that he was satisfied with what he had achieved by the age of five-and-thirty.    With a versatility and serenity rare among those who have once felt the pleasure and excitement of political power and responsibility, he turned to literature, and at Castle Howard and Naworth he produced poems and dramas which, in spite of Byron's sharp attack, who thus avenged himself for the inattention of his guardian on his entrance to public life,[1] though they have had no posthumous fame, gave him a reputation in his day as a man of letters, which was probably a higher satisfaction than would have been the rewards of a political career alone.    And it threw him into closer connection with men of literary and artistic tastes and aims.    Of his writings the poem addressed to Reynolds on his resignation of the Presidency of the Royal Academy is perhaps that which is best worth recollecting.    Carlisle's cultivated mind made him always a liberal patron, and at the sale of the celebrated Orleans collection of paintings he bought the greater part.

Selwyn's letters open with the departure of Lord Carlisle for the Continent.    The young peer was then not quite twenty, but had fallen desperately in love with Lady Sarah Bunbury.    This beautiful and attractive

[1] Carlisle and Byron were not only guardian and ward, but were nearly related ; it is a singular fact that Carlisle declined to introduce him in the House of Lords.

woman had half London at her feet, including the King. For obvious constitutional reasons it was impossible for him to marry her, but day after day the town told how he used to ride to and fro in front of Holland House to catch a glimpse of Lady Sarah. At the drawing room after the royal marriage, at which, by the wish of the King, she was first bridesmaid, Lord Westmoreland, who was an adherent of the Stuarts, knelt to Lady Sarah, mistaking her for the Queen. Selwyn said " the lady in waiting should [must] have told him that she was the Pretender." [1]

Paris was no more able to resist her than London. " Votre milady Sarah a en un succès prodigieux ; toute notre belle jeunesse en a eu la tête tournée, sans la trouver fort jolie, toutes les principantés et les divinités du temple l'ont recherchée avec une grande émulation. Je ne l'ai point vue assez de suite pour avoir pu bien démêler ce qu'on doit pensez d'elle ; je la trouve aimable, elle est douce, vive et polie. Dans notre nation elle passerait pour être coquette. Je ne crois pas qu'elle le soit ; elle aime à se divertir ; elle a pu être flattée de tous les empressements qu'on lui a marquées, et je soupçonne qu'elle s'y est livrée plus pour l'apparence que par un goût véritable. Je lui ai soupçonné quelques motifs cachées, et je lui crois assez d'esprit pour avoir trouvé nos jeunes gens bien sots. Si vous êtes de ses amies, elle vous dira ce qui en est." [2]

The letters for the succeeding year contain frequent references to Carlisle's youthful pass on. Lord Holland had taken his family abroad, and Charles James Fox, whose brilliant public career Carlisle had foretold in verse at Eton, was a congenial companion during a part of his continental travels.

Carlisle at this epoch of his life is an interesting study. Here is a boy of nineteen voluntarily leaving home because of a fascinating woman ; he is anxiously awaiting the delayed green ribbon, and his investiture by the King of Sardinia. He is in close association with the foremost men

---

[1] " Memoirs of third Duke of Grafton," p. 33.
[2] " Correspondance complète du Mme. du Deffand," vol. i. p. 87.

*George Selwyn   Frederick Fifth Earl of Carlisle
and the dog Raton
from a picture by Sir Joshua Reynolds P.R.A.*

of that and a later day.   For three days he is crossing the
Alps, a journey filled with as many hopes or fears of
adventure as could have befallen one a century earlier.

At the time when the correspondence begins, Selwyn's
friend, the third Duke of Grafton, was virtually Prime
Minister, or as it was then termed, " principal Minister,"
for the personal ministerial responsibility of the head of
the Government was, in the days of Chatham, Grafton,
and North, less distinct and less recognised than in the
nineteenth century.   Chatham still held the office of Lord
Privy Seal, which he had accepted on the formation of
his Ministry in 1766.   But by this time ill-health had
rendered him unable to take any part in public affairs.
In October, 1768, Chatham resigned office, and Grafton
became the recognised head of a Ministry the policy
of which he was incapable either of formulating or
directing ; and when in January, 1770, Grafton resigned
office and handed over the Ministry to Lord North, it
released him from a trying and irksome position.

Kindly and shrewd in worldly affairs, and well inten-
tioned as a politician, but wholly lacking in strength of
purpose, the third Duke of Grafton was a man who
obtained the goodwill and lost the respect of his contemporaries.   Between Selwyn and him there existed a
cordial friendship, of which there are many evidences in
these letters.

It is time, however, to let the correspondence speak for
itself; as has been already said, Carlisle was now at Nice.

[1767,] *Dec. 29, Tuesday, de mon Château de Tonder-
dentronk.*[1]—I received your letter of the 8th and 10th,
that is, one part wrote at Antibes, the other at Nice, here
yesterday, which gave me every degree of pleasure and
satisfaction that a letter can give ; it could never have
come more seasonably, than when I cannot possibly, from
the snow without doors, and the Aldermen[2] within, have
any other pleasure.

As I am well furnished with maps, I had recourse to

---

[1] Writing from Matson.          [2] Of Gloucester.

them to follow you in your travels, and had besides the pleasure of hearing that you were well, and knowing exactly where you are, which was an occupation for the whole morning. The Antiquities of France have furnished me with the knowledge of some places through which you have passed. M<sup>e</sup> de Sévigné ¹ did, long ago, bring me acquainted with others ; and sure I am that when she was at Rochers, she could not think more of the Pont de Garde than I should have done, if I had known of your being there.

If you do me the honour to give me in future letters so much detail, I shall be infinitely happy. You may be assured that I shall not communicate a letter of yours to any one, not even to L[ady] S[arah],² who hinted to me she wanted to see your last, without your leave ; but as for burning them directly, I cannot in your absence resolve upon that ; *je les conserverai prétieusement* till your return, and that is all I can promise without your very express commands.

The accident that had like to have happened to you and Charles ³ *ma fait glacer le sang.* I hope it was not

---

¹ Selwyn rivalled Walpole as an ardent admirer of Mme. de Sévigné (1626–1696) through her " Letters " ; he read them assiduously, and passionately collected any information relating to her ; prizing the smallest object that had once been hers as a precious relic.

² Lady Sarah Bunbury (1745–1826), youngest daughter of Charles Lennox, second Duke of Richmond ; great granddaughter of Charles II. ; sister to Lady Holland, Lady Louisa Conolly, and Lady Emily, Duchess of Leinster ; divorced from her first husband, Sir Charles Bunbury, the well-known racing baronet, in 1776 ; married, for the second time, George Napier, sixth son of Francis, fifth Lord Napier, in 1702 ; mother of the distinguished soldiers, Sir Charles James Napier, Sir George Thomas Napier, and Sir William Francis Napier, the historian of the Peninsular War. Constitutional reasons alone prevented George III. from marrying her ; he settled £1,000 a year on her at Napier's death in 1807. She was quite blind when she died.

³ Charles, whenever the name occurs, refers to Charles James Fox (1749–1806). He entered Parliament at nineteen ; at twenty was made a Lord of the Admiralty ; in 1773 a Commissioner of the Treasury ; in 1782 Secretary of State for Foreign Affairs in the Rockingham Ministry ; in 1783 he became again Secretary of State in

Robert that was so heedless. But that, the wild boars, the Alps, precipices, *felouques*, changes of climate, are all to me such things as, besides that they *grossissent de loin*, that if I allowed my imagination its full scope, I should not have a moment's peace.

I shall think no more of anything that may happen unfortunately either to you or me for the next twelve months, than I do in passing from Dover to Calais of the one-inch plank that is between me and Eternity. I have assured myself that as long as the time will appear in passing now, I shall think some time hence its progress not so slow, and I will not add imaginary to real evils, by supposing it possible that I shall not meet you again.

I came down here on this day sevennight, and could I have walked out—but the deep snow has prevented that— I should have passed my time among my workmen tolerably well.

Lord Lisbourne[1] and Williams[2] were to have come with me, but disappointed me. His lordship was hunting a mare's nest, as they say, and fancied he should be this week nominated either of the Admiralty or Board of Trade. He is *fututo de*, and Lord Ch[arle]s Spencer[3] is of the first, and no vacancy in the other.

the memorable Coalition Ministry formed by himself and Lord North under the nominal premiership of the Duke of Portland. When the Whigs at length returned to power in 1806 he was again Secretary for Foreign Affairs in Lord Grenville's Ministry of all the Talents, and died in office. No statesman so little in office ever obtained so great influence in Parliament and in the country.

[1] Wilmot, fourth Viscount Lisbourne.

[2] George James Williams, commonly known as Gilly Williams (1716–1805), son of William Peere Williams, an eminent lawyer; uncle by marriage to Lord North; appointed Receiver-General of Excise in 1774. It was he of whom it was said that he was wittiest among the witty and gayest among the gay, and his society was much sought after. He and Edgecumbe, with Selwyn, met at Strawberry Hill at stated periods, forming the famous group—Walpole's "out-of-town party."

[3] Lord Charles Spencer (1740-1820); second son of third Duke of Marlborough; M.P. for Oxfordshire 1761-1784, and again 1796-1801; filled from time to time several minor political offices.

Vernon [1] has Fanshaw's place at the Green Cloth, and this Greasy Cook dismissed with a sop, but of what sort I know not; however, he thinks himself happy that a dish-clout was not pinned to his tail. March [2] is passing Xmas between Lord Spencer's and the Duke of Grafton's.[3] There is no Oubourn [4]; that family has been occupied, and is now, between recovering a little of his Grace's sight, and niggling themselves into Administration.

I believe I told you of Crawfurd's [5] preferment in my

[1] Richard Vernon (1726–1800), termed father of the turf. He was a captain in the army and a Member of Parliament; it was as a sporting man, however, that he was best known. One of the original members of the Jockey Club, he had a racing partnership with Lord March, and rode in races. His skill at cards and on the turf afforded the means for extravagant living. He married the youngest daughter of the first Earl Gower.

[2] William Douglas (1725–1810), third Earl of March and fourth Duke of Queensberry, in his later years called "Old Q." He was appointed a Lord of the Bedchamber on the accession of George III., and in 1767 made Vice-Admiral of Scotland. Pleasure in all its forms was the sole object of his life, regardless of public opinion; he was good-natured and shrewd, and not without interest in politics and literature. At the time of the King's madness, in 1788, he openly declared for the Prince of Wales, and voted for the regency; he entertained the princes and Fox with reckless prodigality until the King regained his reason, when he lost his place at Court, and prudently retired to Scotland for a time. Among Selwyn's many friends the Duke of Queensberry held the first place. "Hors son milord March, il n'amie rien," writes Mme. du Deffand, in her portrait of Selwyn, whose un-entailed property was left to the Duke of Queensberry, and who survived his friend by nineteen years.

[3] Augustus Henry, third Duke of Grafton (1735–1811). In 1766 he became First Lord of the Treasury in Lord Chatham's Ministry, resigning in January, 1770; and in 1771 Lord Privy Seal in Lord North's Government, stipulating at the same time that he should not be "summoned to any Cabinet." He resigned in 1775, but joined the Rockingham Ministry in 1782 as Lord Privy Seal. On the formation of the Coalition Ministry of North and Fox, in 1783, Grafton left office for the last time.      [4] Woburn.

[5] James Crawford of Auchinames, Renfrewshire. He belonged to the group of fashionable young men who frequented the clubs and played heavily. He was a Member of Parliament. In 1769 he accompanied Charles Fox abroad, and the following year visited Voltaire at Ferney. He was a correspondent of David Hume and of Mme. du Deffand, who always referred to him affectionately as "Mon

letter of last Friday sevennight.  I shall return to London
the end of this week, and go in search of further news for
your entertainment.  The journal which you suppose me
to keep is no other than minutes I make of what I hear.
When you come back from your travels my office of
journalist will cease.

I have no one with me but Râton,[1] but he is in great
health and beauty.  I'm sorry that you told me nothing
of poor Rover ; pray bring him back if you can, and don't
let a Cardinal or any other dog stick it into him.

I find my affairs here, which you are so good as to
enquire after, much as I expected them.  The needy and
tumultuous part of my constituents are daily employed
more and more, as the time of election approaches, to find
me a competitor, and put me, if they cannot, to a needless
expense, but I believe their schemes will be abortive as to
the main design ; and as to money, I must expect to see
a great deal of it liquified and in streams about the streets
of the neighbouring city.

Morpeth I hope will be settled to your satisfaction for
this time by the help of the Duke of Grafton, and in all
future times by no means but what are in your hands.  I
hope as soon as I come to town to find the St. Andrew [2]
ready to be sent, and shall by this post send a quickner to
Hemmins ; if a courier goes before I come, I hope he will
carry it.  Lady Carlisle [3] was to go and see it.  I take it

petit Crauford " ; in a letter in which she urges her desire that he
should become more intimate with Horace Walpole, she writes, " *Vous
êtes melancholique, et lui est gai ; tout l'amuse et tout vous ennuie.*"
Crawford was called the Fish at Eton, a name which clung to him
throughout life.  He had wit and vivacity, but the reputation of being
affected, insincere, and jealous.  Much of his life was passed abroad.
He died in London in 1814.

[1] Râton was a present from Lady Coventry, and Selwyn was much
attached to him.  Sir Joshua Reynolds introduced him in his portrait
of Selwyn and Lord Carlisle which is at Castle Howard.

[2] The Order of the Thistle had just been conferred on Carlisle.

[3] Isabella, Countess of Carlisle (1721–1795) ; daughter of fourth
Lord Byron.  In 1743 she became the second wife of the fourth Earl
of Carlisle, who died in 1758, and was the mother of the fifth Earl.
In 1759 she married Sir William Musgrave.

for granted that Sir W. Musgrave [1] will have an eye to the courier's going. I believe, at least the papers say so, the other two Ribbands are given away ; so yours must be dispatched, of course. What would I not give to see your Investiture ! What indeed would I not give to be with you on more occasions than that ! I know nobody but Charles that I should not envy that pleasure, but *il en est très digne* by knowing the value of it.

I shall be in pain till I hear again concerning Lord Holland [2] ; *il fait une belle defense, mais il en demeure là à ce qu'il me paroit;* I see nothing like a re-establishment. *Ses jours sont comptés au pied de la lettre.* I beg my best and kindest compliments to him, Lady Holland,[3] and to Charles, to whom I wrote by the last post. I desired him to do me the favour to stick a pen now and then into your hand, that I might hear often from you. I shall be extremely glad to have some of your observations upon the places to which you go ; but if that takes up too much time, I shall be contented to know that you are not any more within pistol-shot.

Lord Beauchamp [4] trains on well, as they say, but *il n'a pas le moyen de plaire.* Lord Holl[an]d's criticism upon Beauc[hamp] is not just ; he will get nine daughters if he goes on as he does, before me ; and I thought once it was a hard-run thing between us.

Poor Lady Bol[ingbroke],[5] *quelle triste perspective pour*

---

[1] Sir William Musgrave (died 1800), of Hayton Castle, Cumberland. Commissioner of Customs and a well-known personage in London Society. He was Vice-President of the Royal Society, and filled many useful offices.

[2] Henry Fox, first Baron Holland (1705–1774) ; Secretary for War, 1746 ; Secretary of State, 1735 ; Paymaster General, 1757 ; Leader of the House of Commons, 1762 ; created Baron Holland, 1763. He had at this time gone abroad for his health.

[3] Lady Holland (1723–1774) ; eldest daughter of Charles, second Duke of Richmond. Her runaway marriage to Lord Holland, then Mr. Fox, which, however, proved very happy, created much talk at the time.

[4] Francis Seymour (1743–1822) ; son of Francis, Earl of Hertford, afterwards second Marquis of Hertford.

[5] Lady Diana Bolingbroke (1734–1808) ; eldest daughter of second Duke of Marlborough ; sister to Lady Pembroke. She was celebrated

*elle ! j'en suis véritablement touché.*  Adieu, my dear Lord, *pour aujourd'hui.*  God preserve you from boars of any kind, but one, which is the writer of a long letter ; for mine to you cannot be short, or ever long enough to tell you how sincerely and affectionately I am your Lordship's.

*1768, Jan. 5, Tuesday morning, Chesterfield Street.*—Many and many happy new years to you, some of which I hope to have the pleasure of being a witness of.  When I came to town yesterday from Gloucestershire, I received, to my surprise and great satisfaction, your letter of the 16th of last month, for this is now the second which I have had within a week beyond my expectation.

My answer to the first is now on the road to you, and will, I hope, reach you some time next week.  I don't recollect in any which I have wrote that there was any expression of formality, which you seem to have observed, and which I certainly did not intend, because I know it would not be acceptable to you ; and therefore don't interpret that to be formality, which can be nothing but that respect, which no degree of familiarity can ever make me lose in my commerce with you.

I was surprised to find that Sir Ch[arle]s and Lady Sarah [Bunbury] were in town, and had not been out of it.  The weather has been and is so cold there is no stirring from one's fireside, and so they changed their mind.  I dine with them to-day, when I hope I shall see Harry ; I have not seen him yet.  I have been absent, it is now above a fortnight.  I shall not seal up my letter till I have been in Privy Garden.  I was asked to dine at Lord George's [1] to-day, but am glad that, it being post

for her high character, beauty, and accomplishments.  Two days after her unhappy marriage with Lord Bolingbroke was dissolved she married Topham Beauclerk.

[1] George Sackville Germaine (1716–1785) ; known from 1720 to 1770 as Lord George Sackville, from 1770 to 1782 as Lord George Germaine ; son of the seventh Earl and first Duke of Dorset.  A Member of Parliament and a soldier, he became in 1775 Secretary of State for the Colonies in Lord North's Administration until the fall of

day, I can dine where I may be able to pick up something that will be interesting to you. I don't wish to add fuel, but it is natural to wish that one's letters are made as acceptable as possible.

I have had a message to-day from Sir W. Musgrave, who desires to see me to-morrow ; I will endeavour to see him to-day, as the post goes out ; I don't know particularly what he has to say. I have sent to Hemmins this morning, but he is not yet come to me.

Lord W. Gordon [1] says he thinks his brother will ask for the other Ribband. I long to see the Duke of Buccleugh [2] in his. I can tell you no more at present of Brereton's [3] affair than that he is to be prosecuted. I send you his advertisement, which came out a fortnight ago. I think some answer should have been made to it ; although I think the controversy very unequal, and a paper war with such a low fellow very disagreeable. But the assertions in this advertisement will gain him credit. As I live with but one set of people, I do not hear all the animadversions that are made upon this affair, but I believe there is a certain *monde* where my two friends pass but for very scrubby people ; a bold assertion, and a great deal of dirt thrown, although by a very mean hand, must inevitably have a disagreeable effect.

The night robberies are very frequent. Polly Jones, my neighbour, was a few nights ago stopped, when the chair was set down at Bully's [4] door, and she robbed of 12 guineas.

his chief. His rise to the peerage in 1782 as Viscount Sackville gave cause to some acrimonious debates, which are referred to later, see *post*, p. 186. The Letters of Junius have often been ascribed to Sackville's pen.

[1] Lord William Gordon ; brother of the fourth Duke of Gordon and of Lord George of the Gordon Riots fame. He was Ranger of Windsor Park.

[2] Henry, third Duke of Buccleugh (1746–1812) ; eulogised in Lord Carlisle's well-known verses on his Eton schoolfellows. He succeeded as fifth Duke of Queensberry in 1810.

[3] Colonel Brereton on leaving the army had become a gambler of doubtful reputation.

[4] Frederick St. John, second Viscount Bolingbroke (1734–1787) ;

Lady Bolingbroke has sent her resignation to the Queen, who wrote her a very gracious letter upon it. Bully kisses hand[s] to-morrow ; the others soon after. Lord Gower [1] is the only one who has kissed hands as yet. Fanshaw is not to be in Parliament, so there is so much money saved to him, and his pension consequently in greater security.

I am glad that there is so much care taken of Rover. I think, if he has the good fortune to survive Alps, &c., and ever come to Castle Howard, that he has an establishment for life, and may be a toad-eater of Stumpy's.

I had a letter yesterday from Sir J. Lambert,[2] who says he can contrive to send the Badge safely. I hope he sends my letters regularly. March is still at Lord Spencer's, where he amuses himself, as he tells me, excessively.

I will write more after dinner, when I hope to be more amusing to you. I am glad for your sake and mine that they are still in town. I shall not forget to *faire valoir tous vos beaux sentimens*. I'm persuaded that I shall not be thought borish upon that subject.

Lord March's election at the Old [3] is to be to-night, if

known among his friends as "Bully." He succeeded his uncle, the famous Henry St. John, in 1751, and married in 1757 Lady Diana Spencer, daughter of the third Duke of Marlborough ; the marriage was dissolved in 1768. He married secondly, in 1793, Arabella, daughter of the sixth Lord Craven.

[1] Granville, second Earl Gower, first Marquis of Stafford (1721-1803). Appointed a Lord of the Admiralty in 1749, and resigned in 1751 ; having filled various court offices he became in 1767 President of the Council. He resigned in 1779. Upon Pitt's accession to power in 1783 he became again Lord President of the Council ; in 1784 left this office and was appointed Lord Privy Seal ; in 1786 created Marquis of Stafford ; in 1794 resigned the office of Privy Seal. At first opposed to America's independence, he later declared against the war. He was the father of Lady Carlisle.

[2] English banker in Paris.

[3] A club at White's Coffee House in St. James's Street was formed in 1736. About 1745 so many gentlemen were waiting for admission to its membership, that a second club, known as The Young Club at White's, was established. It had the same rules and was in the same house as the Old Club, the members of which were usually selected from the younger society. In 1781 the Old and Young Clubs were united, and have since been known as White's Club.

you can call a constant ejectment an election. I thank you for your offer of a Circassian in case you travel into Greece ; you must suppose me to be like the Glastonbury Thorn, to receive any benefit by it.

I am also much obliged to you for your hint about Hazard. Foolish, very foolish it is I grant you, and if anything was prevalent enough with me to relinquish so old and pernicious a practice, it would be your condemnation of it. *Heureusement pour moi*, the occasion fails me more than my prudence would serve me, if that offered. The rage there is for Quinze is my great security. Can you forgive these borish letters ; can you excuse my leaving you to go and sup with Sir Ch[arle]s in Privy Garden ?

My dear Lord, you have been very kind in writing so often to me ; the only mischief of it to me will be, that you will have accustomed me to that which I cannot expect, when you are no longer in that state of retreat and indolence in which you have been at Nice. I owe much to your friendship and great complaisance on all occasions, but I cannot expect to interfere with what will occupy you in those places with so much reason. However, whatever you are, I hope I may have leave to assure you from time to time how truly and affectionately I am, and ever shall be yours.

I should be glad to know if all my letters have come to your hands.

[1768,] *Jan.* 12, *Tuesday morning.*—I went to White's to enquire after your ticket, and found The Button with a letter in his hand, which he desired me to direct to you. It was only to tell you that your ticket was a blank : it came up the 2nd instant.

Mr. Walpole's book [1] will not be out this month ; I will send it by the first opportunity I can find. Pray let me know if you have received Hume's Hist[ory], [2] that

---

[1] " Historic Doubts on Richard the Third."

[2] The best English history that had been written up to that time, and the first that made any attempt to literary merit. The first edition was published at intervals from 1754 to 1761. A second edition had been issued in 1762.

Lord Pembroke [1] was to carry for you to Sir J. Lamb[er]t.
The apology for Lord B., that is, Lord Baltimore,[2] I sent
for, but it contained nothing to the purpose, and it was a
title formed to draw people in.

I dined at Crawfurd's on Saturday ; there were Robinson, Sackville, and R[ichar]d Fitzpatrick,[3] who *à la suite
d'une fièvre*, has been attacked with the rheumatism, and
looks wretchedly, and quite decrepid. I went afterwards
and sat an hour with poor Lady Bol[ingbroke] ; she
was very easy and cheerful, *et avec une insensibilité qui
m'en donneroit pour elle ;* but that cannot be. She told
me she had a favour to ask of me, which was, that I
would use my endeavours that she might see her children.
Bully is at present out of town, but to be sure, I shall
have no difficulty in that negotiation. I have supped
at Lady S. several times, and last night went home
with her and Miss B. from the play. *Je profite de
certains momens pour vous rappeller à son souvenir*, if that
was necessary ; they are to dine here, but have not fixed
the day. Little Harry and his French friend are at
Mrs. Blake's in the country. Sir C. will make him

---

[1] Henry, tenth Earl of Pembroke (1734-1794). He married in
1756 Elizabeth, second daughter of the third Duke of Marlborough.

[2] Lord Baltimore had been acquitted of the charge of abduction
which had been brought against him, but the prosecution brought
forward facts sufficient to justify the public indignation that was raised.
He soon after went abroad, and died in Naples in 1771.

[3] Richard Fitzpatrick (1747-1813) ; second son of John, first Earl of
Upper Ossory and Lady Evelyn Leveson Gower, daughter of second Earl
Gower. His sister, Lady Mary Fitzpatrick, married Charles James Fox's
elder brother, Stephen, afterward second Lord Holland. Fitzpatrick
is one of the best known names in the history of the social life of the
last half of the eighteenth century—the Duke of Queensberry left him
a legacy in recognition of his fine manners. He was the talented and
accomplished friend of Fox, whose excesses in gaming and in all the
fashionable follies of the day he rivalled. He served with credit in
the American war ; in 1780 was returned to Parliament ; in 1782
appointed secretary to the Duke of Portland, then Lord-Lieutenant of
Ireland ; in 1783 made Secretary at War. At his death he was a
Privy Councillor, a general in the army, and colonel of the Forty-
seventh Regiment of Foot.

write to you when he returns.   Lady Hertford [1] is actu-
ally (as Lady S. told me last night) Lady of the
B[edchamber].

I expect Sir W. Musgrave to call upon me at three to
take measures about the courier, and Hemmins has promised to bring me the Badge at two.   I shall then have
more to say upon those points.   Parker [2] gave us a great
dinner, but the company was not numerous.   I dine
to-morrow at Lord Barrington's, [3] and, I am told, with
the new Ministers. [4]   I had a little supper at Lady Harrington's [5] on Sunday, *en famille* ;  Lord and Lady Barrymore [6] were there.   She goes on with her pregnancy.

I found Beauc. sitting with his future, [7] *en habit de gala* ;
he soon went away to the Opera, so I had a *tête à tête*.
Mr. Radclif [8] is still talked of for Lady F., but I have not
asked Sir Will[ia]m Mus[grave] if it is true.   He is very
well spoke of, *et le nom est assez beau*.

Quinze goes on vigorously at Almack's. [9]   Lady S. says

[1] Lady Isabella Fitzroy, youngest daughter of Charles, second Duke
of Grafton.   She married in 1741 Francis, first Marquis of Hertford.

[2] George Lane Parker (1724–1791), second son of George, second Earl
of Macclesfield.   He became a general and a Member of Parliament.

[3] William Wildman, second Viscount Barrington (1717–1793).   He
filled various high official and court offices ; he was a Chancellor of
the Exchequer in 1761, and subsequently Secretary at War.

[4] The Bedford faction effected a junction with the Government at
the end of 1767, and Lord Sandwich, and Lord Weymouth, and Rigby
entered the Ministry.

[5] Caroline Fitzroy, eldest daughter of the second Duke of Grafton.
She married Lord Petersham, second Earl of Harrington in 1746.

[6] Richard Barry (1745–1773) succeeded as sixth Earl of Barrymore
at six years of age.   He married Lady Stanhope, daughter of William,
Earl of Harrington.   He was notorious as a skilful gambler.   He is
said to have been an excellent officer, holding a captain's commission
at the time of his death.

[7] Alice Elizabeth, youngest daughter and co-heir of Herbert, second
Viscount Windsor.   She married Lord Beauchamp that year.

[8] John Radcliffe married Lady Frances Howard, Lord Carlisle's sister.

[9] Almack's Club was established by Macall in 1764.   It was subsequently taken over by a wine merchant named Brooks and was
thenceforward known as Brooks's.   This club was primarily formed
for the purpose of high play ; one of the rules reads : " Every person
playing at the new quinze table shall keep fifty guineas before him."

that you have fixed your coming of age as an *époque* for
leaving off that and all kind of play whatsoever.   My dear
Lord, *vive hodie ;* don't nurse any passion that gathers
strength by time, and may be easier broke of at first.   I
am in hopes indeed that when you are *maître de vos biens,*
as the French say, you will not invite Scot, Parker, or
Shafto [1] to partake it with you.   Your condition of life,
and the necessary expenses of it, will not allow that coalition.   I never kept so long from play yet, but I frankly
own I have not much virtue to boast of by that continency.
I know of no good opportunity which I have resisted.   St.
John [2] told me at the play last night that you was to go
and return from Turin alone.   I hope that is not so ; I
shall be very angry with Robert, if he does not take great
care both of you and Rover.   I will finish the rest when I
have seen Sir William.

*Tuesday night.*—Sir W[illia]m sent me word he did not
call upon me to-day because he could not settle with the
courier till Thursday ; and Hemmins did call, and assured
me that on Thursday the Badge should be ready.   I
scolded till I was in a fever ; I believe he will not venture
to put me off any longer.

[1768,] *Jan.* 15, *Friday morning.*—We are at this
moment in some alarm about you, which I hope to find
has been given without any foundation ; however, *en tous
cas,* I hope this will find you at Nice, and not at Turin,
where Lady Carlisle has been told there is a contagious
disorder.   You are near enough that place to have better
intelligence than we.

At play it was the fashion to wear a great coat, sometimes turned inside
out for luck ; the lace ruffles were covered by a leathern bib.   Broad-
brimmed high hats, trimmed with ribbon and flowers, completed a
proper gaming costume.
    [1] Robert Shafto of Whitworth, M.P. for Durham—fond of racing
and betting.
    [2] Henry St. John, called "the Baptist," was a brother of "Bully,"
second Viscount Bolingbroke.   Horace Walpole writes of them as Lord
Corydon and Captain Corydon.   He was a Groom of the Bedchamber,
a Member of Parliament, and a colonel in the army.   He was a man
of wit, universally popular.

I dine[d] with the Duke of Grafton the day before yesterday at Lord Barrington's, who assured me the death of Mr. Shirley would not occasion any delay in regard to you. Sir W[illiam] M[usgrave] and I have been contriving how to save you the price of the courier, which, for going and coming, is above £150. I shall apply to Lord Clive [1] through his former secretary, my neighbour Mr. Walsh. Lord Clive is going to Nice, although I suppose by a slow progress, and can supply this courier's place, *à pas de tortuë*, that will not be inconvenient if you don't leave Nice immediately ; if you do, a more expeditious method may be thought of. But I am very desirous of adding no more expense to that which this Order will cost you.

Almack's was last night very full ; Lady Anne and Lady Betty [2] were there with Lady Carlisle. The Duke of Cumb[erlan]d [3] sat between Lady Betty and Lady Sarah, who was his partner. Lady Sarah, your sister, and His R[oyal] H[ighness] did nothing but dance cotillons in the new blue damask room, which by the way was intended for cards. The Duchess of Gordon [4] made her first appearance there, who is very handsome; so the beauty of the former night, Lady Almeria Carpenter,[5] was the less regarded. We will follow, if you please, the *veteris vestigia flammæ*.

There has (*sic*) been no events this week that I know of, except his Grace of Bedford's [6] appearance at Court.

---

[1] Lord Clive had recently returned from India in bad health. He lived, however, till 1774.

[2] Sisters of Lord Carlisle.

[3] Henry Frederick, younger brother of George III. ; notorious for his dissipation.

[4] Jane Maxwell, Duchess of Gordon, wife of Alexander, fourth Duke. She was a social leader of the Tory party, and a confidante of Pitt. Horace Walpole called her " one of the empresses of fashion."

[5] Lady Almeria Carpenter was famous for her beauty. She was lady-in-waiting to the Duchess of Gloucester and mistress to the Duke. " The Duchess remained indeed its nominal mistress, but Lady Almeria constituted its ornament and its pride " (Wraxall, vol. v. p. 201).

[6] John Russell, fourth Duke of Bedford (1710–71), died 1756. He was appointed Lord-Lieutenant of Ireland in 1762 ; he went as Am-

His eyes are a ghastly object. He seems blind himself, and makes every [one] else so that looks at him. They have no speculation in them, as Shakespear says ; what should be white is red, and there is no sight or crystal, only a black spot. It alters his countenance, and he looks like a man in a tragedy, as in K[ing] Lear, that has had his eyes put out with a *fer rouge*.

I dined yesterday at Lady Sarah's with Mr. and Mrs. Garrick.[1] I say as much as I can of Lady Sarah, and her name shall be in every other line, if it will excuse the borishness of my letters in other particulars.

March leaves Lord Spencer's to-day. He and Varcy like [lie] to-night at St. Alban's, and are to be in town to-morrow. The Northampton Election will cost God knows what. I dine to-day at Ossory's.[2] Lady Sarah,

bassador to Paris, where he negotiated the unpopular Treaty of Paris. He was at the head of the place-seeking politicians called the Bloomsbury Gang, from his town house in Bloomsbury Square ; and when, in 1767, his faction came into power, " the Duke of Bedford, who was worthy of better clients, made a feeble effort to arrive at an understanding with Lord Rockingham about a common policy ; but he could not keep his followers for five minutes together off the subject that was next their hearts. Rigby bade the two noblemen take the Court Calendar and give their friends one, two, and three thousand a year all round ("The Early History of Charles James Fox," p. 132). An overbearing manner and the character of his followers made him unpopular. In 1731 he married Lady Diana Spencer, daughter of the third Earl of Sunderland, and sister of the third Duke of Marlborough. He married for the second time, in 1737, Gertrude, eldest daughter of the first Earl Gower. At the death of their only son, Lord Tavistock, in 1767, the Duke and Duchess of Bedford were harshly charged with want of respect for his memory.

[1] David Garrick (1717–79). In 1749 he married Eva Marie Violette, of Vienna, a dancer who had been received in the best houses in England. "I think I never saw such perfect affection and harmony as existed between them" (Dr. Beattie). Selwyn criticised disparagingly his Othello.

[2] John, second Earl of Upper Ossory (1745–1818). He was the brother of Richard Fitzpatrick and of Mary Fitzpatrick, wife of the second Lord Holland. He was educated at Eton and Oxford. "The man I have liked the best in Paris is an Englishman, Lord Ossory, who is the most sensible young man I ever saw " ("Walpole's Letters," vol. iv. p. 426). He married Annie, daughter of Lord Ravensworth, shortly after her divorce from the Duke of Grafton.

Miss Blake, Sir Ch[arles], &c., &c., dine here on Tuesday. I chose that, being a post day.

I believe that the best thing I can do is to ask Lord Shelbourne [1] for the courier's place. I should be glad of it, if it was tenable with my seat in Parliament. Sir G. Mac sat last night at supper between Lady Bute [2] and his future, who by the way is *laide à faire peur*. I was asking Lady Carlisle which was the most likely, some years ago, to have a Blue Ribband, *du beau-père et du gendre*.

Little Harry is not come to town. Sir Charles goes down into the country next week, but not Lady Sarah that I know of. I expect Hemmins every hour with the St. Andrew. He has so much abuse from me every day, that I believe he wishes that I had been crucified instead of St. Andrew. He swears that one man left the work in the middle of it, and said he would not have his eyes put out in placing those small diamonds that compose the motto.

Mr. Brereton is returned to the Bath, and the street robbers seem dispersed. The hard weather is gone for the present, so that London will be pleasanter than it has been, for the Jockeys and Macaronis.[3] Garrick criticised your picture of mine, which he saw at Humphry's ; he has that and Sir Charles's ; it is like, but not so good and spirited a likeness as Reynolds's [4] certainly. But I am much

---

[1] William Petty, second Earl of Shelburne (1737–1805) ; created Marquis of Lansdowne, 1784 ; he became Secretary of State in Chatham's second Administration, 1766, and resigned office on October 20, 1768, almost simultaneously with Lord Chatham on the fall of Lord North. In 1782 he again became Secretary of State in Lord Rockingham's Ministry, and First Lord of the Treasury on the death of Rockingham. His Government came to an end on the coalition of Fox and North in 1783. He was the most liberal statesman of his time, "one of the earliest, ablest, and most earnest of English free-traders," but he was at the same time one of the most unpopular, a supposed insincerity being the cause of it.

[2] Lady Bute was the daughter of Lady Mary Wortley Montagu.

[3] A society of exquisites drawn from the younger men at Brooks's, noted for their affectation in dress and manner ; travel abroad was necessary for admission to their society.

[4] Sir Joshua Reynolds (1723–1792). Selwyn was his patron and friend. When it was reported that Reynolds would stand as a candidate for the borough of Plympton, and all the town was laughing at him, Selwyn

obliged to you for it. If you sit to Pompeio I shall hope to have a better, and with your Order.

The Duke of Cumb[erlan]d attacked the Duke of Buccleugh last night for wearing his under his coat ; *son Altesse R. a une bâvardise fort intéressante il faut lui rendre justice.*

I should not have troubled you so soon if this alarm from Turin, and the courier, &c., had not filled my head. My best compliments to Lord and Lady Holland and my love to Charles and Harry.[1] Charles is in my debt a letter ; I shall be glad to hear from him. Crawfurd desired me to make his [ex]cuses to you, that he has not answered your last ; he gains no ground ; I think he is *immaigri, et d'une inquiétude perpetuelle qui porte sur rien.*

The Duke of N[ewcast]le[2] seems to have gained strength and life since that manly resolution which he took last week of being no longer a Minister of this country. Let what would happen, he has given a *congé* to his friends to do what they will, and it shall not be looked upon as desertion. That is undoubtedly the most capital simpleton that ever the caprice of fortune placed in the high offices which he filled, and for so long a time.

The last paragraph of this letter can scarcely belong to this date, for the Duke of Newcastle was not in Chatham's Ministry, which was formed on the fall of the first Rockingham Administration in July, 1766.

remarked that he might very well succeed, " for Sir Joshua is the ablest man I know on a canvass."

[1] Henry Edward Fox, youngest son of Lord Holland.

[2] Thomas Pelham-Holles, Duke of Newcastle (1693–1768). For half a century in the front of English political life. In 1724 he became Secretary of State in Walpole's Administration, and continued in office until 1756, having on the death of his brother, Henry Pelham, in 1754, become First Lord of the Treasury. In 1757 he returned as Prime Minister to office with the elder Pitt, resigning again in 1762. In Lord Rockingham's Ministry, 1765 to 1766, he was Lord Privy Seal. Newcastle is a remarkable instance of a man of apparently ordinary capacity holding high office in the State for many years.

[1768,] *Jan.* 17, *Sunday morning.*—We received your Badge at last yesterday. Sir W. Musgrave and I deliberated a great while about the method of sending it, and at last went together to Lord Clive, who sets out for Paris to-morrow, and will take charge of it, as the surest conveyance. The courier was rejected as too expensive, and Mr. Ward as too uncertain. I have enclosed a schedule of what the packet delivered to Lord Clive contains. It is addressed to Sir J. Lambert and Mr. Ward. If he goes to Paris to-day, as he intended, [he] will carry a letter from me to Sir J. L[ambert] with directions for the safest and speediest conveyance of this to you ; I shall write to him again upon the subject on Tuesday.

I wish somebody had received a letter from you by Friday's post, to satisfy us where you was. This idea of an epidemical disorder at Turin has alarmed Lady Carlisle, and I have caught some of the fright of her. March returned yesterday from Lord Spencer's, and the usual company supped at the Duke of Grafton's.

Mrs. Horton [1] sets out for Nice with a toad-eater and an upper servant of the Duke's this next week. The night robbers prove to be soldiers in the Foot Guards, which I suspected ; we have not recovered our terrors, and still go home, as they travel in the Eastern countries, waiting for convoys ; it ruins me in flambeaux's.

Lord Clive will not I think live to go to Nice, but I hope he will get safe to Paris, and then Sir J. Lambert will take care of all the rest. The Badge is pretty, excepting that the shape of it is too long, and the whole seems too large for a young person. But that was the fault of the sardonyx.

The Duchess of Bucc[leugh] [2] is very far gone with child ; but I believe I told you so in my last. I will write the rest when Lady Sarah is gone from my house on Tuesday after dinner.

---

[1] The Duke of Grafton made no secret of his relations with Mrs. Horton.

[2] Elizabeth, Duchess of Buccleugh, daughter of George, Duke of Montagu. She was married in 1767.

*Tuesday night.*—My dear Lord, I have waited till my foreign letters came in before I would finish this, always in hopes of one from you. I have received one by this post from Charles of the 6th of this month ; and he says you was answering one which you had just had from me. This gives me hope that I shall hear from you on Friday.

Lady Sarah dined with me, Miss Blake, Sir Charles, Lord March, Lady Bolingbroke, and Crawfurd. Lady S[arah], &c. went to the Play soon. She received a long letter from Lady Holland while we were at dinner, but only said that Lord H[ollan]d was well, which I was glad to hear. We were 16 yesterday at the Duke of Gr[afton's], a very mixed company. He enquired very kindly after you.

I think I shall have both trouble and expense at Gloucester, as I have had heretofore, but that is all I apprehend, and that I have been prepared for a great while, by expectation. I am in great hopes from Charles's letter that you are still at Nice. Not that I think but, being so near Turin, if there was anything to be feared from the distemper, you would certainly hear it, and not go. Perhaps there are letters from you in Cleveland Court ; I shall send to Sir Wm.[1] to enquire.

The great event at Almack's is that Scott has left off play ; he is, I suppose, the *plena cruoris hirundo*. I am not quite satisfied that Sir J. Lambert is punctual in forwarding my letters ; pray let me know it. Those who have been to see me think your picture very like, but not a good likeness is agreed on all hands ; but such as it is, I am very much obliged to you for it.

I am extremely glad to find that you are applying to Italian, but to anything is useful. You will find the benefit of it your whole life. There are lacunes to be filled up in every stage, which nothing can supply so well as reading, I am persuaded.

I find the last of mine that you had received when Charles wrote his was a month ago ; that makes me afraid Sir J. L[ambert] keeps them. There [they] are no more

[1] Sir William Musgrave.

worth his keeping than your receiving, but they give me the pleasure of assuring you, which I can, with great truth, that I am ever most truly and most affectionately yours.

Intermixed with the personal news which fills the next letter there are allusions to some social and political incidents very characteristic of the time. The Indian nabob, or millionaire as we should now call him, had begun to desire a seat in Parliament for his own purposes, just as the sinecurist did for his, and he was able to outbid the home purchaser. The jealousy with which the Court party regarded the encroachments of these returned Anglo-Indians in their preserves is amusing, especially when we recollect that so great was the venality of the age that a respectable corporation such as that of Oxford did not hesitate to offer the representation of their borough for sale for a fixed sum.

1768, *January 26, Tuesday night, at Almack's.*—I received last night yours of the 9th of this month, for which I thank you most heartily. It is really so much pleasure to me to have a letter from you, that it makes me wish away five days out of seven, and at my age that is too great an abatement. I intended to have called to-day upon Sir W[illiam] Musgrave in consequence of it, but neither he [n]or Lady Carlisle having received any letters (if they are come, he might not have received them), that (*sic*) he prevented me, and called upon me at three o'clock to know if I had had any account of you.

Mr. Ward did not set out the Sunday he intended, that is the 17th inst., but he gave the letter which he was to carry to Sir J. L[ambert] to Mr. Hobart,[1] who was to set out for Paris the day after, that is, the 18th.

---

[1] George Hobart, third Earl of Buckinghamshire (1732–1804). He was returned to Parliament in 1761, 1768, and 1774, and he was manager of the Opera for a time. In 1762 he was made Secretary to the Embassy at St. Petersburg, where his half-brother John, second Earl of Buckinghamshire, was Ambassador; in 1793 he succeeded him. He married, in 1757, Albinia, eldest daughter of Lord Vere Bertie.

Lord Clive did not sail, as Sir W[illiam] M[usgrave] tells me, till last Sunday, so the Ribband and Badge, &c., will not arrive at Paris till next Saturday, or Sunday probably ; but Sir J. L[ambert] will be prepared to have sent these things, by a safe hand to you either at Turin, or Nice. I shall write to him to-night again with a full explanation of all, that no time may be lost.

I conclude you came to Turin last Saturday, according to the letter which I received yesterday, unless Lady Carlisle's letter about the epidem[ical] disorder prevented you, which was wrote the 5th inst., upon seeing Monsieur Viri[1] at the Princess Dow[age]r's Drawing Room. According to the usual course of the post you must then have received that the 19th, the evening of your intended departure, and whether it prevented you or not, is still for me à sçavoir. I hope it did, all things considered. But if you really went to Turin last Wednesday, then you will have been there perhaps near three weeks before your Investiture. I hope no part of this delay will be imputed to me. You will not have passed your time, I should think, ill at a Court, where you was so announced, and to receive that distinction. I am sure, if any time had been lost by my means, I should be very sorry, when you tell me that the going so soon to Turin will accelerate your return hither. For to tell you the truth, I begin to think the time long already, and it is too soon to begin counting the months.

I am extremely glad to find that you had the Marquis[2] with you. I did not like the idea of your travelling alone. Your application to Italian, or to anything, is what will certainly turn to account, because, if I am not much mistaken, yours is the very age of improvement ; but your growing fat must be owing to more indolence than can be salutary to you, and I hope you will take care that that is not too habitual. The inconveniences of it you may not find immediately, but they are certain, and very great, of

[1] The Count de Viry, Sardinian Minister to England.
[2] William Robert, Marquis of Kildare (1748-1805). He succeeded as third Duke of Leinster in 1773.

which I could enumerate very remarkable instances ; but they do not interest me as that does which concerns yourself.    I find by Sir W[illiam] that you have already heard all that your family knows of Lady Fr. ; your great good nature makes me not surprised at your anxiety, but there is no occasion for it, if I am rightly informed.    Your monk's disinterest[ed]ness is a mare's nest ; you will find he expects some gratuity that will amount to more than a certain stipend ; there is no such thing in nature as an Eccle[si]astic doing anything for nothing.

As to Morpeth, the best that can be done at present is done.    I'm persuaded what can be done in future times will depend upon yourself, as I hope and suppose.    I do not wonder that Lady Carl. prefers Reynolds' picture, but I am not sorry to have that which I have neither.    It is a great likeness, though not a good one.

Your seal you will receive with the other things.    You ask me about Lord Tho[mon]d [1] and Will : all [the] party is so broke up at present that they are *au desespoir*. The Bedfords are in extraordinary good humour ; that elevation of spirit does them no more credit than their precedent abasement ; the *æquus animus* seems a stranger to them.    G. Greenv. [2] is certainly—— [befouled] as a Minister, but he is so well manured in other respects that he cannot be an object of great compassion certainly.

I hear you was alarmed in the night by a violent squabble in your retinue.    I hope Robert behaves well ; as a native of Castle Howard I have the most partiality to him, although I really believe Louis to be a very good servant.    I shall be glad to know if Rover is still in being ; he shall have his picture at the *dilitanti* (*sic*), if he returns.

---

[1] Percy Windham O'Brien, Baron of Strichen and Earl of Thomond, brother of Lord Egremont and of Mrs. George Grenville.   He was a Member of Parliament for Minehead, Lord-Lieutenant of the county of Somerset, and a member of the Privy Council.

[2] George Grenville (1712–1770).   Prime Minister and Chancellor of the Exchequer in 1763.   The author of the Stamp Act.   See his character, Lecky, "History of England," vol. iii. p. 64.

I hope you will not travel Eastward but upon the map. *L'appétit vient en mangeant*, but pray let me not find that in respect to your travelling ; I cannot be so selfish as not to be glad that you make the tour of Italy, but I can carry my disinterestedness no further I confess ; more than 18 months' quarantine will be too much for me.

Lord March is much obliged to you for your kind and constant mention of him ; he is extremely well, and not plagued with Zamparini's [1] or anything that I know of. The Duchess of North[umberlan]d [2] according to her present arrangement sets out for Paris, or some place or places abroad, next week. If she is not constantly wagging, as I'm told, she is in danger of a lethargy. Mrs. Horton sets out for Nice on Friday.

There has been a very long debate in the House of Commons to-day upon a motion of Ald. Beckford's [3] concerning a Bill he intends to bring in for the more effectual prevention of bribery and keeping out nabobs, commissaries, and agents of the House of Commons, or at least from their encroachments upon the claims of persons established in towns and boroughs, by descent, family interest, and long enjoyed property ; the principle of his scheme is certainly good.

The Mayor and Corporation of Oxford are to appear at the Bar in defence of themselves, for having offered themselves to sale for £7,500. They had the *honnêteté* to offer the refusal to their old members, who told them in

---

[1] A dancing girl of fifteen and her family, at the moment the object of Lord March's attention.

[2] Lady Elizabeth Seymour, Duchess of Northumberland, generally called Lady Betty. In 1740 she married Sir Hugh Smithson, against the will of her grandfather, the Duke of Somerset, who disliked this marriage for the heiress of the Percys, but there was no power of depriving her of the property, and Smithson succeeded to the title in 1750 ; from this time they both figured prominently in society and politics, and the Duchess's entertainments, where the best musicians performed, were famous.

[3] William Beckford (1709–1770). Alderman and Lord Mayor of London, and Member of Parliament for the City of London. The friend and supporter of Wilkes, he was an upholder of popular rights at a time when men of wealth were usually supporters of the King.

answer to their modest proposal that as they had no intention to sell them, so they could not afford to buy them. I was not at the House, but this is likely to make a great noise. Bully's petition has been presented by Lord Sandw.,[1] and will probably be carried through this Session. Some of the Bishops intend to make speeches against it, as I hear.

Charles Boon has married a squint-eyed, chitten-face citizen with about £5,000 fortune. Sir G. Mac :[2] wedding will be about Monday or Tuesday next. They consummate at Comb, Vernon's house. Sir Ch[arles] is returned from Barton, and Lady Sarah gone to the Opera. You may be sure that we do not pass an hour without mention of you, but, shall I tell you mind (*sic*), when Lady Carlisle tells you that she has seen her at Chapel, and when I tell you that I have dined with her, we certainly mean to please you ; but do we not help to keep up a flame that, in as much as that is the proper description of it, had better be extinguished? *Crescit indulgens isti.* I am sure I shall never say anything to lessen the just and natural esteem which you have for her, but when there is grafted on that what may make you uneasy, I must be an enemy to that or to yourself, and you know, I am sure, how incapable I am of that. I have a long letter

---

[1] John George Montagu, fourth Earl of Sandwich (1718–1792) ; was a party politician whose term of office as First Lord of the Admiralty brought him into general opprobrium ; in private life he was even more severely condemned. With the Earl of March, Sir Francis Dashwood, and others, he was associated with Wilkes in the infamous brotherhood of Medmenham, and later, when they made public the secrets of the club against Wilkes, popular feeling rose high against Sandwich, and he was characterised as Jemmy Twitcher, from a play then running ; the theatre rose to the words "That Jemmy Twitcher should peach me I own surprised me."

[2] Sir George, afterward Lord Macartney (1737–1800). An ambitious young Irishman ; a tutor and friend of Charles James Fox, he had been assisted in his career by Lord Holland. In 1764 he had been appointed Envoy Extraordinary to Russia, and later held appointments as Secretary to the Lord-Lieutenant of Ireland, President of Madras, Governor of the Cape of Good Hope, and Ambassador to China. He married Lord Bute's second and favourite daughter, Lady Jane.

almost every week from my flame also, Mᶜ du Deffands,[1] but these are passions which *non in seria ducunt.* She is very importunate with me to return to Paris, by which (?), if there is any sentiment, it must be all of her side. I should not be sorry to make another *séjour* there ; but if I did, and it was with you, I should not throw away with old women and old Presidents,[2] which is the same thing, some of those hours which I regret very much at this instant. You may assure Lord Kildare that I will do my best about his election at the young club.[3]

[1768] *Feb. 2, Tuesday Morning.*—Yesterday Sir T. Stapleton and Mr. Lee, the members for the town of Oxford, read in their places, by order of the House, the letter which they had received a year and a half ago from the Mayor, Bailiffs, and Council of Oxford to offer them a quiet election, and absolute sale of themselves, for £5,670 sterling ; the sum which the Corporation is indebted, and otherwise as they declare unable to pay. Eleven sign, of which [whom] one is since dead ; all the rest are ordered to attend at our Bar on Friday with the Mace Bearer, &c. Their Regalia has been pawned for their high living. The House was excessively crow[d]ed ; Thurloe and Rigby,[4] for the Duke of Marl[borough's]

---

[1] Marie de Vichy Chamroud, Marquise du Deffand (1697–1780). She married, in 1718, the Marquis du Deffand, from whom she soon separated, and lived the life of pleasure so common in the period. At the age of sixty-two she became totally blind. This misfortune but made her the more celebrated and sought after. In 1764 occurred the quarrel with Mlle. Lespinasse, which divided her salon and left her quite alone with her faithful secretary, Wiart. With the exception of her correspondence with the Duchesse de Choiseul, she bequeathed all her letters to Horace Walpole. She was seventy and Walpole fifty when they met and their famous attachment and correspondence began.

[2] President Hénault (1685–1770). He was President of the Parliament, a member of the Academy, and author of " L'abrege Chronologique de l'Histoire de France." His devotion to Mme. du Deffand lasted until his death, which preceded hers by ten years.

[3] At White's.

[4] Richard Rigby (1722–1788). A prominent politician, he was for many years Paymaster of the Forces ; but was a coarse, hard-drinking place-man.

sake, made weak efforts to bring them off. Some of these people are fled to Calais, as it is said, to avoid Newgate ; it may be that none of them will appear who signed.

Mr. Walpole's [1] book [2] came out yesterday, but I got it from him on Saturday, and my (?) Lord Molyneux carried it for me that morning to Sir John Lamb[er]t to be forwarded to your Lordship immediately. I'm confident that it will entertain you much, and, what is more extraordinary, convince you ; because I have that good opinion of your understanding as not to think that ages and numbers can sanctify falsehood, and that such is your love of truth as to be glad to find it, although at the expense of quitting the prejudice of your whole precedent life. I will not forestall your judgment by saying anything more of this book, but only wish it may afford as much entertainment as it has me. This historic doubter dined with me yesterday, Williams, Lord March, Cadogan, and Fanshaw, *qui m'a demandè à dìner*, at the House.

[1] Horace Walpole (1717–1797) was the fourth and youngest son of Sir Robert Walpole. He was Selwyn's lifelong friend. His biographers place him at Eton with Selwyn, the two Conways, George and Charles Montagu, the poet Gray, Richard West, and Thomas Ashton. On leaving Cambridge he made the continental tour with Gray, but after two years of travel together they disagreed and separated for the homeward journey. In 1747 he bought Strawberry Hill, which he transformed into his Gothic Castle, ornamenting the interior with objects of beauty or curiosity. In 1757 he set up his private printing press, where he brought out Gray's poems and other interesting English and French publications, beside his own productions, which culminated in "The Castle of Otranto," a departure in fiction beginning the modern romantic revival. In 1765 he visited Paris, where he went much into society, and when his celebrated friendship with Mme. du Deffand began. He helped to embitter Rousseau against Hume by the mock letter from Frederick the Great offering him an asylum in Germany. In 1789, nine years after Mme. du Deffand's death, he met the two sisters, Agnes and Mary Berry, who came to live near him at little Strawberry, which he left them at his death. He succeeded his nephew as fourth Lord Orford in 1791, but he preferred the name which he had made more widely known, and signed himself "Horace Walpole, uncle of the late Earl of Orford." The celebrated letters begin as early as 1735 and extend to 1797. Walpole never married.

[2] "Historic Doubts on Richard the Third."

Horry seemed mightily pleased with the success which his new book has met with ; nobody cavils at anything, but here and there an expression ; his hypothesis is approved of from the most reasonable conjectures, and the most indisputable authorities. I would have had Bully [to] have dined with us, but he was engaged to his brother, *qui donne à dîner fort souvent*. I told him, that if he would pay his court to Horry he might give him a lick of his *vernis*, that would do his repu[ta]tion no harm. He is in high spirits ; his divorce is making a rapid progress through your House.

Beauclerck looks wretchedly, and has been very ill. Our Minister,[1] as you call him, goes on very well, but he is now a widower a second time ; his Lady set out for Paris last Saturday. I hope he will not be undermined. The King will never have a servant that will please the public more. I dine with him often *à petit couvert* at March's. I am not desirous that my friends should become ministers ; but if they are ministers, it is fair to wish they may become one's friends. He is yours very cordially, I'm persuaded. He always asks very kindly after you, and seems uneasy that the Order has not yet reached you. He said the other day at dinner, *a'un ton très patétique*, " I shall be much disappointed if in four or five years Lord Carlisle does not give a very good account of himself." *Ministre, ou non ministre, qui tient des propos pareils, n'aura pas grande difficulté à me contenter sur le reste.* I have abandoned him to-day for Lady Sarah, at which you will be neither surprised, [n]or offended. He dines at March's, and I in the Privy Garden.

The D[uke] and D[uches]s of Rich[mon]d are in town. A young man whose name I cannot recollect asked me very kindly after you yesterday, at the H[ouse] of C[ommons] ; he used to sit by your bedside of a morning in King Street ; he is tall and thin.

Dr. Musgrave, the Provost of Oriel College in Oxf[or]d, cut his throat in bed the other day ; he was ill, but he had taken to heart a mistake which he had made

---

[1] The Duke of Grafton.

about a letter of Sir J. Dolben's, who is to be member for the University the remainder of this Parliament. A dispute with the Fellows, as they tell me, arose in consequence of it, and this seized the poor man's brains. He was reckoned very passionate, but *d'ailleurs* a good kind of man. I knew his person and his elder brother, Sir Philip, formerly very well. There is a stagnation of news just at this moment, but as soon as any preferments, peerages, or changes of any kind are known for certain, I will send you word of them.

I dined at the D[uchess]'s or Duke's, which you please, of North[umberlan]d's [1] on Saturday; you are a great favourite of her Grace's. She told me of I don't know how many sheets which you had wrote to Lady Carlisle, giving an account of your travels. All the company almost were of Yorkshire, or of the North; Lord and Lady Ravensw[orth], Sir M. Ridley and his father, the Punch Delaval, Lord Tankerville, &c. Her Grace goes soon to Paris, but has as yet fixed no day.

A disagreeable report has prevailed lately, but I believe without the least foundation, that Crew has lost a monstrous sum to Menil. Almack's thrives, but no great events there. I have ordered the M[arquis] of Kildare to be put up at the young club, at White's. If little Harry is come to town, he shall write to you; others should write to you if I could make them, but I am afraid those wishes are more of a courtier than a friend. I should be sorry and ashamed, by endeavouring to flatter your inclination, if I lost your good opinion, which without flattery I value much.

I sat the other morning with Miss Blake; Lady S[arah], and Sir Ch[arle]s were rode out, and I did not see them. She told me a letter was come from Charles, and there is a rendezvous she said, somewhere, but she could not recollect where. She thought you intended to meet Charles and their family at Spa the end of the summer; if so, I shall not despair of seeing you many months sooner than I can otherwise expect it. I shall

---

[1] Hugh, second Duke of Northumberland (1742–1817).

know to-day at dinner more particularly about it. Lord March thanks you for your frequent and kind mention of him.

My new chaise comes home the week after next. I shall defer making a chariot for some time. I may, perhaps, ask your opinion about a friensh [French?] equipage. March's great room is gilding, and when finished he is to give a dinner to Lady Sarah, and a concert to a great many more. I will finish this *au sortir de table*.

*Tuesday night.*—I dined at Sir Charles's. Harry came to town this morning with his French friend and Academist. He has promised me to write to you next post. Lady Sarah says that if you are not satisfied about the St. Andrew, Hemmins is to blame, not her. She could not get him to come near her ; and the day it was finished, which was the day before it went away, she never saw it.

Charles, I find, is to meet you in April at Rome ; and Lady Sarah the latter end of the summer to meet him at Spa. You do not return to Nice. I do not count much upon hearing from you, but by accident, when you proceed further into Italy.

Sir R. Rich died last night only, so I can know nothing of his preferments yet. Dr. Smith, the Master of Trinity, is also dead, and Dr. Hinchliff asks for his Headship. Lady Sarah was melancholy about Stee[1] ; she hears that his lethargy increases, and thinks it probable her sister may lose both her husband and son in a very short time ; that is a disagreeable perspective. They all desired to be remembered to you. Adieu, my dear Lord, *pour aujourd' hui*. I have no chance of hearing from you by this post, the letters having come yesterday ; so God bless you. I am ever most sincerely and affectionately yours.

[1768,] *Feb.* 16, *Tuesday morning, Newmarket.*—I have just finished a long letter, which, when I came to sand, I have, *par distraction*, covered all over with ink. I came down here on Saturday with March to meet the Duke of

[1] Stephen Fox.

Grafton, who by the by only stayed here that night, and then went to Bury, so that I have scarce seen him.

We are at Vernon's house, that is, dinner and supper ; which he has bought of Lord Godolphin [1] [for] 400.0, Here has been Sir J. More, Bully, and Polly Jones, Vernon's Polly, Mr. Stoneheir,[2] who came with the D[uke] of G[rafton], Sir Charles Bunbury and little Harry, and Mr. Richmond has been here also to lay out Vernon's gardens. Sir Charles has held us a Pharo bank of a night which has cost him £200, a sum, I imagine, not so easily spared at this juncture by him.

March promised that I should be in London again to-day, but you know his irresolution, and the little opposition which I can give to what he desires ; but it is a great sacrifice for me, for you have been so good in writing to me since I left you, that there is not a week that I am absolutely without my hopes of hearing from you, although, when I left you, I should have been glad to have compounded for once a month ; and I'm the more impatient to know what accounts are come by Monday night's post, from what you told me of the gripe, and that you could not go to the French Amb[assado]r's Ball. Harry tells me that he wrote to you, as you ordered him.

Lady S[arah] is in town, and I suppose very happy with the thoughts of a Mascarade which we are to have at Almack's next Monday sevennight, unless in the interim some violent opposition comes from the Bishops. Harry has had here with him a son of Lord Carysfort's [3] from Cambridge. Bully's affair ends with the Session ; as soon as that is concluded, he will be in respect of matrimony absolutely evinculated.

There has been an Almack since I wrote, but no events.

---

[1] Francis Godolphin Osborne, Marquis of Carmarthen, fifth Duke of Leeds. In 1773 he married Amelia, daughter of Robert d'Arcy, Earl of Holdernesse. He was Secretary for Foreign Affairs 1783–91.

[2] Richard Stonehewer, the Duke of Grafton's private secretary. He was a friend of Gray, the poet, and of Horace Walpole.

[3] Sir John Proby (1720–1772). He was created Baron Carysfort in 1752, and appointed one of the Lords of the Admiralty in 1757.

At the other shop, a great deal of deep play, where I believe Ossory has been a great sufferer; the D[uke] of Roxb[urgh]·[1] is become a very deep player also, and at Hazard. I have been, as you justly call it, foolish, but very moderately so, and rather a winner, for which I'm not certainly less foolish. But my caution at present arises from being at the eve of an expense probably for which an opposition at the Hazard table is but a bad *préparatif.* However, all things are quiet as yet, and my own private affairs *en bon train,* according to the present appearances.

The D[uke] of G[rafton] tells me that he wishes to recommend for Luggershall, Lord Garlies,[2] and a son of Sir M. Lamb's. I wish Morpeth [3] could have waited till you come of age. But I hope that in future times everything will be done there and elsewhere which your family consequence entitles you to wish may be done.

The Corporation of Oxford was dismissed on Wednesday last with a reprimand that is to be printed; *un discours assez plat,* as I have heard. That affair has raised up many others, and a multitude of attorneys, who have been hawking about people's boroughs, have been sent for. It is high time to put a stop to such practices, and to check the proceedings of nabobs, commissaries, and agents.

Very luckily for you I cannot find many materials here for detaining you long, so God bless you, my dear Lord. I wish I may be able to contrive some means of abridging the time and distance which seems determined to separate me from you. I am constantly regretting that which I gave up to old women and presidents. But *il est de nos attachemens comme de la santé ; nous n'en sentons pas tout le prix que quand nous l'avons perduë.* I beg my compli-

---

[1] John, third Duke of Roxburghe (1740–1804). In society he was regarded as one of the most agreeable and handsome men of his day, but he is now chiefly recollected as a book collector. The sale of his library in 1812 occupied forty-five days. The Roxburghe Club was inaugurated at the time of the sale.

[2] John Lord Garlies (1735–1806), seventh Earl of Galloway.

[3] The parliamentary representation of.

ments to the Marquis of Kildare ; I am happy to know
that you have a companion, and that it is him.

[1768, *Feb.* 26]. . . .—The Bishops have, as I apprehended that they would, put a stop to our Masquerade,
for which I am sorry, principally upon Lady Sarah's
account.  I shall go this morning and condole with her
upon it. . . . March is very pressing to know if I do
him justice in my letters to you ; he is not very fond of
writing, and therefore deposits with me all his best and
kindest compliments to you.

I thank you for saying that you would have me a few
hours gazing at amphitheatres, and you for the same time
gazing here at something more modern.   That would not
answer my purpose.  I never carried my love of antiquity
and literary researches to that point.  I should be glad to
have a view of Italy, but with you ; and if you should
take a trip here for *a few days*, pray don't insist on my
being at that time in contemplation of the *mazures de nos
ancêtres*.  The last letter which you mention to have
received from me was of the 15th of last month, and you
did not receive it till the 3rd of this.  I hope my letters
come to you, since you permit the writing of them.  I
shall always hereafter put them myself into the post. . . .

A match is much talked of between Lord Spencer
Hamilton and Miss Beauclerk, the Maid of Honour.  I
hope it will not take place.  There is not as much as I
have sometimes lost of a night at Hazard between them
both, either at present or in expectation, and the number
of beggars is increased to an enormous degree. . . .

1768, *February* 28, *Sunday morning, Chest*[*erfield*]
*Str*[*eet*].—I wrote to you on Friday morning, and at
night, just before the post was going, received the
pleasure of yours of the 10th ; so that what I wrote
afterwards was much in haste, and from the impetuosity
of my temper to make my acknowledgments to you.  I
was yesterday at Lady Carlisle's door, to enquire for
Sir W[illiam], but he was not at home.  I asked if they

had had any letters from you, and being told they had
not, I took the liberty to leave word that I had received
one of the 10th, and that you was then very well.

I believe all the apprehensions which M⁵ Viri had filled
us with, are now dispersed, and not fearing anything
from cold, I hope that I shall not be so foolish as to be
thinking of the consequences of heat ; *cela ne finit point.*
I saw Viri at Lady Hertford's at night ; he was unac-
quainted with the particulars of the courier, &c., but
only said that the King, his master, had assured him that
he should invest you with that order, as his Brother ¹
had desired he would, and that it should be done *avec
toute la pompe et l'éclat dont la chose fût susceptible.* He
is a stupid animal in appearance, this Viri.

I had yesterday morning my conference with the
D[uke] of G[rafton] ; he has assured me that I should
have the place of Treasurer to the Queen, added to that
which I already have (without any kind of pension), as
soon as ever one could be found out for Mr. Stone, but
he having been the King's Preceptor there will be some
*ménagement* with him, but the Duke said, if he would not
acquiesce, he insinuated force. The two places together,
if I am not mistaken in the estimate, will be near £2,300
per annum. I'm much obliged to the D[uke] for his
liberal and kind manner of treating with me. I have
succeeded better, I find, in negotiating for myself, than
when I employed another ; but I have this time had to
deal with a person who seemed willing to comply with
anything which I could propose in reason, and has even
gone beyond my proposals ; and I have reason to flatter
myself that his Majesty has not that reluctance to oblige
me, which his grandfather had, and has certainly a much
better opinion of me. Then, if this Election goes off
without an enormous expense, I shall be enabled to pay
off much the greatest part of my debt ; but my impru-
dences have been beyond conception. I hope that that
Providence which has preserved me from the usual effects
of them will be kind enough to let me enjoy some few

¹ George III.

years of ease, and to pass them with your Lordship. I
will not then complain of my lot here, which, were the
cards to be shuffled again, I might mend in some particulars, without perhaps adding anything to the general
felicity of my life.

I went from the D[uke] of G[rafton's] to a little
concert at March's, where was Sir C[harles] and Lady
S[arah]. She and I went up into the rooms above, which
are now gilding and repairing, and I communicated to
her such parts of your letter as I thought would please
her, and which I thought you would be pleased that I
should repeat to her. . . .

*Monday morning.*—Miss Blake[1] did not leave them
till yesterday. She went with Lady S[arah] to Court,
and then Sir Ch[arles] and Lady S[arah] dined at Mr.
Blake's and left her there. I saw Lady S[arah] afterwards
at the D[uche]ss of Hamilton's.[2] The Assembly is there
at present ; Lady Harrington has not been able to see
company for some time.

There is now no talk but of Elections. Lord
Thom[on]d is thrown out at Taunton, and opposed at
Winchelsea, and so it goes on. This is the week I am
in most apprehension of, because I think next, as the
Judges will be then in the town [Gloucester], there can
be no treating nor bustle ; but as yet I know of no
opponent. Sackville sticks close to . . . (*sic*). I was
with her Grace most part of yesterday morning, with
Lord W. Gordon. Harry St. John asks me if you have
mentioned a M^e Château Dauphin ; all Italian news
interests him much. . . .

[1769,] *July* 4, *Tuesday night.*—I have sent to-day

---

[1] Carlisle in a letter refers to her as Selwyn's ward.

[2] Elizabeth Gunning, Duchess of Hamilton and Argyll (1734–1790) ;
a sister of the equally beautiful and famous Maria Gunning, Lady
Coventry, who died in 1760. The Duchess of Argyll, who married
the second time the year following the death of the Duke of Hamilton,
was generally known as the Duchess of Hamilton, and in 1776 was
created Baroness Hamilton in her own right. This untitled daughter
of a poor Irish gentleman was the wife of two dukes and the mother
of four.

for you 45 bottles of the *vin de Grave* and six bottles of Neuilly, and the same quantity is ready to be packed up and sent when I have your further commands. The reason why I did not send the whole at once, was the consideration of the weather, &c. ; when this comes safe, the rest shall follow directly, and then according to my cellar-book you will have had in all ten dozen, that is seven dozen and a half now and two dozen and a half before, of that particular wine, and about a dozen of Burgundy. It goes by sea to Hull. The *Knight* cutter, Thomas Savil, master, Hull, at the custom-house quay. That custom-house quay may mean at London. However, this is the method prescribed by your porter, for I have been at your house to enquire, as well as my servant.

I have wrote to Françès about the *tricoté*, and will send you an account of it by next post. I have regulated the papers to-day, for upon enquiry at the house, I found two were sent you from thence, and the three besides from Jolliffe, which you ordered ; so I bid Jolliffe look to that.

I was at Vauxhall last night with Lady Harrington, Lady Barrimore, Mrs. Damer,[1] Lady Harriot, March, Françès, and Barker. Very fine music, and a reckoning of thirty-six shillings ; fine doings. I had rather have heard Walters play upon his hump for nothing. I dined to-day at James's with Boothby, Harry St. John, March, and Panton. To-morrow Lord Digby and I dine at Holland H[ouse], and on Thursday Harry and I dine at Beckford's with Sir W[illiam] M[usgrave]. Rigby gave a dinner to-day to the Duke and Duchess of Grafton.

The Newmarket people go the beginning of next week. I shall then go into Kent, and the beginning of the week after I shall set out for Castle Howard. I long to see you *dans votre beau Château*. But where is it that I do

---

[1] Anne, only daughter of General Conway. She ultimately became possessed of Strawberry Hill. She devoted herself to sculpture ; the heads that ornament the bridge at Henley-on-Thames are her work.

not wish to see you? If anything is published that is not a mere catch-penny, as it is called, I shall send it directly. I believe the account of the D[uke] of G[rafton] and Nancy is of that sort, but I know no more than the advertisement.

Almack's is extinct. I am writing from White's, which I have long wished was so too.

Bad news from the Colonies. The P[rince] of Brunswick has another son. The people are come from the Installation at Cambridge, but I know no more of what has passed there than you see in the papers. Harry pursues the Bladen, and March will be talked of for Lady Harriot till he does or does not marry her. I wish it decided one way or other. I own I have his happiness too much at heart not to be anxious about it, and hate to have it in suspense.

Lord Farnham has distributed four hogshead of some *vin de Grave*, which he had, among his friends, and they prefer it to that which Wion (?) furnishes us with. I cannot help that, all things are good and great and small, &c., by comparison. God bless you, my dear Lord; I will come, as you have given me leave, as soon as my affairs here will possibly permit it.

I write to-night for ten dozen more of *vin de Grave*.

# CHAPTER III

## 1773–1777, 1779 AND 1780

### POLITICS AND SOCIETY

Fox's Debts—Lord Holland—News from London—Interview with Fox—The Fire at Holland House—A Visit to Tunbridge—Provision for Mie Mie—County business and electioneering at Gloucester—Lotteries—Fox and Carlisle—Highway adventures —London Society—Newmarket intelligence—An evening in town—Charles Fox and America—Carlisle declines a Court post —Money from Fox—Selwyn and gambling—A Private Bill Committee—Selwyn in bad spirits—The Royal Society—Bookbuying—Political affairs—London parks—Gainsborough—The Duchess of Kingston—Selwyn's private affairs—" The Diaboliad " —A dinner at the French Ambassador's—Politics and the Clubs —In Paris—Electioneering again.

A DISTINGUISHED man of letters of the present day has called Selwyn the father confessor of the society of his time : it is a tribute to his friendliness and good sense, as well as to his good nature and patience. Without them he could never have been the trusted adviser of Carlisle in those financial difficulties in which the young peer's friendship for Charles Fox involved him.

It was in 1773 that the crash came in Fox's affairs. His gambling debts had been accumulating. The birth of a son to his elder brother—closing, at any rate for the time, Charles Fox's reversionary interests—caused his creditors to press their claims. Lord Holland was obliged to come to the assistance of his son. It is at this moment that the correspondence which is gathered

in the present chapter begins.  Lord Holland had raised
a large sum with which to pay off his son's debts.  Selwyn
was indignant because it seemed as if creditors less
indulgent than Carlisle would be the first to be paid.  So
in many letters he presses upon Carlisle that he must not
allow his friendship for Charles Fox to outweigh the
monetary claims which he had upon him, and in no
measured terms he condemns the carelessness with which
Fox regarded his financial obligations to his friend.

The correspondence contained in this chapter commences
at the end of the year 1773, after an apparent break of four
years ; there is no doubt, however, that it continued and
the letters from Selwyn have not been preserved.  The
letters in 1773 begin by referring to the financial matters
to which brief allusion has just been made, and which
formed a subject so full of interest and anxiety for
Selwyn.  He has time, however, to give his friend news
of the political and social events of London.  The
American question was becoming more and more important, the Declaration of Independence had startled
England in 1776, and in 1774 Charles Fox had finally
left the Administration of Lord North, soon to become
the leader of the Whig party and the champion of the
American Colonists.

[1773, *Dec.*]—This is the severest criticism which I
have heard passed upon you.  In all other particulars be
assured that you have as much of the general esteem of
the world as any man that ever came into it, and will
preserve the highest respect from it if you will only from
this time have such a consideration, and such a management of your fortune, as common prudence requires.
Charles has destroyed his, and his reputation also, and I
am very much afraid that, let what will be done now,
they will in a very few years be past all kind of
redemption.  You will have been the innocent cause of
much censure upon him, because all the friendship in the
world which you can show him will never wipe off what
he and his family at this instant stands (*sic*) accused of,

which is, setting at nought the solemnest ties in the world, and after the maddest dissipation of money possible, the amassing for his sake £50,000 to pay everybody but those who deserved the first consideration, and without which he could never [be] said to be *free*, and it would [be] a constant reproach to be easy. When there was no idea but of his having £20,000 advanced, which sum was otherwise to have been left him, and I said that such and such persons would be paid first, you did not seem to credit it. Was I right? or not? in my conjectures? If I tell you now, that £16,000 more than the present sum of £50,000 will come, I cannot pretend to say from what quarter, but I mean from the Holland family; and, if I tell you also, that as much more will be borrowed for purposes which do not now exist; I must tell you that I think that these sums will be sent after the others, if you do not strenuously oppose it, and if somebody does not watch over the springs from whence these supplies are to flow.

As to Hare,[1] you will do me the justice to own that I have not said a word to impeach his friendship to you. But I must set him aside as a man capable of transacting this business. It is not *de son ressort*, and I know that he has difficulties to combat with, if he undertakes it, which are insuperable. Now, when I talk of men of business, I will explain myself. I mean three for example: Mr. Wallis, if ever you consult him, Mr. Gregg, and Lavie. I would also seriously apply to my Lord Gower for his

---

[1] James Hare (1749-1804); son of Richard Hare, apothecary, of Limestone; grandson of Bishop Francis Hare; at Eton with Fox and Carlisle, and afterwards entered Balliol College, Oxford. As a young man he was considered more brilliant than Fox, and more was expected of his future. He sat for Stockbridge from 1772-1774, and for Knaresborough from 1781 to his death. Like all of the fashionable men of his day, he played heavily. In 1779 he had become deeply involved in debt, but obtained the post of Minister Plenipotentiary to Poland, which he held until 1782; in 1802 he was very ill at Paris, where Fox made him frequent visits. He died at Bath. Lady Ossory described his wit as " perhaps of a more lively kind than Selwyn's." Storer left him a legacy of £1,000.

advice, and make him a confidant in what relates to this business. He has very powerful motives for interesting himself in it. All others I would silence at once by saying that you had fixed upon particular persons to talk with upon this subject, and that you would not listen an instant to any other. After one or two attempts to discuss the point they would give it up, and, knowing in what channel it was, would be more afraid to trifle with you about it. Charles never opens his lips to me upon the subject, and when Hare was last at my house he did not say a single word relative to it. The bond was not so much as mentioned. To speak the truth, I had rather that they would not, for I should not be able to keep my temper if they did.

I have talked this matter over with persons of established reputations in the world for good sense, knowledge, and experience, and with as nice feelings in points of honour and friendship as anybody ever had. It is their opinion which makes me so confident of my own, exclusive of the arguments themselves, *qui sautent aux yeux*.

Now, as to the expedients. The capital sum,[1] let us call it, £15,000. Let Charles pay immediately £5,000 from the £50,000. I will endeavour a year hence to raise you five more. Let Charles and Lord Stavordale,[2] by their joint securities (and let Lady Holland contribute hers), try to raise the other £5,000, and then this debt is paid ; and when the worst comes to the worst, you will lose yourself only the £5,000, which we shall endeavour to get from your own securities and resources. All this is very practicable with people who are disposed to think of their honour more than of the gratification of their own pleasure.

The Holland family went to Bath yesterday. I took my leave, and it may be a final one, of them on Monday.

---

[1] Fox's debt to Carlisle.

[2] Henry Thomas, afterwards second Earl of Ilchester (1747–1802) ; the cousin and companion of Fox, and as great a gambler. " Lord Stavordale, not one-and-twenty, lost eleven thousand last Tuesday, but recovered by one great hand at hazard."

Charles, it is said, will follow them. What is become of Hare I know not. If you desire a letter to be shown to Lord Holland,[1] Lady H. must shew it. I will speak to you, as I promised, without reserve. I am apt to think that he will *comprehend* what you say very well. It is not my judgment only, but I have heard it said, that a great deal of his inattention upon these occasions has been affected, and that if the same money was to be received and not to be paid, our faculties would then improve. I wish that if he has any left, he would exert them now for the sake of the reputation of his family as well as of his own ; or he will add a load of obloquy to that which has been already derived (?) upon him, on account of the means by which this dissipated wealth has been acquired ; and by this last act of indifference to the honour of his son he will seem to justify all that abuse with which he has been loaded, and they will be apt to apply, what he does not certainly merit, but will nevertheless carry an air of truth with it, and they will say that—

> " Plundering both his country and his friends,
> It's thus the Lord of useless thousands ends."

You see, my dear Lord, with how much confidence I treat you. I have thought aloud, when I have been speaking to you, which perhaps I ought not to have done, but I cannot help it. I hope that you will burn my letters, for if they served as testimonies of the warmth of my friendship to you, they might be ill interpreted by others. . . .

Charles you say has not wrote to you. There is no accounting for that or for him but by one circumstance, and that is, that the gratification of the present moment is the God of his Idolatry. You mention his credit with Lord North.[2] I know for a certainty that Lord North

---

[1] Lord Holland had amassed a large fortune when Paymaster-General, and on this account his unpopularity was so great as to amount to public detestation.

[2] Frederick North, second Earl of Guildford, known in history as Lord North (1732–1792) ; Chancellor of the Exchequer, 1767 ; First Lord of the Treasury, 1770 to 1782 ; Secretary of State, 1783 (March to December) ; succeeded to Earldom of Guildford, 1790.

disavows that which I know he once gave him. "He will," they say, "manage this, and will settle that, with the Minister." Stuff! The Minister, whoever he happens to be, will settle this matter with Charles, and say, "Sir, I know you want me, and that I do not want you, but in a certain degree. Speak, and be paid, as Sir W. Young was." Alas, poor Charles! *Alia promissa dederat.*

You say that you have not had a line from Lady H[olland]; have you then wrote to her? I will add more to this if I see occasion, after I have been to talk with Lavie, who really means, I believe, to serve you with great fidelity, and reasons about this matter with great *netteté* and percision.

[1774,] *January* 18, *Tuesday, Chesterfield Street.*—I received yesterday your extreme kind letter, while I was at Lord Gower's at dinner; which dinner, by the way, or the supplement to it, lasted so long, that I have increased my cough by it greatly, and am so unable to go this morning to Court, that I think now of putting on my clothes in the evening only, and so going, as I did last year, to the King's side, to make her Majesty my bow as she passes from that apartment to the ball-room. We had yesterday at dinner Dick Vernon and Keith Stewart only, besides Lord Gower's family.

I was going home to dine by myself *très sagement et très tranquillement, dans le dessein de me ménager,* when Lord G. was so good as to propose my going home with him; and thinking that to be an opportunity of talking more with him upon you and your affairs, as we did, I could not resist it. I do assure you, my dear Lord, it is a great pleasure to me to see the zeal with which he speaks of you, and your interests, which is not, to be sure, surprising, considering your connection, but it makes me happy that my former intimacy with him begins to revive, which it has gradually done, from the time that you have belonged to him.

Miss Pelham [1] came to Lady Gower after dinner, and

---

[1] Sister of Henry Pelham, niece of Duke of Newcastle (1728–1804). She died at her estate at Esher, in Surrey, leaving a large fortune.

I think intends to go to-day to the Birthday, but such a hag you have no conception of ; and a patch which she is obliged to wear upon the lower eyelid, improves the horror of her appearance. She will kill herself, I make no doubt.

The letter which you have been so good to enclose for my satisfaction, from Lady Holl[an]d to you, does not much elate me, I own ; it is just that of one who is obliged to say a great deal, and finds an inconvenience in doing anything ; and as to Charles's writing to you, you know best how these promises have been fulfilled. If I could direct her Ladyship's good disposition, I should make her show your letter to her to Lord Holl[an]d ; I am persuaded that his faculties are not so entirely lost as not to discern with how much force of reason, propriety, and good nature it is wrote. What he would do in consequence of it, I cannot be quite so sure. Then he might, perhaps, relapse into a state of imbecility, or affected anility, which might deprive you of the advantage which you should expect from it.

Among other things which passed between Lord Gower and me upon the subject of Charles, to which our conversation, by the way, was not confined, I told him that your people of business had proposed that you should sue Charles for the Annuities, and how that advice seemed to shock you. He was not surprised at that, knowing your delicacy and friendship. But sueing Charles, you will find in a short time, has no horror but in the expression. If you are shocked, you will be singly so ; Charles will not be so, it is my firm belief. As soon as Lavie comes to you, he will tell you how far Mr. Crewe has embraced that idea, and what has been the consequence of it. If you will sue Lord H[ollan]d and Mr. Powell, or [for ?] them, in Charles's name, you will do your business. But I do not say that it is time for that.

What I proposed to Lord Gower was only this, and that cannot have nothing (*sic*) *rebutant* in it, to either Charles or you. It is this. To hear Charles's story patiently, but to answer or reason with him as little as possible. To desire that he would be so good as to meet

you at your own house, with Mr. Wallis and Mr. Gregg ;
we will have nothing to do with Lavie, *pour le moment.*
*Il ne respectera pas celui-ci comme les deux autres.*   Discuss
with them before Charles the means of extricating yourself
from these engagements.   Let him hear what they say,
and what they would advise you to do, as guardian to
your children; for there is the *point de vuë*, in which I am
touched the most sensibly ; and whatever Charles has to
offer by way of expedient, by way of correcting their ideas,
whatever hopes he can give, which are rationally founded,
let him lay them before these people in your presence.

Why I wish this is, the [that] he must then have something to combat with, and that is, truth and reason.
Without that, and you two together 'only, or Hare, what
will follow ?   There will be a *flux de bouche*, which to me
is totally incomprehensible, as Sir G. M['Cartney] told
me that it was to him.   *Il fondera en larmes*, and then
you will be told afterwards, whenever a measure of any
vigour is proposed, that you had acquiesced, because you
had been disarmed, confounded.   This happened no
longer ago than last Saturday, with Foley,[1] who related the
whole conference to me, and the manner in which it was
carried on.   "However," says Foley, "I carried two
points out of four, but I was obliged to leave him, not
being able [to] resist the force of sensibility."

I confess that, had it been my case, I should have been
tempted to have made use of M$^e$ de Maintenon's words
to the Princesse de Conti—"*Pleurez, pleurez, Madame,
car c'est un grand malheur que de n'avoir pas le cœur bon.*"
I do not think that of Charles so much as the rest of the
world does, and to which he has undoubtedly given some
reason by his behaviour to his father, and to his friends.
I attribute it all to a vanity that has, by the foolish
admiration of his acquaintance, been worked up into a
kind of phrensy.   I shall be very unwilling to believe that
he ever intended to distress a friend whom he loved as
much as I believe that he has done you.

But really this is being very candid to him, and yet I

[1] See p. 75 (note).

cannot help it. For I have passed two evenings with him at supper at Almack's, *où nous avons été lié en conversation*, and never was anybody more agreeable and the more so for his having no pretensions to it, which is what has offended more people than even what Lady H[ollan]d is so good as to call his misconduct. I do assure you, my dear Lord, that notwithstanding all that I have been obliged by my friendship and confidence in you to say, I very sincerely love him, although I blame him so much, that I dare not own it ; and it will give me the greatest pleasure in the world to see him take that turn which he professes to take. But what hopes can we have of it ?

Vernon said yesterday after dinner, that he and some others—Bully, I think, among the rest—had been driven by the rain up into Charles's room ; and when they had lugged him out of his bed, they attacked him so violently upon what he did at the Bath, that he was obliged to have recourse, as he did last year, to an absolute denial of the fact. The imagination of the blacklegs at the Billiard Table that he was gone over to Long Leate to borrow the money of Lord W[eymouth ?] had in it something truly ridiculous, and serves only to shew that his Lordship had been never trusted by them.

Gregg dines to-day at Lavie's ; I shall go down to meet him there, and perhaps order my chicken over from Almack's, that I may converse more *en détail* with Gregg upon this business of the Annuities. I like his conversation the best, I own, because I see less resentment in it. He speaks to the matters of fact, and not to the characters of the actors, which now is losing of time. God knows how well, and how universally, all that is established.

The women in town have found this a good morsel for their invective disposition, and the terms in which they express themselves *tiennent de la frénésie, et de l'entousiasme.* Lady Albemarle, who is not a wise woman, certainly, was at Lady Gower's the other evening, and was regretting only that Charles had not been consumed in the Fire, instead of the linnets. I am glad it was no worse. I think your fears about the rebuilding of the House are

not so well founded as your satisfaction might be, that
you had not been drawn in to insure it. I think that you
are more obliged to what he thinks upon that subject (for
he said that he did not believe in fire) than to your own
prudence. I am in daily expectation of the arrival of
these late sufferers at Holl[an]d H[ouse]. I wish them
all arrived there, I own, and that they may stay there, and
that there may be no *real* sufferers by the fire, which there
would be if any workmen had begun to rebuild the
House. That would be a case of true compassion.

You desire me to tell you something of Hare and
Storer,[1] &c. Storer, the *Bon ton*, is still at Lord Craven's.
I supped with the *Mauvais ton* at Harry St. John's last
night. I do not dislike him : he does not seem to be at
all deficient in understanding, and has besides *de la bonne
plaisanterie*. Hare is in town, and, if I was to credit his
own insinuations, upon the point of bringing his affair to
a conclusion. But I think that he prepares the world too

---

[1] Anthony Morris Storer (1746–1799), called the *Bon ton*, and
Lord Carlisle, were termed the Pylades and Orestes of Eton, and
the intimacy was continued in later life ; M.P. for Carlisle 1774–
80, and for Morpeth, together with Peter Delimé, 1780–4. In
1781 he succeeded in obtaining the appointment as one of the
Commissioners for Trade, in which Selwyn and Carlisle had so
deeply interested themselves. He was with Carlisle on his mission
to America in 1778 and 1779. During their political connection
he acted as a medium between Fox and North, in whose family
he was intimate. Fox made him Secretary of Legation at Paris
in 1783—Gibbon competing for the office, and when the Duke of
Manchester was called home he was nominated as Minister Plenipotentiary ; six days later, however, his friends were no longer in
power. It was in this year that his long friendship with Carlisle was
broken ; he did not stand for re-election for Morpeth and revoked the
bequest of all his property which he had made to him. Storer never
married. He was universally admired for his versatility and his pro-
ficiency in all he undertook ; he excelled in conversation, music, and
literary attainments ; he was the best skater, the best dancer of his
time. He began his valuable and curious collection of books and
prints in 1781. On these and card-playing he spent more money
than he could afford, but in 1793, at his father's death, he received an
ample fortune. He then occupied himself building and adorning a
property, Purley, near Reading. He left his library and prints to
Eton College, which also possesses his portrait.

much for some change in his condition, for he drives
about in an old chariot of Foley's,[1] as I am told, with a
servant of his own in livery ; and this occasions so much
speculation, that his great secret *diu celari non potest*. I
would advise him to conclude as soon as he can this
business ; *sans cela la machine sera dérangée ; elle ne peut
aller jusques au printems, cela est sur.*

The Duke of Buccleugh has said nothing to us as yet
about our anniversary dinner, but I hope that so good a
custom will not be laid aside. If it is, Richard must take
it up, as it is his birthday, and so I shall tell him. I have
myself, by all which I have said upon the history and fate
of that unfortunate Prince, excused myself from giving any
sort of *fête* at my own house ; but I do not carry my
rigour so far, as not to accept one on that day at the house
of another person. *Voilà le point où ma devotion se prête
un peu.* Your letter to Lord Grantham shall be sent to
the Secretary's Office this evening, and some compliments
from me at the same time. I wish that he was here,
that I might talk with [him] for half an hour upon your
subject.

1774, *July* 23, *Chesterfield Street.*—I received yesterday
a reprieve from Gloucester, and Harris's sanction for my
staying here a week longer ; so that the meeting, and the
report of Mr. Guise and Mr. Burrow's declaring themselves both as candidates upon separate interests, but
secretly assisting one another, were, as Richard the 3rd
calls it, a weak device of the enemy. I found myself
greatly relieved, and sat down and wrote a letter to the
Mayor and Corporation, which I may cite as a *modèle de
vrai persiflage.* I went and dined with Lord Ferrars and
Lady Townshend ;[2] she has received all her arrears, so we

[1] Thomas Foley, second baron (1742–1793). He was noted
for his sporting proclivities ; Fox was his racing partner, and the
money they lost, which included a hundred thousand pounds for
Lord Foley, and its replenishing, was a never-ending source of
gossip.
[2] Anne, daughter of Sir William Montgomery, and second wife of
George, first Viscount Townshend.

have now the pleasure of continuing our hostilities *les pieds chauds.*

Poor Lord Thomond died the evening before last of an apoplexy, with which he was seized the night before. I thought, as well as himself, that he was very near his end, and imagined that it would be this. But the news struck me, for not an hour before he was taken ill he passed by March's door as he was going to take an airing in Hyde Park, with Clever in the chariot. I was sitting upon the steps, with the little girl [1] on my lap, which diverted him, and he made me a very pleasant bow, and that was my last view of him. I had had an acquaintance with him of above thirty years, but for some time past I had seen him only occasionally. He was a sensible honest man, and when he was in spirits, and with his intimate friends, I think a very agreeable companion, but had too much reserve to make a friendship with, and not altogether the character that suits me.

White's begins to crumble away very fast, and would be a melancholy scene to those who remained if they cared for any one person but themselves. Williams gave a dinner to talk him over, which I suppose was done with the *voix larmoyante, et voilà tout.* Lord Monson *a crevé aussi*, and Tommy Alston, who has left a will in favour of his bastards, which will occasion lawsuits.

I have made an agreement to meet Varcy to-morrow at Knowles ; from thence we go to Tunbridge ; so I shall live on Monday on the Pantiles, and on Tuesday return here. I dine to-day with the Essex's at March's ; we supped last night at Lady Harrington's, the consequence of which is to eat a turtle on Tuesday at an alehouse on the Ranelaugh Road, which she has seized from Lord Barrington. I called at Lady Mary's first, and found her *très triste.*

Lady Holland was thought to be dying yesterday, for Lord Beauchamp was to have dined there, and at three

---

[1] Maria Fagniani, Selwyn's adopted daughter. This is the first mention of her in this correspondence.

o'clock a note came from Ste [1] to desire him not to come.
The late Lord Holland's servants, preserving their friendship for my thief whom I dismissed, were so good, when
their Lord died, to send for him to sit up with the corpse, as
the only piece of preferment which was then vacant in the
family.   But they afterwards promoted him to be out-
rider to the hearse.   Alice told me of it, and said that it
was a comfort and little relief to the poor man for the
present ; and Mr. More, the attorney, to whom I mentioned it, said that they intended to *throw him into the
same thing*—that was the phrase—when Lady Holland
died.   I beg you to reflect on these circumstances ; they
are *dignes de Molière et Le Sage.*  How my poor old friend
would have laughed, if he could have known to what
hands he was committed before his interment !

The night before last Meynell lost between 2 and
3,000 ; what the rest did I don't know.   They abuse
both you and me about the tie,[2] and Hare says, it was the
damned[e]st thing to do at this time in the world.   I told
them, as Lord Cowper said in his speech to the Condemned
Lords in the year 16—, " Happy had it been for all your
Lordships had you lain under so indulgent a restraint."
It is difficult for me to say which was the kindest thing
you ever did by me, but I am sure that this was one of
the wisest which I ever did by myself ; and so remember
that I do by this renew the lease for one month more, and
it shall be as if it had been originally for two months
instead of one.   To this I subscribe, and to the same forfeit on my side.   I received a consideration ample enough
if the lease had been for a year.

1774, [*July*] 26, *Tuesday night, Almack's.*—Lady
Holland, as you will see by the papers, died on Sunday
morning between 7 and 8.   I saw Lady Louisa and Mrs.
Meillor coming in Lady Louisa's chariot between 10 and

---

[1] Stephen Fox, second Baron Holland.

[2] A self-imposed restriction on gambling.  The ingenious and rather
childish character of this pledge is described in a letter of December
9, 1775.

11, which announced to me the close of that melancholy history ; I mean, as far as regards my two very old friends. The loss of the latter, I must own, I feel much the more sensibly of the two ; *serrer les files, comme l'on dit à Varnée, n'est pas assez ; la perte ne laissera pas de reparoître*, in that I had counted upon a resource in the one more than in the other.

I went for a minute to see Ste [1] and Lady Mary, and then I set out for the Duke of Dorset's at Knowles [Knowle Park], where I met Varcy, and where I dined ; and after dinner Varcy and I went to Tunbridge. We saw Penthurst (*sic*) yesterday morning, and dined with his Honour Brudenell, who gave us, that is, Varcy, Mr. and Mrs. Meynell, and Sir J. Seabright, an excellent dinner. We were at a private ball at night, and this morning early I set out for London.

Tunbridge is, in my opinion, for a little time in the summer, with a family, and for people who do not find a great deal of occupation at their country houses, one of the prettiest places in the world. The houses are so many bijouzs made up for the occasion, so near the place, so *agreste*, and the whole an air of such simplicity, that I am delighted with it, as much as when my amusements were, as they were formerly, at the Rooms and upon the Pantiles, which are now to me detestable.

I was pressed much to stay there to-day to dine with Meynell upon a haunch of venison, but I had solemnly engaged myself to Lady Harrington, and to her party at Spring Garden, on the road to Ranelagh. We had a very good turtle. Our company were, Lord and Lady Harrington, Lady Harriot,[2] Lady A., Maria Ord, Mrs. Boothby, Richard [3] from his quarters at Hampton Court, Crags, Lord Barrington, Barker, Langlois, and myself.

March went yesterday to Newmarket, and left a letter behind for me, to excuse him to the party ; he returns on

[1] Second Lord Holland.
[2] Lady Henrietta Stanhope, daughter of second Earl of Harrington. She married Lord Foley in 1776, and died 1781.
[3] Fitzpatrick in this correspondence is usually spoken of as Richard.

Thursday. Here is not one single soul in this house, but I came here to write to you *plus à mon aise.* Lady Mary Howard was at Tunbridge, and asked much after you ; Lady Powis, the Duke of Leeds, hardly anybody besides that I knew. Gen. Smith came there yesterday, and I believe was in hopes of making up a hazard table ; at last Lord Killy [Kelly?] said that I might have one if I pleased.

Charles and Ste, &c., are gone for the present to Red Rice. I was in hopes of seeing Storer to-day, but this damned turtle party has kept me so late that I doubt if I shall see him to-night. I met him on the road, as I was going to Knowles, on his return from Tunbridge, and he then told me that he should set out for Castle Howard to-morrow, and would have set out to-day, but that I begged that I might see him first.

They can find no will of Lord Thomond's as yet ; so his poor nephew will by his procrastination be the loser of a considerable estate ; for he certainly intended to have made him his heir, and the attorney had left with him a will to be filled up. But we are never sure of doing any-thing but what we have but one minute for doing ; what we think we may do any day, we put off so many days that we do not do it all.

This reflection, and the experience which I have had in other families of the consequences of these delays, deter-mined me to lose no time in settling, for my dear Mie Mie, that which may be the only thing done for her, and only because we · may do it any day in the week. But I thank God I've secured, as much as anything of that nature can be secured, what will be, I hope, a very com-fortable resource for her. I am egregiously deceived if it will not. As for other things, I must hope for the best. It makes me very serious when I think of it, because my affection and anxiety about her are beyond conception.

I shall not think of setting out for Gloucester, unless there is some new occurrence, till next week. I have had no fresh alarm. The lawyers are going on furiously and sanguinely against the Duchess of Kingston,[1] who is, they

[1] See p. 110 (note).

say, at Calais. Feilding also complains of her ; so *elle s'est brouillée avec la justice au pied de la lettre.* Nobody doubts of her felony ; the only debate in conversation is, whether she can have the benefit of her clergy. Some think she will turn Papist. All expect some untimely death. *C'est un exécrable personage que celui que* (sic) *fait mon voisin.*

James has cut out work enough for himself in Hertford-shire ; *il s'en repentira, ou je me trompe fort.* Adieu ; my best compliments to Lady Carlisle and Lady Julia, and my love to the little ones. I long to see the boy excessively. I hear of your returning to London in September ; pray let me hear your motions very particularly, and if you bring up the children. I am ever most truly and affectionately yours.

[1774,] *July* 30, *Saturday night, Almack's.*—I write my letter from hence, from the habitude of making this place my bureau, not that there is anybody here, or that there was the least probability of my finding anybody here. The last post night I was obliged to have an amanuensis, as you will know to-morrow morning when the post comes in. I had got a small particle of shining sand in my eye that during the whole day, but particularly at night, gave me most exquisite pain, and prevented me from writing to you, which, next to receiving your letters, is one of my great pleasures. So this was *un grand évènement pour moi, par une petite cause.* While the writer was writing, Hare came in, and he said that he would finish the letter for me, but what they both wrote God knows.

Storer I suppose set out yesterday for Castle H[oward], and I take for granted will be with you before this letter. March has been out of town ever since Monday till to-day. He has been at a Mr. Darell's in Cambridge-shire, who has a wife I believe with a black eye and low forward [forehead]. I guessed as much by his stay, and young Thomas who came up with him to town told me it was so.

I supped last night at Lady Hertford's with the two Fitzroys, Miss Floyd, and Lord F. Cavendish [1] ; and to-day, Lady Hertford, Miss Floyd, and Lord Frederick and I dined at Colonel Kane's, who is settled in the Stable Yard, and in a damned good house, plate, windows cut down to the floor, elbowing his Majesty with an enormous bow window. The dog is monstrously well nipped ; he obtrudes his civilities upon me, *malgré que j'en ai*, and will in time force me not to abuse him. He would help me to-day to some venison, and how he contrived it, I don't know, but for want of the Graces he cut one of my fingers to the bone, that I might as well have dined at a cut-fingered ordinary.

I am diverted with your threats that I shall have short letters, because you are plagued with Northumberland disputes. You say that you have every post letters to write, and so you will have them to write for some time, for the Devil take me if I believe that you have wrote or will write one of them. A good *ronfle* for that, an't please your Honour, with about twenty sheets of paper spread about upon the table, and on each of them the beginning of a letter.

You know me very well also in thinking that my heart fails me as the time of my going to Gloucester approaches. I made a very stout resistance a fortnight ago, notwithstanding Harris's importunate summons, and now he plainly confesses in a letter which I received from him to-day, that my coming down upon that pretended meeting would have been nugatory, as he calls it. The Devil take them ; I have wished him and his Corporation in Newgate a thousand times. But there will be no trifling after the end of this next week. The Assizes begin on Monday sevennight. Then the Judges will be met, a terrible show, for I shall be obliged to dine with them, and be in more danger from their infernal cooks than any of the criminals who are to be tried, excepting those who will be so unfortunate as to have our jurisconsult for their advocate.

[1] A distinguished soldier, afterwards Field-Marshal (1728–1803).

7

I would not advise you to be unhappy about Caroline's [1] want of erudition ; a very little science will do at present, and much cannot be poured into the neck of so small a vessel at once. I agree with you that it is not to be wished that she should be a *savante*, and she will know what others know. I have no doubt there is time enough for her to read, and little Morpeth [2] to walk.

There is, I grant you, more reason to fear for Hare. Boothby [3] assures me that as yet no prejudice has been done to his fortune. I have my doubts of that, but am clear that he runs constant risk of being very uneasy. But there is no talking to him ; he has imbibed so much of Charles's *ton* of *qu'importe, que cela peut mener à l'hôpital.*

Lady Holland [4] will be removed on Monday, and my thief one of her outriders. All Lord Holland's servants, since he had that house at Kingsgate, have been professed smugglers, and John, as I am informed, was employed in vending for them some of their contraband goods, for which he was to be allowed a profit. He sold the goods, and never accounted with his principals for a farthing ; and so now they place him to sit up with the corps[e] of the family, and to act as one of their undertakers, that they may be in part reimbursed. This is the *dessous des cartes, qui est véritablement comique, et singulier.* Ste, &c., will be here about the end of the week.

I hear that the night that Charles sat up at White's, which was that preceding the night of Lady Holland's death, he planned out a kind of itinerant trade, which was going from horse race to horse race, and so, by

---

[1] Eldest daughter of the Earl of Carlisle ; married, 1789, John Campbell, who was created first Lord Cawdor ; she died 1848.

[2] George, Lord Morpeth, afterwards sixth Earl of Carlisle (1773-1848). In this correspondence Selwyn often refers to him as George. Selwyn had a strong affection for him, and treated him with sympathy and tact.

[3] Sir Brooke Boothby (1743-1824). One of the fashionable young men of the period. He devoted himself particularly, however, to literary society, and published verses, and political and classical works. He lived for a time in France, and was a friend of Rousseau.

[4] Lady Holland died on July 24th.

knowing the value and speed of all the horses in England, to acquire a certain fortune.

I learned from Bore to-day, that Sir G. M'Cartney is a debtor to the family as well as myself, and his debt is to the amount of five thousand pounds, which I am afraid he will find it difficult to raise.

Blaquiere and George Howard are to have two Red Ribbands on Wednesday. There is no end to the honours of your family. I have entrusted Lady Carlisle's picture, I mean your grandmother's, to Linnell, to be framed and cleaned, and then it will be sent to Castle Howard. March I hear goes to Huntingdon next Tuesday.

I think that I shall set out on Thursday next, or if my heart fails me, not till Saturday. I shall then be time enough to meet these Judges, who do not begin to poison and hang till Monday. Lady Mary has promised to make me a present of the little antique ring which you gave to Lord Holland.

Did I tell you that I saw Lord Ilchester?[1] He shewed me a letter which he had received from Ste on his mother's death, and some trifling things which had belonged to Lord H[olland]. Lord Ilchester was extremely pleased with this mark of his affection, and indeed the letter was a very kind and well-bred letter as any I ever read.

I find Lord Thomond most excessively blamed in having neglected to make his will, so that he has died at last *en mauvaise odeur* with his White's friends. I cannot but think, as he was so remarkably methodical, that he intended, by making no will, that the estate should go where the law directs, especially as the second son of his brother has besides so ample a fortune.

Williams has been giving a different account of the public money left in Lord Holland's hands from any which I ever before heard. He, Walters, Offley, and March dined at White's. I called in there after dinner. Williams said that a calculation is made of what the

---

[1] Stephen Fox, first Earl of Ilchester (1704–1776), the elder brother of Henry, first Lord Holland.

interest of that money will amount to from this time to the settlement of the account ; and that it is to be made capital, and is part of what is due to the public. I protest I don't understand him, nor do I conceive what the residue of the personal estate will amount to ; but not to much, as the opinion of the family is. The reports, and belief of those who are not in the secret, are out of all credibility.

Lady Holland's second will, or codicil, will not be opened till the family returns to town. Everybody is inquisitive to know if you and Foley are safe. *Il est merveilleux l'intérêt que tout le monde prend à tout ceci, aussi bien qu'au mariage de notre Prince, dont je ne saurois vour dire des nouvelles.* Meynell, Panton, and James are in Hertfordshire, and the highty-tighty man at Port Hill in the damnest (*sic*) fright in the world about the small-pox. I hope the poor devil will get over it.

Adieu, my dear lord. If I was prevented from writing by last post, *cette fois-ci je m'en suis bein vengé.* . . .

I see your porter every morning in the grove, as he returns from Islington, where he is drinking the waters ; he looks a little better, but not much. They have lent him a horse to ride there, and he says that he finds the air where he is to agree better with him than that of the country.

Pray tell Shepardson that I ask after her, and my compliments to Mr. Willoughby, if you see him. I have demonstrated to Sir G. Metham that I [am] originally a Yorkshire man, and that my name is Salveyne ; and he says that the best Yorkshire blood does at this time run through my veins, and so I hope it will for some time before the circulation of it is stopped.

The duties of a country gentleman and a Member of Parliament, the boredom of a visit to a constituency could not always be avoided by Selwyn. Thus the two following letters are written from Gloucestershire.

[1774,] *Aug. 9, Tuesday, Gloucester.*—I set out from London on Saturday last, as intended, and came to Matson the next day to dinner. I found our learned

Counsel in my garden ; he dined with me, and lay at my house, and the next morning he came with me in my chaise to this place for the Assizes. I have seen little of him since, being chiefly in the Grand Jury chamber, but I take it for granted that till this morning that he set out for London his hands were full of business, and the two men condemned were his clients, who were condemned only *par provision* till he had drawn up the case.

This town has been very full of the neighbouring gentlemen, and I suppose the approaching elections have been the cause of it. I am not personally menaced with any opposition, but have a great dread of one, because the contentions among those who live in the country and have nothing else to do but to quarrel, are so great, that without intending to hurt me, they will stir up trouble and opposition, which will be both hazardous and expensive. I am tormented to take a part in I know not what, and with I know not whom, and my difficulty is to keep off the solicitation of my friends, as they call themselves, who want a bustle, the expense of which is not to be defrayed by themselves.

I do assure you that it is a monstrous oppression of spirits which I feel, and which I would not feel for an hour if I had nobody's happiness to think of but my own, which would be much more secured by a total renunciation of Parliament, Ministers, and Boroughs than by pursuing the emoluments attached to those connections. However, as it is the last time that I shall ever have anything to do of this kind, I will endeavour to keep up my spirits as well as I can ; but I must declare to you that it is an undertaking that is most grievous to me, that I am ashamed of, and that neither the established custom of the country [n]or the nature of our Government does by any means reconcile to me.

I have dinners of one sort or other till Tuesday, and then I purpose to set out for London, unless some unforeseen event prevents me. Horry Walpole has a project of coming into this part of the world the end of this week, and, if he does, of coming to me on Saturday. I shall be glad to converse with anybody whose ideas are more intelligible than those of the persons I am now with. But I do not depend much upon seeing him.

The weather is very fine, and Matson in as great beauty as a place can be in, but the beauties of it make very little impression upon me. In short, there is nothing in this eccentric situation in which I am now that can afford me the least pleasure, and everything I love to see in the world is at a distance from me. All I do is so *par manière d'acquit, et de si mauvaise grace*, that I am surprised at the civility with which I am treated.

I am in daily hopes of hearing from yon. I am sorry that the children are to be left behind ; that is, that their health, which is a valuable consideration, makes it prudential. I shall be happy when I see them again, but it is not in my power to fix the time any more than the means of my happiness. . . .

Storer has little to do than to sing, *Se caro sei*, and to write to me, and therefore pray make him write. Richard the Third is to be acted here to-night. I will go and see an act of it, *pour me desennuyer*.

[1774,] *Aug.* 13, *Saturday, Matson.*—As you are one of the first persons who occupies my thoughts when I awake, so it shall be a rule with me hereafter, when I am to write to you, to make that my first business, and not defer, as I have these two last posts, writing till the evening, when it is more probable, at least in this place, to suffer some interruption. This looks like an apology for what I am sure needs none ; it requires much more, that I seem to have established it as a rule to trouble you so often. I have not here the shallow pretence of telling you some little occurrence[s] which can hardly be interesting in the Parish of St. James's, but when they are confined to this spot. I can have no reason for pestering you with them, but *par un esprit de bavardise, ou pour me rappeler plus souvent à votre souvenir ; ce que votre amitié a rendu pour moi très inutile.*

I have this whole week been immersed in all the

provincial business of a justice, a juryman, and a candidate ; and yesterday was forced to open my trenches before the town as one who intended to humbug them for one seven years more.

> J'ignore le destin qui le ciel me prepare,
> Mais il est temps enfin qu' larbe se declare.

I entertained the whole Corporation [of the City of Gloucester] yesterday at dinner, and afterwards made them a speech, which I am glad that nobody heard but themselves. However *i'ai réussi*, I do not mean in point of eloquence, but I carried my point ; and if it was possible to judge from the event of one meeting only, I should think that there would be a peaceable election, and the expense not exceed many hundred pounds, and those given chiefly to the service of the city. But if [I] did not make my escape, and parry off all the proposals made to me by the people whose whole employment is to create disturbance, I should soon be drawn into a contest from which I should not escape but at the expense of thousands.

At night I heard that Mr. Walpole is here ; I was then at Gloucester ; so I hurried home, and have now some person to converse with who speaks my own language. He came yesterday from Lady Ailesbury's, and stays with me till Tuesday, and then I hope we shall return to London together. I am to have the satisfaction of another festival on Monday, on which day Mr. Walpole proposes to go and see Berkley and Thornbury Castles.

I have had the advantage of very fine weather, and should have had all the benefit of it if I was in any place but where my mind has so many disagreeable occupations, and my stomach so many things which it cannot digest. But it is chiefly their liquors, which are like so much gin. The civility which they shew me, I may say indeed the friendship which I have from some of these people, make me very sorry that I cannot prevail on myself to stay a little longer with them ; but in regard to that, I can hardly save appearances, either by staying, or by forbearing while I do stay to shew them what a pain it is to me.

Your friend Mr. Howard, who is to be Duke of Norfolk, and who by his wife is in possession of a great estate in my neighbourhood, takes so much pains to recommend himself to my Corporation that we are at a loss to know the source of his generosity. I have no personal acquaintance with him, but as a member of the Corporation have a permission to send for what venison we want. He has some charming ruins of an abbey within a mile from hence, with which I intend to entertain Mr. Walpole, and if that is not enough, I must throw in the *mazures* of this old building, which, I believe, will not hold out this century.

Horry tells me that a scheme has been formed, of replacing Charles, but that Lord North will not hear of it. I should certainly myself have the same repugnance. But as I love Charles more than I do the other, I wish that, or anything which can put him once more in a way of establishment. I shall however not have any hopes of that, till he is less intoxicated than he is with the all sufficiency, as he imagines, of his parts. I think that, and his infinite contempt of the *qu'en dira-t-on*, upon every point which governs the rest of mankind, are the two and (*sic*) chief sources of all his misfortunes.

Ste, they tell me, has come to a resolution of selling Holland H[ouse] as soon as possible, and of rebuilding Winterslow. If Lady Holland had not died just as she did, I believe that I should have had him and Lady Mary here for some days, which I should have liked very well.

I have got a prize in Barbot's Lottery, as it may be Conty has told you. I left a man in London, when I came away, with a commission to see that justice was done me, and to send my pye, if I should have one, into Kent. Mine is *à quatre perdrixs* (*sic*); so I have no reason to complain of Conty's Lotteries, for I have had a prize in both of them.

If you intend to buy a ticket in the State Lottery, I should be glad to have a share of it with Lady C[arlisle], Lord Morpeth, and little Caroline, that is, one ticket between us five. Three of my tenants joined for one in the Lottery two or three years since, and they got a £20,000 prize. I made a visit to one of them the other day, whose farm is not far off, and he had made it the prettiest in the world ; and he has three children to share his £10,000, for one moiety of this ticket was his.

Pray make my very best compliments to Lady C. and Lady J.,[1] and give my hearty love to Caroline ; and as for the little Marmot, tell him that if he treats his sister with great attention I shall love him excessively, but *s'il fait le fier*, because he is a Viscount and a Howard, I shall give him several spanks upon his *derrière*. Make Storer write to me, and make Ekins read Atterbury till he can say him by heart.

By the end of August, Selwyn had escaped from Gloucester and was again among his friends and in his favourite haunts in London.

[1774,] *Aug.* 25, *Thursday night, Almack's.*—Here are the Duke of Roxb[urgh], Vernon, James, and Sir W. Draper at Whist ; Boothby, Richard, and R. Fletcher at Quinze. I dined to-day at the Duke of Argyle's [2] at a quarter before four. He and the Duchess went to Richmond at six. The maccaroni dinner was at Mannin's. My eyes are still very painful to me at night, and I do not know what I shall do for them. I hear of no news ; that of the Duchess of Leinster's [3] match is very *équivoque* ; and extreme their drawing-room.

I [am] in constant expectation of being sent for again to Gloucester, and begin (*sic*) a canvas. I think if I prevent it, and an opposition, I shall be very vain of

[1] Lady Juliana Howard was Lord Carlisle's youngest sister. She died unmarried.

[2] John, fifth Duke of Argyll (1723–1806). He had married for his second wife the Duchess of Hamilton, *neé* Gunning, the famous beauty.

[3] Lady Amelia Mary (1731–1814), daughter of Charles, second Duke of Richmond, as celebrated for her beauty and charm as her sisters, Lady Holland, Lady Louisa Connolly, and Lady Sarah Bunbury, The reference is evidently to her approaching second marriage to Mr. Ogilvy.

my conduct. There is nothing so flattering as the
shewing people who thought that they could dupe you,
that you know more of the matter than they do. I know
too little to be active, but have prudence enough to
take no steps while I am in the dark upon the suggestion of others who cannot possibly interest themselves for
me. But I really think it will be a miracle if this is not
a troublesome and expensive Election to me. However,
I will not anticipate the evil by groaning about it before
it happens. . . .

The Duke of Newcastle is to bring Will Hanger into
Parliament, but what is to pay for his chair to go down
to the House the Lord knows; they tell me that there
is absolutely not a shilling left.

The correspondence of 1775 begins with the frequent
story of Charles Fox's debts. It has been well said of
Carlisle, that each fresh instance of prodigality in Fox
"affected his generous heart with anxiety for the character,
the health, and the happiness of his friend before he
found time to compute and lament its calamitous influence
on his own fortunes."[1] Selwyn's solicitude for the welfare
of his friend urged him, as we see in the following letter,
to something like impatient expostulation on his forbearance
and good nature.

[1775 ?] (*Beginning wanting.*) . . . Gregg wants me
to dun Charles. He lost last night £800, as Brooks
told me to-day. He receives money from More the
Attorney. He forestalls all he is to receive, and unless
the importunity begins with you, mine will avail nothing.
Besides, I fairly own that I cannot keep my temper.
My ideas, education, and former experience, or inex-
perience, of these things, make me see some things in
the most horrible light which you can conceive, and I
am far from being singular. Pray write a letter to
Charles, *à tella fin que de raison;* otherwise there will
be no ability left, and then it will be to no purpose.

[1] "The Early History of Charles James Fox," p. 460.

What *ménagement* you choose to have with him is more than I can comprehend. I can conceive the intimacy between you. Your delicacy of temper, ten thousand *nuances de sentiments*. But I can never conceive that all feeling, all the principle, &c., should be of one side only. If you don't press it, he will not think it pressing, and will say so; that must depend upon what you choose to reveal. He may not think you want it, or may think that all mire in which he wallows is as indifferent to you as to him. *Je me perds dans toutes ces reflections.* My God, if they did not concern you, I should not care who were the objects of them.

1775, *Aug.* 1, *Tuesday afternoon, from your own house, below stairs.*—I came from Richmond this morning on purpose to meet Gregg here to dinner, and we have had our leg of mutton together; a poor epitome of Roman greatness. I believe, as Lord Grantham told me, few have so little philosophy as I have. You have a great deal, having a much more manly understanding. . . .

I have been misunderstood about Stavordale, because just what you tell me you approve of is what I meant to propose, or if I had any conception beyond it, it was from a sudden thought which I retract. I have said a few words to Charles, but I do not find that he has more intercourse with him than you have. He says that there can be no doubt of the validity and payment of the debt, and there is no anticipation of it. But it is not to be expected that Charles should think more of Stavordale's debt than his own. He lost in three nights last week 3,000, as he told me himself, and has lent Richard God knows what; the account, and friendship, and want of it, between them is as incomprehensible to me as all the rest of their history. It is a mystery I shall never enquire into, when what concerns you is out of the question. I never heard of the same thing in all the first part of my life, and it shall be my own fault if I hear any more of it.

I rode over yesterday to Lord Besborough's at Roe-

hampton, on purpose to see Lord Fitzwilliam,[1] and had
a long discourse with him in the garden.  He was excessively pleased with the account which I gave him of
the present state of your affairs, together with your manner
of expressing yourself about them.  Every word which
dropped from him discovered the real interest which he
took in whatever concerned you, and his affection for
you.  He is a very valuable young man.

Hare went away without being certain that he was
to go to Castle H——.  He will excuse me if I don't
rely upon his resolutions in parties of pleasure.  But
I should have been glad to have known for a certainty
that he was to have set out.  I believe March's money
and mine helped to grease his wheels.  March deserves
to have lost his, because he was the seducer.  I could
not have lost mine if he had kept me to my obligation ;
but I will not resign my fetters any more.  Welcome,
my chains ; welcome, Mr. Lowman, the keeper.  I am
glad it went no further.

[1775, *Aug.*?].—I am just come from Almack's.
Many are gone to the Thatched House,[2] to sup with *the
ladies*, as they call it.  These ladies are Lady Essex and
Miss Amyas(?).  Richard won last night 1,300 ostensible, besides what he pocketed to keep a *corps de reserve*
unknown to Brooks.  For Brooks lent him 2,300, and
then laments the state of the house.  He duns me for
three hundred, of which I am determined to give him
but two ; as he knows so well where to get the other
hundred, which is that Richard owes me, but seems
determined that I shall not have.  Charles is winning

---

[1] William Wentworth Fitzwilliam, second Earl Fitzwilliam (1748–
1863).  He began at Eton his lifelong friendship with Fox and Carlisle.
In 1794 he was appointed Lord-Lieutenant of Ireland.

[2] The Thatched House Tavern in St. James's Street stood on
the site of the present Conservative Club.  Various well-known
clubs were in the habit of meeting here, notably the Society of
Dilettanti which was formed in 1734, of it Walpole wrote that
" the nominal qualification is having been in Italy and the real one
being drunk."

more, and the quinze table is now at its height. I have set down Brooks to be the completest composition of knave and fool that ever was, to which I may add liar

You say very true, that I have been in a bank, that I have lost my money, that I want to get it back ; but it is as true that I shall make no attempt to get it back till my affairs are quite in another posture from what they are at present ; so pray give me no flings about it, for I lay all the blame upon March, who should not have contributed to it.

[1775,] *Sept.* 1, *Friday, Richmond.*—I have omitted, contrary to my usual custom, two posts, the writing to you, which being out of course may perhaps make you at a loss to guess what is become of me. I am here with Mie Mie, and shall be so for ten or twelve days longer, and then the weather being cool and the days grown short, I shall find the evenings too tedious to myself and not very beneficial to her, which would undoubtedly be with me the first consideration. My journey to Castle H[oward] I would not postpone, if the postponing of it was the prevention of it.

But as I am determined to go there, and it is not as I apprehend material whether it be the first week of this month or of the next, I have submitted to those who desire to govern me in this matter, and that is in regard to Luggershall. My lawyers and Mr. T. Townshend,[1] who is the heir of entail to that estate, have entreated me not to omit any longer the holding what they call a Court Leet.

Mr. Grenville's Bill, as I apprehended that it would, has made it very dangerous to omit any forms which the law prescribes, and the failure of what I am enjoined as lord of the manor to do by the charter would certainly

---

[1] Thomas Townshend (1733–1800), afterward first Viscount Sydney, was Selwyn's nephew. He was Secretary of War in 1782, and in 1783 Secretary of State, when he initiated the policy of sending convicts beyond the seas as colonists. Sydney in Australia was named after him. His second daughter married the second Earl of Chatham, and his fourth daughter married the fourth Duke of Buccleugh—"the beautiful, the kind, the affectionate, and generous Duchess" of Sir Walter Scott.

be very prejudicial upon an enquiry, and perhaps lay me open to an opposition, which could never be made to my interests or property there without such negligence.

For this reason I must either postpone my journey to Castle H[oward] till after that, or make my stay there if I go before too short. This is my present arrangement, which, however important it may be represented to be, should be altered if I could be essentially useful to you or to your affairs by it. I beg that you will not omit to acquaint Mr. Gregg with this, who will see immediately the necessity of it.

I could indeed have set out as I originally intended so as to have met you upon your return, and should have done it if I could have prevailed upon M[arch ?] to have allowed me to do what I am now doing, by which I flatter myself to bring about what will be in many respects of use to that little infant, who has very little thought bestowed upon her but by my means. It is a sore grievance to me, but it is my lot and I must endure it.

My excursions to town are not above once in six days. On Saturday last on my return hither I was indeed very near demolished. My coachman thought fit to run for the turnpike, as the phrase is, and against a four-wheeled waggon with six horses. He seemed to me to have very little chance of carrying his point, if it was not to demolish me and my chaise, but almost sure of succeeding in that. I called, roared, and scolded to no purpose, *il ne daigna pas m'écouter un instant*: so the consequence was, what might be expected, he came with all the force imaginable against the turnpike gate, [and] set my chaise upon its head. Mr. Craufurd was with me, and on the left side, which was uppermost, and we were for a small space of time lying under the horses, at their mercy, and the waggoner's, who seemed very much inclined to whip them on, and from one or other, that is, either from the going of the waggon over us, or the kicking of the horses, we were both in the most imminent danger. Lady Harrington was in her coach just behind us, and took me into it, Mr. Craufurd got into Mr. Henry Stanhope's phaeton, and so we went to Richmond, leaving the chaise, as we thought, all shattered to pieces in the road. This happened just after I had finished my last letter to you, and which I think had very near been the last that I should ever have wrote to you, as those tell me who saw the position in which we for some time were.

*Postscript. Richmond, Saturday morning.*—I received to-day yours from C[astle] H[oward] of last Monday, the 28th August, and you may be sure that it is no small pleasure to me to find by every letter which I receive, that there is such an attention to your affairs, as is really worthy your understanding and capacity. You will find your account in it, by preventing *ennui* in yourself and roguery in others, besides a thousand train (*sic*) of evils that are inseparable from dissipation and negligence. I hope that you made my compliments to Mr. Nicolson ; *il a l'air d'un personnage très respectable, d'un homme affidé et sur.* I cannot afford to wish any period of mine, at ever so little distance, to be arrived, but I am tempted to wish that I was two years older, for this reason, that I am confident your affairs, and the state of your mind, will be pleasanter than it has been in for a great while. So my wife [1] has made you another agreeable visit for a fortnight, as she called it. I am sorry for what you tell me of the visit which was not made. I don't love excuses, but perhaps there may be some which need not give any jealousy of want of true affection. I hope you will receive mine as such, or I would set out for C[astle] H[oward] directly. I have totally laid aside the thoughts of going this year to Matson, or even to Gloucester. I have no engagement, but to be one day at Luggershall, but that with difficulty can be dispensed with. Neither Lord N[orth] or his Parliament, or anything else shall prevent me from going to you when you desire it.

But the alteration in the little girl is so visibly for the better, since she has been in this air, and Mrs. Craufurd acts so much like a guardian to her, that I am in hopes by degrees to be the means of placing her where my

[1] A joking allusion to one of his friends.

mind will for the present be easy about her, and that she may be brought up with that education that, with the help of other advantages, may in some measure recompense her for the ill fortune of the first part of her life. This is, if my heart was laid open, all that you could see in it at present, except the anxiety which is now almost over in regard to you.

For I verily believe that what has happened, although it came upon me like *coup de tonnerre*, and has given me a great deal of bile, and my stomach I find weakened from that cause, more than from any other,—for I'm more and more abstemious every day,—yet I now see that all will end well, and that in the meantime neither you [n]or Lady C[arlisle] will make yourselves uneasy by placing things before you in a wrong light.

I will speak to Ridley when I go to town, but scolding increases my bile, and so to avoid it I sent that coachman who had like to have destroyed me this day sevennight out of my sight, and his horses, without seeing him.

You say that C[harles] will receive four or five thousand from Lord S[tavordale ?] upon the same account. *Je le crois*, and others will soon after receive it from him, but I am afraid not you. You may be sure that he said nothing to me of that ; he does not talk of his resources to me, except that of his Administration, which you will be so just to me as to recollect that I never gave any credit to, because he knows how I desire that those resources may be applied. On the contrary, when I spoke to him the other day about your demand, I was answered only with an elevation *de ses épaules et une grimace dont je fus tant soit peu piqué.* But it is so. I shall say no more to him upon that or any other subject than I can help. *La coupe de son esprit, quelque brillante qu'elle puisse être, n'est pas telle qui me charme, et luisera par la suite pour le moins inutile.*

I am now going in my chaise to dine at Mr. Digby's, *où cette branche de la famille ne sera pas traitée avec beaucoup de ménagement;* and first I am going to write a letter

to my Lord Chancellor to thank him for a living which
he has given to a friend of mine at Gloucester, accompanied with the most obliging letter to me in the world.
This and yours have put me to-day in very good humour.

We had an assembly last night at Mrs. Craufurd's for
Lady Cowper, Lady Harrington, Lady H. Vernon, &c.,
and Mie Mie was permitted to sit up till nine. She
wanted to see "an sembelly," as she calls it, and was
mightily pleased. . . .

[1775,] *Oct.* 7, *Saturday night.* — I returned from
Luggershall yesterday, a day later than I was in hopes
to have come, for I was made to believe that the Court
Leet, which was my object in going, would have been
held on Wednesday ; however I passed a day extraordinary
better than I expected in that beggarly place. I made an
acquaintance with a neighbouring gentleman, who has
a very good estate, and a delightful old mansion, where
I played at whist and supped on Wednesday evening. He
is a descendant of the Speaker Smith, and son of that Mr.
Ashton whom we saw at Trentham, or whom I saw there
the first time I went, and who was an evidence against me
at Oxford 30 years ago—a sad rascal ; but the son is *un
garçon fort honnête*, and he received me with extraordinary
marks of civility and good breeding.

We have the same relations, and his house was furnished
with many of their pictures. There was one of a great
grandmother of mine, who was the Speaker's sister, painted
by Sir P. Lely, that was one of the best portraits I ever
saw. I wish Sir J. Reynolds had been there to have told
me why those colours were so fine and looked as if they
were not dry, while all his are as lamb (*sic*) black in
comparison of them. I am to have a copy of this
picture next spring.

I shall appoint Gregg on Monday to meet me on
business, and I will therefore defer talking upon that
subject till I have seen him. Storer dined with me
to-day. Hare and Charles I am told have lost everything
they had at Newmarket. General Smith has been the

8

winner.  Richard also is stripped.  No company in town as yet, or news.  I have been writing Gloucester letters to-night about this damned contest till I am blind, so I must be short.  Ridley has assured me that he has sent the books.

Have you read the Anecdotes of M^e du Barri ?  They are to me amusing.  The book is I think a true picture of the latter end of the life and court of that weak wretch Louis XV., not overcharged, and so many of the facts being incontestable, you may take the whole story for a true one, no one part being more improbable than another.  Will you have it sent ?  It is dear, half-a-guinea ; *un recit trop graveleux pour être recommandé aux dames.*  My most affectionate compliments, and so adieu.  My eyes grow too dim to write, but are infinitely mended.

I dine to-morrow at the Ambassador's, and after dinner we go to make our visits at Richmond to Lady Fawkener, and to Petersham.  I thank you for your idea of Emily ^1 : *j'en profiterai ;* I can depend upon no other's.

In the midst of the news of the gaieties of the town, of the begging of political placemen for a higher rank in the peerage, we now come upon the question of America.  The English people had not yet appreciated the momentous struggle into which the King and his ministers had drawn their country.  The flippancy with which Selwyn alludes to the rebellion is indicative of the general state of opinion even among those who were constantly at the centre of political affairs.  The battle of Bunker's Hill had been fought on the 17th of the preceding June, and yet to Selwyn the struggle beyond the Atlantic was merely a " little dispute."

[1775,] *Oct.* 11, *Wednesday m[orning].*—I went last night after I had sent my letters to the post, which by the way was not till past ten, to Lady Betty's.  There

---

^1 Edward Emly, Dean of Derry.  Selwyn always writes of him as " Emily " : in a letter of March 24, 1781, he calls him " Mr. Dean Emily."

were with her Lady Julia, Gregg, and a Mr. Owen at
whist. There were Hare, Delmé,¹ and his odd-looking
parson, who came to town to christen the child. I went
from thence and supped at Lady Hertford's, with Lord
Fr[ederick] Cavendish, Mrs. Howe, and the Beau Richard,
who is returned from Jamaica. His friend Colonel Kane
has got the start of him since he went *dans la carrière
politique, mais le bon Colonel est un peu plus intriguant que
son camarade ; celui-ci est certainement un charactère bien
sauvage, un mélange d'irlandois et de Creol, et avec tout cela,
un fort honnête garçon.* . . .

You pant after news from America ; there are none
*pour le moment.* But you may depend upon it, if that
little dispute interests you, I will let you know, *quand le
monde sera rassemblé, tout ce que j'apprens, et de bon lieu.*

Charles assures us that nothing is so easy as to put
an end to all this, but then there must be a change of
Ministry, *quelconque*, no matter what, as a preliminary
assurance to the Insurgents ; and then for the inference,
under any change he can't allow himself to take an
employment, and lay more money upon shark[s ?]. But
there will be no change yet, I am confident, and when
there is, he will as much want another.

They now doubt of Southwell's peerage,² after all the
bustle in our country. All the claimants for new peerages
oppose it with their clamours, as if this was a creation,
and taking it for granted that the King is to accept their
interpretations instead of his own. I suppose, if he
fulfilled all his engagements upon that score, there would
be an addition to the House of Lords equal to the present
number.

*Ergo*, if I was King, I should expunge the whole debt,
and begin *sur nouveaux fraix.* I think that I should

¹ Peter Delmé, married in 1769 to Lady Elizabeth Howard, Lord
Carlisle's sister ; he was called Peter the Czar, in allusion to his great
wealth, which, however, he and Lady Betty very much reduced by
high play. He shot himself in Grosvenor Square, April 10, 1770.
² Thomas George, third Baron Southwell (1721–1780), was created
Viscount Southwell in July, 1776.

have answer ready to make to my Minister against those promises. I should tell him, if my affairs required a Sir G. Hawke or who[m] you please to be made a peer, it should be down [done] *sur le champ*, but I would not be hampered by engagements. *Qu'en pensez-vous, Seigneur ?*

I take it for granted that Lord Gower will be here soon. I have desired Gregg to wait on him with an account of all that has passed in your affairs during my regency, because Gregg will be better able to state the matter to him, and to explain the necessity I have been under, by an unexpected increase of demands, of transcending the bounds of the deed, as well as to satisfy him upon your own domestic economy, which is certainly by all accounts irreprehensible.

[1775,] *Nov.* 16, *Thursday night, the Committee Room of the House of Commons.*—I received last night, but late, your much wished-for and expected letter concerning the Bedchamber ;[1] which, containing what it did, and the style of it being what it was, I carried this morning to Lord G[ower], who seemed perfectly satisfied with the option you had made, and the manner in which you expressed yourself in relation to himself. Lord North dines with him on Saturday, when he intends to expatiate more at large upon your views, and to urge further your pretensions to some more advantageous situation.

I must say for the Bedchamber, you could not have a more honourable post or at the same time a more insignificant one. I ventured to tell Lord G. that I believe (*sic*), notwithstanding the demur you made upon it, if it had been a point with him that you should have accepted it— I did believe that you would. I thought that I ran no risk in making on your behalf that compl[imen]t, as he seemed to be so perfectly agreed with me that it was better not to accept it.

He entered with me on the last account from the Colonies, which is undoubtedly much more favourable

---

[1] Lord Carlisle declined the offer of a Lordship of the Bedchamber, see Trevelyan's " Early Life of Fox," chap. iv.

than was expected by friends, or enemies ; and it agreed so perfectly with the private letters which I have seen, that I could not but credit it. It is my real belief that the Opposition will be disappointed, and those who have joined them upon speculation and resentment, not a little vexed at being duped. It is impossible to answer for events, but these must be such as are very little expected or probable, before there can be any breach in the present Ministry, or the King obliged to make a change in it.

Burke's speech [1] to-day was three hours and twenty minutes. Lord Ossory has hoisted his flag, and spoke. It is now about 9 o'clock ; it will be midnight in all probability before we rise, for none of the leading persons in Administration has spoke, or the principal squibs of opinion. Charles is down, but has not yet spoke. I am more desirous myself of hearing Lord G. G[ermaine] than anybody. He looks very confident, and I take for granted is prepared for all kind of abuse.

Rigby came to me in the House last night to know if I had heard from you, adding, " I hope to God that he will accept the Bedch[amber]." I was not more desirous that you should, because that was his opinion. I thought that Lord G[ower] had been talking to him, but he assured me that he had not ; so from what quarter his intelligence came I know not. Lord G. thought that it was most probable from Lord North. If you had made that your option, I should have proposed that you should at the same time have been sworn into the Privy Council, as an earnest that more was intended, and in a Line of Business, and I think that they would not have objected to it.

Adam Hay, Lord March's Member for Peebles, died yesterday, I am afraid to say suddenly, because it is a suspicious word, and will be more so in his case, as I

---

[1] On November 16th Burke moved for leave to bring in a Bill for composing the present troubles and for quieting the minds of his Majesty's subjects in America. The motion was negatived, after an important debate, a little before five o'clock in the morning, by 210 to 105 votes.

believe Fortune has not been favourable to him. But
I do not believe anything of that sort ; his general state
of health has been bad for some time, and I was told that
his last and fatal attack was in his bowels. The two
Lascells and (*sic*) dined at his house not a week ago.
Sir R. Keith comes in, in his room. Lord N[orth] and
Lord Suffolk recommend him. March has demurred
upon it, but seems not determined for particular reasons.
I have been employed about this, this whole day at Court,
and then with Lord North, and going backwards and
forwards. March will not do what he should, at the
time it ought to be done, and then things are in confusion,
when they should be adjusted, and carried into execution.
It is to no purpose endeavouring to persuade him ; if
you tell him what may happen, he silences you with some
adage, or a *qu'importe*, and so drives everything off till he
does [not] know what party [*parti ?*] to fix upon.

[1775,] *Dec.* 9, *Saturday* m[*orning*], *at home.*—By
accident you will receive no letter from me to-morrow,
but by no accident *fâcheux.* For the future, however
I conclude my day, I will begin it by writing to you,
when the day comes that I am to write.

Yesterday I dined at Lord Gower's ; there were the
B[isho]p of Worcester, Lord Stanley and Lady Betty,
Lord March, Storer, K. Stewart, and *la famille ; en vérité
votre beau-père est bien servi ; le diner fut superbe.* I
was obliged, without staying for my coffee, to go to the
House, where we were till about ten. I hope that it
is the last day of business before the Recess.

I sent your letter last night to Lady Carlisle, and wrote
to her myself. But I will defer no more writing to
anybody till the evening, excepting to Ald. Harris, who
is at present very clamorous for a letter, for he has not
heard from me in God knows how long a time, and at
this minute I have mislaid his last letters.

I have contrived to wrench out of Charles's black
hands 50 pounds for Spencer, by watching the opportunity of his play, and should have got from anybody

but himself one thousand of the £1,500, for he had won that, and more, the other night, and it was to have been paid to him the next morning. I sent immediately to Gregg, and it was my design to have carried your bond to Brooks, who should have intercepted the 1,000 for his own use, and then I should have applied the same sum afterwards to the tradesmen ; but he was too quick for me, and sett [sat] up and lost it and more to Lord Stavordale. I know that he could have pleaded his debt to Lord Cholmondly, and to Brooks himself, &c., neither of whom probably would have received a groat ; but that matter is over for the present. However, Brooks has promised me that (*sic*), if any event of this kind happens again, to avail himself of it, for your convenience.

I have taken the liberty to talk a good deal to Lord Stavordale, partly for his own sake and partly for yours, and pressed him much to get out of town as soon as possible, and not quit Lord I[lchester] any more. His attention there cannot be of long duration, and his absence may be fatal to us all. I painted it in very strong colours, and he has promised me to go, as soon as this Sedgmoor Bill is reported. I moved to have Tuesday fixed for it. We had a debate and division upon my motion, and this Bill will at last not go down so glibly as Bully hoped that it would. It will meet with more opposition in the H[ouse] of Lords, and Lord North being adverse to it, does us no good. Lord Ilchester gets, it is said, £5,000 a year by it, and amongst others Sir C. Tynte something, who, for what reason I cannot yet comprehend, opposes it.

The comparison of me to Arlequin, I allow to be in a great measure just. The events have frequently called his (*sic*) to my mind. But I beseech you do not say that you do not desire to hinder me from a favourite amusement. If it was an innocent one also, *passe ;* but it is not only dangerous, but in its consequences criminal, and there is no dependence upon any one man breathing, who pursues it with the *chaleur* which I have done. How can I expect another man to trust me, if I cannot trust myself ?

Therefore, although March has dissolved the tie,[1] I beg that you will lay me under some sort of restriction about it. I do not speak this from having now suffered, for I have not, as I told you before, since March last ; that is, by the event. But I have been susceptible [since ?] then more than once, and it has been my good fortune and not my prudence which has kept me above water.

What I propose is, to receive a guinea, or two guineas, and to pay twenty, for every ten which I shall lose in the same day, above 50, at any game of chance. I reserve the 50 for an unexpected necessity of playing in the country, or elsewhere, with women. All things considered, it is the best tie, and the tax the easiest paid, and restrictive enough, and twenty guineas you will take ; and if you tie me up, I beg my forfeitures may go to the children, and then perhaps I may forfeit for their sake, you'll say. I really think it will be a wise measure for me, and a safe one; and let this tie be for this year only, and then, if it is demonstrable that my fortune is impaired by not playing, the tie will be over, and not renewed the next. In the mean time, and till I shall hear your sentiments upon this, I must avoid going to Almack's, and so I will. . . .

I dine to-day at Harry St. John's, and to-morrow at Eden's[2] ; and on Monday all the St. Johns in the world, old and young, dine here.

Lord Northington[3] brought me home two nights in his coach, and in one of them the conversation turned upon you. He said there was nobody had a better idea

---

[1] See *ante*, p. 77 (*note* 2).

[2] William Eden, Lord Auckland (1744–1814). He was educated at Eton and Oxford ; called to the Bar in 1769. In 1778 was one of the peace commissioners to America with Lord Carlisle, accompanying him later to Ireland as secretary. Between 1785 and 1789 he filled appointments as ambassador successively to France, Spain, and the United Provinces. In 1789 he was created Baron Auckland in Ireland, and in 1793 raised to the English peerage. He married Eleanor, daughter of Sir Gilbert Elliot and sister of the first Earl of Minto.

[3] Robert Henley, second Earl of Northington (1747–1782), a friend of Charles Fox. The main event of his political life was his tenure of the office of Lord-Lieutenant of Ireland in the Coalition Ministry in 1783.

of what a gentleman should be than Carlisle ; that you was so throughout. There is a singularity and frankness in some people's manner of delivering their sentiments, by which they receive great advantage. You remember Sir R. Payne's way of describing you, which was still more odd ; he said if anybody looked through the keyhole at any time to see how you behaved when you was alone, that he was sure there would be no more impropriety in it than if you had a hundred eyes upon you. I don't like commending you myself, but I like to hear others do so, and especially when they speak about what they think, and when what they think has the air of *vérité* in it.

I hope you make my compliments to Ekins, and that he has by this time read Atterbury quite through. I do not propose the Bishop as a pattern for anything but for eloquence ; and for argument, *on n'en trouve pas, chez lui.*

I think that Storer, John St. John,[1] and I, shall set out in about ten days. My coach, cloak, and muff are ready. Adieu most affectionately. My respects to Lady C[arlisle] and my love to the children, and last of all do not despair of me about Hazard, for it being what I love so much, is precisely the reason why I shall be more upon guard in respect to it. I do not mean by this to limit, but the *ense recidendum ;* every other *parti* is delusive and childish.

[1775,] *December* 12, *Tuesday night.*—General Scott is dead ; *sic Diis placuit.* Bully [2] has lost his Bill. I reported it to-day, and the Question was to withdraw it. There were 59 against us, and we were 35. It was worse managed by the agents, supposing no treachery, than ever business was. Lord North, Robinson, and Keene divided against. Charles said all that could be said on our side.

---

[1] John St. John (1746-1793), third son of John, second Viscount St. John, a typical specimen of the macaroni. He was an M.P. from 1773 to 1784, held a sinecure post as Surveyor-General of Land Revenues. He wrote some political pamphlets, a play, and an opera. The play was a tragedy—" Mary Queen of Scots " ; it was acted at Drury Lane with some success in 1789, Kemble and Mrs. Siddons taking the leading parts.

[2] Lord Bolingbroke.

But as the business was managed, it was the worst Question that I ever voted for. We were a Committee absolutely of Almack's ; so if the Bill is not resumed, and better conducted and supported, this phantom of £30,000 clear in Bully's pocket to pay off his annuities vanishes.

It is surprising what a fatality attends some people's proceedings. I begged last night as for alms, that they would meet me to settle the Votes. I have, since I have been in Parliament, been of twenty at least of these meetings, and always brought numbers down by those means. But my advice was slighted, and twenty people were walking about the streets who could have carried this point.

*December* 14, 1775.[1]—I was much disappointed yesterday in not receiving a letter from you. I dined here and alone and was in hopes that a letter from you would have come or I should have dined out for my spirits at present are not good, nor can I contrive that they should be better, and yet *je ne donnerai pas la mort* though nothing in the world has happened, but *j'ai les dragons noirs et fort noirs l'avenir me donne des horreurs*, but *brisons la pour la present :* I have bought to-day at Lord Holland's sale of books, " Dart's Antiquities of Westminster Abbey," a very complete copy on large paper. But I paid £6 for it, which is £2 more than it has been usually estimated at. Dr. Baker has promised to propose me for the Royal Society, and I will be of as many societies as I can which may serve for dissipation and to avoid what I have more reason to dread than anything in the world. I am sure a grand coup de malheur at play would oppress me beyond anything.

I hope that apprehension will keep me from it, and you must assist me. Don't say, he knows it, it is to no purpose speaking to anybody. . . . Speaking does operate if you esteem the person who speaks, and those who are silent have an indifference about what happens to their friends which I know you have not. There is an old translation of Plutarch two hundred years old by

---

[1] This letter was not included in those printed by the Historical MSS. Commission.

Amyot, in twelve or fourteen volumes 12mo. bound in blue maroc. Gibbon tells me that it is a very rare and valuable book, one of the first translations which was in that language, and has infinite merit. The print is not good enough for me, it will come high and I seldom read. I must buy quartos now, large letter, and books of another kind which amuse me more. Lady Holland has got well again. Scott has left £200,000 and two daughters who divide it. . . . I hear some good news is come to-day from America. I shall know more of it from this dinner I am going to. I have no mind to go, but cannot recede. I hope that my spirits will be the better for it, but it is the gloomiest day I ever knew. The Duchess of K[ingston] is in a great fright for the consequences of her trial. Where she is to be tried is not yet decided. Most people I take it for granted wish it may be in Westminster Hall. Lord Mansfield opposes it. It is near five so I shall take my leave. I wrote this for fear this dinner and a nap, etc., might prevent my writing. My respects to Lady C. and the dear children.

In this last letter Selwyn notes the arrival of news from America. But he preferred to let his friend Storer forward the political information of the moment to Carlisle, so that a letter of Storer is sometimes supplementary to one of Selwyn. The following is a continuation, so to say, of that which Selwyn wrote on the same date.

*Anthony Storer to Lord Carlisle.*

[1775, *December* 14, *Portugal Street.*—I did not give Selwyn my promise concerning our expedition to Castle Howard, and therefore should not have mentioned it to you ; but if I am not able to come, it will be some comfort to me to know that you will have him and St. John ; so that if you fail of getting any politics out of George, I think you must be very unlucky if you have not, what you wish, a boar (*sic*) of politics from the other.

I assure you, at least so it appears to me, that American politics are very much altered. Taxation and the exercise of it are totally renounced. You never hear the right mentioned, but in order to give it up. The rigid politician of last year, such a man for instance as Wellbore Ellis, stands now almost single in the House of Commons.

You ask me if the *Intercourse Bill*,[1] as it is called, cuts off all commerce and communication with the Islands.  You may guess why it is called the Intercourse Bill; it is *lucus a non lucendo*.  The Americans are neither to trade with the West Indies or Great Britain ; they are not interdicted any commerce with us, but they are to be treated, both themselves and their vessels, as enemies in open time of war, and the captures are to become the property of the commanders and the sailors.

This is the winding up of our catastrophe.  If it lasts more than one year, it seems even to moderate West Indians to be totally ruinous to them.  What seems to affect them most by the passing of this Bill is not the fear of starving, which they have their apprehensions of, but the danger there is of their being taken on false pretences by the men of war that are to protect them, or by the Americans, on whose coast they are always obliged to pass very near.  In short, every West Indian, except Jack Douglas, is in the utmost consternation.

Parliament, that is, the House of Commons, have done their business ; we are now waiting for this Bill to pass the Lords, and then we adjourn for the holidays.  The day before yesterday, the Sedgmoor Inclosure Bill, in which Lord Bolingbroke was very much interested (G. Selwyn was Chairman for and in the Committee) was thrown out, owing to some irregularities—some differences in the Assent Bill and the House Bill.  As you have had something to do with enclosures, you understand those two words, so I need not explain them.

It is true I have spoke, and as you say, and as I meant, not brilliantly. *Le mieux est l'ennemi du bien*, is a very favourite maxim of mine. Perhaps, as this is one of my great undertakings, it is more owing to you, than to any other motive.  I know you will laugh at me, for saying so, but I really believe it.  I said a few words, too, upon your Morpeth business, which encouraged me perhaps to do afterwards, what I did with respect to Mr. Oliver's motion.

Lord G. Germaine's coming into office seems to have been a greater acquisition on the side of Government, than on his.  Office adds dignity and respect to some men ; others, who derive no dignity from it, generally lose by it.  This I think Lord G.'s case.  He seemed to speak with much more weight, before he was in office.  The Ghost of Mindon is for ever brought in neck and shoulders to frighten him with. Willes [Wilkes] and Sawbridge have attacked him more than once with the British Cavalry ; and thus, he must either turn absolute knight errant, or else put up quietly with constant affronts.

The news-papers must have given you the general features of this year's politics.  The complexion of them, I own, is somewhat altered ; and so much, that I dare say you will hardly know 'em again.  You will soon grow used to them, however, and upon very little acquaintance, will be as intimate with them as ever.  So much for the affairs of the

---

[1] The American Prohibitory Bill, to prevent trade and intercourse between the American Colonies and Great Britain and the West Indies.

Nation. You, who hear no politics, will be astonished at this boar (*sic*), but must excuse it from me, who hear nothing else.

Indeed, there is another operation which breaks in upon this subject, *i.e.*, the game of Commerce. Lady Betty has taken to this game, and she makes all the world, *bon gre, mal gre*, play at it till five o'clock in the morning. I live there almost ; what with Balls, Bt (?), Tessier, Commerce, Supper, and Quinze, I am never out of the house. They have invited me to go to the Oaks, this Christmas, but if Castle Howard is too far, the Oaks, I assure you, will be much farther. I rather think I shall go for a fortnight to Bath. You have heard of Gen. Scott's death. George's motto for his achievement is—*sic Dice placuit* ; and for his sarcophagus—*Dice Manibus*, &c. . . .]

[1775,] *Dec.* 19, *Tuesday.*—I write to you before dinner, and before I have all the opportunities which I might have before night of sending you news, for fear that it should happen as it did last Saturday, that I fall asleep, and so let pass the hour of the post. The cold drives me to the fire, and the fire into a profound nap, in which every earthly thing is forgot ; but it shall happen no more, that a post goes without something to indicate my existence.

Last night and the night before I supped at Lady Betty Stanley's. Their suppers are magnificent, but their hours are abominably late ; however, they do not discourage my Lord of Worcester from staying them out. We are very merry, all of us, and I think Mrs. North the merriest of us all. At 2 this morning, the Bishop and I were almost left alone ; the rest of the company were in their domino's, and going to the Masquerade. I have seen nobody to-day to tell me what passed there. I have been with Mie Mie at Gainsborough's,[1] to finish her picture. I thank you for inquiring after her ; it has been one of my comforts that she has escaped any of these colds. She seems to grow very strong ; so far, so good.

Sir G[eorge] M'Cartney and Lady Holl[an]d dined here yesterday, and we had the contrivance to keep our

---

[1] Gainsborough was at this time living at Schomberg House, Pall Mall, and therefore was a near neighbour of Selwyn. This portrait is not to be found among Gainsborough's existing works.

party a secret from Craufurd, for, although he was engaged to two other places, he told March that he should have been glad to have come, and certainly would, if he had known it. I think verily he grows more tiresome every day, and everybody's patience is *à bout*, except Smith's and Sir George's.

Sir G[eorge] has been telling me to-day, that Lord Stormont is coming from France, and is to have Lord Marchmont's place, who is satisfied by the peerage of his son, and that Lord Harcourt will stay but a very little while longer in Ireland. This must produce in all probability other removes.

I dine to-morrow with Lord Gower, Lady G[ower], Lord and Lady Waldegrave, l'Ambassadeur, and Monsr. Tessier, at Bedford House. I shall know, perhaps, something more of this then. Her Grace has suppers for the class I dine with to-day, but I am not of them. Monsieur Tessier is to read to the Queen, and till then, will read no more ; he goes down to pass his Xmas at Wilton. I wish, for Lady Carlisle's entertainment, that you had him for two or three days, at Castle H.

I should, with your approbation, have been glad to have carried him with me. I shall be glad to bring anybody, but I have no prospect, but of John St. John. Storer tells me that he goes to the Bath. Eden would be excessively happy to go, if it was for a few days only, but his attendance at this time seems scarcely to be dispensed with. Our last news from America are certainly not good, but it does not alter my expectations of what will be the issue of the next campaign. It is a great cause of amusement to Charles, but I see no good to him likely to come from it in the end.

I wish to know, if I could, precisely your time of leaving Castle H[oward]. I should be glad to contrive it, so as to return with you. You will be here for the Trial,[1] I take for granted. It will be altogether the most

[1] Elizabeth Chudleigh, Duchess of Kingston (1720–1788). The celebrated public trial of the Duchess of Kingston for bigamy took place in Westminster Hall, April, 1776. It was proved that she had

extraordinary one that ever happened in this or I believe any other country.   It is a cursed, foul pool, which they are going to stir up, and how many rats, cats, and dogs, with other nuisances, will be seen floating at the top, nobody can tell.   It will be as much a trial of the E[arl] of B[ristol] as of her, and in point of infamy, the issue of it will be the same, and the poor defunct Duke stand upon record as the completest *Coglione* of his time.   The Attorney and Solicitor General have appointed Friday, as I hear, for a hearing of what her Bar can say in favour of a *Noli prosequi*, which is surely nothing.

Selwyn, as we see by the preceding letter, represented the optimistic spirit of the English people in regard to the American War.   His friend Storer, though one of the Court party and a place seeker, shows a much truer appreciation of the actual condition of affairs.   With a keener interest than Selwyn in political matters he sometimes, as already mentioned, took his friend's place as Lord Carlisle's correspondent when political interest was aroused. In the letter which follows he perceives clearly the future course of the struggle.

*Anthony Storer to Lord Carlisle.*

[1775, *Dec.* 29, *Bath.*—I broke off very abruptly in my last, telling you that Oliver's Motion came into Parliament in so strange a form, that it met with very little encouragement ; Wilkes counted twelve who divided with him on the main Question, and he dignified them by calling them his twelve Apostles.

---

privately married Augustus, second son of Lord Hervey, but the marriage was not owned.   She lived publicly with the Duke of Kingston and finally married him during Mr. Hervey's life, but at the death of the Duke, who left her all his disposable property, proceedings were instituted against her and she was found guilty.   She afterwards went to St. Petersburg, where she gave an entertainment for the Empress Catherine said to be more splendid than had ever been seen in Russia.   She bought an estate near St. Petersburg, calling it by her maiden name of Chudleigh, where she intended to manufacture brandy, but found herself so coldly treated by the English ambassador and Russian nobility that she removed to France, where she became involved in a lawsuit regarding the purchase of another estate ; chagrin at loss of the case caused her death.

Sawbridge had attacked the present Administration for their intended folly of taking up four other persons besides Mr. Eyre upon the news of that plot, that made so much noise for a day or two at the opening of Parliament ; and said that some person in Administration had very wisely objected to it, because instead of having the Wilkes, there would immediately be five.

To which Lord North answered by saying, though he might believe a Buckingham House Junto might do a great deal, yet he had so much respect for Mr. Wilkes, as not to imagine that they could easily make another person at [all ?] similar to him ; that he had seen the difficulty of such an undertaking by observing, that gentlemen who made it the whole object and study of their lives to resemble him, had failed in the attempt. He ended by quoting—*Non cuivis homini contingit,* &c. ; some of the Treasury prompted him—*Ex quovis ligno non fit Mercurius.*

We divided twice that day, besides having a third Question. The order of the day was first put, then the previous Question, and the main one. So that Wilkes and his party divided with us upon the previous Question. Lord North upon this desired, while the minority was in the Lobby, that gentlemen would stay for the main Question, as we should not have some of the present majority with us. Upon the whole, I never saw a Question in Parliament treated with so little respect.

Now I ought, according to the course of proceedings, give you some account of Hartley's ; but as he has printed his speech, I will not take that out of his hands, which he has so much more right to. He spoke for above two hours. Good God ! I shudder even now at the thoughts of it. No one can have a complete idea of a boar (*sic*) who has not been in Parliament.

Thus you have seen an epitome of what we have been about ; what we are to do, you are more likely to know than I, having a direct avenue to the Cabinet ; but I believe it is scarcely in their power to say what we are to do. Whether we are to send Russians, or French, or what nation the troops are to be of, I cannot guess. They say Russians cannot go on account of the ice in the Baltic ; and then if they could, they say the French and Spaniards would not let them. We are playing *três gros jeu,* and in every way a losing game.

As for conquering America, without foreign troops, it is entirely impossible ; and I think it pretty near a certainty that the Rebels will be in possession of all America by the spring. By the news of Fort St. John's and Chambley, and the investiture of Quebec, their diligence and activity is wonderful, and it must end in the possession of all N[orth] Am[erica]. They have taken a store-ship, and have several ships at sea. *De peu à peu nous arrivons ;* if they go on so another year—*fuit Ilium et ingens gloria*—we shall make but a paltry figure in the eye of Europe. Come to town, and be witness to the fall, or the re-establishment, of our puissant Empire. . . .]

Little of Selwyn's correspondence in 1776 and 1777 has been preserved. Possibly he wrote less, and made a long stay at Castle Howard. "I have more *bon jours* and *bon soirs* for her *en poche*," referring to his little child-friend, Caroline Howard, "than I shall be able to give her during the whole time I shall stay at Castle H." For the despatch of political news he trusted, as he often did, to Storer. "I hope that Storer gives you a more particular account of what is said in the House than I can do. What is he employing himself about? Why won't he attempt to say something? What signifies, knowing what Cicero said and how he said it, if a man cannot open his mouth to deliver one sentence of his own?" But Storer, like many able and cultivated men, was more critical of his own powers than those who want both talent and knowledge. He was not, however, altogether neglectful of Selwyn's wishes, and he presently sent Carlisle some political news, but of no great interest.

Selwyn himself was in somewhat low spirits, he was as we know troubled by Mie Mie's parents, and he longed for the society of Carlisle and his family.

[1777, *Feb.*,] *Tuesday night.*—. . . As to my own situation I cannot say it is a happy [one], although I have so much more than I could have expected. I have, indeed, for the present all I ever wished, but I have also the strongest assurances given me that at all events things shall continue for some time in the state in which they now are. But whoever upon that concludes that I must be easy is either ignorant or indifferent to the feelings of mankind. The bare possibility of be[ing] rendered so unhappy as I should be made upon a change of their resolution, or from the operations of caprice and *travers*, I say the mere apprehensions of that, even slightly founded, prevent my mind from being in that *équilibre* which is absolutely necessary to my tranquillity. We are, I say, at present going on very well, in as good and regular a progress of education as it is possible; both Mie Mie and I as

9

tractable as it is possible ; *et troubler ce ménage seroit une cruauté sans example.*

I have also to grieve at other times for a great deprivation of part of my happiness ; that, I mean, to which you contributed, Lady C[arlisle] and your children. There is a *hiatus valde deflendus ;* indeed, a *lacune* which I do not know how to fill up, and I sigh over the prospect of it perpetually, and without seeing my way out of it.

I have, at another part of my day, a scene, which time or use cannot reconcile to me. I see my mother's strength grow less every day, without any consolation, but that her mind does not decay with it. In short, my dear Lord, as I have often told you, *j'ai l'esprit et le cœur trop tracassés* for me to be happy at present, and all I can say is that I might, by untoward accidents, be more miserable, and these are removed from my view *pour le moment ;* but I wait for a period of time when I shall be relieved from uncertainty of what may happen, and when I may live and breathe without restraint and apprehension. That period will, as I imagine, arrive in about two months, and till then *les assurances les plus fortes sont trop foibles pour mon repos.*

It is some time since I have had a long letter from you. I hope to have one of some sort or other to-morrow. I hope all goes quietly, at least Gregg says that you write cheerfully. *On s'accoutume à tout,* they say, but I know and feel very sensibly that there are exceptions to that adage.

The author of a new Grub Street poem, I see, allows me a great share of feeling, at the same time that he relates facts of me, which, if they were true, would, besides making me ridiculous, call very much into question what he asserts with any reasonable man. I do not know if you have received this performance. If I thought you had not, paltry as it is, I should send it to you. The work I mean is called "The Diaboliad." [1] His hero is Lord Ernham. Lord Hertford and Lord Beauchamp are the chief persons whom he loads with his

---

[1] "The Diaboliad, a poem dedicated to the Worst Man in His Majesty's Dominion," London, G. Kearsley, 1777.

invectives. Lord Lyttleton [and] his cousin Mr. Ascough are also treated with not much lenity ; Lord Pembroke with great familiarity, as well as C. Fox ; and Fitzpatrick, although painted in colours bad enough at present, is represented as one whom in time the Devil will lose for his disciple. I am only attacked upon that trite and very foolish opinion concerning *le pene e le Delitté* [*ed i delitti*], acknowledging [it] to proceed from an odd and insatiable curiosity, and not from a *mauvais cœur*. In some places I think there is versification, and a few good lines, and the piece seems to be wrote by one not void of parts, but who, with attention, might write much better.[1]

I forgive him his mention of me, because I believe that he does it without malice, but, if I had leisure to think of such things, I must own the frequent repetition of the foolish stories would make me peevish. Alas ! I have no time to be peevish. *Quand on a le cœur gros, et serré, comme je l'ai souvent à cette heure, il est rare que l'on a de l'humeur ; l'âme est trop sérieusement attaquée et touchée pour prêter attention à de petites choses ; chez moi, je suis triste, je soupire, mais je ne gronde plus, je ne m'emporte pas.*

Richard, I hear, goes in about a fortnight. Fish Craufurd thinks, as I am told, that Lord O[ssory ?] should

---

[1] "The Diaboliad " was a social satire : in it the devil was supposed to have grown old, and being anxious to find a successor for his throne visits London. He appears to a gambling party :—

"With joy and wonder struck the parties rise !
Hell is worth trying for . . . cries ;
Pigeons are left unpluck'd, the game unplay'd,
And F—— forgets the certain Bett he made ;
E'en S-l-n feels Ambition fire his breast
And leaves half told, the fabricated Jest.

 .  .  .  .  .

The murmurs hush'd—the Herald straight proclaim'd
S-l-n the witty next in order nam'd,
But he was gone to hear the dismal yells
Of tortur'd Ghosts and suffering Criminals,
Tho' summoned thrice, he chose not to return,
Charmed to behold the crackling Culprits burn
With George all know Ambition must give place
When there's an *Execution* in the case." (Pp. 3 and 17.)

pay his debts ; that is, give him £40,000 from his own children, *pour le délivrer des Juifs.* He pays already to one of them out of his £300 a year, which he meant to have paid to his brother for a more comfortable maintenance.

I dined on Sunday at the French Ambassador's ; a splendid and wretched dinner, but good wine ; a quantity of dishes which differed from one another only in appearance ; they had all the same taste, or equally wanted it. The middle piece, the *demeurant,* as it is called, a fine Oriental arcade, which reached from one end of the table to the other, fell in like a *tremblement de terre.* The wax, which cemented the composing parts, melted like Icarus's wings, and down it fell. Seventy *bougies* occasioned this, with the number of persons all adding to the heat of the room. I had a more private and much better dinner yesterday at Devonshire House.

[1777, *Aug.*?] .... I am convinced that I shall be free some time hence from that agitation of mind with which I am now so tormented, and from those almost constant sinkings of my spirits ; but, my dear Lord, you may be quite assured that *des plaies comme les miennes ne se referment pas bientôt,* and when they do they have altered the whole constitution of the mind to such a degree as never to let it feel as it did before. But *brisons là.*

Mr. D'Oyley tells me that no important news is likely to come from America before the 20th of this month. Lady Cornwallis told me yesterday she expected some much sooner. Mr. D'Oyley's picture of affairs was not a joyous one, but he gave an infinitely better account of them to me than I have had from anybody else.

The Opposition affects great spirits, and to be sanguine about a change of men and of measures. *Je n'en crois rien.* Charles said last night if I would give him five guineas he would give me 100 if I lost my place. He must get one himself to justify my accepting the proposal. The match of tennis stark naked was not played, which I am sorry for. Another red Ribbon vacant, Sir C. Montague. Clinton anticipated that which Lord Inchiquin had.

I saw Horry W[alpole] yesterday for a few minutes ;
*his distresses* are, Lord O[rford's] lunacy, and the Duchess
of Gloucester's situation if his R[oyal] H[ighness] dies,
who will probably come and die in his own country. I
wish these were mine, and I had no other, but we cannot
choose our own misfortunes ; if we could, there is nobody
who would not prefer being concerned for a mad nephew
whom they did not care for, or a simple Princess whom
they would laugh at, *si l'orgueil ne s'en mêloit pas.*

The great rendezvous of the White's people has been
at my Lord Cadogan's, as that of the Macaroni's at Lord
Egremont's. *Adieu pour aujourd'hui ;* I need not conclude, as this letter does not go till Tuesday.

*Monday morning.*—At Almack's last night :

| | | | |
|---|---|---|---|
| Duke of Grafton, | Lord March, | 2 Craufurds, | Sir W. Draper, |
| Lord  Egremont, | Varcy, | Thompson, | Sir C. Davers, |
| Jack      Town- | Barker, | Lord  North[ing- | Self, |
| sh[en]d, | Hare. | to]n, | Boothby. |
| W. Hanger. | | Foley. | |

There was no news last night, and but little play.
Boothby loses regularly his 300, and, if he had a run in
his favour [has] nobody to furnish him with materials to
profit by it. Lady Harriot came again to fetch her
husband in their *vis à vis*, and I crammed myself in too.
I left Draper and Sir C. Davers travelling through the
worst roads of Canada, Triconderaga (*sic*), and the Lord
knows what country. But it was so tiresome that I was
glad to leave them in the mud in[to] which their conversation had carried them.

Lord North[ingto]n is very sour about Lord
Cov[entry]'s treatment of his sister, and talks of going
to Crome to expostulate with him about it. I hope that
he will not. It will do the cause no good in any respect.
I am for leaving everything for the present, bad as it is,
where the ill stars of them all have placed them.
Cov[entry]'s mind will take another turn, and [he will]
do of his own accord perhaps more than he ought.

Mademoiselle D'Eon goes to France in a few days ; she
is now in her *habit de femme,* in black silk and diamonds,

which she received from the Empress of Russia, when she was in the army and at her Court as minister. A German of her acquaintance has promised Lady Townshend to contrive that she and I shall have a sight of her before she goes. She met her grandson coming to town in a chaise and four, *ventre à terre*, from Brighthelmstone ; he dined with us. Storer's attachment at present, as he says, is to Lady Payne. O'Brien gets £9,000 a year, and the title, by Lord Inchiquin's death.

The absence of Lord Carlisle as a Commissioner to America caused a break in the correspondence. Selwyn was much abroad during his friend's absence, and the distance between England and America was prohibitive of letters frequent. Two, however, from Paris in 1779 give an insight into Selwyn's life abroad. He resumed the correspondence in 1780. He was not well ; he was being pressed to go to "that abominable town" of Gloucester. He hated electioneering, but it is from Matson that the next letter, in the midst of the General Election of 1780, is dated. He lost his seat—perhaps not without regret—for he returned to the less irksome representation, if such it could be called, of Ludgershall.

[1779,] *April* 18, *Sunday, Paris.*— . . . I have managed in regard to my lodging as I once did in regard to poor Mr. Pottinger, whom I wanted to avoid and so asked him in my confusion to dine with me, which you cannot forget that he accepted. I wished above all things to be lodged as far from a certain Lady[1] as I could, and I have so contrived it, that for the present I am next door. I intend for the future to describe her by that name, that is, La Dame, as Lord Clarendon does the Duchess of Cleveland. I will for the rest of my life mention her as little as possible ; but when I am forced to speak upon her subject I will take care not to call her by her name, and I am the more authorised so to do, as she

[1] The Countess Dowager of Carlisle, whose proposed marriage to a foreign baron met with opposition from her family and friends.

has called me by every name but that by which I should be described, and that is your friend.

The Barone servante is gone to England, as you perhaps know, and perhaps she is now on his (*sic*) road back. However I shall be quit I hope for a distant bow ; for although honest Iago had taken as much care as possible that he should cut my throat, a much better friend took care that he should *not*; which is the Maréchal B[iron].[1]

I went yesterday to the Maréchal for the first time ; he was in his levee room ; it was the day that the officers of the *Gardes françoises* always dine with him. . We dropt upon him once [again ?] the same day ; but this was at noon, and he was giving audience. He took me out immediately into another room, and after some civil reproaches for not having been there before—for some English, who dine with him on a Friday, had told him that I was come—he entered into a very particular conversation upon that very disagreeable subject, upon which he spoke with all the reason and good nature and propriety imaginable.

I said for you everything which I could conceive it would be agreeable to you that I should say. I found it very acceptable, and his respect for you so great, and so much real kindness mixed with it, that having in my coach a picture of Caroline, which I had intended for the Duchesse de la Valière, I desired him to accept of it, and I think he received it as well as I could for her sake have wished him to do. I believe he will think that Lady Dunmore's daughters will not be the only beauties that we shall be able to produce. He was delighted with it. I gave him also another of Admiral Keppell,[2] which is an extraordinary good one. Caroline's was not a good impression, which I am sorry for. I gave my other where I dined to M[e] de la Vaupalière, to be a pendant to your

[1] Armand Louis de Gontaut, Duc de Biron (1753–1794). Though he joined the Revolutionists he perished on the scaffold.

[2] Admiral Lord Keppel (1725–1786), second son of second Earl of Albemarle. He was a Whig in politics, and was First Lord of the Admiralty under the Rockingham Administration in 1782, and was soon after created a peer. "I ever looked on Lord Keppell," Burke said, "as one of the greatest and best men of his age."

own, and you must send me one of Lady C[arlisle], ill as
she is represented, that the collection may be complete.

What he said besides was inevitable. I am unwilling
to repeat it. I wish that there was not so much truth in
it. I wish that it could be remedied, but that is impossible, for the only step towards it, which is returning to
her family, and to yours, she is determined not to take ;
she will return no more to England I believe, if she can
help it, unless [to] be totally abandoned and plundered
everywhere else becomes a necessary inducement.

I am at Galan's, at the Hôtel de Bourbon, next door to
where we used to lodge, what is now called l'Hôtel de
Danmark. But I must remove, for one apartment will
not do ; we must have three ; one for Monsieur le
Marquis, another for the child and her people, and one
for myself. So I think I must go for the present to the
Parc Royal. Every kind of house has been offered to
me, to induce . . .

[1779,] *Avril* 18, *Sunday night, Paris.*[1]—I wrote to
you this morning, as I hope that you will know. This
afternoon I find *tous mes projets pour le présent sont
suspendus.* I am obliged to set out to-morrow for Lyons.
It is so unexpected, that it is by much the greatest
*embarras* I ever felt, and a monstrous exercise of expense
to me. But Mie Mie will be there to-morrow. *Les
parens ont changé d'avis,* and I must go to Lyons to fetch
[her]. God knows how much further I would go to
conduct her safely, but I was made to believe there was
no occasion for it. I expected her here on Friday next,
or on this day sevennight. *Combien de tems faut-il que je
sois le jouet des caprices des autres?*

Mrs. Webb also is not in a good state of health for
travelling so far or so fast. I have had a letter from
Warner ; he has seen the Baron, who was charged, I
find, with a commission to you. . . .

I shall write to you from Lyons ; but when I shall
hear from you the Lord knows, and I want to hear how
the children do.

[1] See *ante,* p. 11.

*Ma patience et ma persévérance sont inépuisables sur ce qui regarde Mie Mie. Je me croyois tranquillement établi ici. J'aurai des entretiens avec la mère, qui ne sont pas toujours composés avec du miel. " Helas ! Rende mi figlia mia." Voila où j'en reviens. Adieu. Ayez un peu de pitié de tous mes embarras, qui ne finissent pas.*

[1780,] *Sept.* 11, *Monday morning,* 7 *o'clock, Matson.*— You will receive a long letter from me to-day ; and this will come to you on Wednesday ; so by these repeated courtesies you will see that I have no repugnance to writing, although *you* have, and that I am very well pleased to go on in my old way of scribbling, as long as I am convinced that it is agreeable to you. But a line now and then is comfortable, for, as Lady Macbeth says, " the feast grows cold that is not often cheered," or something of that sort ; so a correspondence is awkwardly maintained, and is a contradiction in terms when it is on one side only.

At present I am afraid that I shall be particularly tiresome, because, much against my will, they have filled my head with Election matters, and will not allow me a moment's time for anything else. I have no comfort, but that it will be concluded on Thursday, or Friday, but till then, what I shall suffer from folly and impertinence, and from everything that is disagreeable, cannot be described.

There is a party here called the True Blues, who lead Sir A. H. and I [me] about, as if they had purchased us, to show in a fair. They cost me, some years ago, twice two thousand pounds, by opposing me, and now are doing all they can to make me pay four for befriending me ; and these people have given Administration such an idea of their own omnipotence that I should have never been forgiven, if I had not yielded to this importunity. I am assured that it will succeed, and that both Sir A. and myself shall be returned, but my credulity does not extend to that point. It is very probable, indeed, that by this effort I may retain my own seat, which I did not care for, but to attempt the other does as yet appear to me a great piece of extravagance, considering the party which we have to contend with, who have had their secrets well kept, and been very industrious for two years in bringing about this opposition, whereas this scheme of the Tories has not been taken up with any support, but a fortnight ago.

My best and ablest friends here are dead ; their survivors supine and superannuated ; their connections new Whiggs and Reformers, and Associators ; myself grown quite indifferent upon the point ; and the principal Tories, such as the Duke of Beaufort, &c., and those who would have been active, if they had been desired to be so half a year ago, never spoke to. Mr. Robinson,[1] in his letters to me, has always spoke in the plural number, *our friend and I;* so it is a scheme adopted by both, I am to suppose, and a hazardous one it is. But one Member they will have, I believe, and I wish they had fixed upon any one but me to be their choice.

Sir Andr. goes upon the surest grounds, because I believe that he will be franked to a certain point, and is sure of a seat in another place, if not here. He is really a very agreeable man, and seems to penetrate into the characters of the people he has seen very well. He entertained me much yesterday with his account of my old friend the Duke of Newcastle. He speaks of you in terms of the highest esteem.

We stole away the day before yesterday from our keepers, to dine here, which was a great relief, but we were jobed (*sic*) for it at our return. I get here time enough to go to bed, that is about 11 o'clock, and I do not leave this place till about nine, that is till Mie Mie and I have breakfasted together.

We have a committee sitting at what is called the

[1] John Robinson (1727–1802), the son of an Appleby tradesman. He grew wealthy by marriage and inheritance, and locally influential. He became member for Westmoreland in 1764. In 1770 he was appointed Secretary to the Treasury, which office he retained till Lord North's fall in 1782. He was the business manager of the Ministry, and had in his hands the distribution of the party funds and patronage. He was an honest, able, and cool man of affairs, who regarded politics wholly from a business point of view.

New (?) Inn, which has been built, and never repaired, three hundred years since; and here this swarm of old Jacobites, with no attachment to Government, assembles, and for half an hour you would be diverted with their different sentiments and proposals. There is one who has a knack at squibbs, as they call it, and he has a table and chair with a pen and ink before him, to write scurrilous papers, and these are sent directly to Mr. Raikes. I wish to God that it was all at an end.

> What sin, to me unknown,
> Dipped me in this? My father's, or my own?

I am very glad that you have so quietly abandoned a contention for Carlisle. When these things come to us without trouble it is very well; but when they do not, I do not know one earthly thing that makes us amends, and it is not once in a hundred times that you are thanked for it. . . .

I am *old indeed*, as the papers say, and if not *trained up in ministerial corruption*, I am used to all other corruption whatever, and of that of manners in particular; and the little attention that is paid to what was in my earliest days called common honesty, is now the most uncommon thing in the world. . . .

Let me have the pleasure of hearing that you are going on well in Ireland,[1] for the loss of that I should have in being there with you, which is impossible. Keep yourself, as you can very well do, within your intrenchments, that no one may toss your hat over the walls of the Castle. I dread to think what a wrongheaded people you are to transact business with for the next three years of your life. But I am less afraid of you from your character, than of another, because I think that you will admit, at setting out, of no degree of familiarity from those you are not well acquainted with. I hope that Eden goes with you. I have a great opinion of his good sense and *sçavoir faire*.

[1] Lord Carlisle had this year been appointed Lord-Lieutenant of Ireland.

# CHAPTER IV

## 1781

### THE DISASTERS IN AMERICA

A drum at Selwyn's—George, Lord Morpeth—Dr. Warner—Sale of
the Houghton pictures—The House of Commons—Pitt's first
speech—Selwyn unwell—Play at Brooks's—London gaieties—
Fox and his new clothes—Gambling—The bailiffs in Fox's house
—"Fish" Crawford—Montem at Eton—Mie Mie's education—
Second speech of Pitt—Lord North—A Court Ball—Society and
politics—The Emperor of Austria—Conversation with Fox—
Personal feelings—American affairs—Lord North and Mr. Robinson—State of politics—London Society.

THE year 1781 will remain memorable as that in
which the connection of England with her
American Colonies was finally broken. The surrender of
Cornwallis at Yorktown on October 19th impressed the
Government with the futility of a contest which the
country had already realised, and which would have at
once caused a change of administration if the House of
Commons had been truly representative of the opinion
of the country ; "a sense of past error" wrote the Duke
of Grafton in his autobiography, "and a conviction that
the American war might terminate in further destruction
to our armies, began from this time rapidly to insinuate
itself into the minds of men. Their discourse was quite
changed, though the majorities in Parliament were still
ready to support the American war, while all the world
was representing it to be the height of madness and

folly."[1]  But though the country was oppressed by
taxation, and disgusted at the want of success of its armies,
society in St. James's Street took the national disasters
with perfect composure.  It troubled itself more about
the nightly losses of money at the card-tables of Brooks's
than of soldiers on the Delaware.  It lived in the same
kind of fatalism as the House of Commons and the King,
who, with characteristic obstinacy, refused to bow to the
force of events, and kept in office, but not in power, a
minister who did not believe in the policy which he was
compelled to support in Parliament.  From contemporaries
the cardinal events of history are obscured by the course
of their ordinary social or political life.  To us, who can
see them so large and momentous, it appears strange that
they do not fill a greater place in the public mind of the
period.  Selwyn constantly hearing of the course of the
vital conflict between England and her Colonies, fills his
correspondence with details of the day, mingling remarks
on facts which have become historical with the latest
story of the clubs.

1781, *Feb.* 1, *Thursday morning, Cleveland Court.*—
. . . I saw Lord Gower yesterday morning ; he is grown
very corpulent, and his face fuller of humour than I ever
saw it.  While this humour keeps out he will be well,
but when it returns I am afraid the consequences will be
fatal to him. . . .

We dined at March's yesterday.  Boothby, James,
Williams, Offley, Lord W. Gordon, Dr. Warner,[2] and
myself.  The place of rendezvous for the morning is I
believe, the Park, and it is a reconnoitring party too.  Where
the Prince sups, and lies, and with whom, are the chief
objects of the politics of a certain class of people.  All

[1] Page 314.
[2] Dr. John Warner (1736–1800) was the son of a clergyman and
educated at Trinity College, Cambridge.  He took orders, but had a
literary and social, rather than theological, bent.  He was a confi-
dential friend of Selwyn's, and after his death wrote a defence of him
in regard to witnessing executions.

agree that at present the agreement between him and the King is perfect. The speculation is only how long it is likely to last. His Royal Highness stoops as yet to very low game. In some respects it may be better. You will have heard of Captain Waldgrave's success with the two Dutch ships, and the French merchantman, if I am right.

To-day is to be one of violent attack upon Lord Sandwich and Palliser. Charles makes the motion. We shall have a great deal of abuse, and reply and declamation from Bourk [1] [Burke], and vociferation from Lord Mahon, and perhaps a long day ; and I must go down early, because I was yesterday when the House was called a defaulter ; so I shall dine there, and after dinner I will collect upon paper what I hear of the transactions of the day.

I read yesterday in the P[ublic] Advertiser an account of your box at the play. I am not knowing enough in what is called humour, to be sure, if that was such, and pure invention, or not. I hear that you did not produce yourself enough, but retired too much within the box, which did not please the Irish, who do not so well comprehend what it is to be out of countenance. I wish to know if Lady C[arlisle] will find for Caroline masters to her satisfaction, and a country house. I have not seen as yet Lord Fitzwilliam, or had any answer about the pictures. Eden they tell me calls too soon for coffee. But upon the whole, the reports concerning you, and your Court, and your ministers, &c. is [are] good. I do not expect this business in which you are engaged to be quite *couleur de rose.* I hope you will preserve your health, and the peace of your mind, your temper, and your fortune. I am in no pain about anything else.

Lord W[——] had yesterday an air more *égaré* than usual ; he is *enlaidi, et mal vêtu, et enfin il avait plus l'air de pendard que son frère. Vous pouvez bien vous*

---

[1] Edmund Burke (1729-1797). The only political office that the great publicist ever held was that of Paymaster of the Forces for a few months under Lord Rockingham and the Coalition Government.

*imaginer que nous n'avons pas parlé de corde, pas même celle du mariage.* The Maréchal de Rich[e]lieu was told that the mob intended to have hung me, but *que je m'en suis tiré comme un loial chevalier.* This was their notion in Paris of the mob which insulted me at Gloucester.

[1781,] *Feb. 11, Sunday morning, Cleveland Court.*—I received your letter of the 5th, yesterday, in the afternoon, and another of the same date from Dr. Ekins, at the same time the day before : why they did not come together, I know not. But so it has happened, I believe more than once before, since my connections with Ireland, which I wish to God were at an end. There is one indeed which will plague me, while I live, and that is an annuity upon Mr. Gore's estate, which I must sue for as regularly as it becomes due.

I was prevented from writing to you yesterday by I do not know how much disagreeable occupation. I had a Drum, and that began early ; I was to prepare for it, I was to be served in *ambigu*, and it was to be the easiest, most agreeable, best understood thing in the world. It was to my apprehension the very *antipode* of this. I do not know how my company felt, but I was not at my ease a moment. I had a Commerce table, and one of Whist. My company were Middletons,[1] Bostons,[2] Townshends, and Selwyns.

March came to the door at eleven, but hearing that supper was served, and almost over, and perhaps hearing of the company too, he went away ; they were all good kind of people, and who I dare say had conversation enough in their own families, but although we were all related, we had not one word to say to one another. There was Mr.

[1] George, fourth Viscount Middleton (1754-1836); son of George, third viscount, and Albinia, daughter of the Hon. Thomas Townshend. He married first, in 1778, Lady Frances Pelham, daughter of Thomas, first Earl of Chichester, who died in 1783.

[2] Frederick, second Baron Boston (1749-1825), son of Sir William, first Baron Boston and Albinia, daughter of Henry Selwyn. He married, in 1775, Christiana, only daughter of Paul Methuen.

Methuen, Lady Boston's father, who seems to be a shrewd entertaining man, if he was where he found himself at home. The cook, the housekeeper, and *Maître Jacques* all exerted themselves, and did their parts tolerably well, but *rien n'a pu me mettre à mon aise*, and the more I tried to be at home, the more I was *désorienté*; so I believe I shall try some other kind of party for the future ; otherwise I may say *que le jeu ne vaut pas la chandelle*. But now for your letter.

George's subject is not the first in course, but it has taken the first place in my thoughts. I do assure you that I am not his puff. What I tell you of his reading is literally true ; but it is not reading that expresses it, for I could have said as much if he had read nothing but the History of Cinder Breech and that kind of biography. He read with me English History, and stopped for information, and showed an uncommon thirst for it. He asked me as many questions in the History of George 1st concerning the South Sea Scheme, the prosecution of Lord Macclesfield, and the Barrier Treaty, as another boy would have asked me about Robinson Crusoe. He likes other books too, and it is agreeable to hear him talk of them. For which reason I should be glad, if you approved of it, that he had a choice of books, to a certain amount— a little library—as many as would fill a small bookcase. Mr. Raikes tells me that he is remarkably careful of his books, and therefore was not displeased that those which you gave him I had well bound, and that it was a fair edition. An early love of books will produce a desire to read, which amusements may suppress for a time, but is a constant resource against ennui. I have been years without looking in a book, and God knows in my long life how few I have read ; but when it has happened that I could, *par force*, do nothing else, I have collected together a number, began a piece of history, and have thought at last the day too short, because I wanted to read more ; and this I attribute to having once read, although it was but a very little. Rollin was the first author I read by choice. . . .

I am in hopes that your kindness to Storer will take
place ; *il en est digne, soyez en assuré, sur ma parole.* I
never doubted, I was quite persuaded indeed, that you
would do what you have done, and properly too. I have
been told that he is to have this place, but I have not seen
him much lately. I hope that he will dine here to-morrow,
or on Tuesday, when all the Gregg family comes, and it
may be, Dr. Warner. Your letter to Hare was sent to
him by the post of the day that I received it, and you will
have had information of it, I doubt not, by this time. He
was not that day in town. You desired it to be sent,
without loss of time. I therefore lost none. But unluckily he was on the road, although nobody knew it ; he
must have received it a few days after, so I suppose by
this time he has acknowledged to you the receipt of it.
I shall send your letter to Dr. Warner to-day, and invite
him to meet Mr. Gregg's family at dinner here on
Tuesday. . . . I believe him to be a perfectly honest
man ; he is uncommonly humane and friendly, and most
actively so. But he has such a flow of spirits, and so
much the *ton de ce monde qu'il a fréquenté*, that, had I been
to have chose a profession for him, it should not have
been that of the Church. There is more buckram in that,
professionally, than he can digest, or submit to. The
Archbishop, who has been applied to in his favour, by the
late Mr. Townshend, said he was too lively, but it was the
worst he could say of him. Lord Besborough served him
once essentially, and esteems him. The family of Mr.
Hoare, the banker, has assisted him, and so he has been
able to support his mother and his nearest relations, whom
his father, with a great deal of literary merit, had left
beggars. I have given you this succinct history of my
doctor, whom you have enlisted into your corps. I was
once before obliged to write his character for Lord Ossory,
when he settled himself in Bedfordshire, and Lord Ossory
has found it true in all particulars.

The K[ing] has told my friend M. that Lord Cadogan [1]

[1] Charles Sloane, third Baron and first Earl Cadogan (1728–1807).
The house at Caversham Park was destroyed by fire in 1850 and re-built.

wants to sell his house at Caversham, for why, I know not.    Lord Walpole's eldest son is to marry Lady Cadogan's sister.    Churchill, *du côte du falbala, ne réussit pas mal;* his sons, I am afraid, one of them at least, has [have] not managed so well.    But I would myself sooner have been married to [a] Buckhorse, than to that [A]Esop Lord C.    The Zarina repents of her bargain, and, it is said, will give no more than 20,000 for the pictures.[1]    If that is not accepted, Lord Orford make [may] take them back.    He gets an estate of near £10,000 a year by his mother's death.    Her will is all wrote in her own hand, and not one word, even her own name, rightly spelt.

Few events in the annals of the House of Commons are more remarkable than the sudden rise of Pitt.    His maiden speech—in support of Burke's Bill for economical reform —placed him at once in the first rank of parliamentary orators.    " I was able to execute in some measure what I intended," was Pitt's own modest account of this speech in a letter to his mother.    The opinion of the House of Commons and the town was wholly different : his speech was regarded as masterly—astonishing in one so young and new to Parliament.    Selwyn had not heard it, but in the following letter he tells Carlisle of the general impression it had made; and on June 13th he gives his own critical opinion of Pitt's third speech.    The detailed description by Storer, who supplemented Selwyn's letters of the debate of February 26th, adds to our knowledge of this memorable debate.

[1781,] *Feb.* 27, *Tuesday.*—I have received no comfort or pleasure for some days, but what I had last night by a letter from Mrs. Sowerby to Lady Gower, and which Lady Gower was so good as to send to me.

[1] The gallery of pictures at Houghton, collected by Sir Robert Walpole, was, with some reservations, sold by the third Lord Orford, to the Empress Catharine of Russia in 1779. " Private news we have none, but what I have long been bidden to expect the completion of the sale of the pictures at Houghton to the Czarina " (Letters of Walpole, vol. vii. p. 234.) The date of the sale and of Selwyn's gossiping allusion are not reconcilable.

I find by that that the children at Trentham are well, and that Charlotte is so altered for the better as to be *méconnoissable*. But of you and of Caroline, Lady C., Louise, I know nothing. The weather has been so wet that I have not proposed to Storer his visit to George, of which I shall profit. For my own pleasure, I long to see him.

We were in the House of Commons last night till half [an] hour past twelve. The majority of our side against the second reading of Burke's Bill,[1] and in fact, by a following question of rejecting it, was of 43, if I mistook not. I was not in the House to hear anybody speak a syllable, nor do I ever wish it. I believe there is no actor upon the stage of either theatre who, repeating what the author has wrote, does not, at the same time, recite his own private sentiments oftener, than our pantomimes in Parliament.

The chief subject of C. Fox's harangue yesterday was an *éloge* upon economy, and Jack Townshend,[2] who spoke for the second time, rehearsed these maxims of his preceptor. Jack did better than the time before, but was so eclipsed by Mr. W. Pitt, that it appeared to impartial people but an indifferent performance. This young man, Mr. Pitt, gained an universal applause.[3] I heard Lord N[orth] say it was the best first speech of a young man that he had ever heard. It was a very crowded House, but there were there neither Mr. Dunning, Mr. Barry, or General Burgoyne. This was matter of speculation.

The P[rince] of W[ales] is said to have a kind of carbuncle. Mr. Delmé told me that Lady B[etty] had heard from her mother, and that she talked of being here in April. Indeed I see no feasibility in any other scheme, although many would to her passions appear more eligible.

[1] For the better regulation of Civil Establishments, and of certain public offices, and for the limitation of pensions, and the suppression of certain useless, expensive, and inconvenient places.

[2] John Townshend (1757–1833); second son of the fourth Viscount and first Marquis of Townshend. He was returned for the University of Cambridge in 1780, and lost his seat in 1784 when Pitt was elected.

[3] See Storer's letter. *Post*, p. 132.

Lord Althorp [1] is to be married before the 10th of March —that is all that Lady Lucan would tell me. I hear of no more news. The Emperor is expected or it is hoped will assist us, at least with his mediation. There is all my foreign politics. The regaining America or having any kind of peace from that quarter is with me *à perte de vuë*.

I wish the spring was a little advanced that I might walk out, for nothing but George can make me stir out of my room, except in fine weather, and I have a hundred places to call at. I do not tease you, or ever will, about writing, but pray get some one person in your allegiance to write to me for you. I want neither anecdotes, or sentiments, or politics, but I want to know frequently how you all do. The Attorney General told me last night that there was no expecting an account of you but from me ; *j'eus honte de le détromper*. I am supposed to have letters constantly from my Lord Lieutenant, and I give myself so much air at least as not to deny it.

*Anthony Storer to Lord Carlisle.*

[1781, *Feb.* 28.—I have not wrote to you so often as perhaps I ought to do, and as I really wish, because in regard to everything that passes on this side the water at present, the newspaper is a very authentic chronicle. The debates in Parliament are not frequent, and when they do happen Mr. Woodfall reports them very much at large, and almost always faithfully. In regard to the *chronique scandaleuse*, there is no occasion for any report, as the Session seems a maiden one. These two heads, which Selwyn does not in general interfere with, I should have thought fell under my department, and I should certainly [have] told you all I knew but for the reasons which I have given. I take it for granted Selwyn writes to you principally about Lord Morpeth, as I perceive he is in general uppermost in his thoughts, and the subject on which he converses *le plus volontiers avec moi. Le seul bien qui nous reste, &c.*

We had a debate on Monday, when Mr. Pitt for the first time made such a speech, that it excited the admiration very justly of every man in the House. Except he had foreseen the particular species of nonsense which Lord Nugent was to utter, his speech could not be prepared ; it was delivered without any kind of improper assurance, but with the exact proper self-possession which ought to accompany a speaker. There was not a word or a look which one would have

---

[1] George John, afterwards second Earl Spencer, K.G. (1758–1834) ; married March 6, 1781, Lavinia, daughter of the first Earl of Lucan.

wished to correct. This, I believe, in general was the universal sense of all those who heard him, and exactly the effect which his speech had on me, at the time I heard it.

Mr. Sheridan did very well ; he said a very [few] words in answer to Mr. Courtenay, each word being exactly placed where it ought to be—*quasi tesseratâ emblemate*—as if he had studied them a week beforehand, and had read them instead of speaking them. His harvest at the Opera House is likely to be very successful, for his Saturdays and Tuesdays are so full, that he is going even to attempt the Thursdays. Vestris' Ballet people think too long. " It is impossible that an English audience should be satisfied. They don't know when they have got a good spectacle, and think that finding fault is the only way to pass for judges." Such are the words of his Honour, the prophet Brudenell. John St. John says that the Baccelli is thrown away in the part of Nannette ; *au lieu d'être danseuse, elle n'est que la Colombine.* This he takes from the Baccelli, and the Duke of Dorset. John acts a strange underpart at the theatre. Mademoiselle Baccelli's runner is not so honourable an employment as being Lord North's.

Selwyn lost within this week a large sum of money. He was so *larmoyant* the other morning, that I did not dare to ask him any questions about it. Delmé has sold all his hunters, and sold them at very extraordinary prices ; his hounds too sold excessively well ; it was fortunate at all events to part with them, but the people who bought them, according to all accounts, were as mad as he had been in keeping them. . . .

In Monday night's debate neither Dunning [n]or Barry was in the House ; that looks very like a measure ; it is impossible that should be mere accident. Opposition were without several of their plumpers that evening, either from their being ill or their being out of town. Lord Robert and Lord Edward for instance were ill ; Ned Foley and his brother-in-law, out of town ; Lord Howe and Doily not in the House, with more that do not occur to me. Burke acted with his usual bad judgment in not letting Sir Fletcher Norton speak before him, but rather pressing his privilege of bringing in the Bill, to speak before him ; consequently Sir Fletcher did not speak at all. It was a debate of young members entirely. Neither Charles Fox or Lord N[orth] spoke. There is a Select Committee upon East India affairs sitting, at which there is a great deal of curious evidence given relating to the manners, customs, and religion of the Gentoos. I was there one morning, and was very much entertained with the accounts of the witnesses. A Brammin, who is now in England, was examined on Monday. *Voici, milord, assez de détails.*]

[1781,] *March* 24, *Saturday.*—. . . Mr. Potts has just left me. I have been freer from pain these last 29 [or 24 ?] hours. I am now to bathe three times a week, take opiate going to bed for some nights, and begin a

course of bark.  I take nothing after my coffee, besides,
except Orgeat.  I have quite relinquished *nasty Brooks's*,
as Lady C[arlisle] calls it.  I am with the sexagenary of
White's, *et de cette manière je passe le tems assez tranquillement.*

12 *o'clock.*—Here comes a letter from George for Lady
C[arlisle], brought to me by a gardener of Mr. Raikes,
under his cover.  Lord Deerhurst has sent a formal proposal of marriage by Lord Ligonier to Lady something
Powis—Lord Powis's sister, who, to save appearance of
repulse, has returned for answer that she will take three
or four days to consider of it.  This I have from
Williams.  He and his father have constant altercations
upon this subject.  Lord Cov[entry] does not object to
the plan of marriage, but says it is not practicable, on
account of circumstances.  I shall hear nothing of the
matter from the parties themselves.  *Ce n'est pas mon
affaire, et je ne m'en mêlerai pas, aux signes de perdre les
bonne graces de ce belle-mère.*  Lady M'Cartney has wrote
to me to hire my house ; but one thing I am resolved
upon is, not to let it to an acquaintance.  I shall keep it
in its present state till these things at Avignon are determined upon.

I dine to-day at the Bishop of Salisbury's, and to-morrow
at Lord Lisbourne's.  I was to have gone for a day with
Lady Fitzw[illiam] to Roehampton, if these damned
spasmodic complaints *ne m'étoient pas survenus.*  However, Potts assures me that I shall be well again, but that
I must take more care of myself.  *Je le crois.*  I have a
great mind, as you may imagine, to see you again, and
Lady C[arlisle] and Caroline, and all of you, and I have
*d'autres raisons qui m'attachent au monde, et je n'en suis pas
dégoûté parce qu'il est comme il a toujours été et comme il
sera à toute éternité.*  I am very angry with Emily, that
he will not write to me ; is he afraid that his style is not
good, or of what ?  . . .  The play at Brooks's is
exorbitant, as I hear ; Grady and Sir Godfrey Whistler
and the General and Admiral are at the head of it.
Charles looks wretchedly, as I am told, but I have scarce

seen him.   Richard is in high cash, and that is all I know
of that infernal house.   Adieu ; my respects to Lady
Carlisle, and my most hearty love to the children.   My
best compliments to Mr. and Mrs. Eden, and to Crowle,
and pray rub Mr. Dean Emily's ears till he writes to me.

It is not desirable that those who present a correspondence for perusal should play too much the part of a
showman.   Letters speak for themselves.   Yet that which
Selwyn wrote on April 14th may well be pointed to as
giving, in a few lines, a reflection in miniature of the
events grave and gay which were then interesting London
society.   We see it vividly, how people were admiring
Lady Crawford's new chair, remarking parenthetically
of bad news from across the Atlantic.   But society was
less frivolous perhaps than it seemed ; the distance from
America, the length of time which elapsed between the
happening of an event and the news of it in England, the
meagreness of the intelligence when at length it arrived,
prevented the public imagination from being aroused, and
so public interest and opinion lay inert.

[1781,] *April* 24, *Tuesday noon*, 1 *o'clock.*—   .        .
   P.S.   *Tuesday afternoon*, 3 *o'clock.*—. . . Vary has just
dropped in upon me, and says that news is come from
Arthburnot (*sic*), that there has been a skirmish with the
Fr[ench] Adm[iral], and it was a kind of drawn battle ;
that General Phillips has joined Arnold with 2,000 men.
He came to ask after George ; *il ne sçait pas encore, à
quel point le monde s'intéresse pour lui.*   My best and most
affectionate respects to Lady Carlisle, and my love to
Caroline, and to her sisters, not forgetting Louisa, *chi gia
non sovra di me.*
   Two balls ! very fine, Caroline.   Mie Mie will have
seen but one, and that is Mr. Wills's annual ball.   But
we are very well feathered for that, *à la Vestris.*   I had
not the ordering so much ornament, and when it is over,
and we have had our diversion, I shall read a lecture upon
heads, which I wish not to be filled with so many thoughts

about dress.   But she coaxed Mrs. Webb into all this *à mon insçu*, and then I cannot be Mr. Killjoy ; so *pour le moment* I seem to approve of it.

We have been at one opera, and instead of other spectacles, I propose to go for the first part of the evening to Ranelagh, *quand la presse n'y sera pas.*   Lady Craufurd's new chair is, as Sir C. Williams said of Dicky's, the charming'st thing in town, *et les deux laquais qui la précèdent attirent les yeux de tous les envieux et envieuses.*

Sir Alexander comes and dines here with March, and is as easy as ever was Sir Jos. Vanheck, and lives with his friends now upon the same foot as before this acquisition of honour.   I am told that you have a receipt as Lord Lieutenant to make knights yourself.   But I suppose if you intend me such an honour I must come and fetch it. I suppose you do everything that is Royal except touching for the Evil, which would be the most useful *fleuron* of the Crown if it was effectual.

Storer was out of spirits yesterday at dinner, and I found out afterwards that he had been losing, like a simple boy, his money at Charles's and Richard's damned Pharo bank, which swallows up everybody's cash that comes to Brooks's, as I am told.   I suppose that the bank is supported, if such a thing wanted support, by Brooks himself and your friend Jack Manners.   It is a creditable way of living, I must own ; and it would be well if by robbing some you might pay others, only that *ce qui est acquis et* [*est?*] *jetté par la fenêtre, et si l'on paye, on ne s'acquitte pas.*

[1781,] *May* 16, *Wednesday night.*—I was engaged to dine to-day at Lady Ossory's,[1] but I called in at Lady Lucan's, and they obliged me to send an excuse, and so I dined there, and dine at Lady Ossory's on Saturday.   I

---

[1] Anne, only child of Lord Ravensworth.   In 1769 she was divorced from the Duke of Grafton and shortly afterward married the Earl of Upper Ossory.   She was a correspondent of Selwyn, and of Walpole, who called her "my duchess."   She was "gifted with high endowments of mind and person, high spirited, and noble in her ways of thinking, and generous in her disposition."

found myself with a party of Irish, Dean Marly, and Lady Clermont, and with her Mrs. Jones, whom I was ravished to see, for she had given a ball where Caroline was, and commended her dancing, and I tormented the poor woman with such a number of questions about her, that I believe she thought me distracted. It is hard upon me to be so circumstanced that I cannot see what would give me so much pleasure, but *on ne peut pas ménager le choux et la chèvre*. If it pleases God that I should live, I shall have that, and for a time a great deal more, for I think that I must be quite wore out with infirmities, and blindness must be one, if seeing Caroline appear to advantage will not give me pleasure. . . .

I saw Charles to-day in a new hat, frock, waistcoat, shirt, and stockings ; he was as clean and smug as a gentleman, and upon perceiving my surprise, he told me that it was from the Pharo Bank. He then talked of the thousands it had lost, which I told him only proved its substance, and the advantage of the trade. He smiled, and seemed perfectly satisfied with that which he had taken up ; he was in such a sort of humour that I should have liked to have dined with him. His old clothes, I suppose, have been burned like the paupers at Salt Hill.

[1781,] *May* 21, *Monday* m[*orning*].—. . . Yesterday about the middle of the day, passing by Brooks's, I saw a Hackney coach, which announced a late sitting. I had the curiosity to enquire how things were, and found Richard in his Pharo pulpit, where he had been, alternately with Charles, since the evening before, and dealing to Adm. Pigott only. I saw a card on the table—" Received from Messieurs Fox & Co. 1,500 guineas." The bank ceased in a few minutes after I was in the room ; it was a little after 12 at noon, and it had won 3,400 or 500 g[uineas]. Pigott, I believe, was the chief loser.

At Devonshire House there had been a bank held by Sir W. Aston and Grady, and that won 700. Martindale cannot get paid, because, as Charles says, he is not allowed to take money from the bank ; he means for the payment of debts, but yet I hear some are paid, such as O'Kelly and other blacklegs. But there are at this time two executions in his house, and Richard's horses were taken the other day from his coach, as Lady Ossory tells me.

Charles says that he is *accablé de demandes, comme de dettes, et avec la réputation d'avoir de l'argent, il ne sait où donner de la tête. A vous dire la verité, si j'avais une tête comme la sienne, ou je me la ferois couper, ou j'en tirerois bien meilleur parti que ne fait notre ami; son charactère, son génie, et sa conduite sont ègalement extra-ordinaires et m'est [me sont] incomprehensibles.*

Lord G. Cavendish is to be married to Lady Eliz. Compton, it being agreed that the Cavendish family must be continued from his loins. *Me la Duchesse fait des paroles, mais non pas des enfans.* I hear that she has won immensely, *et avec beaucoup d'exactitude, ce qui n'est pas fort ordinaire aux dames.*

Harry St. John has been here to ask me to hold a bank to-night at his wife's, and I had an invitation from Mrs. Crewe [1] also this morning to come to her, and I suppose for the same purpose. *Je renonce à tout cela; les inconvéniens en sont innombrables;* all my play at present is confined to a rubber at whist, and a little Pharo with Ailsford, and perhaps two or three more. *Le grand évènement c'est la perte or la gain de* 50 or 80 guineas.

4 *o'clock.*—Come home to dinner. No letters as yet come from Ireland. Lord Egremont tells me that Digby is sent after La Motte Piquet.[2] I went to Miss Gunning's to carry her a parcel of francs, but I did not find her at home. I expect to see Mitchel back in a few days; the wind, as I am told, is favourable for his return.

The post has brought me letters from Holyhead, but no other, so what kind of passage my dear little boy has had over the sea I am still to know. But he was,

---

[1] The fashionable beauty, "whose mind kept the promise was made by her face," as Fox sang; the woman whom he said he preferred to any living. She was the daughter of Sir Everard Falkener, and was married to Mr. Crewe in the same year (1764) as her sister who became the celebrated Mrs. Bouverie.

[2] Commander of the French fleet.

I doubt not, safe with you on Friday, and will I hope in God remain so. I met Sir N. Thomas to-day, with whom I had some conversation about him. I do not perceive that he has a very favourable opinion of the Irish climate, for those whose lungs are not very strong. I hope to hear that Louisa is better. My love to them all most cordially, and to Lady Carlisle with my best respects at the same time. What a cursed affair to me is this Lieutenancy of Ireland, and a damned sea between us! Lord Buckingham shewed me last night an infernal ugly gold box which he had received from the town of Cork, and such another I understood that you would have. Adieu; I have heard no news to-day.

Our club at White's *commence à tomber; la grande presse n'y [est?] pas; c'est un asyle toujours pour les caducs, et pour ceux qui n'ont pas une passion décidée pour le jeu.*

[1781, *May* 29.]—You must know that for these two days past, all passengers in St. James' Street have been amused with seeing two carts at Charles's door filling, by the Jews, with his goods, clothes, books, and pictures. He was waked by Basilico yesterday, and Hare afterwards by his *valet de chambre*, they bein[g] told at the same time that the execution was begun, and the carts were drawn up against the door. Such furniture I never saw.

Betty and Jack Manners are perpetually in a survey of this operation, and Charles, with all Brooks's on his behalf, in the highest spirits. And while this execution is going on in one part of the street, Charles, Richard, and Hare are alternatively holding a bank of £3,000 ostensible, and by which they must have got among them near £2,000. Lord Robert since his bankruptcy, and in consideration of his party principles, is admitted, as I am told, to some small share in this.

What public business is going on I know not, for all the discourse at which I am present turns upon this bank. Offly sat up last night till four, and I believe has lost a good part of his last legacy. Lord Spencer did not sit up, but was there punting at 4. Now the windows are open at break of day, *et le masque levé, rien ne surprend qu' à qui tout soit nouveau, et ne ressemble à rien que l'on ait jamais vu depuis le commencement du monde.* There is to-night a great ball at Gloucester House; it is the Restoration Day, and the birthday also of Princess Sophia. Lady Craufurd is now dressing for it, with more roses, blood, and furbelow than were ever yet enlisted (?). My love and thanks to my dear boy for his letter, which I will answer.

[1781,] *May* 31, *Thursday.*—If I did not send you *tous les petits détails de ma vie,* as insignificant as it is, our correspondence must soon cease, which is one of the greatest pleasures to me, or rather comforts, in your absence. I trust to others the information of things of more consequence. I have, then, if this is not disagreeable to you, a perpetual source of intelligence, for although *je ne fais rien qui vaille,* I am always doing or hearing something, as much as those who are employed about more important matters, and if among these a circumstance happens to interest or amuse you, *je ne serai pas fâché de vous l'avoir mandée.*

The diversion of seeing Charles's dirty furniture in the street, and the speculations which this execution has caused, *avec tous les propos, et toutes les plaisanteries qui en resultent*—all that is now over, and he is established either at his Pharo table, or at his apothecary's, Mr. Mann, who, as a recompense for the legacy which was left by his father and not yet paid, has Charles for a lodger. Jack Manners does not scruple to say that he knows for a certainty that this bank has won to the amount of £40,000, but then Jack does not scruple to lie when he chooses so to do. I cannot conceive above half the sum to have been won; but then, most of it has been paid.

Trusty's advancement to a share in this bank, and his new occupation of dealing, was what I had a great curiosity to see; and although he is, as you know, *fort chiche de ses paroles,* he is obliged for the time that he is upon duty to say "The King loses," and "The Knave wins," and this for some hours, while Charles and Richard are in bed.   Hare is also indefatigable, but what his share is, or what have been his profits, I know not.   Never was a room so crowded or so hot as this was last night.   I could not stay, or chose so to do.   The punters were Lord Ossory, Lord C. Spencer, Admiral Pigott, General Smith, Lord Monson, Sir J. Ramsden, &c., &c.

To-day I dine at Lord Ossory's with Lord Robert and Harry Conway, *qui m'avoient demandé à diner*, but it was by Ossory's desire to his house.   I mentioned to Lord Ossory the offer which the Duchess of Bedford had made me of Streatham, and I was much blamed for refusing it.   If the offer is made again I shall accept it, and it will serve me for a villa till I have hired another.

The Fish came a few evenings ago to dine at Brooks's after the House of Commons was up, but hearing by accident that Lord North dined at White's he went thither, and ordered some champagne and burgundy from his own house for his Lordship's use.   He got a dinner by this means the next day at Rigby's with Lord Mansfield and the Chancellor, and then he came to Ossory, and gave himself a thousand airs upon this invitation.   I have told you perhaps that a nephew of Lord Chedworth's, the heir of his title and estate, got into the same scrape at Epsom as Onslow did at the Exhibition ; *ceci prouve la force d' une passion qui est hors de la nature ; les autres ont leurs bornes, et de la discrétion jusqu'à un certain point.*

I went from dinner yesterday to the House of Commons, and came just time enough to be in a division upon some American question, God knows what.   I was received in the House with a laugh, because three parts out of four believed me to be with you in Ireland, as *bouffon de la Cour*.   This the morning papers had in-structed them to believe, and such is the notion I believe that the writers of those papers have of my talents and turn.   You have not told me that Lady Carlisle is with child, but I hear it from other hands.   Be so good as not to let me be ignorant of these probable events, in which my affection to her and to you is so much interested.

I sat a great while the other morning with Miss
Gunning at St. James's ; Sir Robert was with her.   She
is afraid of having the measles ; her sister has them at
present.   The Ball at Glouc[ester] House was magnificent,
and their Royal Highnesses gracious *al maggior segno*.
They call the others, " the people in Pall Mall," and
the man in Pall Mall calls the Duke[1] " the Warden
of the Forest," and distinguishes him by no other name.
I wonder that they do not let other people find names for
them both, who know them better than they do themselves.

Montem[2] is to be a fine sight, that is, a great concourse
of people will be there, I suppose, on their Majesties'
account.   Mie Mie wants to go.   If the Townshends,
that is Mary and Lady Middleton, had offered to be
troubled with her, I should have consented and gone
there myself.   I have made no preparations for the
Birthday, but thinking where I shall go to avoid it ;
or for yours, but I will ; Storer shall dine with me that
day, *et ceux que je crois vous être les plus attachés*, and
we will drink the health of their Excellencies, *cela du petit
dauphin*, of my dear little Caroline, *et ainsi du reste*.
Pierre tells me that she is not so tall as Mie Mie is
at present ; *en dédommagement de cela elle est cent mille fois
plus robuste.*   As to myself, *j'ai un ménagement pour ma
santé incroyable.*   For I am determined, if it pleases God,
to live to see you and all of you again, but when or where,
that must be left to the chapter of accidents.   Emily has
left off writing to me ; he wrote to me twice *pour faire
votre éloge, ce qui ne fut fort peu nécessaire*, and there was

---

[1] Of Gloucester.

[2] In the time of George III. and up to the date when it was
abolished in 1847, Montem at Eton was a school holiday, an "event,"
as we should now say, of the London season.   Of its origin nothing is
known, but the ceremony of a procession in military costume " ad
Montem " to a mound near Slough, now called Salt Hill, can be traced
back to the sixteenth century.   Visitors were offered salt by some of
the boys, and in exchange gave money.   The amount collected after
payment of the expenses belonged to the captain of the school.—
" History of Eton College," by H. C. Maxwell-Lyte, p. 450.

an end of his epistolary correspondence. Pray goad that Dean [1] who slumbers in his stall, and make him write. . . .

[1781,] *June* 1, *Friday* m[*orning*].—I am at this moment employed *fort pédagoguement.* I have taken into my own department Mie Mie's translations out of English into French. That is, I am at her elbow when she translates, and by that means can see what faults she makes from insufficiency, and what are produced from carelessness. She is very much so if left to herself, but is very much improved, as I perceive. But Mrs. Webb can be of no use in this, and so I have the task when Labort is not here. I hope that Caroline has somebody to read French with her who has a real good pronunciation, other- wise it will take *un mauvais pli,* which will not be so easy to recover, and it is better not to speak a language at all than without some sort of grace.

To-day I give a dinner to the bankers ; the two not upon duty come here at five, and when the other two come off they will find here *des réchauffés ;* to the Duke of Q[ueensberry] and Mr. Greenville, and to two chance comers ; it may be Boothby and Storer, or Sir C. Bunbury. It is too hot to go out to-day. I have seen nobody, and the rise and fall of the bank is not as yet added to the other stocks in the morning papers. It is frequently declared from the window, or gallery, *aux passans.* Pigott was there this morning at four, and from May the 31st (*sic*) at night, that is, from Tuesday night, about nine. The account brought to White's, about supper time, was that he had rose to eat a mutton chop. But that merits confirmation.

Young Pitt made yesterday on the Accounts another speech,[2] which is much admired, in which there was *du sel, et du piquant, à pleines mains.* Charles *en fut enchanté,* and I hear that the satire of it was pointed strongly

---

[1] Edward Emly, Dean of Derry.

[2] Pitt's second speech, on May 31st, was against a Bill to continue an Act for the appointment of commissioners' accounts. The Opposition were defeated by 98 votes to 42. The speech attracted great notice.

against Lord N[orth]. It wanted no other recommenda-
tion to the party who dines here to-day. Sir J. Irwin will
be soon with you. I supped with him at White's, and
with Lord Glendower and Lord Westmoreland, &c., &c.,
and I concluded my sitting with a little bank to Harry
Carteret, Sir W. Gordon, Lord Ailsford and General
Grant, and to no others. I had them in great order. I
do not allow the opposite no greater sum than 5 guineas,
and such byelaws as these I oblige the observance of, and
I won 120 guineas. They waited till near one before
I had finished my prosing, and telling old stories at supper
to the two young men. When they were finished, I
retired and opened my bank.

Charles's house is now going to be new painted, and
entire new furniture to be put into it, belonging to I do
not know who[m]. He was security for an annuity of
Richard's, and so suffered this seizure on his account. It
is a strange combination altogether, and is now more the
subject of conversation than any other topic, and it serves
me also as one to fill my letter. *Si le récit vous ennuye,
vous n'ignorez pas le motif que j'ai à vous le faire.* I
suppose that you are not always at audiences, and that you
may like sometimes to know what passes in circles from
whence everything of moment is excluded, and where you
may be again, to relieve yourself from business.

To-day I expect a letter from Warner, and of great
decision and importance as to the matter about which he
has been employed. But if I see him come in while
I am at dinner I shall not be surprised. If I have a letter
I will send you the substance of it, for I may not go
out again after dinner, or only to Lady Harrington's.
My bank is not like that at Brooks's ; there are a great
many *lacunes*, and it is not above once in I do not
know how long that I can get such a party as I had last
night.

Ossory's new house is delightful, and the furniture
mighty well chose. I have not met yet Lord Euston
there, as I expected. But I have dined there less this
than former years.

[1781,] *June 2, Saturday morning.*—Charles Fox has desired me to send Gregg to him, and is to discharge the annuity for which you are bound, and, I hope, to pay off the arrears at the same time. I have wrote to Gregg, to desire that he will lose no time, as Charles's property is of a very fluctuating kind. My dinner of yesterday was a very agreeable one to me, and seemed to be so to the rest. But Charles had forgot, when he promised to come to me, that he was engaged to the Duke of Grafton. The rest came, for this remarkable sitting at Pharo was over yesterday morning about seven o'clock, and so shall be my further account of it. The event is so often repeated that it becomes less extraordinary. But I have known of no other to entertain you with for some days past. General Craigs sets off for Ireland in about a week or ten days. I shall send my box of things for the children, either by him or Mr. Kinsman. . . .

The Montem is put off from Monday till Wednesday, for the convenience of their Majesties, who are to be there. The Queen will not have prayers read in the manner that they have been used to be there; she sees it [in] the light of a comedy acted, and therefore, improper. Doctor Young, the Fellow, has just been with me, to ask me if I could borrow a regimental suit of clothes, sash, and gorgette from some officer of the Guards, of my acquaintance. I intend to ask Richard, for the boy who is to wear it is, by Doctor Y[oung]'s account, of Richard's height. If I had known it before, I could have sent to Matson for a sash which my father wore at the battle of Blenheim, where he assisted as Aid-de-Camp to my Lord Marlborough. It will be a very lucrative campaign for the boy, who is captain. His name is Roberts ; he is a son of one of the Fellows.

Storer's business is not, from what I have accidentally heard, in so great forwardness as I was in hopes that it had been. There must be two vacancies at the Board before he has a very good chance, if he has any. Lord Walsingham has no inclination to quit ; it is a scene of business which he likes. Mr. Buller has been many years in Parliament, and I am afraid that his pretensions will preponderate above the friendship or good-will which Lord N[orth] professes to Storer. I picked up this by accident as I was going out yesterday airing with Mie Mie, after my company had left me. I met Lord Brudenel, and I collected this from his conversation, for he did not tell it me directly. But this and everything else, trifling or not, I think myself obliged to let you know, *et enfin ne rien laisser au boute de ma plume.*

But I am particularly desirous to inform you of what concerns Storer, because I am persuaded that you wish to serve him. Your protection ought to be a valid one, and Lord N[orth] will not, I should imagine, choose to displease you ; as to myself, *maintenant que mes ongles sont rognés comme ils le sont*, he will treat me with what indifference he pleases, and I know no remedy for it, but what is worse than the disease. Then it is more supineness, insensibility, and natural arrogance than any desire to use me worse than another. He has no tact in point of breeding, and he lays all his business on Robinson's[1] shoulders, who has behaved worse to me than any man ever did ; but I must take shame to myself for that, because, if I had rejected his first proposal of standing for Gloucester, by his suggestion, against my own reason and inclination, he would never have dared to have treated me ill any more. I hope to be rich enough in a year or two more, if I live, to be as much a patriot as I happen to choose ; but it is a *fichu matier*, as times go, and nobody of common sense ever gives you any credit for it. I shall be contented only, if, instead of making a bargain with a Minister, I can be in circumstances good enough to sell him one, if he uses me ill.

[1781,] *June* 5, *Tuesday.*—. . . I know of nothing remarkable at the Birthday yesterday. I put on the best clothes which I had, about nine at night, to make a bow to their Majesties *sur leur passage*, as they went to the

---

[1] John Robinson, Secretary to the Treasury.

ball room, and there the Queen stopped and said some
very gracious things to me, which my great deference to
her Majesty made me not understand, but I bowed and
thanked her, supposing that she said something that
interested me. The King's face was turned the other
way, and he did not see me, but I was taken notice of
*dans l'antichambre du Roi*, and so it was very well, and it
was there that I saw my nephew Broderick, who had just
had an audience of the King. His Royal Highness's [1]
equipages are very becoming, and give some little splendour to the Court. I could tell poor Guerchy now that
we had not *des vaisseaux* only, but *des carro[s]es* ; we
have *des Princes*, God knows, *à foison*. The Princess
Royal seems a very agreeable young woman, but I had
only a transient glance of her. Her air and manner
seemed good. One coach came by after another in their
liveries, and each stuffed with royal children, like a cor-
nucopia with fruit and flowers. Bory got I do not
[know] how many of my servants, by some *escalier
dérobé*, to see the ball-room and some of the dances ; he
has a back stairs interest through that of Lord Trentham's
nurse, and being himself the State Trumpeter in a
neighbouring kingdom, is of some note and importance,
and all is at my use and service. He is a very honest
good creature. I wish that I had room for him here in
this house instead of in Chesterfield Street. Bob grows
every day more and more attached to him, but I cannot
dawdle him as Horry Walpole does Tonton, for Mᵉ du
Deffand's sake, nor does he seem to expect it. He has
the *accueil* of a respectable old suisse in my hall, where I
meet him on coming home in a *posture couchante*. Adieu ;
till I have letters, remember me kindly to all, but to the
dear children in particular. It is a great grievance to me
not to see them. *Je vieillis, et je m'en apperçois.*

[1781,] *June* 11, *Monday evening.*—. . . The
Duke of Q[ueensberry] dined here to-day, and, by an
accident, the Duke of Dorset. I had also Mr. Selwin

[1] The Prince of Wales.

who was a banker in Paris, a worthy man, but a more
splenetic one I never knew, with an extreme good understanding. We are of the same family, by his account,
although I do not know the degree of affinity in which
we stand to each other.

To-morrow I find a Motion [1] is to come from Fox concerning America, to which he may, contrary to his
expectation or wishes, find in the friends of Government
an assent. People now seem by their discourse to despair
more of that cause than ever. There has been wretched
management, disgraceful politics, I am sure ; where the
principal blame is, the Lord only knows ; in many places,
I am afraid.

The Duke of Gloucester is going to-morrow, as I hear,
to Brussels, to meet the Emperor. I hope for our sake
that they will be *deux têtes dans le même bonnet*, but *la
différence en est trop évidente*. That between our master
and his son is not less, if report says true. They have
great reason to be uneasy, I believe, but they must, when
they reflect, think, that their own conduct has been very
much the cause of it, and that they either have not read
history, or forgot it.

The Pharo bank goes on, and winning ; *cela s'entend*.
The winnings are computed to be 30,000. Each of the
bankers, to encourage him in his application and to make
him as much amends as possible for the waste of his constitution, is entitled to a guinea for every deal from the
bank ; and so our Trusty is in a way of honest industry,
dealing at the pay of a guinea every ten minutes. There
is also an insurance against cards coming up on the losing
side, which is no inconsiderable profit to the underwriters.

Offly has had unexpectedly fallen to him, by way of
legacy, an estate of some hundreds a year, which enables
him to punt till past five in the morning.

---

[1] On June 12th Fox moved that the House should resolve itself
into a Committee to consider the American war, at the same time
moving a further resolution that Ministers should take every possible
measure to conclude peace with the American Colonies. The Motion
was rejected by 172 to 99.

I had a very pleasant day yesterday at Gregg's, and as often as I mention these excursions I have a long dissertation from the Duke [of Queensberry] upon the folly of having a country house at above ten or fourteen miles distance from London ; which reflections will end in nothing but a condemnation of what he has, and never procure the enjoyment of that which I am sure he would like above all things if he had it.   His uncertainty is in some measure the cause of my own, but shall not govern it, beyond the present year.

Craigs sets out for Ireland on Thursday.   I am concerned at the account which you give me of Ekins.   I hope to hear no more of your own gout.   But if you feel symptoms of it, pray do not conceal them from me.

I go to-night to Marlborough House,[1] and there is also a promenade at Bedford House,[2] but it is announced that no candles will be lighted.   My nephew Broderick is to have a £500 gratuity, and a Majority, and Lord Cornwallis [3] will solicit leave for his purchasing a company in the Guards.

Pray remember me most kindly to Lady Carlisle, and my hearty love to all the children without exception or preference.   If George is to come here again, let me know it.   If not, I shall not expect it.

Charles's house, like a phœnix from the flames, is new painted, and going to be new furnished, with certain precautions to keep his furniture *à l'abri de*

[1] Marlborough House was designed by Wren ; it reverted to the Crown in 1817.

[2] Bedford House, built in the reign of Charles II., covered the whole of the north side of what is now Bloomsbury Square.   It was sold and pulled down in 1800.

[3] Charles first Marquis Cornwallis (1738–1805).   In early life Cornwallis was both a soldier and a politician.   Though one of the few men opposed to the taxation of the American Colonists, he felt bound as a soldier to serve against them and was undoubtedly the most able of the English generals.   In 1786, at the urgent request of Pitt, he became Governor General of India and did not return to England till 1793.   In 1798 Cornwallis again entered the public service as Lord-Lieutenant of Ireland and occupied that position at the time of the Union.   At his death he was again Viceroy of India.

*ses créanciers.*  You have heard how he has liquidated the annuity for which you was engaged.  There are still arrears due to you, to a considerable amount. This Pharo Bank is held in a manner which, being so exposed to public view, bids defiance to all decency and police.  The whole town as it passes views the dealer and the punters, by means of the candles, and the windows being levelled with the ground.  The Opposition, who have Charles for their ablest advocate, is quite ashamed of the proceeding, and hates to hear it mentioned.

I hear of neither deaths, marriages, or preferments ; public news come to your knowledge sooner, and with more authenticity, than through me ; so I have no more to say at present, but to beg that I may hear from you as often as possible, and that I may have the satisfaction of knowing that you are well.  These assurances cannot be too often repeated to me, who am interested by every degree of affection in knowing whatever concerns you or yours.

My best compliments to Dr. Ekins, and my love once more to George, and to his sisters.  He has wrote as often to me as I expected.  I shall never, as long as I live, forget his assurances upon that head, the *tone* and air with which he said it, and the cordiality of it.  *Il a indubitablement le meilleur des cœurs possibles.*

[1781,] *June* 13, *Wednesday m[orning]*.—As I think, after having wrote a long letter to Dr. Ekins, I shall have little to say to you, so I take only this vessel of paper for my purpose.  Mrs. Webb and I are going to consummate our unfinished loves at Streatham, and to reside there at times for the next six weeks.  I shall make use of this opportunity to fix myself in a country house for next year, and perhaps the Duke of Q[ueensberry] may do the same, for from that distance to about ten miles further we have agreed is the best to answer our purposes.  We must necessarily have two houses, that purity and impurity may not occasionally meet.  Lady Ossory has negotiated this matter for me, and this morning I shall go to Bedford House to do homage, as a tenant-at-will.

I heard yesterday young Pitt ; I came down into the
House to judge for myself. He is a young man who
will undoubtedly make his way in the world by his
abilities. But to give him credit for being very extraordinary, upon what I heard yesterday, would be absurd.
If the oration had been pronounced equally well by a
young man whose name was not of the same renown, and
if the matter and expression had come without that prejudice, or wrote down, all which could have been said
was, that he was a sensible and promising young man.
There is no fairer way of judging.

Lord Cambden's son acquitted himself but very ill ;
however, Lord Chatham did him the honour to say that
he sees he will make a speaker, so we must give him
credit for what he may *do* by what Lord Chatham has
*said*.

If I wanted reputation, and to be puffed, and could
afford to pay for such nonsense, I would certainly be in
Opposition, and sit in the House in the places where
Ossory and Lord Robert and young Greenville sit. But
the difficulty would be to extol my speaking when I
said nothing.

The guinea a deal is now deemed too much, so Charles
has published a new edict, and they have only five guineas
an hour, by which Lord Robert cannot earn in a day
more than Brooks gets by furnishing cards and candles.
Pigott has found out that punting is not advantageous,
and has left it off. The General is not yet of the same
opinion. Lord Spencer, Mr. Heneage, Offley, &c., are
*des culs de plomb*, and the bankers' coaches are not ordered
till about six in the morning.

Lord Abergavenny's son is certainly to marry Robinson's daughter. He gives her £25,000 down, which
does not pay all the young man's debts. Lord A[berga-
venny] gives them a thousand a year. He is a weak,
good-tempered young man, or, as the King of Prussia
called an acquaintance of mine, the Comte de Bohn, *une
belle bête*.

Robinson seems rejoiced that he is to be allied to the

Nevills, and that his posterity is to have the bear and ragged staff, red roses, and portcullises for their insignia. Malden, to console himself for the infidelity of Mrs. Robinson, is gone to Bruxelles with his Royal Highness.[1]

[1781, *June* 13,] *Wednesday, 4 o'clock.*—P.S.—I have been at Bedford House, and performed my homage. I dine at Streatham on Sunday, and in the course of the next week go to settle myself there. I met Admiral Biron in my way back, and had some discourse with him on the subject of his sister.[2] He spoke to me about her with great good nature and reason, but said that the correspondence was between his wife and her, and seemed to hint, if he was himself consulted, he should advise her better. He expects her home, from the tenor of her letters to Mrs. Biron, so perhaps, after all, she may come. If she does, Bory and I shall prepare a reception for her.

Storer is coming here to dinner. He lives now with Mr. Walpole ; has his lodging at Strawberry Hill, as an antiquarian. March dines here also. There are to be two more promenades at Bedford House on a Monday, and then she [the Duchess] goes to Ouburn [Woburn] for the rest of the year.

The bank won last night, as Lord Clermont [tells me?], 4,000 ; that must have been chiefly of the General ; but of the bankers, those who deal, punt also ; so they may have contributed.

At Streatham I shall be within two miles of Gregg, so we shall have together a great deal of discourse about you. Admiral Biron was the other day at Castle Howard, and saw little Elizabeth, who was very well. I like the Admiral much.

P.M. (*sic*).—Poor Storer is gone away in great dudgeon. March fell asleep on one side of him, and I on the other, the moment that the cloth was taken away. He was not last night in the Division, or made any bargain. He has been all this day at Charles's auction, to secure for him his books. All his things were upon sale yesterday and

---

[1] The Duke of Gloucester.
[2] The Countess Dowager of Carlisle.

to-day. Some of his books are very scarce and valuable. I wonder that, knowing himself liable to such an attack, he did not keep them at Brooks's, where they would have been for ever unmolested.

Mrs. Elliot is returned from France, and I have seen her in a *vis-à-vis* with that idiot Lord Cholm[ondeley]; so I suppose that is to go on as it did.

My servants tell me that Sir J. Irwin sets out for Ireland to-morrow, but that I believe is not so ; I understood him last night that it would be a month before he went. He said that he should go no more this Session to the House of Commons. I believe that Mr. Robinson will find it very difficult to muster so many of his troops as were assembled there last night, any more this year. It was insufferably hot and dull.

I wish that Storer would be in humour with them till the Session was over, and say nothing. If then nothing is done, he may begin his grumbling. W. K. and John, I take it for granted, report these things, if they happen to hear of them. He will succeed at last, I do not doubt ; in the meantime, *le meilleur parti est de se taire*.

Lady Julia, as I understand, is to meet Lady B[etty?] in the country, and come up with her to town. What a *fracas* we shall have when my Lady Dowager arrives ; and if she does not, I see no end of her vexations. The Admiral says that she talks of coming. . . .

[1781, *June*] 18, *Monday night.*—I saw this morning Lady Julia, who looks very well, and has no brogue. I sat a great while with her and Lady Betty, and talked over with them our foreign affairs ; but no letter is come from Warner, although a mail is, as I see by the papers, arrived both from France and from Flanders. The Jamaica fleet is safe at last, and the Emperor [1] declares Ostende to be a free port. The two Houses will rise yet this month, and this is all that I know of public matters.

---

[1] Joseph II., Emperor of Germany ; he died in 1790. In 1781 he had declared the Barrier Treaty no longer binding. See his character, Lecky " History of England," vol. v. p. 218.

Charles, from paying his debts, proceeds to make presents ; he is now quite *magnifique avec une abondance de richesses.* Varey dined with me to-day, Storer, and Lord Carmarthaen.

I have now settled with my servants to go to Streatham on a Saturday after Mie Mie's dancing, and to stay there till Tuesday noon, and this every week, during the time that I shall stay in this part of the world ; and if I can get no one else to be with me on those days, I shall take Lobort (?), which will be a benefit to Mie Mie.

The Duke of Gloucester is returned from Bruges, where he passed two days with the Emperor. What object there was in this expedition besides that of seeing the Emperor, I do not know. But a cat looking on a king, could not, in all probability, have more innocent consequences. Malden, I suppose, is come back with him, as his conferences with his Imperial Majesty could not be more interesting, after his R[oyal] H[ighness] was gone.

Lord Cornwallis's letter to Mr. Webster's father on the death of his son *est très touchante.* The town empties extremely. I reckon my stay to be from this time about five weeks. Belgiosioso told me last night that he had had letters from Milan, by which he was informed that the M. Fagnani was gone quite mad. He has been stone blind a considerable time, and I take for granted both these misfortunes are come from the same cause, that is, mercury. His experiments to ease the one probably occasioned the other. I never hear one syllable from any of the family ; I hope in God that I never shall, or poor Mie Mie either. It grows every day less likely, and yet when I am out of spirits that Dragon, among others, comes across me and distresses me ; and the thought of what must happen to that child, if I am not alive to protect her. You will not wonder then, that I am afraid of being left to my own reflections : *elles sont quelque fois fort tristes.* Clubs are better for dissipation than consultation ; all which being considered makes me wish myself not alone, or so much in public. But to find a person who really interests themselves (*sic*) about you, and is able and

willing to give you such advice as applies immediately to
your case, is of all things in the world most difficult to
meet with, but the most comfortable when you do, and is
the utmost service which I ever expect from anybody in
this world, and yet what I despair of finding, in the circle
in which I move.   I will not fatigue you with any more
*bavardise.*   Remember me most kindly to Lady Carlisle
and my cordial love to all the children, and pray let me
know how my dear little George goes on.

[1781,] *June* 19, *Tuesday.*—Last night I went, when I
came from airing, to White's, where I stayed in the
Chocolate Room till I went home to bed, that is till 12—
Lord Ashburnham, Williams, and I—hearing Lord
Malden's account of the Emperor, and of the manner of
his living, and travelling, and behaving.   It was very
amusing and circumstantial.   He is really a great prince
*dans tous les sens,* and by Lord M[alden's] account
a sensible man, with a very amiable address and behaviour.

He talked of the excessive gaming here, and of Charles
Fox, and he spoke of him not in terms of very high
esteem.   Speaking of his talents and oratory, he said, " *Il
suffit qu'il dite (dise ?) des injures.*"

What of business there was passed between his R[oyal]
H[ighness] and the Emperor ; Malden was not of that
Cabinet.   I suppose nothing essential is as yet concluded
between them.   He promised the Princess Sophia, when
he took leave of her, that he should certainly be returned
on Sunday, and kept his word very punctually ; so something may transpire through her R[oyal] H[ighness's]
channel.

While I was hearing these things, I was called into the
vestibule by Gregg, who communicated to me your letter,
which corresponded with the last which I received from
you.   It is a pity that Warner should not know your
just idea of what is right or wrong.   I am and shall be
very uneasy till I hear from him.

I observed, in your letter to Gregg, that you press him

to solicit the payment of the arrears from Charles. I had mentioned it in mine to you, as you will find in a few days. But you will not be surprised at anything which that boy does ; you must know not half an hour before Fawkener said that he left Charles a loser [of] 5,000 to General Smith at picquet, and [he] was then playing with him a £100 a game.

I go to-night with Mie Mie to the Opera in Lady Townshend's box, to see this famous dance of Medea and Jason. The girl had not in her head to go this year any more to the Opera, but Lady Townshend made this party. It will be *étouffante* ; Vestris, it is said, dances for the last time.

The Emp[eror], I forgot to tell you, said that he had now in his pay, and ready for service, 300,000 men and 40,000 horse. I have heard before the same thing. He is attentive to the greatest detail ; he travels and lives in journeys, and at such places as Bruges and Ghent, with the utmost temperance and simplicity. He refuses audiences to no one individual, [so] that he is occupied with that and his reviews from very early in the morning till it is dark. He speaks French without the least accent whatsoever. He has a dark complexion, *bazané*, but very lively eyes, and fine teeth, and a most manly carriage, with great affability. We all went home to bed in admiration of this Emperor.

He received a letter from Belgioi[o]so while the Duke of G[loucester] was there. I have no doubt but what passes at Brooks's makes part of the despatch. He reads all our papers in English, so I asked Lord Malden if he said anything of my jokes, and was mortified to find that they had escaped his Imp[erial] Majesty's observations. But he has read some of them, *sans doute*, so I may have the same vanity as poor Dick Edgcumbe had, of think-ing that the Emperor of Constantinople had from the windows of his seraglio heard him play upon the kettle drums.

I heard no more of an approaching Peace. Dr. Gemm assures me that the French will make no overtures towards it, and that we must ask it ourselves. The Emperor does not seem to be of opinion that we shall subdue our Colonies, but thinks our cause a just one. He does not seem favourable to the French, or to like his sister the French Queen. He said one day, *Que la bongress* (?) *ma sœur aime la France ; that*, if she does, deserves another reflection ; *his* is not a just one ; *elle aime les dames françoises, cela n'est pas à douter. La Princesse de Carignan et M<sup>e</sup>. de Polignac en sont témoins.*

Gregg has been here for [a] quarter of an hour ; he came to desire that I would meet Lord Ravensworth at dinner at his house next Sunday. It is the day I go to Streatham. I have told you that I have now fixed to be there from Saturday till Tuesday m[orning] each week during my lease. I asked Gregg when he went into the North ; he has fixed no time. I asked him if he went alone ; he said yes. It is an idea of mine that he would not dislike the carrying Mrs. Gregg and his daughter with him, if while he went into Cumberland he had your permission to leave them at Castle Howard. I have thought it proper to hint this to you, because, if you cho[o]se to make him that offer, you may. He does not expect it ; and I do assure you that I will not say one single word to him to let him understand that I had mentioned [it]. I do not, indeed, believe that he would like that I should ; so whatever you do, I beg not to be committed.

I believe that I shall take it upon myself to speak to Charles about these arrears, for he has that good humour in his composition, that he never takes anything amiss that I say to him, and I am sometimes very free in telling him how opposite my sentiments are to him, and to his conduct. I should rather say to his conduct, for, personally, I love him, as he would have had no doubt, if he had been like other reasonable people ; *car avec les défauts les plus insignes il y a quelque fois un brin de raison dans la pluspart des hommes ; mais en lui, ce qui est defectueux, l'est radicalement.* He has adopted it with so much earnestness that there is no room for reproof or hope of correction.

[1781,] *June* 22, *Friday.*—I must begin my letter of to-day by contradicting the piece of intelligence with which I concluded my last.   I went to Lady Betty's yesterday after dinner, who was gone with Mr. Delmé to Bray, till Wednesday.   I saw your porter, who is established there, and he told me that no letter from abroad was come ; so this came from the vague report of servants who never comprehend truth, or tell it.

I went to White's, and there met with Lord Lough-borough, who goes the Oxford Circuit.   He finishes at Stafford, and from thence goes to Ireland.   He desired me to go upstairs into the supper room with him, to which I had consented, but Williams and Lord Ashburn-ham,[1] and he and I assembled around the cold stove, till the supper was forgot, and I fell asleep.

I walked home, but called in at Brooks's as I passed by ; Hare in the chair ; the General chief punter, who lost a 1,000.   The bank concluded early a winner, 12 or 1300.   Charles, *de côté ou d'autre*, told me that he had won 900.   I said that I was informed from the Emperor that he had lost lately 8,000.   He said, in two days, at various sports.   I hinted to him that I had a suit to prefer. He guessed what it was, and begged that I would not just then speak to him about money.   He was in the right.   I meant to have dunned him for yours.

I told him that I had been reading his character in the Public Advertiser.   The writer says that his figure is squalid and disagreeable.   I told him that my opinion coincided with half of that account, that he was un-doubtedly squalid, but if by his figure was meant, as in French, his countenance, it was not a true picture.   He said he never cared what was said of his person.   If he was represented ugly, and was not so, those who knew him would do him justice, and he did not care for what he passed in that respect with those who did not.   The *qu'en dira-t-on ?* he certainly holds very cheap, but he did [not ?]

---

[1] John, second Earl of Ashburnham (1724–1812).   Lord of the Bedchamber to George III.

explain to me exactly to what extent proceeded his indifference towards it. I then went home.

To-day we have a late day in the House, but I shall go and dine first at Lord Ashburnham's in the King's Road, and to-morrow to my villa at Streatham. I have bought Johnson's Lives of the Poets,[1] and repent of it already ; but I have read but one, which is Prior's. There are few anecdotes, and those not well authenticated ; his criticisms on his poems, false and absurd, and the prettiest things which he has wrote passed over in silence. I told Lord Loughborough[2] what I thought of it, and he had made the same remarks. But he says that I had begun with the life the worst wrote of them all.

Charles was yesterday very abusive upon Johns[t]on.[3] Lord N[orth] said in his reply that the gentleman was at a great distance ; that if he had been on the spot, he would have given him as good an answer then as he had done on other occasions. We shall sit, I believe, till about the 11th of next month. John says, in regard to the East India business, we are now all afloat. It is à recommencer. I should, if I was the Minister, put [it ?] into his hands for dispatch.

[1] The first *livraison* was published in 1779 ; Johnson completed the work in 1781.

[2] Alexander Wedderburn (1733–1805). He was appointed Solicitor-General in 1771 and Attorney-General in 1778. He was created a peer as Lord Loughborough on his appointment as Chief Justice of the Common Pleas. In 1793 he reached the Woolsack, and in 1801 was created Earl of Rosslyn. Beginning political life as a Tory, he presently became a Whig and an opponent to Lord North ; then he took office under him. A member of the Coalition Cabinet of Fox and North on its fall he became leader of the Whigs in the House of Lords, only to conclude his official life as Lord Chancellor in Pitt's administration.

[3] George Johnston (1730–1787), sometimes called "Governor" Johnston ; a naval officer. He became Governor of West Florida in 1763, in 1768, having returned to England, he became member for Cockermouth, and in 1778 he was appointed a commissioner to treat with America, from which, by reason of a partisan letter, he was obliged to withdraw. In 1779 he was appointed commodore of a small fleet. In 1781 he was again returned to Parliament. He was a violent and self-advertising politician.

Mr. Raikes has sent to me this morning to know how George does. I sent him word that he was very well, that I heard from him, and that he had particularly desired to be remembered to him.

1781, *Nov.* 17, *Saturday night.*—I do not know how I shall conclude my letter, but I begin it in no better spirits than I can have, when I reflect, as I can never help doing, upon a loss which I sustained this day; it is now thirty years, and which as many more, although they will certainly annihilate the reflection of, can never repair. I will not be so unjust to the kindness which I have received from you and some others as to say that when I lost my father I lost the only friend I could have, but I most undoubtedly lost the best, and being to-day where that happened, and more at leisure to recollect it, *je la sens, cette perte, avec la même vivacité aujourd'hui, que je ne l'eusse faite que depuis trois jours.*

I set my heart therefore particularly on receiving to-day a letter from you, *et la voici.* It is a great consolation to me, as that it proves to me, with manifold other arguments, that whatever may be your occupation, you will find a moment to tell me, what if you did not I should have not the least doubt of, and that neither business or distance will deprive me of the place which I have always maintained in your mind and regard.

But *mes jérémiades ne sont pas encore finies.* The Castle air, by which I find the health of the children must be in some measure affected, and your own to be made a sacrifice to I do not know what, is to me a great grievance, and one to which I know as yet no remedy. The only one is to return here, and the sooner you do the better, and the happier we shall both be, I am sure.

*Ce retardement de la poste, aussi, si cela n'est pas un malheur excessif, il ne laisse pas d'être un très grand inconvénient;* and I have only to comfort myself that when it was the most necessary to the ease of your life to have my letters come to you more exactly, that is, when the poor little boy was so ill, that then they came with more expedition, *et qu'alors et les courriers et les vents aient eu également compassion de ce que vous avez senti à cette occasion. . . .*

Gregg is to go to Neasdon to-morrow from Mitcham ; he has dined here once ; when his business will permit it I shall see him again. I have already hinted to him what you have desired as to his account. He desires it as a satisfaction to himself as well as to you. Delmé does not please him by his conduct in any manner, and I think that he will, if he undertakes anything for him, do it more to oblige you than for any other reason.

I am very sorry to hear such an account of the affairs of that family, and of so little disposition to do what is necessary to set them to rights. If the estate and the resources were forty times what they are, such dissipation and want of management must undo them.

I am very glad that Storer is coming, and when he does I hope that he will come and attend with better grace that that has been done, which has been done (*sic*) for him. But the point of the cause to which he is to advert, and the only one, is the part which you have acted by him, and the benefit which will accrue to him from it. He has, when he reflects, a great deal of sense, and his heart is very good ; therefore I look upon his present humour to be rather *un effervescence* than the result of much reflection.

The town is at this moment, as much as I can judge of it, as great a solitude as it has been at any time these two months past. But we are at the even of *beaucoup de tintamarre, comme de nouvelles.* Lord Cornwallis's situation is as critical, both for himself and for this country, as any can possibly be ;[1] and if George, in his History of Greece, and of Nicæas in the expedition to Syracuse, can find a parallel for it, I cannot ; no more than a remedy, or a reparation for all the losses which we have and must sustain, if we are not successful. Till I see the issue of this cast, I will not conclude, what the Duc de Châtelet told me to be true, that it is *une cause perduë.*

[1] See *post* p. 164 note.

I will take the first opportunity of speaking to Gregg about your not writing to him, for he has been waiting for a letter from you, with unusual impatience, and I will write to Boothby if he does not in a few days return to town. I was with Ekins last night, and I stayed with him till ten. He is more crippled than I ever knew him to be. He is going to change his house, from which change, as of posture, he derives some comfort. It matters little from what hope[s] we derive comfort while we hope them.

Lady Mary H[oward] is very angry with me, as Lady Townshend assures me, for not having been near her. The truth is, that when I carried George to wait on her the day that he was in town, before his going to school, her room was quite insupportable, and for that reason I could not allow him safely to stay there.

Mr. Walpole, more *défait*, more *perclus de ses membres*, than I ever yet saw any poor wretch, is gone to-night to the play-house, to see the Tragedy of Narbonne. The gout may put what shackles it pleases on some people ; *on les rompt, et la vanité l'emporte.* He seems as able to act a part in the drama as to assist at the performance of it.

Poor Barker has lost all the hopes which he ever had of resource. His uncle, from whom he had great and reasonable expectations formerly, is dead at Constantinople, and without a groat. He has now, poor man, *pour tout potage*, Lady Harrington's dinner and compassion, and the one is as late and uncertain as the other. If his own relation, with his enormous wealth, and after such unexpected and unmerited good fortune, does not assist him, he will for ever pass with me for a man *destitué de sentimens comme de principes.* But, perhaps, not knowing more than I do of the connection and of the persons, my judgment may be severe and unjust.

My dear Lord, to what an unreasonable length have I spun out this letter. But from my disposition of mind to-day, and being alone, or *en famille* only, I did not think that I should be very concise. To my own *tristes reflections* you have added more, and the account[s] which

I have of your health, and of what it may be, and of the Castle air, &c., do by no means aid me on this occasion. I will fairly own to you, that, *à quelque prise que ce soit*, I wish this administration of yours in Ireland was at an end ; and if no other ever began, I should be as well contented, unless, what is impossible, it could be exempt from those solicitudes which do not seem in any degree to be suitable to your constitution.  However, it will be not what I think or feel which must determine that question.  I am only sorry that whatever be the burthen, I can take no part of it, for you, on my own shoulders. You have given me one occupation,[1] and for that I am much obliged, because, while no adverse accident happens, it will be one of the pleasures of my life, and not an inconsiderable one neither, and will, I hope, be one of those indisputable marks of affection with which I am, ever have been, and shall remain your[s].  My best and most cordial respects to Lady C[arlisle] and my love to the children, and my compliments besides to whom you please.

[1781, *Nov. ?*] 27 [26 ?], *Monday night.*—Storer came to town this morning, as he proposes to tell you to-night ; he dined with me.  I met him first in the street, as I was returning from Lincoln's Inn.  He had been, as he was engaged to do, to Lord Loughborough, to whom he had made a promise of going on his arrival.  Neither the air or the *bonne chère* of the Castle have [has] done him any harm ; *il a bonne mine.*  He has left me to go to Brooks's, and perhaps to the Cockpit [2] ; but as that is a compliment to the Minister rather than as a support of Government, he shewed no great *empressement;* nor could I inspire him with a zeal which I have not myself.  I am not a solicitor of any future benefit from those who are in

[1] Probably to look after Lord Morpeth during his father's absence in Ireland.

[2] The Treasury was on the site of the Whitehall Cockpit, which had been placed there by Henry VIII.  It was converted into offices for the Privy Council in 1697.  The Ministerial meetings being held there, the word, in political slang, was used for a meeting either of Ministerialists or the Opposition.

power, and when I require no more than common civility, they must not be surprised, if I [do] not pay what I do not receive.

We have had a blow, for the cause is a common [one]. This surrender of Lord Cornwallis [1] seems to have put *le comble à nos disgraces.* What has been said about it, either at White's or *parmi les Grenouilles* at Brooks's, I know not.[2] I have not been out but for an hour before dinner to Mr. Woodcock. I received the first news of this yesterday from Williams, who dined with me, but you may be sure it was a subject he did not like to dwell upon, and I chose to talk with him rather of old than of modern times, because of them we may be agreed ; of the present, whatever we think, we should talk and differ in discourse widely.

This evening I have had your letter of the 20th. I am diverted with your account of my two Irish friends. They are so completely of that cast, that I cannot but imagine that they meant to be of your side. Richards was sent away quickly for that purpose by my Lord Chamberlain, as my Lord told me. The other I have but a slight acquaintance with. I only guessed, as he desired a letter of introduction to you, that he meant to profess, by that, attachment. I had no doubt that in neither the one [n]or the other it was disinterested, but I own that I was so far their dupe that I imagined that they would not begin with opposition. Kingsman['s] proposal of being your private Secretary, without a previous acquaintance, seems to be an idea quite new ; what crotchet the Beau Richard has got in his head the Lord knows.

Storer has drawn to me a very pleasing picture of your present situation, satisfaction, and domestic felicity. All that gives me pleasure enough, as you may imagine ; but when he talks to me of the length of time that you may stay, and the probability of it, I am *au desespoir.* I see

---

[1] The news of the surrender of Cornwallis at Yorktown on October 17, 1781, was received in London on November 25th.
[2] See letter from Storer, November 26th, *post.* p. 165,

myself deprived of my best resource for the passing of my life agreeably, when the greatest part of it is already gone. If I dwelt on this long I should be *désolé*. I will there [fore] endeavour to think only of what is a consolation to me, that you are all well—*en bonne odeur*—that it is the beginning perhaps of a very career—that I may see some part of it—that I have little George here from time to time, and the pleasure of looking after him, and as I hope to your and to Lady Carlisle's satisfaction. You think, I am afraid, that I nurse him too much. . . .

Storer as usual supplemented his friend's letter by the following note :—

*Anthony Storer to Lord Carlisle.*

[1781, *Nov.* 26, *Monday.*—I arrived in town this morning, time enough to do all in my power to send to Gregg, to try if I can get a qualification to take my seat to-morrow. My qualifications have been always embarrassing to me. I have too attended the Cockpit to-night, where there were a great many long faces. What we are to do after Lord Cornwallis' catastrophe, God knows, or how anybody can think there is the least glimmering of hope for this nation surpasses my comprehension. What a stroke it is ! but it still seems determined to pursue the game, though we throw nothing but crabs. . . .

Selwyn meant to treat you to-morrow with a Georgic. Everybody that I meet seem[s] to think that you did right in dispatching Mr. Flood. I am so loaded with questions about Ireland, that I have no time as yet to make any myself about England. Indeed, the attention of everyone is confined to our situation in America. The Speech from the Throne contains the same resolution which appeared in times when we seemed to have a more favourable prospect of success, of continuing the war, and of claiming the aid of Parliament to support the rights of Great Britain. Charles has a Cockpit to-night, as well as Lord North. The blue and buff Junto meet in St. James' Street to fix upon their plan of operations for to-morrow.

With regard to private news, I find Lady Worsley is run away from Sir Richard, and taken refuge with some gentleman whose name I do not know in the army. I must go and pay my respects to my father.]

Parliament opened under the shadow of the disasters in America on November 27th. The Speech from the Throne showed no appreciation of the gravity of the national situation, and the policy of the Government was at once challenged by Fox, who moved an amendment to the

Address.  It was negatived, however, by 218 to 129 votes.
The House of Commons though it supported the Minister
was conscious of the folly of his policy, and on the
following day the Opposition again challenged the
Government on the Report of the Address.  The result
was again a defeat—more nominal than real—of the
Opposition by 131 votes to 54.  Two days later
(November 30th) on the motion that the House should
go into Committee of Supply, Mr. Thomas Pitt (afterwards Lord Camelford) the uncle of William Pitt, who
from character and position carried great weight, rose to
object to the Speaker leaving the chair.  In other words,
he moved a vote of want of confidence in the Government.
The House again supported Lord North by their votes,
though the impossibility of continuing the ministerial
policy was obvious to all.  " If measures and conduct are
not to be changed we are completely undone," wrote
Selwyn in the beginning of December—but he had no
idea of supporting his opinion by his vote : there were
many others who thought and acted as he did.

[1781, *Nov.*] 28, *Wednesday.*—It is you see with me,
that I address you, *veniente die comme decedente.*  I sent
you some account of the H[ouse] of Commons last night
before the division ; we were about 89 majority.  I got
home between two and three.  I can no more go to
Brooks's to hear a *réchauffé* of these things, or assist at
the incense offered to Charles, or his benediction and *salut*
to those he protects.  The reserve at White's tempts me
as little, and so I think my own pillow the best resource
after these long days.

Young Mr. York brought me home, who commended
your Speech, and the manner in which you spoke it.  He
was present.

The terms of the Capitulation are now come, and
everything known which has happened, and in a few
days more everybody will be as indifferent as ever, except
in their political language, about [what] will happen.

I spoke to Keene about Richard's conduct ; he laughed,

and well he might ; he said, Poor Beau ! he does not
mean to oppose ; it was only in that instance where the
Sugar Islands were concerned, that he dissented, and there
he was by his property personally interested ; well then,
for this time *passe*, as private motives must and will ever
supersede public considerations ; so on that ground,
*et pour le coup*, he is excusable.   But when Lord Hertford
would not admit of his staying one day at Rayley with
his son, to shoot, lest he should not be in time to give
you the fullest assistance and concurrence possible in all
your measures ; this deviation could not but make me
smile, as well as his friend Mr. Keene.

As to the other, he is a puppy *du premier chef.*   I
could not refuse to his solicitation a letter of introduction,
he himself being a Member, and having a brother-in-law
also in the House.   But I could not doubt neither from
his discourse but he meant to support you ; and although
I must have known that it was an interested motive which
actuated him, that matter I left for your consideration.
His father I knew well, God knows, and every step which
I take in this House reminds me of him, *malheureusement
pour moi*, and why I do not choose to say or to think of,
now that he is dead, and is better judged than by me.
However, none of my resentment to him descended to his
son, and when he made himself known to me I was as
willing to receive him as if his father had behaved better
towards me.

Gregg and Storer will dine here to-day.   Storer says
that he wrote to you last night.   What should or could I
add to the account which the papers now give of the
debates ?   Charles is for my part the only one I can bear
to hear, but although it be impossible for him to do anything but go over and over again the old ground, make
the same philippics, it is entertaining to me, and I can
hear him (which is a singular thing) with the same
pleasure and attention as if I gave ample credit to what he
said, with such talents, and with such good humour, as is
at the bottom of all that pretended acrimony.   It is as
impossible not to love him, as it is to love his adversary.

The unfeelingness which he applied yesterday to our Master, characterises much more the Minister.  Charles aims sometimes at humour ; he has not an atom of it, or rather it is wit, which is better, but that is not his talent neither, and they are indeed but despicable ones in my mind, *et de tous les dons de la nature celui qui est le plus dangereux et le moins utile ;* but Charles's poignancy and misapplication of truth, making the most known falsehoods serve his person [purpose ?] better, in all that he is admirable.  His quotations are natural and pleasing and *à propos*, and if he had any judgment or conduct, or character, [he] would, and ought to be, the first man of this country.  But that place, I am assured now, is destined for another.  I said in *this* country, not in Ireland.  Whenever that happens, I do assure you neither Barbados nor any of the Sugar Colonies shall interfere in my political conduct ; but Barbados [is ?] *à d'autres*, and in a very short time I believe.  Now my next sheet shall be for the evening.

No, I must go on, for here is just come into my room a man in black ; I did not ask him his name.  I suppose by his mourning he belongs to Mr. Fraser.  He has brought me your letter to George, which I longed for. . . .

*Wednesday night.*—I did not go to-day [to] the House, but there has been there a *réchauffé* of yesterday's debate.  I hear there has been a political event.  My Lord Advocate's speech has given great jealousy to Administration.  There are now three parties on the Court side of the House, the King's, Lord North's, and [the] Lord Advocate's, on which is Rigby and the Chancellor.

The Fish did not vote last night, which he was much impatient to discover to Charles, with one of his fulsome compliments.  Mr. Pitt's speech to-day has made a great noise.

[1781,] *Nov.* 30, *Friday* m[*orning*].—I have sent my coachman this morning to Neasdon, with your letter to George, and two or three ripe pears, which he desired, so

that before I seal up this letter, I shall be able to let you
know how he does.    I wrote to him to excuse my not
answering his letter, which came to me on Monday, but I
have made him amends by sending him yours.    I hear
that Lord and Lady Gower will be in town this evening,
so I suppose that they will go and make him a visit.    When
any of these are to be paid, I shall be a candidate for a
place in the coach.

The reason why I did not send your letter before was
that I have had no leisure to think of anything but what
I would have avoided thinking of, if I possibly could, but
the truth is that I cannot divert myself of thinking
upon what must occupy everybody's mind, which is, our
public calamity and disgrace.[1]    They are become too
serious and irretri[ev]able, in my opinion.    I have had
superadded to these my own private mortifications, and I will
be so frank as to own I feel them too amids[t] what is of
more consequence.

I have also had a great deal of conversation with Storer,
have heard his grievances, and I think that he has had
very just cause to complain, and if I wish or desire him
to be pacified, it is not that I do not think he has had
great provocation.    But he has taken the only just and
true line of reasoning and acting for him, which is to do
whatever is the most consonant to your plan and idea,
acknowledging as he ought, avowing, and giving me
authority also to say, that he thinks himself obliged to
*you* and to *you* only for the situation he has.

To the obligation which you have laid him under, and
of which no one can be more sensible, Lord North might
have added one of his own, which was, to have done what
you required, and had a right to require, *de bon cœur*,
with a good grace.    Instead of that, he has permitted a
little attorney,[2] upon whose good judgment and liberality
he reposes for all the great conduct of his Administration,
to job away from Storer and Sir Adam Ferguson half a

[1]  See Storer's letter of December 1, *post*. p. 172
[2]  John Robinson, Secretary to the Treasury.

year's salary, in order to put one quarter more into the pocket of Lord Walsingham, who had the pride, acquired by his title, of disdaining to be in a new patent, and so pressing that the old might not expire till he had received £200 more salary.

Mr. Robinson intended to have come to me on Sunday to speak upon this subject, as if it concerned me, before I had seen Storer, or knew what he authorised me to say, forgetting all his own impertinent behaviour towards myself. It is the true picture of an indolent, selfish Minister, and of a low Secretary.

March dined at my house with Greg and Warner ; he had them all to dispute with, so I had few words to say. But without knowing one syllable of the story, and from mere contradiction, he supported the Secretary in his conduct, that is, he took that line as his advocate. He will in some instance or other receive the same treatment, sooner or later, from the same persons, and then what I would have said the other day will have its force.

I have told you this, that you may know how you stand in the H. of Commons, and that *there* no one can pretend to divide with you any obligation. I have dwelt the more upon it from knowing what language has been held by Lord N[orth's] toadeaters about Storer. You will always hear of his acting agreeable to you, and that is what he ought to do, and what will give to you the weight which is due to you.

I supped last night at Brooks's with Lord Ossory, and chiefly on his account. There was a large company besides : the D[ukes] of Q[ueensberry] and of Devonshire,[1] Percy Windham, Charles Fox, Hare, Lord Derby, Mr. Gardiner, Richard, Belgiosioso, &c., &c. I stayed very late with Charles and Ossory, and I liked my evening very much. A great deal of the political system from Charles, which he expatiated upon in such a manner as gave me

---

[1] William, fifth Duke of Devonshire (1748–1811), married, in 1774, Georgina, daughter of John, Earl Spencer, the well-known beautiful Duchess of Devonshire ; their daughter, Georgina Dorothy, married George, successor to the fifth Earl of Carlisle.

great entertainment, although, in all things which regard the K[ing] and his Government, I differed from him *toto cælo*. Lord D[erby's ?] nonsense was the only drawback upon the rest. He is the most *méchant singe* I ever knew.

Hare opened the Pharo Bank in the great room, but had so few and such poor punters that Charles and Richard was [were] obliged to sit down from time to time as decoy ducks. The Bank won, as Hare said, about a hundred, out of which the cards were to be paid. I do not think that the people who frequent Brooks's will suffer this pillage another campaign. Trusty was there to go into the chair, when he should be called upon. I told him that I was extremely sorry that he had quitted the *Corps de Noblesse pour se jetter dans le Commerce*, but it is at present his only resource. I cannot help thinking that, notwithstanding our late disasters, Bob's[1] political tenants will be very tardy in remitting him their rents. But between Foley House, and the run of Mr. Boverie's kitchen, with his own credit at Brooks's, and his share in and affinity to an opulent Bank, and flourishing trade, he may find a subsistence.

The D[uche]ss of Marlborough,[2] I hear, is already laying a scheme for marrying Lord Blandford to a great fortune, so by that any hopes which I might have had of my dear little Caroline being Duchess of Marlborough are blasted. I am told, that Miss Child's alliance is in her Grace's contemplation. I saw Ekins yesterday; he mends very slowly. Lady Althrop is breeding, Lord Harrington has another son. Lord Sandwich looks near to death with fatigue and mortification.

Burke (?) said in the House the other day that he had so little credit that his evidence was not good even against himself. All this may be, but he is the last of all his Majesty's Ministers which I shall give up. He has experience, assiduity, e[t] *du zèle*. Whether he has blundered or not I cannot tell, or been obliged to adopt

[1] Lord Robert Spencer ?
[2] Caroline, only daughter of John, fourth Duke of Bedford.

the blunders of others.  He has judged right in one thing, if he ever had it in his head to make a friend of me.  For he has been always extremely civil, and indeed that is not only a *sine quâ non* with me, but all that I have to ask of any of his Majesty's Ministers, and that I am intituled to at least.

Now do I wish that my coachman was come back, that I may hear how my dear little friend is, and at night I will let you know.

*Anthony Storer to Lord Carlisle.*

[1781, *Dec.* 1.—I received your short note with an enclosed letter for Boothby, which I sent into the country to him.  You laugh at me when you talk about the tears at the Drawing Room.  I confess *to you* that I left Ireland with a great deal of regret.  If you had not packed me off to Parliament, I suppose that by Christmas I should almost have thought myself happy to have established myself in Dublin.  There is a great misfortune in your being Lord Lieutenant, not only to yourself, but to your friends—for *en fait des femmes*, you can neither do anything for yourself, nor can you for me ; so that [I] having no confidant but yourself, all my tender messages are perfectly put a stop to.  I hope Trentham has made greater advances amongst them since I left Ireland than he did whilst I was there.  He takes time to consider and moves but slowly on to the siege.

During the few days I have been in town, I have had as much of Parliament, Levee, and Drawing Room as if I had been in Dublin.  I have been nothing but proper things.  Lord Loug[h]borough, whom I called upon, has got the gout ; but that is what I need not tell you, for he said that he should write.  We had no Irish conversation, for the Duke of Queensberry was with me, and we made but a short visit.  I understand from Delmé, who came up the first day of the meeting of Parliament, that Lady Betty is coming up to town next week to lay in.

Town is very full, and the Opera is really infinitely better in every respect than ever I yet saw it or ever expected it to be.  Perhaps coming from what is very bad in Dublin makes me find what was only moderate before exceedingly good now.  The roof of the theatre has been raised, and the loftiness at present of the house makes it look really well.

For the same reason it is perhaps that I was so much struck the first day of Parliament.  Charles Fox, who did not speak as well as he usually does according to the opinion of many, yet in mine was astonishingly great.  I never attended to any speech half so much, nor ever did I discover such classical passages in any modern performance.  Besides [th]at, I owned, he convinced me.

I wished not to talk to you of political events, but nothing else is thought of.  The events that are passed are not half so melancholy as the prospect which is looked to. The Supply was opposed by Tho[mas] Pitt, for the first time since the Revolution, yesterday. I did not hear Mr. W. Pitt, which I regret very much, as it is said that he even has surpassed Charles, and greater expectations are formed from him even than from the other.

There surely must be some change or alteration in Administration. Lord George Germain seemed to lay a very heavy charge the first day of the Sessions against Lord Sandwich, but what will come of it, it is difficult to say. Speculation upon political events, however justified by seeing what ought to be, is not always to be depended upon. You can judge better than I can, because you have probably sure information, and I can only form conclusions by what everyone sees and knows. From what Lord Germain said, C[harles] Fox told him that when he impeached Lord Sandwich, he should consider him as a principal witness.

The most melancholy events are predicted with regard to the W[est] Indies. Indeed it is true that everything is now at the mercy of the Enemy, and it is their fault if any possessions whatever, either in N[orth] America or in the W[est] Indies, remain under the British Empire. Our affairs in Ireland go on pretty well, and that is the only place where they do. [The] Lord Advocate made a downright, open speech, but Lord Geo[rge] did not understand it ; though parts of it, by what the Advocate has said in *private*, were most probably levelled at *him*.]

[1781], *Dec. 4, Tuesday morning.*—I found, when I came home last night, this letter from your son, which I enclose. Dr. Ekins shewed me a letter from him yesterday, which was with less mistakes in the writing, and was verily (*sic*) prettily expressed, but it was shorter. I find my idea of the Provostship will never do. There are other arrangements for him, and the Provostship, as I hear, will be given to Dampier, Mr. North's tutor.

Burke's Motion is withdrawn. The Opposition thought this was exactly the proper moment to increase and inflame the quarrel between us and the Americans. Unluckily for them, Government is in possession of a letter from Mr. Laurens,[1] in which he expresses himself perfectly satisfied with the treatment of him, in all respects ; so this was communicated to Burke. I heard of no other business yesterday, or of any news, but Lord Cornwallis, it is said, goes to Paris. I do not envy him the civilities which he will receive there.

[1] See note p. 200.

Monsieur de Maurepas[1] heard of our defeat just before he died, and expired with a line of Mitridate in his mouth, which sounded as well I suppose as a *Nunc-dimittis*, and was as sincere :

*Mes derniers regards ont vu fuir les Romains.*

An old coxcomb ! I wish that I could live to see our hands *trempés dans le sang odieux de cette nation infernale*, rather than our *petits maîtres* here, *in Caca du Dauphin, Bouë de Paris, Bile repanduë du Comte d'Artois, ou vomis* (sic) *de la Reine. Ce sont les couleurs les plus à la mode, et pour le Carnaval qui vient.*

Lord Loughborough has the gout, and is confined to his bed. To-day I have all the Townshends and Brodericks to dine here, and Mie Mie goes after dinner to the Opera with Lady Payne, so I must be dressed to be her beau, which, if it was not for the pleasure of being assistant to her, would be *souffrir le martyre.*

We shall adjourn next week, I believe, till after the Queen's birthday. There was a talk yesterday of changes in the Admiralty, but without foundation. Lord Lisbourne, who dined with us yesterday at Lord Ashburnham's, did not seem to think that there would be a change of any sort. I hope he means as to *men then* only ; for if measures and conduct are not to be changed we are completely undone, supposing anything of that *now* left to do.

The Duke of Newc[astle's] youngest son is at Lisbon for his health, and not likely to live. What is become, or will become, of his eldest God knows. His Grace's pride has settled everything upon Sir H[enry] Clinton, for the sake of the name, and Oatlands is to be sold and no vestiges left, of his infinite obligations either to Lord Torrington or to the Pelhams. He is £200,000 in debt, and will, if Lord Lincoln marries, of which nobody

---

[1] Jean Frédéric Phélippeaux, Comte de Maurepas (1701–1781), Minister of Marine under Louis XV., but banished through the influence of Mme. de Pompadour ; recalled by Louis XVI., he was made first minister, and though himself more courtier than statesman, succeeded in his policy of the recognition of the United States, and brought into the Ministry such men as Turgot, Malesherbes, and Necker.

doubts, have probably £6,000 a year to pay in jointures to Lady Harrington, and Lady Hertford's daughters, and when this and the usual charge upon the maintenance of great houses is defrayed, he will leave nothing to Sir Henry but the expense of his own monument. He is a complete wretch, and no one ever deserved more to be so.

Earlier in this year Walpole had written to Sir Horace Mann: " Mr. Fox is the first figure in all the places I have mentioned, the hero in Parliament, at the gaming table, at Newmarket." The sentence with which Selwyn, half angry and half amused, concludes the last letter of 1781, emphasises the extraordinary and commanding position which Fox held at this critical moment in the House of Commons.

[1781,] *Christmas Day, Tuesday m.*—. . . . I dined yesterday at Lady Lucan's. The dinner was at first designed for George and Mie Mie, but upon my explaining myself to Lady Lucan concerning that [his objection to their dining out late], this dinner took another turn, and was at their usual hour ; so instead of them, I met Lady Clermont, Sir R. and Lady Payne, Mr. Walpole, and Mr. Gibbon.[1] There were a few at Brooks's, and Hare in the chair to keep up the appearance of a pharo bank, but nobody to punt but the Duke of Rutland and Fish Craufurd. Charles, or Richard, if he is there, never fail[s] ; and at their own bank they will lose a thousand in one deal, and win them back in the other ; but Richard, as I was told, lost *tout de bon* 7,000, the other night, to this bank, in which Hare and Lord Robert have a twelfth. The whole manœuvre, added to their patriotism, their politics, &c., &c., are incredible.

I am going to dine to-day at Delmé's ; he has promised me some plum porridge. His son is to dine here with George. Lady B[etty] brings him at half-hour after two. On Friday I dine at Keene's, and in the

---

[1] The historian (1737–1794).

evening George and Mie Mie come, and George may renew his addresses to the young lady. Lady Lucan desires that we should choose King and Queen at her house. I have myself no objection to anything but the dinner abroad.

*Tuesday night.*—No letter come. At Delmé's the D[uke] of Q[ueensberry], Storer, Hanger, and G. Fitz-williams, Lady Ann, and the family. . . . Hare holding the Bank. The punters are, Charles, *par intérêt*, Fish Craufurd, *par complaisance*, and the D. of R., *par bêtise*. Storer's patent is at last passed,[1] as Gibbon tells me. I hear no more ; it is likely, for this next week, to be a great dearth of news. For be the West India Islands taken, or secured, it will be no matter I suppose of concern till Charles has made a speech about them.

How close were the ties of friendship which united Selwyn with Storer and Hare has been told at the beginning of this volume : the following letter will add to the picture of the group of friends and of the diversions of London society at this moment.

*James Hare to Lord Carlisle.*

[1781, *Dec.* 29.—I stayed at Foxley till the middle of October, and then came to Town, where, for want of other amusement I chose to take the diversion of Hazard at the House in Pall Mall, and lost near £4,000 in three nights to a set of fellows whom I never saw before, and have never seen since. Though it has generally happened to me to begin the winter without a guinea, I did not make up my mind to it this year so easily as I have done formerly, because I knew that I deserved to be poor for having been fool enough to lose my money at Hazard instead of saving it for Pharaoh.

Richard played at the same place, and lost 8,000 gs., which he paid immediately, though he had declared to me a few days before that he had not a quarter of that sum in the world ; but you know how to estimate his veracity on these subjects as well as anybody.

Charles, in the October meetings, lost about £10,000, the greatest part of it on Races, and the rest to General Smith at picquet. The general opinion was, that Charles was extremely partial to horses of his own confederacy ; this he denies, and of course is angry to hear suspected, but you and I shall not be very backward to believe it to have been the case.

---

[1] See p. 74 note.

Most of the joint annuitants agreed to a proposal made to them by Richard and Charles, viz., to receive £6,000 immediately, and the remainder by instalments in three years. One of them refused to accept this proposal, and seized soon after the meeting four of Charles's horses, which were of trifling value, and therefore bought in again at a small expense by Derby, in whose name they now stand ; whether some time or other his protection may not be insufficient, I shall not pretend to say, but it is not quite out of the reach of possibility.

Thus, you see, the Bankers did not meet at the beginning of the winter in the same opulent circumstances as they had parted in at the end of the last campaign. Lord Robert and I proposed to have our share increased from a twelfth to an eighth. Charles consented, but Richard refused, and we remain on our former footeign (*sic*). The Bank has already won considerably, and would probably have done still better if money was not very scarce, as most of the punters retain their passion without the means of gratifying it.

You will be surprised · when I tell you that Richard is our most valuable punter, and has lost this year full as much as his share of the winnings of the Bank ; and as he would not agree to my having a larger share, I have no great remorse in taking his money. Last night he lost £13,000, and Charles above £5,000 ; all the other players won something, but not a sum at all equal to our partner's losses. Pray do not mention this, unless you hear it from some other person, as probably you will.

The club at Brookes's is very ill attended, and Brookes enraged to the last degree that gentlemen should presume to think of anything but making his fortune. He complained to Charles that there was £17,000 owing to the house, which is a most impudent lie ; and even if it were true he would have no reason to complain of the balance, as he has £15,000 belonging to the proprietors of the Bank in his hands, for which he pays no interest, though he receives at least 5 per cent. for all money owing to him.

There are two Clubs lately formed, both consisting of young men, and chiefly of different parties in politics. Goostree's [1] is a small society of young men in Opposition, and they are very nice in their admissions ; as they discourage gaming as much as possible, their Club will not do any harm to Brookes's, and probably not subsist a great while ; it seems to be formed on the model of the celebrated Tuesday Night Club. The other is at Welche's,[2] in St. James's Street, consisting of young men who belong to Government ; and poor John St. John, whose age and zeal for Government particularly qualify him to be a member, has hitherto met with objections on the ballot, which I hope will be withdrawn on another trial of his interest, and that the Town will have the advantage of his management at the next Masquerade, which that Club is to give after Xmas.

·  ·  ·  ·

[1] See p. 191.          [2] See p. 190.

13

Boothby has just told me that James finds himself in such bad circumstances that he is obliged to sell all his horses, and give up hunting entirely ; but as James is in Town, and has not said one word to me about it, I am in hopes that it is not exactly so : the Prince is rather a dark painter, and fond of placing the principal figure in the shade. The Prince himself, I am afraid, is rather distressed, as he never games, and it is observed invidiously enough by people who do not love him, that he must be poor, as he has grown so much more agreeable than he used to be.

Crawford was giving himself great airs the other day on having taken Longchamp, the man who keeps the rooms at Newmarket, into his service as cook, but on enquiry it appeared that he had taken one of his brothers : the Fish was unspeakably mortified to find that his cook was not a man of so great celebrity as he had imagined, and gave his first dinner yesterday with a determination to condemn the cook's performance, whether good or bad. I am very ill qualified to tell you the scandalous history of fine ladies, not having been at one assembly this winter. . . .

Lord Salisbury sacrifices his whole time and fortune to Hertford-shire popularity, and six years hence may perhaps reap the reward of his labours by bringing in a Member for the county, after an expensive contest. . . .

Lord Morpeth looks remarkably well : I hope George's fondness will not spoil him, for he is the prettiest boy I ever saw.]

# CHAPTER V

## 1782

### THE FALL OF LORD NORTH

Fox's political principles—The fifth Duke of Bedford—A little dinner —A debate in the Commons—The attack on Lord George Germaine—Beckford—An evening at Brooks's—Pitt and his friends— Possible changes in the Cabinet—Faro at White's—A story of the Duke of Richmond—An address to the King—A levée—Play and politics at Brooks's—Government and the Opposition— Selwyn and his offices—The position of the King—Fears of change of administration — The King's objections to Fox— Probable debates—Political prospects—Debates and divisions— The fate of the King's friends—Illness of Lord Morpeth—Annoyance of Selwyn at the state of affairs—Fox and Selwyn—Fall of Lord North — A new Ministry — Official changes — Fox and Carlisle—Carlisle's position—Morpeth and Mie Mie.

THE year 1782 is memorable for the fall of Lord North. It was more than the end of a Ministry, to a great extent it was the end of the system of personal government by the sovereign. "The King," wrote Selwyn, "on March 27th, will have no more personal friends, as Lord Hertford says ; there will be no opposition to that in this new Government, what a cipher his Majesty will be you may guess." Selwyn had no great respect for the King, and not much liking for his minister, Lord North. "I see him in no light, but that of a Minister, and in that I see him full of defects, and of all men I ever yet sate down to dinner with the most disagreeable. But he is so, in part from a scholastic, puritanical education, to which has been superadded the flattery of University parsons, led captains, and Treasury dependants. Without this, he would· have been a pleasant companion. He has parts, information, and a good share of real wit, and [is], I believe, not an ill-tempered man by any means. But with all this, he has *un commerce qui me rebute*. As to what he says, or promises, it is *sur la foi de Ministre* and *credat Judæus*, but I never will." (May 15, 1781.)

But like many others Selwyn had grown accustomed to the existing method of carrying on the government and obtaining majorities in the House of Commons. He had seen much of political corruption and official influence, and having no high political standard he had come to regard the system of George III. and North as normal and constitutional. He had, too, a fear of a ministry in which Fox and his friends should take a leading part. In Selwyn's mind Fox was connected with the wildest gambling and with a carelessness in regard to monetary obligations which he considered to be almost criminal. There were many others who shared this opinion : it was one thing for a gambler to hurry from the card-table in St. James's Street to the floor of the House of Commons and delight alike Ministerialists and Opposition by a brilliant attack on the Government : it was quite another for him to be responsible for the affairs of the nation. George III. and Lord North were men of business. Fox was a man of pleasure, and those who were most intimate with him at the clubs were the last— very often—to desire to see him a Minister. " From a Pharo table to the headship of the Exchequer is a transition which appears to me *de tenir trop au Roman*, and those who will oppose it the most are those whom he has been voting with and assisting to ruin this country for the last ten years at least." Selwyn underrated the need for Fox's great abilities in office ; so powerful a debater could not be used by a party in opposition only. But he certainly expressed a feeling which existed in the minds of many.

Selwyn's letters which were written at this crisis give a lively description of the dismay which the change of Ministry produced among those who had begun to consider Lord North's Government as a part of the established order of things. The Court party had hardly taken the Opposition seriously ; there were many who had grown to suppose that nothing could overturn the individual authority of the King, and they were puzzled and surprised at the impending changes.

In the first of the following letters there is an account of a curious academic discussion at Brooks's on the theory of government, in which Fox took part. Those who listened to him hardly realised that presently he would be the most important member of a new government. It would not be easy to find a clearer picture of Fox at that extraordinary time than is given to us in these letters ; the apprehension and the affection felt by his friends, the contrast between his social bonhomie and his political fervour is conspicuously presented. We understand his greatness better when we see him moving among his contemporaries, good-natured, indifferent to what was said or thought of him, telling his opinions without hesitation—a giant among political and intellectual dwarfs.

Again in the midst of the gambling, the supper parties, and the gaieties of the town, there is the continual sombre shadow of an important constitutional change—a system and a Cabinet were falling under the deep resentment of the country. Neither the King, the Ministry, or its supporters appeared to appreciate that, even in an age when public opinion was chaotic and often hardly audible, there must come a time when a day of reckoning was certain for a Government which had discredited and injured its country.

We see the apprehensions, the personal expectations, the littlenesses of political society. Then comes the final crash when, after twelve years of opposition, the Whigs take office, watched half with fear and half with contempt by those who had been unable to understand the forces which had produced this inevitable result.

[1782,] *Jan.* 8, *Tuesday.*—I did not go to bed this morning till seven, and got neither drunk, or gamed. The Duke of Rutland,[1] Charles Fox, Belgiosio [Belgiojoso], Gen. Smith, and I supped at Brooks's, but it was pure conversation between Charles, the Duke, and I which lasted so long.  Our chief and almost only topic was that of Government, abstractedly considered, and speculations about what would be the best for this country ; Charles's account of his own principles in that respect ; his persuasion about mine ; his Grace's lessons from Lord Chatham, and commonplace panegyric upon that unparalleled statesman, and the utility to the public derived from paying his debts and maintaining his posterity.  The principal is, that hereafter people in employment will be indifferent about the emoluments of office, persuaded that a grateful country like this will not suffer the wife and children of great characters to go unprovided for, or their tradesmen unpaid, and a great deal of this sublime nonsense.

Charles was infinitely agreeable, or I could not have stayed so long.  A quarrel, he says, had like to have happened at Quinze between the General and the Fish. The General told the Ambassador[2] how rich he was, and how well the English (meaning, he said, people of distinction, such as his son) were received both at Brunswick and at Vienna ; lied immoderately about the affairs of the India Company ; and was ten times more at his ease than ever, to shew Belgiosio that he had the *ton de cour.* Charles shewed me two of Brooks's cards ; on one he was Dr. £4,400, on another Cr. £11,000.  This was the Rich Bank he belongs to.

[1782,] *Feb.* 4, *Monday morning.*—You will not expect me to give you so soon any more account of George than I shall have from Sir John Eden, who intends to go either

[1] Charles, fourth Duke of Rutland, K.G. (1754–1787).  He was Pitt's first Lord-Lieutenant of Ireland, and died in office at the opening of a promising political career.
[2] Belgiojoso.

to-day or to-morrow to Neasdon, and who will bring me word how he does.

I was at Lord Gower's last night ; and I saw there the Duke of B[edfor]d,[1] who, I must own, surprised me by his figure, beyond measure ; his long, lank, black hair, covering his face, shoulders, back, neck, and everything, disguised him so that I have yet to know his figure ; I can but guess at his person. Why this singularity at 17 years of age ? *cela n'indique pas un esprit solide.*

They saw the astonishment which this exhibition created in me, and Lord Gower laughed, and said, "You perhaps do not know who it is ? " Indeed I did not. *Je devine seulement que sa figure n'est pas laide.* His *chevelure* was like that which I see in a picture of the grand Condé. If there is anything of that hid under this disguise *je lui passerai cette singularité*, and yet, if your sons or either of them should have all which Monsieur le Prince possessed, and Colbert too, I had rather that they would not be singular. It may divert, but can never add to the respect which they might otherwise have.

I went with Lord Trentham to the Speaker's, and returned to Lord G[ower], but had no conversation either with him or the Countess. When they go to Neasdon, I hope that they will carry me with them. When George meets me, he accosts me with these words, " *Quomodo vale* (sic) my *petite sodale ;* " *où il a pêché cette plaisanterie* I do not know. His namesake, Lord G. Germain,[2] is to kiss hands this morning for the title and peerage of Sackville. Drayton, it seems, goes to the Beauclerks, if he becomes Duke of Dorset and has that estate.

My dinner yesterday with Fawkener and Warner at Mr. Crespigni's was a very agreeable one indeed ; *la chère plutôt bonne qu'exquise ; excellent vin.* You will not

---

[1] Francis Russell, fifth Duke of Bedford (1765–1802) ; succeeded his grandfather in 1771. He was badly educated, indifferent to public opinion, liberal and independent in political views, a consistent follower of Fox. In later life he showed great interest in the advancement of agriculture, by practice and experiment.

[2] See note *post* p. 186.

forget Warner, I hope, when the opportunity offers, *afin qu'il soit dans le cas d'en tirer de sa propre cave.* We generally close the evening around the fire in the card room at White's, *à forte peu de fraix;* Williams, Lord Ashburnham, Vary, Fawkener, &c. ; that is, those who either sup, game, or sit up. The season of all that is over with me, and I have little inclination left for either of them. I am quite well, *vu mon âge,* and as likely to see you again as any other who is a *sexagénaire, et même davantage.* It is the chief part of my *Litanie.*

I talked of Caroline last night with Lady Ann, till I could ask no more questions about her. I am glad that her dancing is admired. We have here Mademoiselle Théodore, who takes Mr. Willis' (?) place till the season is over. She has half a guinea a lesson, but it is to stay an hour. There is a good account of Johnson's prices, but he himself is gone to Lisbon to be married ; whether that will be a prize, is *à sçavoir.* That of the Duke of Newcastle's [1] (*sic*) is already condemned, at least by his Grace, but *hæ nuptiæ sunt veræ* nevertheless. Lord Cornwallis is, I believe, going to inhabit my house till midsummer. That has been a heavy charge upon my hands, instead of a profit.

We have now nearly reached the climax of the political interest and excitement which had been growing greater since the memorable session of 1781 began. To appreciate the letters which follow, it is necessary to bear in mind some of the main parliamentary incidents of this particular period. On February 7, 1782, the House of Commons resolved itself into a Committee to inquire into the present state of naval affairs. Fox in an elaborate speech reviewed their course for the preceding five years, and concluded by moving " that there has been gross mismanagement of the naval affairs of Great Britain during the course of the year 1781." The supporters of the Government were as little satisfied with the

[1] Thomas, third Duke of Newcastle (1752–1795). He married in this year, the second daughter of the Earl of Harrington.

administration of the navy as the Opposition, and the debate, which was concluded by another remarkable speech from Fox, resulted in a virtual defeat of the Administration. The Opposition were in a minority only of 18 votes. On February 22nd a different ground was chosen by the Opposition for their attack, General Conway moving an address that the war in America should no longer be pursued. The noticeable change in the feeling in the House of Commons, crammed as it was by place-men, is clearly exemplified by the result of the division. On this occasion the Government were only able to defeat the Opposition by one vote, 194 to 193. On February 27th a similar address was again moved by Conway and an attempt by the Government to adjourn the debate was defeated by 234 to 215 votes. The address was then carried without a division. Selwyn looking at events from what was, politically speaking, a somewhat non-party point of view, is obviously puzzled as to how the crisis would end. He tells us, too, of the formation of a group of young politicians under Pitt. He ascribes to the future Prime Minister the organisation of a party, though hitherto these meetings at Goosetree's have been regarded chiefly as social gatherings.

[1782,] *Feb.* 8, *Friday, the Fast Day.*—We were not up last night till near three this morning ; our numbers were 205 and 183. Our majority was but *mince,* but it was a popular Question, but Lord Sandwich is not a popular man ; but I have lived long enough to have remembered other ministers less popular, if possible, and who have been since reverenced, and by the most respectable among those who had traduced them. Charles made two speeches ; the last was much animated. Admiral Keppell spoke, and so did Sir E. Dering, drunk, *sicut suus mos est ;* but he says in that *ivresse des vérites vertes, et piquantes.* He is a tiresome noisy fool, and I wish that he never spoke anywhere but in the House of Commons.

*Saturday.*—I was prevented from continuing this letter yesterday, by a visit from Lord Digby, who assured me that to the best of his judgment you had nothing to fear from that quarter which has now and then alarmed me not a little. I dined at Lord Ash[burnham's] : Lord Frederick, Williams, Sir J. Peachy (?) and old (?) Elison. I do not perceive that Lord Carm[arthen] has got any repu[ta]tion from his violence against Lord George.[1] The attack surprised, [and] had not been concerted with anybody ; he had revealed his design but to one, as he said, and that I am told was Lord Pembroke, *une tête digne de cette confidence.*

It was a Motion cruel and illmannered, and not becoming one man of quality to another ; at the same time an unpardonable insult to the Crown. Lord de Ferrars, I hear, has found out a precedent for it, as he thinks, in King James 1st['s] time, but a precedent of what ? of ins[o]lence to the Crown ; it was in that reign begun, with impunity. If there could be any hesitation in this peerage, this motion must have confirmed it.

Lord Abingdon spoke like a perfect blackguard, and Lord Shellbourne, in a speech which Lord Cov[entry] calls such a model of perfect oratory, to exemplify the contempt which the late King had of Lord George, quoted not only his own words, but imitated his manner—two of his grand-children, the Princes, in the House. This part of his speech was a pantomime fitter for the *tréteaux*

---

[1] Lord George Sackville Germaine, on his resignation of the Secretaryship of the Colonies, was, in February, 1782, created a peer as Viscount Sackville of Drayton Manor, Northampton. Thereupon the Marquis of Carmarthen brought forward a motion in the House of Lords that it was derogatory to the honour of the House that any person under the censure of a court martial should be raised to the Peerage. The motion was defeated, but was repeated on February 18th after Lord Sackville had taken his seat. Though personal in its form, this was simply a Parliamentary attack on the Ministry and the Crown. Sackville had at the battle of Minden, in 1759, disobeyed the orders of Prince Ferdinand of Brunswick, the Commander-in-Chief, by refusing to advance with the cavalry. In the following year he was dismissed by court martial from the army. The use made of an event more than twenty years old illustrates the temper of the Opposition. The subject is referred to in a subsequent letter, see p. 188.

*des boulevards* than for a chamber of Parliament. However, Lord George will take his seat next week, and
what he will do, or be, afterwards, God knows. Ellis [1]
has his place.

Poor General Fraser died of an emetic, which occasioned
the bursting of a vessel. Lord Talbot has had another
warning, and so has Lord R. Bertie, and neither can
live long. I was last night at Lady Lucan's, to see
young Beckford, [2] who seems to possess very extraordinary talents ; he is a perfect master of music, but
has a voice, either natural or feigned, of an eunuch. He
speaks several languages with uncommon facility, and
well, but has such a mercurial turn, that I think he may
finish his days *aux petites maisons;* his person and figure
are agreeable. I did not come till late, and till he had
tired himself with all kind of mimicry and performances.
The Duchess of Bedford [was] there, and Lady Clermont.

There is a picture engraving at the man's house in St.
James's Street where your picture is to be engraved.
His design is ingenious ; it is the story of Pharaoh's
daughter finding Moses in the bullrushes. The Princess
Royal is introduced as Pharaoh's daughter, and all the
other ladies, celebrated for their beauty—the Duchess
of Devonshire, Lady Jersey, &c. &c. ; *on briguera les
places.* The portraits will be originals, and the whole,
if well executed, will be a very pretty print. I would
have a pendent to it ; and that should be of Pharo's sons,
where might be introduced a great many of our friends,
and acquaintance, from the other side of the Street. I

[1] Welbore Ellis, appointed Secretary of State for the Colonies
March 8, 1782.

[2] William Beckford (1759–1844), son of the well-known member of
Parliament and Lord Mayor. As a boy of nine, he came into possession of a property of a million. " Neither his genius nor his fortune
yielded what they would have produced to a wiser and better man.
. . . Hardly any other man has produced such masterpieces with
so little effort." He was the author of "Vathek," an Oriental romance,
and other works. He was an enthusiastic collector, and he made
Fonthill, where he lived in later life in eccentric seclusion, a complete
museum.

am so taken up with business this morning, that I did not endeavour to make a party with Lord Gower to go and see George. Gregg has wrote me word that he shall ride that way to-morrow.

[1782,] *Feb.* 19, *Tuesday morning.*—I wish that I could repeat and describe, as well as I can hear and attend to what is said to me, when people speak sense and to the purpose, and are not trying to mislead you. When I went to Brooks's it was in search of the Duke ; [1] there I found him at dinner, altercating Lord Sackville's cause, and Stirling, with Charles, Lord Derby, &c., &c. You may imagine with what candour and fairness his arguments were received. I am, it is certain, a friend to him, and not to Charles, but all partiality or prejudice laid aside, I think my friend as good a reasoner as the other ; but one employs his faculties in the search of truth, and the other in disguising it and substituting falsehood in its room, to serve the purpose of Party.

I soon left them and went to White's ; I like the society there better. There was a dinner also for the Lords, and there was Lord Loughborough, Lord Buckingham, Duke of Dorset, Lord Cov[entry], Lord Ash[burnham], &c., &c., &c. I stayed with Lord Loughborough, Lord Ash[burnham], and Lord Cov[entry] till past two this morning. The Duke changed his court and came to us, to plead in the common pleas, but with us there was no dispute. There was one who would have disputed if he could, which was Cov[entry], but Lord Loughborough has such a variety of incontestable facts concerning the affair of Minden, the opinions of foreign officers relative to P[rince] Ferd[inand's] whole conduct in respect of Lord George, the faction and partiality and injustice in the proceedings of the court martial, with so many arguments and precedents against the Question of yesterday, that poor Cov[entry] had not a word to say but that he had been soliciting privately—which I do not credit—the Lords in Opposition not to bring on this

---

[1] Of Queensberry.

Question, which at the same time he rejoiced at. Lord Ash[burnham] is among many others one whom Cov[entry] is practising constantly his astucity upon, and whom he thinks that he deceives. I was extremely entertained.

I have no liking and esteem for Lord Sack[ville], or ever had, any more than acquaintance with him, but from the first to the last I have believed that he has been sacrificed to the implacable resentment of P[rince] Ferd[inand], the late Duke of Cumb[erlan]d, and the late King, helped on by all the private malice and flattery in the world ; and all which I heard last night, of which I cannot have the least doubt, confirms me in that opinion. I am clear in nothing concerning his personal merit, or defects, excepting of his abilities, and when these could be of any use to Party, they were extolled, and his imperfections forgot. He was invited to take a share in Government by the people who think, or have pretended to think, him a disgrace to the peerage.

I am sorry for it, but Lord Carm[arthen [1]] has in all this made but a miserable figure. I am sorry, from wishing well towards him, that I had not been apprised of this. I could have assured him of what even the best of his own party would think of his Motion, after it was made. I know that Lord Cambden [2] was strongly in his private opinion against it. [The] Lord Chancellor [3] spoke out I hear ; his speech was admirable, *en tous points ;* and upon the whole, I believe Lord Sackville to have been infinitely more served than hurt by this proceeding.

I saw on Brooks's table a letter directed to you from Hare, so I hope that it was to give you an account of these things, partial or impartial. I have no doubt but his account will be an amusing one. I left him in his semicircular nitch at the Pharo table, improving his fortune every deal. I wish Monsieur Mercier would

[1] See note, p. 58.
[2] Charles Pratt, Earl Camden (1713-1794). Lord Chancellor in 1766 ; the friend of Pitt (Lord Chatham).
[3] Thurlow.

come here and write a Tableau de Londres as he has that of Paris, and that he would take for his work some anecdotes with which I could furnish him.

It is thought that we shall be run hard in the House to-morrow. And so we shall, but we shall not be beat, as Charles gives out, and does not believe. I suppose our majority will be about twenty. Absentees in the last Question on both sides will now appear. I hope that Government will send two Yeomen of the Guard to carry the Fish down in his blankets, for he pretends to have the gout. He should be deposited *sur son maniveau*, and be fairly asked his opinion, and forced to give it, one way or the other, *en pleine assemblée*, for at present it is only we who can tell *s'il est chair ou poisson*. . . .

[1782, *Feb.* 19 ?] *Tuesday night, 8 o'clock.*—I saw Lord R. Spencer and Lord Ossory to-day, who tell me that they suppose that we shall carry the Question by ten, if the Question is put ; but it is imagined rather by them that the Ministers will give it up. Ellis has added another footman to his chariot, and is a Minister in form, and fact, and pomp, and everything. Lady Ossory is just come to town. Lord Clarendon has wrote a copy of verses upon Lord Salisbury's Ball, which the Essex's are so kind as to hand about for him. The verses are not numerous. There are not above two stanzas, and not good enough to suppose that they had been composed even in his sleep ; so much nonsense and obscurity and want of measure and harmony I never saw in any composition before. But as they love to laugh at his Lordship in that family, so, as he had the absurdity to communicate them, they are determined that they shall not be suppressed. . . .

Weltie's Club [1] is going to give a masquerade like that given by the Tuesday Night's Club. I hear that all the different parties in Opposition are determined to draw

[1] Weltzie's Club was at No. 63, St. James's Street. Weltzie was House Steward to the Prince of Wales, by whom the Club was established, in opposition to Brooks's.

together in this Question, how much soever they may differ afterwards, in hopes, I suppose, by their united force, to destroy this Administration. Young Pitt has formed a society of young Ministers, who are to fight under his banner, and these are the Duke of Rutland, Mr. Banks, Lord Chatham, &c., &c., and they assemble at Goostree's.[1]

To-morrow no post goes, as I am told, and on Thursday Storer shall give you an account of what will have passed in the House ; he will do that better than I can.  He attends at his Board very exactly.  You have done a great thing for him, and no one seems more sensible of it.  Lord Cov[entry] would have persuaded me to-day that things were going very ill in Ireland, but till I hear it from you I shall not believe it.  All my accounts hitherto have had a different tendency.

I hear from one quarter that a change of some sort in Administration is determined upon, and that the Chancellor has the task of composing those jarring atoms to prevent the King's Cabinet from being stormed.  That Lord Sheilbourne will be taken in, *de quelque manière ou d'autre*.  Storming a Cabinet is a phrase coined in my time, to express what I cannot pretend to say that I do not understand, but how the fact is practicable, *invito rege*, will be for ever a mystery to me, and if it happens with his consent I am yet to learn how the Cabinet is storm[ed].  I will never believe but if a prince very early in his reign had a mind to set a mark upon those who distinguish themselves in Opposition with that view, he would never have the thin[g] attempted.  It may be necessary to change measures and men, but why it is necessary that particular men must be fixed upon you, whether you will [or] not, I do not conceive, nor will ever admit as [a] possibility, while the Laws and Constitution remain as they are ; so with this I wish you a good night.

[1] This club was at No. 5, Pall Mall, which was occupied by Almack's before it was taken over by Brooks' in 1778, and removed to St. James's Street.  Goosetree's was quite a small club, of about twenty-five members, of whom Pitt was the chief.

[1782, *Feb. ?*] 26, *Tuesday m[orning]*, 11 *o'clock.*—. . .
I went last night, after the children were in their beds, to
White's, and stayed there till 12. The Pharo party was
amusing. Five such beggars could not have met; four
lean crows feeding on a dead horse. Poor Parsons held
the bank. The punters were Lord Carm[arthen], Lord
Essex, and one of the Fauquiers; and Denbigh sat at
the table, with what hopes I know not, for he did not
punt. Essex's supply is from his son, which is more
than he deserves, but Malden, I suppose, gives him a
little of his milk, like the Roman lady to her father.

A very large company yesterday at Lord Rocking-
[ham's]. The whole Party pretends to be confident of
their carrying the Question to-morrow, if people are
properly managed and collected. I do not believe it, but
they do. The main point will not be more advanced in
my opinion.

[1782,] *March* 1, *Friday.*—George seems so well to-
day that there does not seem wanting the *coup de peigne.*
I have not heard a cough to-day. We have been walking. It is the finest day that ever was, and we are
going in the coach to meet one part of His Majesty's
faithful Commons, who go to Court at two o'clock with
their Address. People are either so close, cautious, or
ignorant, that among those I converse with I can be
informed of nothing which is to happen in consequence
of the last majority. It may be nothing at present, but
the Opposition is in great glee, to judge from their
countenance. I shall know before I sit down to dinner
not only the K[ing's] answer, but the manner of the
answer also.

Lord Ossory is this morning gone to the Levee, and
others of his sort, I suppose, with a design to countenance
and spread the credit of their coming in. Fish, as I hear,
doubles and trebles all his flattery to Charles, and now
and then throws in a compliment to Lord N[orth], not
being quite sure of what may happen, and then adds, " In
that respect I will do him justice; I do not think better

even of Charles, as to that " ; and goes on in this style till the whole room is in a laugh.

But now I have a story to tell you of his Grace the Duke of R[ichmond].[1]   Lord Rawdon, I hear, came over from Ireland for no earthly reason but to oblige his Grace to a recantation of what he had said in the H[ouse] of L[ords] about Haines.   He wrote to him here a very civil but a very peremptory letter, and at last Lord Ligonier [2] went to him, at Lord Rawdon's request, with the words wrote down which his Grace was to use, on his subject.   At first the Duke hesitated, but Lord L. said that he recommended it to him to read it over carefully, and then decide ; that he was limited as to time, and hinted that, upon a refusal, he should be obliged to come with another message.   The Duke complied very judi-ciously, and a speech was made accordingly ; and Lord Huntingdon was present, and heard justice done to his relation.   The Duke was conscious of the part which he was forced to take by what he said to Lord Lothian and to Lord Amhurst ; and this, as I am told, is the third time that his Grace has been compelled to make these *amendes honorables*.   I am glad to have heard this, because so much *méchanceté* deserves this humiliation.   It may be that in telling me the story, it was aggravated, but I believe the *fond* of it to be true, and that his Grace deserves this and ten times more, and so probably Mr. Bates will directly or indirectly let him know.

*Saturday morning.*—Mr. Walpole came to me last

[1] Charles Lennox, third Duke of Richmond (1735–1806).   He was a Whig of strong liberal opinions.   In 1782 he joined Lord Rocking-ham's Cabinet as Master General of the Ordnance.   He resigned office when Fox and North came into power in 1782.   In 1783, on the fall of the Coalition Ministry, he joined Pitt's first Administration, from which time his opinions grew more conservative.   In 1795 he gave up office but continued to give an independent support to Pitt. Richmond's handsome person, high station, love and patronage of the fine arts, and his political ambition and capacity, combined to make him one of the first men of the time.

[2] Edward, Earl Ligonier, died 1782, of the Irish peerage, and a general in the English army.   His grandfather was a native of France, and a Huguenot.   His uncle was Marshal Lord Ligonier.

night, as George and I were playing together at whist with two dummies (for Mie Mie and Mrs. W[ebb] were gone to her dancing academy), and he stayed with me till near eleven ; so I was obliged, finding it so late, only to scrawl out three words to let you know that the little boy was quite well. . . .

I do not find upon discourse anything exaggerated in the least in regard to his Grace.   Lord L[igonier], to those to whom he chooses to talk upon this subject, is very explicit, and from these I had it.   It was the same with Mr. Clavering and Colonel Cunning[ham].   Now for the Address.   I saw all these *brouillons* and their adherents go by ; that starved weasel, Charles Turner, in his coach, grinning and squinting : Wilkes [1] in his ; Charles F[ox] and Ossory, laughing in Charles's chariot, *à gorge deployée*. They were not detained long.   The King beheld them come up the room with a very steady countenance, and one which expressed a good deal of firmness.   I have been told by several that he is shrunk, and does not look well. I have heard that the Chan[cellor] sat up with him the other night, and till five in the morning.   Of this I know nothing.

He made them the only answer which he could, in my opinion, have made with any propriety, had he been less displeased than he has reason to be with these people. But he laid such an emphasis upon the words, " By the means which shall seem to *me* the most conducive," &c., &c., that the answer was by no means acceptable, or the reception ; and what will follow from it and what [be] voted upon it, the Lord knows.

Next week will be one of bustle, and I will beg Storer to be circumstantial in all he relates to you of the House of Commons, as I shall myself, as far as it shall come to my knowledge.

At the Levee Charles presented an Address from Westminster.   The King took it out of his hand without

[1] John Wilkes (1727-1797).  He first made use of the power of the press in politics.   In 1782 his election for Middlesex was finally pronounced by Parliament to be valid.

deigning to give him a look even, or a word ; he took it as you would take a pocket handkerchief from your *valet de chambre*, without any mark of displeasure or attention, or expression of countenance whatever, and passed it to his lord-in-waiting, who was the Duke of Queensberry. It was the same with Sir Jos[eph] Mawbey. He spoke to none but one word, and it was inevitable, to Admiral Kepple, who had *bouché son passage*. When he was upon the throne the Chancellor was at his right hand, and looking with such a countenance as affords to the people of Brooks's much occasion of abuse. Arnold[1] was behind the throne. The King looked much displeased with Mr. Conway, the mover, at the right hand of the Speaker.

I do not find that they expect any immediate changes to follow from this, but so various is the discourse at White's and at Brooks's among themselves, that it is difficult to collect anything which is worth recording.

I went last night to Brooks's, and stayed with them all after supper, on purpose to hear their discourse, which is with as little reserve before me as if I was one of their friends. Charles says that it was some comfort to him to have frightened them, at least ; but he was so candid to me as to own that from the beginning of this *émeute* he could not perceive in me the least expression of fear or disquietude whatever, and that, to be sure, he did not like.

The truth is, I have made up my mind to whatever shall happen. I wish the King to be master, and he may be so, if he pleases, I am confident, and all whom I saw at Brooks's last night *anéantis* as politicians, if he will stand but firm upon the ground on which he now is.

[1] Bendict Arnold (1741–1801). Arnold, after brilliant military services on behalf of the revolted Colonists, had entered, in 1780, into negotiations with General Clinton to give up to the English commander the position of West Point with its stores. Major André was sent to him on behalf of the English general. Arnold's treachery was discovered, and he had barely time to escape to a British sloop. In 1782, after being given the rank of Brigadier-General in the English army, he came to London.

Sir G. Cooper [1] tells me that two only were lost by the disappointment of the Loan. Several Scotch members went off, for reasons but too apparent, and which justified but too much the character given of them. Mr. W. lays this upon Rigby's agitated, restless humour and intrigue, but how much he has contributed to this bustle I am sure I cannot tell. If I was in his circumstances, I should not be disposed to hazard any change.

The Taxes, which were to come on on Monday, are put off till Wednesday. Questions will be followed by questions, but all will not be carried by a majority against Government, if the King expresses an inclination to yield as to measures and to be resolute as to men.

I own that to see Charles closeted every instant at Brooks's by one or the other, that he can neither punt or deal for a quarter of an hour but he is obliged to give an audience, while Hare is whispering and standing behind him, like Jack Robinson, with a pencil and paper for mems., is to me a scene *la plus parfaitement comique que l'on puisse imaginer*, and to nobody it seems most [more] risible than to Charles himself.

What he and his friends would really do with me, if they had me in their power, I cannot say, but they express in their looks and words nothing which I can fairly interpret to proceed from ill-will. I have been lately not so contentious or abusive as formerly, no more than I have flattered them, and my appearance among them is from mere curiosity, and to amuse you by my recitals more than from any other motive.

The correspondence must again be interrupted to continue the narrative of the parliamentary struggle. On receipt of the King's answer to the Address which, it has already been stated, was carried without a division, Conway moved another hostile resolution, to the effect

---

[1] Sir Grey Cooper, died 1801, one of the Secretaries of the Treasury from 1765 to 1782, and again under the Coalition Ministry. Noted for his administrative ability and accurate knowledge on questions of finance.

that those who should advise the further prosecution of the American war should be considered enemies of the country. This was also carried without a division, but Lord North still remained in office.

On March 8th, therefore, the attack was renewed, Lord John Cavendish bringing forward a resolution which concluded with the words, " That the chief cause of all these misfortunes has been the want of foresight and ability in his Majesty's Ministers." The Government were still able to depend on their place-holders, and averted a direct defeat by carrying the order of the day by ten votes.

The Opposition was as obstinate in assault as the King —for it was virtually he against whom the attacks of Fox and his friends were being pressed—was in defence, and on the 15th of March a direct resolution of want of confidence was only defeated by nine votes.

Notice was promptly given of a renewal of the struggle on March 20th, but when that day arrived Lord North came down to the House of Commons and announced the resignation of the Government. It was one of the momentous declarations in English history. It virtually proclaimed the independence of the American colonies and the beginning of a new epoch of ministerial responsibility to the House of Commons. Among the frequenters of St. James's Street the first thought was how would their own political fortunes be affected. Fox's declaration that an end had come to a political system was received with incredulity. To Selwyn it was a time at once of annoyance and interest. He feared for his sinecure offices; he had, as has been already pointed out, grown accustomed, like many others, to the Administration of the King and Lord North. He had no personal liking for the fallen Minister, and he had watched the career of Fox from boyhood with mingled admiration and disgust. He could not realise him as a Minister.

[1782,] *March 6, Wednesday morning.*—I told you, in my letter of Monday, that I should write to you yesterday, and so I should have done, if there had

anything come to my knowledge more than what you
see in all the public papers, and which must be of
equal date with my letter.

What conversation I have with the people at Brooks's
or White's upon these matters is really not worth putting
down. Those who are out, and wanting the places of
those who are in, either for themselves or for their friends,
talk a language which has much more of phrensy in it
than common sense, which, in the most rational and the
best tempered, seems as much out of sight, as the spirit of
the Constitution itself.

You will laugh at my mentioning that, because you will
not conceive that I understand it ; perhaps I do not, but
I perfectly remember how [I] have ;heard and read it
described to be, and it is as different from what our
present Patriots or Whigs represent it, as the Government of the Grand Senior [Signor].

Poor Fitz[willia]m, whom I really love on many
accounts, held me in conversation last night, his brother
only being present. I do not know if he was in earnest,
but I suppose that he was. He had worked himself up
to commiserate the state of this country, nay, that of the
King himself, [so] that I expected every instant that his
heart would have burst ; but to speak more to my
passions, he lamented, in the terms the most *attendrissants*,
your situation, and how much your pride, and feelings of
every kind, must be hurt, and that for no estate upon
earth he would be in your perilous state.

I begged for a little light, and to know if there was a
possibility of salvation in any position in which our affairs
could be placed. He asked me then with the utmost
impetuosity, what objection I had to Lord Rock[ingham]¹
being sent for. You may be pretty sure that if I had

¹ Charles Watson Wentworth, second Marquis of Rockingham
(1730-1782). Rockingham was twice Prime Minister, in 1765, until
the formation of Chatham's Administration, and again in 1782, on the
fall of Lord North. He owed his political position to the fact that he
was a peer with large possessions, and was at the same time an honest
politician. Thus he became the head of that group of politicians known
as the Rockingham Whigs.

any, I should not have made it.    I contented myself
with asking how he intended to begin his operations, to
which I was answered in two Latin words, *de novo*.

If that should be, and the *in nova fert animus* should
take place, we must as individuals be meta[mor]phosed
indeed, and what will become of the public neither he,
Burke, Charles, or any one of the Cavendishes I suppose
knows or cares.    But I think that Lord N[orth's] peremptory assurance of yesterday, together with the King's
strong expressions of resentment for the manner in which
he has been treated, may suspend all this nonsense for the
present, and leave us at leisure to regret something of more
essential consequence to the public than whether Charles
and Hare live in St. James's Street, or at the Treasury.

To-day we have the Taxes, which are heavy enough of
themselves without all the speeches made to oppose them ;
to-morrow I know nothing of ; and on Friday we shall
have another trial of skill between the Privileges of the
Crown and the Prerogative of the People.    In the meantime there is in the larder the loss of Minorca and of St.
Kit's,[1] with good hopes of further surrenders, to feed our
political discontent, and private satisfaction.    I have a
new relation, as you know, that is the most zealous Con-
stitutionist, according to his own notions, that ever was,
and he has honoured me lately with very long conferences ;
*ma porte ne lui est jamais refusée, cela s'entend.*    But I can
only ask questions for information, and even my doubts
or ignorance are not acceptable, but we part always upon
very good terms, because I always appear attentive, and
so he presumes that of course I must be more instructed
than when he came to me.

Charles has attempted more than once to feel my pulse,
but finding them (*sic*) beat pretty much as usual, he
augurs no good from it.    I have only desired, if they are
resolved to turn me out, to have three months' warning,
that I may get into another place, which I shall certainly
have if I go with the same character which I had in my

[1] St. Christopher's was taken by the French, and Minorca by the
Spaniards in January, 1782.

last.   I am sober, and honest, and have no followers, and although I used to be out at nights and play at the ale-house, I have now left it off.

I was asked last night at Lady Buckingham's, and am ashamed of my laziness in not going.   I dine with his Lordship on Saturday, and to-day I am going with Mie Mie and Mrs. W[ebb] to Mr. Gregg's, who has got a little ball for a dozen children of her age, because it is the birthday of one of his own.

Arnold's being behind the King's chair when the Address came up has given great offence.   They will not suffer soon an enemy to the Americans to come into the guard room.   I think that Arnold might as well have paired off with Laurens ; [1] it would have conciliated matters much more.

. . . Poor Lady H[ertfor]d['s] civilities in inviting so many of the Opposition to her Ball, afford a great deal of mirth.   Charles did not go ; he has not leisure for those trifles.   Hare and Lord Robert have the drudgery of dealing between them.   Your kinsman Walker is a *cul de plomb* at the table, and has lost, I believe, both his eyes and fortune at it.   He seems so blind as not to see the card which is before him.   Keene seems to have surrendered in his mind this *forteresse*, so I take for granted that he knows how little a while it will last.

I wish I could know at this moment for a certainty what is to become of you and me.   I talked long with Gregg about this when Storer had left us.   It is my opinion, from all I hear of your circumstances and my own, that we shall be both reduced to £2,000 a year each, and as great as the inequality is between us in all other respects, in that we shall be equal, and the alternative is to submit to the terms imposed by the new people, which

[1] Henry Laurens (1723–1783), President of the American Congress in 1777 ; he resigned in 1778, and was appointed Ambassador to Holland, but was captured by the English at sea and imprisoned in the Tower.   After his release he was sent by Washington to Paris to negotiate for a new loan, and in 1783 he signed there the preliminaries of peace with Franklin, Adams, and Jay.

may be very humiliating to us both. If you are not an object of their justice, of their esteem, and respect, you will, I am sure, not consent to be one of their mercy only. I shall feel the deprivation of two parts out of three of my income, but I hope that I shall have enough left for Mie Mie's education, and to supply possible losses to her in other respects. If I do that, and am lodged up two pair of stairs in a room at half a guinea a week, as I was when I lodged with Lord Townshend and Lord Buck[ingham] in 1744 or 5, I will never utter an impatient word about *le retour de mon sort*, whatever injustice may have been done me. If the storm falls upon you only, I am willing that you should avail yourself of anything in my situation, by which you can be assisted. But I shall never bear with patience the insults which I know would be offered to you, if these people had their terms, in their full extent.

The King, I hear, is in good spirits, and went yesterday to Windsor to hunt, so I hope he knows that he is in a better situation than I fancy him to be. If it is not so, and he can make up his mind to it, I must envy him his insensibility. But I think that if he had one atom of it, and heard a hundredth part of what I hear from those who are forcing themselves into his councils, he would lose his Crown, and his life too, rather than submit to it. It is better certainly to be kicked out of the world than kicked as long as you live [in] it, whatever his Grace may think. But the Duke intended to insult, and not to be obliged to apologise.

A peace, I find, of some sort is negotiating with Mr. Adams.[1] Lord Cov[entry] dropped hints of a great deal which he knew of this matter, but could not reveal. No credit seemed to be given yesterday at dinner, either to his intelligence or credit with the new people, and he had a very dissatisfied look. Two of the Bedchamber are to be left, Lord Ailesford and the Duke of Queensberry, but the Duke's other place will be annihilated.

---

[1] John Adams (1735–1826), afterwards second President of the United States, then in Paris.

The Duke of R[ichmond] affects to say that he will take nothing, and when this is repeated there is a laugh, thinking how suddenly his Grace is changed, for lately he took anything, and what no man living would have taken but himself ; he has met with more of this at Chichester. His pride must have suffered of late immensely. Lord Huntingdon dined with us yesterday, and we had the whole story *en détail*, from the beginning to the end. Mr. Bates pines in his confinement for a sight of the papers ; it will not be long, I daresay, before his resentment is gratified.

It is certainly a great consolation to me, in this trouble and public disgrace to the King, and private distress to myself and to you, that you stand, as you do, upon such high ground in point of reputation ; not a mouth is open against you, not a person but is ready to say, that no one ever executed a great office so becomingly or so judiciously as you have done. But I am afraid not of your conduct, but of your decline, and therefore wish for a timely retreat if possible. That others may repent of it, is true, but a good man and one who meant the good of his country only would never wish to have Administration pass out of your hands into those of such a calf as they now talk of.[1]  But things must have their course ; they are grievous to me, but not unlooked for.

If I had had any conception that this storm would have come so soon, I could have supported it with less embarrassment ; but I must now bear up against it, as well as I can, and so must you, for *si tout sera perdu, horsmis votre honneur*, there is no help for it. *Le Roi ne s'est pas encore rendu.*

As to Ireland, you have passed over that subject very slightly with me, but the approaching troubles or danger of them could not be a secret from me long. As accounts were exaggerated, so I was in hope no part of them were [was] true, but it is manifest to me now, from what I hear, that there are materials in that country for the greatest confusion, *tôt ou tard*. There is a spirit of independency,

[1] The Duke of Portland, who subsequently succeeded Lord Carlisle as Lord-Lieutenant of Ireland.

and impatience of Government, and an aversion to rule, which has infected every part of his Majesty's dominions. It is to me wonderful that with all this he preserves his health, for to public distress is added the utmost degree of domestic infelicity, and no prospect of a change for the better.

Charles did not go to Lady Hertford's ball last night, although invited, in so *distinguishing a manner*. The Duke of Devonshire told him that twenty ladies had kept themselves disengaged in hopes of having him for a partner. Mie Mie goes to-night to the Theodores' benefit, with Lady Craufurd and Lady something Aston. I shall stay at home with George and get Fawkner to be her beau, if I can. I could not parry this off, but am in pain about it.

[1782,] *March* 12, *Tuesday.*— . . . Dr. Ekins and I dined yesterday at Lord Gower's, when I received your letter of the 6th, and Lady G. one from Lady Carlisle. Lord G. and I had a good deal of discourse on the present state of things, but my curiosity led to know chiefly how any alterations would affect you in your present situation. He seemed to think not at all. What may become of Storer, of me, or of John St. J[ohn] is another thing. These people, by long opposition, hunger, and engagements, are become very ravenous ; and Charles, as far as he should be concerned, I am persuaded, would have no consideration upon earth but for what was useful to his own ends. You have heard me say that I thought that he had no malice or rancour ; I think so still, and am sure of it. But I think that he has no feeling, neither, for any one but himself ; and if I could trace in any one action of his life anything that had not for its object his own gratification, I should with pleasure receive the intelligence, because then I had much rather (if it was possible) think well of him, than not. However, I am inclined to believe, that whenever there is anything like a settlement in Government, he will find himself disappointed and mortified, and he will then see that he has been doing other people's work, and not his own.

Brooks's is at present a place open to great speculation
and amusement and curiosity, and I go there and talk
there, but it is without heat, or anything which makes it
in any respect disagreeable to myself or others.    If
that was not my temper I should not go among them.
Boothby said last night to me, that he thought that they
were not so *cock-a-hoop*, as he phrased it, and Lord
G[ower] said that he believed, what may be true, that
they become frightened at their own success.    It is
much easier to throw things into confusion than to
settle them to one's own liking.    Troubled waters are
good to fish in, it is true, but sometimes in searching for
a fish you draw up a serpent.    I have much more
admiration of Charles's talents than opinion of his
judgment or conduct.

[1782,] *March* 13, *Wednesday m[orning]*.—Two packets
of mine were sent yesterday to the messenger who was, as
Sir S. Portine told me, to set out for Ireland last night at
nine.    I intended to have sent another by the post ; but I
had not materials enough, and I found myself indisposed
with my cold, and could do nothing but drink tea by the
fireside at White's.

The story of St. Christopher's tells well at the outset,
and gives *me* at least, who am sanguine, great hopes, but
the Opposition still is incredulous as to good news, and
the same intelligence which they dispute the authenticity
of to-day, would be, to-morrow, if they were in place,
clear as proofs of Holy Writ, clearer indeed than those
are to the greatest part among them.

I was assured last night, that the King is so determined,
as to Charles, that he will not hear his name mentioned in
any overtures for a negotiation, and declares that the
proposal of introducing him into his councils is totally
inadmissible.    I should not be surprised if this was true
in its fullest extent.    I can never conceive that a King,
unless he and his Government differ from all others, can
do otherwise.

Friday is our great day of struggle ; some changes I

should think must be, but Denbigh,[1] who is a good cal-
culator as to numbers, says that we shall have eight more
than last time.   That will make but a paltry majority;
however, if it be so, we shall brush on, I suppose, live
upon expedients, and hope for a more favourable crisis;
and then we shall be soon prorogued, and so give time for
an arrangement in which our poor master will have better
terms.

I said to Sir S. Portine yesterday, by way of conversation, that I wished you was here to take the seals.   He
said that undoubtedly you might have them, when you
came over, and so I suppose you may.   But I am sure it
is not the station I [in] which I the most wish to see you.
As to Ireland, I have no doubt, as you say yourself, but
that you have touched your zenith, and if circumstances
permitted it, I wish to God that you was returned.   No
one can have done better than you have, in all respects,
*et de l'aveu de tout le monde;* but you are, I see, *non nescius
auræ fallacis,* and in Ireland the winds rise suddenly, and
are violent and blast, *quand on y pense le moins.*

You have, I understand, made Mr. Cradock one of
your Aid de camps, which has pleased the Duchess of
Bedford much; *elle se louë continuellement de la lettre
qu'elle a reçuë de votre part; elle se vante du credit qu'elle
a aussi après de vous.   C'est un beau garçon, et très digne
de sa protection à tout égard.*   I know him a little myself;
he seems a very right-headed, well-bred young man, and
when we played together, as we have done at Kenny's,
he showed me particular civilities, so I was glad to hear
of the kindness which you have had for him; but I
had never heard that he had any such thing in contemplation. . . .

I fancy that Wyndham[2] is returned for Chichester, but
by a very slender majority.   Betty's patriots spread it
about yesterday that Lord N[orth] was out.   What use
that lie was to be, which must be contradicted an hour

---

[1] Basil, sixth Earl of Denbigh (1719–1800).  He was Master of the
Royal Harriers, and was deprived of his office by Lord Rockingham.
[2] Percy Charles Wyndham was returned March 11, 1782.

after, is difficult to say; perhaps to get a vote or two of ours to go out of town, or some such flimsy scheme. I hear that we shall be about twenty. Conway was at the Levee yesterday, and scarce noticed; the King talked and laughed a great deal with both Rigby and the Advocate, who were on each side of Conway.

I was at night at Brooks's for a little while; it was high change, all sorts of games, all kinds of parties, factions, arrangements, whispers, jokes, &c., &c. John in better spirits; he had had a cordial from Brummell, Lord N[orth's] secretary. Storer plays his whist at White's. Nobody at supper there but Lord Fr. Cavendish, Lord Weymouth, and one or two more. My circle around the fire in the card room breaks up at about twelve, and the Duke of Q. generally joins us towards the conclusion, and when he has talked himself out of breath at Brooks's.

Charles dined yesterday, I believe, at Lord Rockingham's; I saw him about five in great hurry, and agitation. What is to be done, may not probably be concluded upon till the Easter holidays, and by that time I hope to hear that his Majesty has been better served in the W[est] Indies than in other parts of the world.

Negotiations for peace are much talked of. I hope that we shall first have a little success, and then go with our proposals to Versailles. Monsieur de Vergennes[1] says, that *si l'Angleterre veut avoir la Paix, il faut frapper à ma porte*, and the sooner we are in his cabinet for that purpose the better. If we do not begin there, I am afraid, as Lord Bolingbroke says, we shall be suing for it elsewhere, and at the gates of every other palace in Europe.

I have received an anonymous letter from Ireland, dated Dublin the 6th inst. I call it anon[ymous], because I believe the name of R. Thomas to be feigned. The hand is a good one, and of a person of fashion. He makes a demand of £500, which he says that he must have by my

---

[1] Charles Gravier, Comte de Vergennes (1717–1787), Minister of Foreign Affairs under Louis XV. His policy had been to humble England by assisting the United States.

means. The place I am to direct to is specified. Ekins will carry over the letter. I rather suppose it to be from a lunatic. He talks of not selling his voice, but I have no more light into his scheme, or who the man is.

There is to be a great Drawing Room to-day, because Lord G[eorge] and his bride will be presented, and with them come La Noblesse, that is, the heads and tails of a hundred great families, to which these young people are allied. *Her* head runs upon nothing but dress, and expense; she is rather plain, as I hear, but not disagreeable. She has made great terms for herself; her pin money is 1,500. She will give up no part of her fortune to her husband. It is settled upon the children; a jointure in proportion.

I saw the Duke of Bedford coming out of Charles's yesterday, so there is another Duke for him to lead by the nose. For him he is, I suppose, obliged to Ossory. Young Pitt will not be subordinate; he is not so in his own society. He is at the head of a dozen young people, and it is a corps separate from that of Charles's; so there is another premier at the starting post, who, as yet, has never been shaved. I hope George will have a little more patience, but he is, as I hear, the first speaker in his school, and by much the most beloved, which pleases me more than if I saw the seals in his hands.

[1782,] *March* 16, *Saturday morning*, 10 *o'clock.*—We divided this morning between one and two; our majority was nine, the numbers 236 and 227. I came home; my cough is so bad that I shall put off all my engagements to dinner, and stay at home, I believe, till I have got rid of it. But there is to be another trial of skill on Wednesday. Charles's arrogance both in the House, and out of it, is insupportable. I can neither think or speak of him with patience. Gilbert voted with us, Sir J. Wrottesley against us, Lord Trentham went away, McDonald with us. This is Denbigh's way of calculation; he was positive that we should have 30, or at least 22.

But good God! what a Government is this! if the

King has not the power of choosing his own Ministers. It is enough, when he has chosen them, that they are amenable to Parl[iamen]t for their conduct. But if it is in the power of any man, on account of his Parl[iamen]t-[ary] talents, to force himself upon the King and into Government, when his private character would exclude him from ever[y] other station, or society, I wish for my own part not to belong to that Government in any shape whatever ; and it would satisfy my mind infinitely more, that, while things remained upon that foot, that neither of us were in any kind of employment whatsoever. But I do not presume to dictate to you. You can see and feel for yourself, with as much discernment and sensibility as another.

Lord North was thought to speak better, and with more spirit than before. I could not go down into the H[ouse] to hear the Advocate, I was so oppressed with my cold. You will see the substance of the speeches in the Chronicle ; I suppose that you have all our papers. Storer will write to you, and tell you of his conversation with Charles, but do not say that I anticipated the account. I must talk with Gregg upon the subject of your return here, for neither the removal, or the mode or the time, will be weighed by any other scales than those of their own convenience. . . .

The Fish voted with us, and upon the merit of this assistance, and at this important crisis, I suppose something was founded, for when the H[ouse] was up, he was never from Lord North's elbow. Notwithstanding Charles's impatience, it will not be settled all this [month?] till the Easter holidays, and how it will be settled then, I do not conceive. They talk now of Barré for Rigby's place. I have never once heard my nephew's[1] name in any part of the arrangement, but he has, I presume, a situation fixed in his own mind, as adequate to his consequence. Young Pitt expects to be sent for from the circuit to the Cabinet, but not in a subordinate capacity. George has not sent from Neasdon any proposals to the K[ing], so I suppose

[1] Thomas Townshend.

[he is] waiting till he can negotiate a Peace.    I wish that
I could overhear him in his rhetorical mood.

[1782, *March* 16,] *Saturday noon.* — Lord G[ower]
assured me that he knew that at this juncture there was no
arrangement ; that there certainly would be, and soon ;
that it was impossible to guess at the disposal of the parts.
That Charles would be, and has been, a thorn in the side
of his party ; that the Ministers would not suffer him to
rule, nor would the country gentlemen endure him.    But
you might be recalled ; that it was not now an object of
ambition to be the Governor of Ireland ; that he thought
it would have been a lucky event for you, and that it
would have afforded you an occasion of resigning, the
best that you could have had ; for things would grow
worse, and that hitherto all had been well, and that you
might now come away without reproach ; but that your
circumstances opposed this option.    He was, on account
of the great expense and your love of show, afraid how
these would be hurt ; that he could not help being
alarmed, notwithstanding the prospect Mr. Gregg held
out of saving, at one time, to provide against the extra
charges of another.

I own that these reflections have often struck me, and
very forcibly, and makes us in a sad dilemma and per-
plexity about what can be done.    He assured me that as
soon as he knew anything, I should be informed of it.    I
told him that I wish[ed] we had our four members, which
could not be, unless Lord Meilbourn could be made by
some consideration to vacate his seat ; but if we had, I
would risk my fortune in Government with yours, and
take my chance, and be served in the second place, when
those had the administration with whom we could draw.

What these will do, and in what manner they will treat
the King's friends, the Lord only knows.    Charles made
it an objection, your attachment to the King ; that was
beginning well.    He has none, God knows.    His countenance to Hare or Fitzpatrick are [is] no proof of it to
me.    People can like and protect those who are sub-

15

servient to them, and persecute them when they are not.
Had he been capable of a good sentiment, he would have
had one for you.   Instead of that, he puts your fortune
into immediate danger, by a sacrifice of his honour and
engagement, and when he has done that, you and those
attached to you are treated as mercenary, and illiberal,
because you desire to be rescued from the impending ruin.
Not a hundredth part of what has been said on this
subject comes to my knowledge, but enough to fill me
with horror and indignation.

While I was writing, and just before my dinner came
up, I saw Mr. Cook, who brought me your letter.  You
needed not to have cautioned me against asking after
matters of state.   Those nearer to me are no objects of
curiosity, further than you are concerned in them.   It is
a pleasure to have such a recent account of your being
well.   I wish *my* letters could go as speedily to *you*, to
prevent the *radotage* incident to letters of an old date.
Your correspondence with Lord Hilsborough will soon
cease ; who[m] you will have to write to afterwards I
have not heard.   It may be Charles.

Hare and Richard came into White's just before dinner.
I stopped there to hear what was going on.   They can
talk of nothing but the demolition of the last Ministry,
and *abbai[s]sement* of his Majesty, but of this they speak
without reserve.  Lord Cov[entry] was there, as malignant
and insulting as possible.   It requires some degree of
temper to refrain from a reply to these things, but I shall.
I have made up my mind to these *revers ;* no future
minister can hurt me, for none will I ever trust.

Lord North and his Secretary, Robinson, have acted
such a part by me that I should never have believed anything but a couple of attorneys of the lowest class to have
done ;  but my conduct has been uniform, and not
changed towards the King, whom I have meant, though
unsuccessfully, to support.   Had I been a bargain-maker,
I could have made as good a one with the Opposition as
another, and could have justified it better.

I hope that in about a week more, I shall be able to

send you such intelligence as will put us both out of doubt of what is or ought to be done. Lord G[ower], I believe, six months ago, wanted to be at the head of affairs ; he might now, but will not.[1] Nothing but the worse management on earth in our leaders could have brought things to such an issue.

[1782,] *March* 18, *Monday m[orning]*.—I am sorry to begin my letter with telling you that George is again in my house, but so it is. Mr. Raikes brought him to me, and little Eden to the surgeon's, on account of his chilblains, yesterday morning in a post chaise. Sir N. T[homas] came, and he ordered George to be blooded, which he was directly, and wrote other prescriptions. I believe there was some James's powder taken last night, and he is to help his cough with something in a certain degree emetic. His pulse were [was] above a hundred, and his cough very troublesome, but there is nothing that forebodes any mischief. I do not hear of the least apprehensions of that. Dr. Ekins was here, and Mr. Nevison. Lady G[ower] could not come on account of her cold. Lord G[ower] will be here this morning. . . .

I have no objection to declaring my own [opinion], but I beg you and Lady Carlisle to know that what is done now, if it is with my opinion, it was not in consequence of it, for I have been perfectly passive. Dr. Ekins went done to Whitehall to acquaint Lord and Lady G[ower] with this, who approved of what was done, and last night I was there myself ; and Lord G[ower] and I had more conversation with him upon this horrid situation of affairs. That I should be much disturbed about them, on your account, and my own, is not extraordinary. I have, in certain circumstances, fixed and determined in my own mind what would be most becoming for us both to do, and what in the end would be most advantageous, but I shall not obtrude my advice upon you, whose judgment I

---

[1] " Attempts were made to induce Shelburne and afterwards Gower to construct a Government but they speedily failed " (Lecky, vol. iv. p. 203).

hold in higher esteem, infinitely, than my own, and whose temper is more equal. But I will say what I believe to be the state of things now, and what they probably will be, and you will judge the best, it may be both for yourself and me.

I called in at Brooks's last night, but avoided all conversation, and will for the future with any one belonging to the party. Their insolence, their vanity and folly, and the satisfaction expressed in their countenances, upon fancying themselves Ministers, and going into the place of them, as they think, and to drive the K[ing] from every shadow of power and dignity, is no object to me now of mirth ; so, as I cannot help it, or approve it, and shall get nothing by a dispute with such people, I am determined to act for my own part—what I think is becoming me to do—to resign all ideas of pecuniary advantage, if I cannot have them upon the terms I like, and wait for better times.

The P[rince] of W[ales] supped the night before last at Lord Derby's ; there were as I am told no less than six courses ; the women were Lady Payne, Lady Jersey, perhaps Lady Meilbourne ; I have not as yet been informed of particulars. He stayed there till six, and then, I hear, carried Charles home in his coach. He canvassed in the last Question against his father. Lord Meilbourne stayed away at his instigation. In this he has acted contrary to his engagements. He says that he purchased his seat at Luggershall.[1] It is a falsehood. If he did, he has not paid the money he ought for it ; but both Lord N[orth] and Robinson have acted in this, towards me, in the most scandalous manner in the world, and I will inform the K[ing] of it myself by an audience, if I can find no other means of doing it.

I warned Lord North over and over again of this *supercherie*. I knew his intention, and he was so weak as to neglect the means of pinning this fitz scrivener, [this] fitz coachman, this fitz cook to his word, and putting it

[1] Lord Melbourne was returned with Selwyn as M.P. for the borough of Ludgershall on September 12, 1780.

in his power to use me in this manner, as if he had bought of me a seat in Parliament, which no man living ever yet did, but the King himself.

Lord Gower told me last night, that it might be a week before it was possible to guess in the least how things would [be] settled ; he believed that the King would not send for you from Ireland, unless you chose it. I think, and so I told him, that *that* was more than the King himself could answer for.

I am now confident they would give it to the Duke of Dev[onshire] if he would accept it ; he will not, and the Duke of Portland, that jolt-headed calf, certainly will.[1] I wish to have nothing but Buckinghams and Portlands for their subalternate ministers as long as they are at Court, and then their damned Administration will be over in six months, and they sunk into the herd of the people, and the contempt which they deserve from any man of sobriety and character.

Rigby and Lord G[ower] were in another room in close conference a great while. The negotiation has been carried on, but at present broke off, between the Chancellor and Lord Rock[ingham]. Burke's Bill, they say, is insisted on, that is, a Bill which, while they promise the public to carry into execution, they are determine[d] shall be rendered [as] ineffectual as this they broke off. The Chancellor went yesterday out of town.

The thought of a new Administration is so prevalent with Charles that he would not go to Newmarket. I heard him last night tell his people that he saw no reason, when he was Minister, that he or his assistants in Administration should sit upon the Treasury bench. The merry and the sad, as my Lord Clarendon says, have employment enough, while these actors are dressing themselves up for the play, and rehearsing their parts.

[1782,] *March* 19, *Tuesday*, 11 *o'clock, morning.*—. . . . Gregg dines with me to-day. He has been ever since

[1] The Duke of Portland succeeded Lord Carlisle as Viceroy of Ireland on the formation of the Rockingham Ministry.

Friday last at Saffron Walden, so I have as yet not seen him. I have a great deal to say to him. The seeming impossibility of your staying in Ireland agreeably to your own sentiments, and the inconvenience which returning suddenly will be to your private affairs, gives me at this moment not a little disquietude, and Lord G[ower] cannot help it, by any lights which as yet he has himself.

I saw Charles last night, and by accident was alone with me [him] ; he stretched out his hand to me with great good humour. I could have asked him an abundance of questions, and could have reasoned with him a great while. For although in that sphere he has much superiority to me, he has not the faculty of persuading me in the least of what I know to be without reason, and a great part of which he knows to be so himself. However, I did not, for fear of betraying a want of temper which could be of no use, and I asked him no questions, lest he should interpret them ill, and think that I wanted to deprecate his vengeance or solicit his favour. He must be reduced to his former despair before I shall discuss these matters with him pleasantly.

He spoke of all coming to a final issue now within a very short space of time ; he talked of the King under the description of Satan, a comparison which he seems fond of, and has used to others ; so he is *sans ménagement de paroles*. It is the *bon vainqueur et despotique ;* he has adopted all the supremacy he pretended to dread in his Majesty. It seems a dream that I survey his figure, and know his history. His talents are great, but talents alone never operated in this manner.

When he said how few days we had to subsist, I uttered in an humble voice, " Πολλα μεταξυ πεσει " ; I have forgot to write my Greek. To that he said, " You are in the right—that is the only reflection which can be suggested for your comfort, but it is next to an impossibility." He talks of us so much as an Opposition, that even the Wine Surplus, which we call a majority, is forgot, and I wonder he does not in his sleep walk into St. James's with the seals of his new Government in his hand. He told me that he would make me a Baronet, for my vote to-morrow night. The Duke of Dev[onshire] said gravely, "A vast price for one vote only!" Charles Turner has seriously insisted upon it.

The Fish told Lord N[orth] the other night, after the Division, that he had only three bottles left of that champagne which he liked so much, and if he would come and dine with him they were at his service. Lord North replied, archly enough, "What! *still*, Mr. Craufurd, may I dine with you?"

[1782,] *March* 21, *Thursday* m[*orning*].—In the midst of all that multiplicity of distress and confusion in which I am at present, as well as the public, I will not omit to let you know that, excepting the cough, George is very well. . . . What happened yesterday in the H[ouse] of C[ommons], of which you will by various channels know the particulars, with many more in a few days, must for ever astonish you, if you were not sufficiently apprised of the characters of the persons concerned. I hear that the Duke of Montagu at Windsor, the day before, told the King of the impossibility of continuing the Administration.

Lord N[orth], when he went to the King, was told abruptly of these intentions; and then He (*sic*) sent for the principal persons in Administration, and those who had assisted him, and having thanked them, went down to the House to declare this in his place in the manner in which you will, I suppose, see it described in the papers.[1]

The old Ministry is at an end, and of what materials the new one will be composed, the Lord knows. The insolence, the hard heartiness (*sic*), brutality, and stuff, which these people talk, altogether give me the worst apprehensions of what they will do, and I have only to hope that from this, which seems so irreconcilable to reason, decency, or the usual practice of Government, some system will be formed that I shall like better.

As to Lord N[orth], what happens disagreeable to him

[1] See *ante* p. 197.

he merits in greatest degree, and if the King chooses to acquiesce in all this ill treatment of him, I see no reason why I should be offended, or feel more for a man's disgrace than he feels himself. He might have prevented it; he seemed to wish that he could; he now seems not affected by it; but *je courerois risque d'extravaguan[ce] si je continuois sur le chapitre.*

I stayed at Brooks's this morning till between 2 and 3, and then Charles was giving audiences in every corner of the room, and that idiot Lord D.[1] telling aloud whom he should turn out, how civil he intended to be [to] the P[rince], and how rude to the K[ing].

*Thursday night, 9 o'clock.*—George is going on as before, no fever, but a cough. Sir N. T[homas] has forbid his going out as yet. I took him out airing yesterday in the middle of the day for an hour, but to-day he has had some physic.

Lord Gower and I were a long while together at Whitehall; we both agreed that, *rebus sic stantibus*, it seems impossible that you should stay in Ireland. Hare informs me that they do not mean to remove you. I should wonder if they did, for such an account as I have of the state of Ireland is terrible, and I am sure one cannot wish to send a friend to weather such a storm. The best thing for you would be their sending another in your room, but, if they do not do that, the next is to desire to be recalled, when you know who these Ministers are. You must expect a pause for some time in your political *carrière*, and you must in that interval practise a great economy, which will do you infinite credit, and then, upon a new turn of affairs you will be called with more lustre into a better situation. This was Lord Gower's opinion, and is mine.

Charles assured me, not half an hour ago, that the King had sent for nobody, that all was as much at a stand as before the Creation. Nobody knows what to make of it. But a Ministry must be formed by Monday. It is thought that my nephew will be Chancellor of the Exchequer and C[harles] Fox the Secretary of State, and of

[1] Probably Lord Derby, Edward, twelfth Earl (1752–1834).

the rest I know nothing, of that nothing like intelligence
(*sic*). It is imagined that Lord Rock[ingham] and Lord
Shelbourn cannot agree.

The King had no Drawing Room, only the Queen
between him and Lord Robert ; Lady Sefton next to
Fitzpatrick ; the Prince between the D[uchesse]s of
Devon[shire] and Cumberland ; on the other side of the
Duchess of D[evonshire] the Duke of Cumberland.

When I left the House, I left in one room a party of
young men, who made me, from their life and spirits,
wish for one night to be twenty. There was a table full
of them drinking—young Pitt, Lord Euston, Berkley,
North, &c., &c., singing and laughing *à gorge deployée* ;
some of them sang very good catches ; one Wilberforce,[1]
a M. of P., sang the best.

I shall go at noon (?) to Whitehall, and write again in
the evening. I dine at home to-day, but to-morrow at
Lord Ossory's. I would not leave my house when George
was here, but Mrs. W[ebb] has a care of him, and attention
to him in everything, as much as Mie Mie. Poor Lady
Craufurd wished to go to this Ball. I did not know, or
would have contrived it for her. She was at Lady
Hertford's, but the Duchess is so (*sic*) at Gloucester
House, so that cannot be, upon admissible terms.

Lord Sheilbourn was at Dev[onshire] H[ouse] the
whole night, which seems to countenance the report that
Lord R[ockingham] and he cannot act together. *Plût à
Dieu que la discorde, cette déesse si utile en certaine occasions,
voulût bien se mêler de cet arrangement; ce seroit bien à
propos.* But there is no agreement among them but which
tends to create confusion. Tommy T[ownshend] and his
family seemed in high glee. Lady Middleton's daughter
danced with my cousin of Westmoreland ; *il est tant soit
peu gauche, sa danse a fort peu de grace.* The women
looked extremely well. Lord George presented to me
his bride ; she is her father *toute crachée*, but not so handsome. Charles has not bought a good coat yet upon the

---

[1] William Wilberforce (1759–1833), the abolitionist and philan-
thropist ; at this time M.P. for Hull and one of Pitt's closest friends.

change in his affairs.    I thought that his former calling
would have supplied [it?].    Mrs. Bouverie [1] at supper.
Many ladies who had not received cards were sure it was
a mistake, and sent for them.    This was an additional
pleasure to those to whom they were sent, for here was a
school for scandal as well as for dancing.    Lady Warren
played at Pharo ; the Prince at Macco, and the Duke of
Cumberland.    John, with a very handsome coat, satin,
*couleur de maron*, and an *appliqué* of silver and *des diamans
faux*—a coat *d'hazard* sent from Fripier's in the Ruë de
Roule.    The Duke and I did not receive our cards till
five o'clock.    It was such a snow and hail and rain when
we were coming away as never was seen.

I am glad my dear little boy is in this house now ; I am
sure that he would run a great risk out of it, just at this
time. . . . He is mighty busy in making out his Latin
with Littleton's Dictionary, which I have given him. . . . I
left Lady Gower and Lady Ann and the Dunmores at the
Ball.    The Duchess of Bedford has invited me to Bedford
H[ouse] to see your letter to her. . . .

Storer carries this off with such seeming spirits as are
certainly more becoming than an apparent dejection.    But
I dread to think to what, I verily believe, that he will be
reduced.    I utter no complaint, but I feel the danger
I am in, and the distress which it may occasion to me, and
still more Lord N[orth's] abominable treatment of me.
If I had resented it, as many would have done, I know
what might have been said.    But I have acted my part
well and steadily, and when I have done all which becomes
me to do, I shall make up my mind to the event.

[1782, *March* 22,] *Friday m[orning]*, 11 *o'clock*.—
George seems very well ; his cough is considerably abated,
but the weather is so remarkably wet and bad, that Sir
N. T[homas] wishes him to stay within.

I was at Devonshire H[ouse] till about 4, and then left

---

[1] The fashionable and courted beauty.    The portrait of her and of her
sister, Mrs. Crewe, together as shepherdesses, by Sir Joshua Reynolds,
in 1770, attracted much notice.

most of the company there. All the new supposed
Ministers were there except Lord Rock[ingham], who
had probably other business, and perhaps with the K[ing].
Rigby assured me that some one was sent [for?], and
if Charles did not know it, he was more out of the secret
than he thought that he had been. To be sure, the
arrangement is *entamé, la pillule est avalée, et bien des
coulœuvres après.* Charles I left there ; I believe that he
had heard what did not come up to his full satisfaction,
so probably a little water is mixed with their wine. We
shall know to-day, for this strange situation of things
cannot remain till Monday ; *la machine n'est pas construit
à pouvoir aller jusques à là.*

I conversed privately a good while with Lord Ashburnham. I have the greatest opinion of his judgment
in the conductive part of life. I really believe, if any
man ever went through life with consummate discretion,
it has been himself, and he has preserved his reputation at
the same time, or else I should not give his conduct this
*éloge.* He asked me after you in the most obliging and
interesting (*sic*) manner, and solicitude about the part you
would act, not hinting a doubt of your not performing it
well, but with great expressions of esteem. He hoped
much that you would take this opportunity, as he said,
of leaving Ireland. He said that it would be laying the
foundation of a very brilliant situation to you at another
time. He is very much in the right. I could not, to be
sure, explain all the difficulties in the way of this. There
are none, indeed, comparatively speaking.

Hare writes to you ; he expresses a tenderness for your
interest ; *je ne la révoque pas en doute,* but his interests
and yours are not the same. These new people will wish
you perhaps to stay, and say it is from regard to you. If
you believe it you will deceive yourself. If they will send
another, so much the better ; let their friend stay to
govern Ireland when Ireland is what it will be. But if
they talk of keeping you there, wait to see the Ministry
established, and then ask for your recall. I hope that you
will not reflect a moment with concern upon the straights

to which you may be reduced by way of expense. We will do all we can to arrange this matter, but honour and figure, as you know, cannot he added, or taken from you, by expense. That is not the scale in which the respect which all the world owes and is ready to pay you and Lady C[arlisle] will be weighed. If you came from Holyhead in the stage waggon, it would only be more reputable to you. There was a strong instance of that in the story of this Duke of Newcastle's father. Lord Gower tells me that Lord Rock[ingham] is personally not attached to you from provincial reasons. I never adverted to that consideration.

The K[ing] had a most narrow escape hunting on Tuesday. His horse ran away with him ; he was thrown on a gate ; he seems to be marked out for a people (*sic*) to be distressed and disgraced in every way possible. Burke was last night in high spirits. I told him that I hope, now they had forced our entrenchments and broke loose, that he and his friends would be compassionate lions, tender-hearted hyænas, generous wolves. You remember that speech of his ; he was much diverted with the application. Our fête was very brilliant indeed, and well conducted ; there was a supper for at least 300 people ; eight rooms where there were tables. The Prince *l'astre de la nuit, couvert de faux brilliant* (sic) ; *c'est un beau cavalier.* The Duchess of Cumberland was there, but not the Princess Royal. It was proposed, as is said, that the Duke of Gloucester should be Commander in Chief.

[1782, *March*] 23, *Saturday night.*—George goes on well, but Sir N. T[homas] will not let him go out. The weather is worse than it has been at any time this winter. Leveson has been all this evening at my house to play with him.

Nothing as yet arranged, and we meet on Monday. It is imagined that we must then adjourn till Friday ; about that there will be a bustle. Lord Gower was sent for yesterday morning by the King, and was with him a great while. I was this morning at Whitehall. The Chanc[ello]r was there. Gregg showed Lord G[ower] your accounts ; they are better than he expected. Charles expressed to me last night more than once an anxiety lest you should be in Opposition, and asked me if the Master of the Horse would please. I could give him no answer to that, but that it depended upon circumstances. He said Lord Cadogan's place would do for Lord Foley. That this Revolution · which he brought about was the greatest for England that ever was ; that excepting in the mere person of a King, it was a complete change of the Constitution ; and an era ever glorious to England, and a great deal of such rhapsody. Richard insolent to a degree.

I was a good while to-day with Lord G[ower] ; still of opinion that your return here would be the most favourable event that could happen to you. Ossory hinted to me this afternoon that the King would see Lord Rock[ingham] to-night. Hanger assures me that Charles is better disposed to me than to anybody, but that I have enemies who surround him ; so there is one friend in a corner.

On Monday I expect some envious dissertations in the H. of C. on the nature of the new Government. The Duke of Gloucester won't be Comm[ande]r in Chief for two reasons ; one is, that the Duchess can be admitted at Court ; and the second is that Lord Rock[ingham] will not permit it. It is meant to take the Army out of the K. hands, and that would be putting it into them. have no more for to-night. My love and respects to your fireside. shall see Caroline again with great pleasure indeed, and the little boy.

[1782, *March* 27,] *Wednesday night*, 10 *o'clock, at home.*—The Cabinet Council ¹ kissed hands to-day, and

---

¹ The new Cabinet. The Rockingham Ministry consisted of Lord Rockingham, First Lord of the Treasury ; Lord Thurlow, Lord Chancellor ; Lord John Cavendish, Chancellor of the Exchequer ; Charles James Fox, Secretary for Foreign Affairs ; Lord Shelburne, Secretary for the Home and Colonial Departments ; Admiral Keppel,

Dunning with the rest. He is Chancellor [of the] Duchy of Lancaster and a peer. At this I was surprised. Ashburn[h]am is kept, and all the Bedchamber. Lord Hertford is delivered up at discretion ; either he or his son Isaac must be sacrificed. But his Lordship has not been thought the father of the faithful, or so himself. Their trimming has released his M[ajesty] from any obligations to protect them.

The Duke brings me word from Court that I am safe, but how I do not comprehend. To take away my place, which is to be annihilated in two months by Burke's Bill, [is absurd], and a pension I would not receive, but as an appendix to a place or as a part of it. But the D[uke], whose friendship for me is very *vif*, on some occasions, has fished out this for me. I could not go to Court, my temper would not permit. I could have seen my R[oyal] master on the scaffold with less pain than insulted as he has been to-day. I am going out to hear all that passed, and how he bore it. From my parlour window I saw Mr. Secretary Fox step into his chariot from his office, and Lord Shelbour[n]e and Dunning from the other office. The Levee was not over till near five, that is, the audiences, a most numerous Court—souls to be saved, and souls not to be saved.

Warner dined here, and Storer. Mie Mie went to her Academy, so I stayed at home to keep George company. He was upon the dining table hearing Warner, Storer, and I [me] talking over this political history, with an attention and curiosity which would have charmed you, as well as the questions he asked. He looked like a little Jesu in a picture of Annibal Carraci's listening to the Doctors. He has been reading to-day speeches in Livy, with the French translation. We gave him sentences this evening to construe. It was wonderful how well he did them. The weather grows fine, and I shall desire leave to carry him back till the 25th of next month, for he is very well ; the cough which [he] has is trifling. He has no heat ; he looks delightfully.

I was with Lord Gower this morning. The Chan-c[ello]r dined there to-day. I talked with Lord G. about you ; he has explained your situation, and I suppose has told you that arrangements will be made here to your satisfaction. I see some comfort in all this. *Nous reculerons pour mieux sauter.* Your return will mortify some of the Opposition, who hope to keep you a year in Ireland out of charity, to insult you, and for their convenience. Lord Carm[arthen] solicits this with *chaleur* and impatience. I believe there is in this *tant soit peu de malice, et pour se venger,* for he will have your Lieutenancy in the County too. He has lost himself with me entirely. A thousand traits of him have crowded upon me, which a little partiality to him had obscured.

I was asked to dine at Derby's to-day with the new Ministers ; I could not accept it. Prudence forbid[s] that, as well as want of temper. What I said or did not say would have been ill interpreted, so I refused.

Charles has taken a house in Pall Mall. Sheridan is his secretary. What becomes of Hare and Richard I know not. Richard has provoked me beyond measure by his insolence and unfeelingness about everybody and everything. The Garters are for the Duke of Portland, D. Devonshire, Duke of Richmond, and one of the Princes.

My nephew, Secretary at War, and Burke, Paymaster. This was what he hoped for, I mean Tommy. The C[hancellorship] of the Exchequer not determined upon it [yet ?]. Lord John Cav[endish] balances about it. Young Burke, Secretary of the Treasury. Another ball at Devonshire House. I long to see you, Lady Carlisle, and the children. This is the only balm in all this infernal business. But *vous avez un beau rôle à jouer,* but you must have patience for the present and, as George says, wait the event. This is *à plusieurs facettes.* I will now go to White's for more intelligence, and write more if I can, but it is half-hour after ten.

[1782,] *March* 29 [30?], *Saturday m[orning]*, 8 *o'clock*. —I could not write last night but a few lines, but if I could, many pages would not have been sufficient, or any force of language which I possess strong enough to express all I feel from reading your letter of the 22nd instant. Although my friendship, and tenderness for what concerns you, may not be greater than that of . . . (*sic*), my judgment has on this occasion been, as I perceive, more corresponding with your sentiments, which I have spoke from the dictates of that pride which I can adopt on your account, but would be presumptuous on my own. I hope, in avoiding one inconvenience, that I have not fallen into another, but if I have, the mistake can be easier corrected if necessary.

When Charles has expressed to me, as he did more than once, an anxiety about your conduct, and an uneasiness lest it should be in opposition to his own, I contented myself with saying, that it was impossible for me to know what you would do, but I was in no pain about it ; that if he could, as I had heard him say that he could in very strong terms, answer for your ready judgment on all occasions, so I would answer for your honour, which two things made me sure that you would always act as became you, and that, therefore, I was in no pain upon that head ; that whatever might happen disagreeable to you, or to me, we were both prepared for it. And when I have expressed a curiosity concerning the disposal of offices in general, I have been sometimes taken up *shortly*, *impertinently*, and *dirtily* by that jackanapes, Lord D., and he has said, " Your friend will not stay in Ireland."

I have then only answered, " My Lord, my wishes are that he *may not*, and it is most probable that he *will not*, desire it ; but you are quite mistaken if you suppose that in these arrangements I have any anxiety or curiosity about him." All that is an object of my love and esteem is quite independent of other people's resolutions ; and as for what regards myself, I am not indifferent, I own, and I shall wish to know how I may be treated by those to whose power I am delivered up, but I have never asked one question concerning it. I shall provoke no man's anger unnecessarily ; it is my only solicitude to let people see that if they oblige me by good treatment, they oblige one whom they do not despise, and who has acted in all circumstances like a gentleman.

I have, I find, from what I have been told by the Party, the credit of having behaved better and calmer on this occasion than many of my fellow convicts. What I have felt I have felt like a man, and that I have not attempted to deprecate by pretending that I thought myself to blame.

But, my dear Lord, this has been merely exterior, for at home and alone I have been greatly depressed, both on your account and on that of others. I have felt for the honour and credit, and sufferings, of a person to whom I can only be attached by principle. For the sentiment of personal affection does not arise for objects of such in-equality. I do not know how to account for it, but I have had, and still have, such a share of *that*, as would make one think that with the air of France and with the language of the country I had imbibed all the prejudices of their education. My thoughts about your distress, and of those dear children, which seem to belong as much to me as to you and Lady C., have really affected me at times in a manner which would have exposed me any-where out of my own room, and to anybody else but to Dr. Ekins, who knows how naturally, and justly, I feel for you.

I have in the last place been touched, as I must be, with the great difference of my own circumstances, such as they were and might have been, and such as they would be if all this impending mischief had its full effect. The loss of three thousand pounds a year, coming after debts created by imprudence, and which might otherwise have been soon liquidated, is a blow which I confess that I was not pre-pared for, and if I could not feel it for myself, I must have felt it for you. Born for your use, as Zanga says, I live but to oblige you, and as soon as I become unprofitable to you, I shall feel then the most sensibly, how imprudently I have acted, and how unjustly I have been dealt with. I have, as I have told you before, not had yet the courage to look upon that ledger, where I saw once so fair an account, and where I must now make myself so many rasures. *Stabant tercentum nitidi in præsepibus altis.* I must now see myself reduced in comparison to a narrow or at least a circumscribed plan, and without a possibility of assisting one object of my affection without hurting another.

However, gloomy as the prospect has been, it may clear up, and I could, if it was right, encourage hopes and anticipate a perspective that is not unpleasing to me.

I shall see Lord G[ower] to-day, who will tell me more particularly how things have been settled since yesterday, when I was with him. It is an idea of my own that he has contrived an arrangement for you, which, while it relieves your distress, saves, I hope, your honour. I have myself as much dreaded as you could do, your being thought of as an object of mercy, and I trust that so near a relation will dread that for you, as well as myself, and that if he secures you from injustice that he will secure your credit at the same time. I have my eyes opened now upon the intrigues of a Court more than they were in all the former part of my life, and of all people I believe that I shall be the last for the future who will be the dupe of Ministers.

The new Government, for it is more that than merely a new Administration, has given me quite a new system for my own conduct. If they have by violence &c. got into places from whence I would have excluded them, if now they should behave rightly in them, and the country becomes better and safer for their conduct, it would be folly not to assist them. But I am, above all things, desirous that both your assistance and my own, such as it is, should be more wished for by them than their assistance wished for by us.

I think that you stand clear of all which can humiliate

you at present. No one's conduct in every circumstance, so far as regards your administration in Ireland, can be more universally commended. You do not desert, but retire, when those who are at the helm, if they have confidence in your understanding and honour, mistrust your inclinations towards themselves, and you leave to their friends and dependants a business from which no honour can be derived.

You are not driven from your post, because they will have recalled a man manifestly more willing to leave it, than they to profit of the resignation. They would have kept you perhaps for their own sakes, although they would do nothing for yours, and they would have made you a tool, but cannot, as they know, make you a friend but by behaving well towards [you] and towards their country.

Your private circumstances, if known to be embarrassed, are known at the same time not to embarrass you. Your chop and your pewter plate will reproach others sooner than they can reflect disgrace upon yourself. The *audax paupertas*, however, *is not* necessary, but great economy *is*. I myself will give you an example of it, and contribute every atom in my power to ease your mind from what will most sensibly and naturally affect it. What interest in Parliament is left me shall be yours, and if my little bark, sailing in attendance upon yours, is able to assist you, I shall be happier in that circumstance than from any which I could otherwise have derived from it.

But we may perhaps all act in concord for the present. I am told, I do not [know] how true, that no hostilities are intended towards me ; *nous verrons*. I can never be used by any set of Ministers so ill, or with such indignity, as by those who are removed. . . .[1] said last night that the executions were now near[ly] over. I will open my mind to you. I think both his and Richard's language in all this transaction has been to the last degree indecent, and I am sure, unless these two are better advised, they will do their chief more disservice than any ill-conduct of his own. When people of low birth have

---

[1] An erasure.

by great good luck and a fortunate concurrence of events
been able to obtain, from lively parts only, without any
acquisitions which can be useful to the public, such situa-
tions as are due only to persons of rank, weight, and
character, it is surely an easy task *not to be* insolent.    It
is all I require of them ; I envy no man his good fortune,
ever so undeserved, while he shows no disposition to
offend others.    But with all this I have not been provoked enough to express my resentment, or mean enough
to deprecate that of others.

I was last night at supper with Charles, but not one
syllable passed between us.    He knows that I see him in
a situation where I cannot wish to see any one who has
aspired to it and obtained it by the means which he has
used.    No one admires more or thinks more justly of his
abilities than I do ; no one could have loved him more, if
he had deserved it ; what his behaviour has been to the
public, to his friends, and to his family is notorious.
Facts are too stubborn, and to those I appeal, and not to
the testimonies of ignorant and profligate people.    However, if hereafter you can reconcile yourself to him and
to his behaviour towards you, I will forgive him, and
although I desire to lay myself under no obligation to
him, I will remember only that he is the child of those
whom I loved, without interest or any return.

George wonders to see me write so much to you ; he
is so well that I will carry him to school on Monday,
without consulting any person. . . . He has read
more Latin *to me* than I have *to him*, for my breath has
been affected by the cold, or I should have read more
with him ; but he has hammered out his Latin with the
dictionary and what assistance I can give him, and con-
strues it wonderfully well.    He will be at school till the
25th of next month, and then I propose exercise abroad,
and the Modern History of Europe at home, and French ;
for to speak the truth he is defective in the pronunciation
of that, for want of practice. The Theodore's coming here
obliges me to have my nieces dine here, to see her.    I'm
afraid people will come to see Mie Mie dance *par billets*.

# CHAPTER VI

## 1786–1791

### THE CLOSING CENTURY

Political events—At Richmond—The Duke of Queensberry's villa—
Princess Amelia—The King's illness—The French Revolution—
Proposed visit to Castle Howard—In Gloucestershire—Affairs
in France—The Émigrés—Society at Richmond—The French
Revolution—Richmond Theatre—French friends—Christening
of Lady Caroline Campbell's child—Selwyn's bad health—Death.

OF the series of political events which in rapid succes-
sion followed the formation of the Rockingham
Ministry, the death of its head, the accession to the
premiership of Lord Shelburne, the resignation of Fox,
and lastly the coalition between that statesman and his old
antagonist Lord North, Selwyn tells us nothing.    His
correspondence with Carlisle came to an end for the time
when his friend was recalled from Ireland in 1782.    Thus
the last group of letters has rather a social and a personal
than a political interest.

For a number of years Selwyn had been in a constant
state of alarm lest he should be deprived of his sinecure
office of Paymaster of the Board of Works.    Burke's
scheme of economical reform had been a constantly
threatening cloud to him.    The passing of this Bill,
which that statesman had so persistently but unavailingly
pressed on the House of Commons, had, however,
been made one of the conditions on which the Rockingham Ministry came into office.    It became law in

1782,[1] and under its operations Selwyn was deprived of his office. But in 1784, when Pitt was safely in power, Selwyn was appointed to the equally unarduous and lucrative post of Surveyor-General of Crown Lands. He was thus able to enjoy the last years of his life in affluence, and enjoy them he did, in spite of failing health. His letters are still gay, showing unabated interest in the world around him. He retained that remarkable sympathy for the young which had characterised his life. The children of Carlisle had grown out of childhood. Lord Morpeth was going to Oxford,[2] Lady Caroline was married. His adopted daughter, the Mie Mie of so many of the preceding letters, had become a woman, and the care and affection with which Selwyn had watched over her growth and upbringing was now transferred to her well-being and pleasure in the first society of the country.

It is a charming picture—the old man without a wife or children of his own finding in the friendship of young and old all that his kindly and affectionate nature required. It heightens our ideas of the breadth and the depth of friendship when we see how it can compensate for the lack of those natural relationships which are supposed to be the solace of advancing years. Of political events in England during the period covered by this last correspondence the most important was the mental illness of the King. It began early in November, 1788 ; it ended in the spring of the following year. On the 23rd of April, 1789, the King, the Royal Family, and the two Houses of Parliament attended a thanksgiving service at St. Paul's. But in the interval important constitutional debates had occurred in Parliament on the question of the Regency. That the Prince of Wales should be Regent both Government and Opposition were agreed ; but whilst Pitt and the Cabinet desired to place certain limits to his power, Fox and the

---

[1] 22 Geo. III. c. 82, 1782. An Act for enabling his Majesty to discharge the debt contracted upon his Civil List Revenues, and for preventing the same from being in arrear for the future, by regulating the mode of payments and by suppressing or regulating certain offices.
[2] He matriculated at Christchurch, October 19, 1790.

Whigs regarded his assumption of the office as a matter of right, and held therefore that he should have the powers of the Sovereign. The constitutional question was complicated by personal feeling, so that all London society was ranged on one side or the other. Selwyn was a ministerialist, though he seems to have kept a cooler head than many of his friends. But the rapid recovery of the King rendered these discussions abortive and put an end to the political hopes and fears which were aroused by his illness. Pitt remained in office, the Whigs in opposition.

Presently, however, the French Revolution became all-important. Events in France were watched with the keenest interest by Selwyn, to whom many of those who figured in the tragic scenes in Paris were personally known. But he regarded the state of affairs in France with greater calmness than many, though he was shocked at revolutionary violence. It is, however, the picture in these letters of the society of the French émigrés in and about London that gives so much interest to the last group of correspondence. Of this, however, it will be more fitting to speak when the letters which touch on it are reached.

[1786, *Oct.* 25,] *Wednesday m., Richmond.*—I was in London on Monday, but returned hither to dinner. I propose to go there this morning, and to lie in town. I am to dine with Williams, who is quite recovered, as I am ; he is kept in London, Lord North being there, on account of his son's ill health—Mr. Frederick N[orth].[1] I hear no news, and am sorry that that which Lord Holland told me is not true, of his uncle's annuity, which I mentioned in my last.

The Princess Amelia [2] is thought to be very near her

[1] Frederick North, afterward fifth Earl of Guildford (1766–1827), the famous Greek scholar. He was Lord North's third and youngest son.

[2] Princess Amelia (1783–1810) was the youngest and most beloved of the children of George III. Always delicate, the King was constantly concerned about her, and her dying gift of a ring with a lock of her hair is said to have helped to bring on his last mental illness.

end ; there is to be no Court to-day, which is unusual on this day of the Accession. But I do not know that the Princess's illness is the cause of it. I intended to have gone to the Drawing Room and have put on my scarlet, and gold embr[oidery], for the last time. Pierre I believe has contracted for it already. I cannot learn from any of your family when you propose to return ; I hope in less than three weeks. I wrote to Lady C[arlisle] yesterday.

I have no thought myself of settling in London, nor am I desirous of it, while the Thames can be kept in due bounds. At present it is subdued, and all above is clear after a certain hour, and my house is the warmest and most comfortable of any ; and when I came here to dinner on Saturday last, having given my servants a day's law, everything was in as much order, as if I had never left it.

The Duke [of Queensberry] dines with me when he is here, a little after four, and when we have drank our wine, we resort to his great Hall,[1] *bien éclairée, bien échauffée*, to drink our coffee, and hear Quintettos. The Hall is hung around with the Vandyke pictures (as they are called), and they have a good effect. But I wish that there had been another room or gallery for them, that the Hall might have been without any other ornament but its own proportions. The rest of the pictures are hanging up in the Gilt Room, and some in a room on the left hand as you go to that apartment. The Judges hang in the semicircular passage, which makes one think, that instead of going into a nobleman's house, you are in Sergeants' Inn.

[1] Queensberry Villa, which stood by the riverside, was purchased by the Duke of Queensberry in 1780. It was built by the third Earl of Cholmondely in 1708, and subsequently became the property of the Earl of Brooke and Warwick, and then of Sir Richard Lyttleton. It was purchased by John Earl Spencer for his mother, the Countess Cowper, on whose death, in 1780, it was sold. The Duke of Queensberry bequeathed the house to Maria Fagniani (Mie Mie). In 1831 it became the property of and was rebuilt by Sir William Dundas. The old house was of red brick with a balcony running round it above the first floor windows. ("The History and Antiquities of Richmond," by E. B. Chancellor, p. 160 *et seq.*)

There is, and will be, a variety of opinions how these portraits should be placed, and with what correspondence. I have my own, about that and many other things, which I shall keep to myself. I am not able to encounter constant dissension. I will have no bile, and so keep my own opinions for the future about men and things, within my own breast. I am naturally irritable, and therefore will avoid irritation ; I prefer longevity to it, which I may have without the other. I have had a letter from Lady Ossory, who is impatient to tell me all that has passed this summer in her neighbourhood, but she is afraid of trusting it to a letter. I can pretty well guess what kind of farce has been acted, knowing the *dramatis personæ*. The Duke of B[edford ?] was to wait on her Grace. . . .

I thought that Boothby had been with you. Mrs. Smith assures me that you have fine weather, and fine sport ; so I wish the fifth-form boy [Lord Morpeth] had been with you, and his sister Charlotte, to make and mark his neckcloths.

I hear no more of Eden, but my neighbour Keene's conjectures on his refusal, which are very vague, *et tant soit peu malignes.* I expect more satisfaction to-day from Williams : not that I want really any information about him. I have already seen and known as much as I desire of him ; he is a man of talents and application, with some insinuation, and cunning, but I think will never be a good speaker, or a great man. But what he is I do not care.

My best compliments to the Dean,[1] and Corbet. I have not heard from you, nor do I expect it. Mrs. Smith says, that sometimes you do not return till 8 in the evening. Then I suppose *que vous mangez de gran appétit, et que vous dormez après;* so how, and when, am I to expect a letter ? Write or not write, I am satisfied that you are well, and be you, that I am most truly and affectionately yours.

I shall keep this half sheet for the news I may hear in Town, and as this letter is not to go till to-morrow.

[1] Dr. Jeffrey Ekins, Dean of Carlisle (1782–1792).

*Thursday m., Cleveland Court.*—I met no news in Town when I came, but the Princess Amelia has at present, in Dr. Warren's [1] estimation, but a few days to live.  If her own wishes were completed in this respect she must have died yesterday, being on the same day in October that the late King died.  It is a pity that she should not have been gratified.  But she still hopes it will be in this month, that she may lose no reputation in point of *prévoyance*, which would be a pity.

It is not an unnatural thing, with our German family, to make a rendezvous as to death, and it has in more instances than one been kept.  K[ing] G[eorge] 1st took a final leave of the Princess of Wales, afterwards Queen Caroline, the night before he went to Hanover for the last time ; and the Queen afterwards prophesied that she should not outlive the year in which she happened to die.

But her R. H. is firm and resigned, and, as Dr. Warren says, declares herself ready.  She flaps her sides as she sits up in her bed, as a turtle does with its fins, and says, " I am ready, I am ready."

I heard yesterday that I have lost two other friends, whom I valued as much, and for the same reason, that their faces were familiar to me for above five and forty years.  I mean little Compton, Bully's friend and minister, and Sturt of Dorsetshire, both victims to the gout.  I am also told that Sir G. Metham is dying. . . .

Harry Fox is to have a tolerable good fortune with his wife, which I am glad of.  But that she could like his person would amaze me, if I did not know that, for particular reasons, women will like anything.

In the summer of 1788 Selwyn was laid up by an illness.  " Mr. Selwyn has been confined in Town by fever and I have not seen him since the royal progress was intended," wrote Walpole to Lady Ossory in July.  The visit of the royalties to Matson took place

---

[1] Richard Warren (1731-1797).  The most eminent physician of the time.  He was a man of great ability and judgment.  In 1762 he was appointed physician to George III.

later. "Mr. Selwyn, I do not doubt, is superlatively happy. I am curious to know what relics he has gleaned from the royal visit that he can bottle up and place in his *sanctum sanctorum*." Such was Walpole's news in August to the same correspondent. Selwyn recovered from his illness, and left Matson to join the Carlisles. "The Selwyns I do not expect soon at Richmond for the Carlisles are going to Cheltenham; but so many loadstones draw him, that I who have no attraction seldom see him." But in the autumn Walpole could again enjoy his friend's society—for as the following letter to Lady Carlisle shows he had returned to Richmond for a time.

[1788,] *November* 2, *Richmond.*—It must seem, dear Lady Carlisle, very shabby that on this day I do not afford a sheet of gilt paper for my letter to you, but it is to no purpose giving any other reason when I have that to give of having none by me. But truth on plain paper is better than a compliment without sincerity, with all the *vignettes* which could be found to adorn it, and nothing can be truer than that I rejoice at the return of this day, which gave birth to what I have on so many accounts reason to value and esteem. I wrote yesterday such a long epistle to Lady Caroline, as would have worn out anybody's patience but hers. . . .

Miss Gunning [1] is I find at the Park with Mrs. Stewart, and to-morrow morning I shall go in my coach to see her. I wish it were possible for her to accept a corner in my coach, and go with me to C[astle] Howard, but I am afraid that it is not. I take for granted that you have fixed upon the 20th for our setting out, and that you intend that Lord Morpeth should come to my house the

[1] Charlotte Margaret, daughter of Sir Robert Gunning, K.C.B., Minister at the Courts of Copenhagen, Berlin, and St. Petersburg. Miss Gunning, who was Maid of Honour to the Queen, must not be confused with the two celebrated sisters of an earlier period, or with Miss Elizabeth Gunning, a well-known and much-talked-of beauty at this time.

day before, which will be on Monday fortnight. He wishes to have leave to come from Eton on Saturday, and, as he has told me in a letter which I have received from him to-day, he has hinted it to his father. I promised to second his motion, and I hope it will be complied with. . . .

I shall remove with my family to town from hence in about ten days. As yet we have leaf and verdure and air, and the country is very agreeable. We have a few to associate with, and not too many. Old Mrs. Crewe is my passion, and her house free from that *cohue* with which others are filled ; and as we have no connection with those who make a public place of this situation, I find it a much more private one than I expected.

The Duke seems for this year to have deserted us. Monsieur de Calonne engrosses all the time which he can spare from Newmarket. Frederick St. John's match is, as I am told, at an end. But then the Duchess of R[utland's] widowhood is just begun. I have lost myself the opportunity of being his rival. Her Grace was in this house last summer with me, and alone, but how could I foresee the event which has since happened ? and a *survivance* at my age could not be thought an object. I do not hear who are to compose the next Court at the Castle. You see whom the papers name, and perhaps can say who are the most likely to go there. . . .

The correspondence from 1788 to the end of Selwyn's life is entirely with Lady Carlisle. Carlisle himself appears to have been much in London during that period, and thus in companionship with his old friend. But letter-writing had become at once a habit and a necessity. It was—and can always be where there is what he has called an *epanchement de cœur*—an unceasing pleasure and solace. There is only required pen, paper, and ink, and the last bit of news, the thought of the moment can be written down and exchanged with the friend at a distance. It matters not that the letter does not reach its destination for some time to come.

In the transcribing of the thought, there is the sharing of it with another, and imagination anticipates its reception.

[1788, *November*] 20, *Thursday, Cleveland Court.*— George, you know, set out on Tuesday, and to-morrow I hope that you will see him, and as well as when I took leave of him.   I will own fairly to you, that it was some degree of anxiety to me, that he had no servant to go with him so long a journey. . . . When I left him in Grosvenor Place I came here to write to you a letter, . . . but condemned it to the flames.   This Lord C., with whom I have breakfasted, has reproved me for : he was sorry that I did not send it ; you should not be left out of the secret, you should know as much as your neighbours, &c.   You shall do so, if I can furnish you with any intelligence, and although you never tell me anything which I have not seen before, a fortnight past, in the Gazette, I shall not use the same reserve with you. I intend to write constantly to you, or to my Lord, what comes to my knowledge, true or false, and when I may cite the authors of my news I will, and what I ought to keep secret I must, but I think that there will be no occasion for that ; I desire to be trusted with no secrets myself.   Those who are, tell them soon enough for me. . . .

The account of the K[ing] this morning in the papers, and which, to a certain degree, is generally true, is as bad as it can be, and from such information I dare say, with regard to his health or the continuance of his disorder, the whole world can have but one and the same opinion. But I am obliged, I find, to be cautious of saying in one place what I am ordered to believe from authority in another ; and when I am enquiring or saying anything concerning the present state of things, I am precisely in the situation of Sir R. de Coverley, enquiring, when he was a boy, his way to St. Ann's Lane.   Nothing, it is supposed, will be said to-day in either House.   We shall meet about three or four, and agree to adjourn, about

which I hope and presume there will be no difference of
opinion.  Lord C[arlisle] thinks that there will not, and
that the adjournment will be for a fortnight.

To-day, I have heard, is fixed upon to speak reason to
One who has none.  Dr. Warren, in some set of fine
phrases, is to tell his Majesty that he is stark mad, and
must have a straight waistcoat.  I am glad that I am not
chosen to be that Rat who is to put the bell about the
Cat's neck.  For if it should be pleased (*sic*) God to
forgive our transgressions, and restore his Majesty to his
senses, for he can never have them again till we grow
better, I suppose, according to the opinion of Churchmen,
who are perfectly acquainted with all the dispensations of
Providence, and the motive of his conduct ; I say, if that
unexpected period arrives, I should not like to stand in
the place of that man who has moved such an Address
to the Crown.  If the Dr. should, as it was told me,
say simply that he must be under government, the K.
will not be surprised at what, *bon gré, mal gré*, has
happened to him so often.  But what happens, when it
comes to my knowledge, I will write it, and something
or other I shall write to C[astle] H. every day. . . .[1]

[1788, *Nov.* 26 ?] *Wednesday m*[*orning*].—I have had
the infinite pleasure of receiving your letter this morning,
so I shall write to you to-day, and not to Lord C., and I
am the more glad to do so, because I think it but fair, as
you have married him for better, for worse, that you
should divide my nonsense and importunity between you.
*Je laisse courir ma plume*, which would be abominable and
indiscreet, if I was not writing to one who is used to hear
me say a thousand things which he attributes to passion
and perverseness, and is not for that the less my friend.
Then I like, when my mind and heart are full, and I
cannot open the budget before him, to evaporate upon
paper, which provokes no tart reply.  I wish that we
were agreed upon every point of consideration in the

---

[1] This and all succeeding letters are written to Lady Carlisle.

Grand Affair [1] which occupies the whole country, so naturally, but I am afraid that we are not, yet he will not be angry with me.    For when I change my mind, or my rage is abated, it will be more from cool and friendly advice from him than from anybody, and to make me, as I have told him, quite reconciled to measures.    I must, besides, seeing they have not all the evil tendency which I expect, be persuaded that he will be considered as he ought to be, and that they think one person of character, as well as rank, is no disparagement to their connection, but on the contrary will give some credit to it.    I shall say no more to you upon this matter.

The K. is so much in the same state he was, and there is so little appearance of any immediate change, that I am not, for the present, solicitous about it.    There must be a new Government I see, and it may be a short or a lasting one, for it will, or ought to depend entirely upon his Majesty's state of mind.    For my own part I am free to confess, that if I only see his hat upon the Throne, and ready to be put upon his head, when he can come and claim it, and nothing in the intermediate time done to disgrace and fetter him, as in the [year] 1782, I shall be satisfied.    It is a sad time indeed, and if the Arch[bisho]p pleases, I will call it by his affec[ted ?] phrase, an awful moment.

I pity the poor Queen, as you do, most excessively, and for her sake, I hope that a due respect will be paid to the K., and while he and she were grudged every luxury in the world, by those mean wretches Burke, Gilbert,[2] and Lansdown, all kind of profusion is not thought of to captivate his R[oyal] H[ighness].[3]    In short, I shall be glad, if his Majesty has lost his head, to hear that the P. has found it.    I have given him as yet more credit than I would own, for I will not be accused of paying my court to him while, I say, I see the K.'s hat only upon the Throne.

[1] The question of the Regency during the King's illness.
[2] Thomas Gilbert (1720–1798) ; known for his reform of the poor laws.        [3] The Prince of Wales.

I know that you will say that I am heated with a zeal that in three months' time may be out of fashion. It may be so ; but I rather believe myself that this misfortune will add greatly to the veneration which the public has of late had for his Majesty, and make it more necessary for his successor to be cautious *with whom* and *how* he acts. He has *beau jeu*, I hope he will make a right use of it. The K. will be soon removed and in a *carrosse bourgeois*, but whether to the Q[ueen's] House or to Kew I cannot learn for certain. I should prefer Kew, if the physicians did not by that sacrifice too much of the care which is due in their profession to the public.

I cannot get sight of the D.,[1] the P[rince] will have him to himself. I am now confined ; my cough must be attended to, or it will increase, and perhaps destroy me. Mie Mie is an excellent nurse, and a most reasonable girl indeed. If her mother was so, I should hear no more of her. But there will be still *du ménagement nécessaire à avoir* ; however, I have no fears of the issue of it.

Mie Mie, I believe, will be glad, when your L[ad]y [ship] comes to town, to go to the Chapel with Lady Caroline ; you will tell me *tout bonnement* if you should have any objection ; *à tout évènement* she will have a pew somewhere. She can no longer support the idea of belonging to no communion, that *en fait de salut* she should be *ni chair ni poisson*. She pleases me in that, and I shall be completely happy to see her established in the Protestant religion, provided that it is her own desire. But my profession is not that of making converts, *et je ne veux me charger de l'âme de personne*.

My dearest William,[2] pray mind your Billiards ; whatever you do, do not apply to it slovenly, wish success in it, and be so good, for my sake, as to love reading ; you may entertain me, if you do, with a thousand pretty

[1] Duke of Queensberry, who at this juncture, though a member of the King's Household, markedly allied himself with the Prince of Wales's party.
[2] Second son of Lord Carlisle, born December 25, 1781, died January 25, 1843.

stories of Hector and his wife, of Romulus and Remus, and at last we may come to talk together of M. de St. Simon. Learn to make a pen, and write a very large clean hand, and then I shall love you, if possible, more than I do at present.

Frederick,[1] what would I give to see you Regent with a Council, and Tany that Council. You say nothing to me of Lizy or Gertrude ; my love to them.

George must certainly be grown, but I do not perceive it. I perceive that he is strong and well, and I hope he will have a great deal of hunting, *sans être trop témé-raire*. My hearty love to Lady Caroline. Mie Mie and I have not laid aside the thoughts of that which is so connected with our wishes and affections, but I see no immediate prospect of doing or hearing anything one likes as yet.

I was in hopes that when Lord C. came here next, you and the family would come with him. I cannot bear the thoughts of not seeing you till after Christmas. The winter will appear terrible (*sic*) long to me, who have so little pleasure here besides that of going in a morning to Grosvenor Place ?[2]

To-day I have a bill sent me of £100 12s. od. laid out for the poor King, who ordered me to bespeak for him the best set which I could get of the glass dishes and basons for his dessert. The Regency may perhaps not want them, thinking that they have no occasion for any dessert, and that they can do without it : perhaps so, *nous verrons*. Old Begum, as they call her, is more absurd, I hear, than ever.

I was sorry that I could not dine yesterday at White-hall, but I shall not dine out of my room for some time. Wine is my destruction, with the cold that I endure after it. I shall keep myself, if I can, from any complaint that will prevent my going to Parliament. The rat-catchers are going about with their traps, but they shall not have a whisker of mine.

[1] Third son of Lord Carlisle, Major 10th Hussars, killed at Waterloo.
[2] Lord Carlisle's town residence.

Lord C. sets out you say on Monday next ; then I shall see him, I suppose, on Wednesday ; he will not hurry up as he did down, and then I am afraid I shall hardly get access to him.   Charles you know is come ; I have not heard anything more of him.   The papers say that Pitt and the Chan[cell]or [1] went to Windsor together in one chaise, and he and Dr. Graham [2] in another.   I want to know, how he has relished Sheridan's [3] beginning a negotiation without him.   I have figured him, if it be true, saying to him, at his arrival, as Hecate does to the Witches in Macbeth, " Saucy and [over] bold, how did you dare to trade and traffic, &c., and I, the mistress of your charms, the close contriver of all harms, was never called to bear my part," &c.   I will not [go] on to the rest of the passage,[4] for fear of offending.   I hope that I shall not have offended you by anything which I have said ; if I do not, you shall hear from me as often as you please.   Be only persuaded that I am most truly and devotedly yours.

[1788, *Dec.* 4?] *Thursday morning.*—I begin my letter to you this morning, and at an early hour, before I can have been informed of anything, but I do so to shew you that I am impatient to obey your commands, and that I intend to write to you as often as I can pick up anything which I think will interest or amuse you ; in which I shall

---

[1] Lord Thurlow.

[2] Dr. Graham (1745–1794) ; a noted quack doctor.   Returning from America, he claimed to have learned marvellous electrical cures from Franklin, and advertised impossible discoveries ; he declared he could impart the secret of living beyond the natural span of life.   He became fashionable, received testimonals from many well-known persons, and occupied part of Schomberg House, Pall Mall, where Gainsborough had his studio.

[3] Richard Brinsley Sheridan (1751–1816).

[4] " Or show the glory of our art ?
    And, which is worse, all you have done
    Hath been but for a wayward son,
    Spiteful and wrathful, who, as others do,
    Loves for his own ends, not for you."   (Act 3, scene 5.)

not forget that George and Caroline are now of an age to take some parts in public affairs. What is of a more solemn and profound nature and secrecy, such as the deliberations of the Cabinet, that you will learn from those who will relate them to you with more precision and authenticity. Of these, if anything transpires to me, it must be through Jack Payne,[1] Lord Lothian,[2] or Trevis, and these are such confused and uncertain channels that there will be no dependence upon the veracity of them. *Ils ne laissent pas pourtant de donner leur avis de tems en tems, et d'en parler après, à ce que j'ai ouï dire.* So that *de côté ou d'autre* you are sure to know something, and perhaps what may not come to the knowledge of those who furnish materials for the daily papers.

The K. is undoubtedly in a state in which he may remain, and a deplorable one it is; deplorable and deplored, I believe, by every honest and feeling man in this country. But he has now a comfort which, as the poet says, none but madmen know. You, nor any belonging to you, I hope in God will ever know what it is; but he diverts himself now, as I hear, without his reason, precisely in the same manner as I have seen the children do, before they had any, and from this account you will have a just conception of his *present* state.

There was a meeting last night at Lord Sydney's,[3] and another at the Cockpitt, and what was said and done the public papers will, I doubt not, more fully relate than I can. I could not stir out or see anybody after Lord Carlisle, who dined with me, went away, except the Duke, who now sups every night with H.R.H. and his

---

[1] Captain John Willett Payne, known as "Jack Payne," was secretary to the Prince of Wales.

[2] The Marquis of Lothian (1737–1815) belonged to the "fast set." He commanded the first regiment of Life Guards, and was a favourite of George III., whom he deserted at the division caused by his first attack of insanity; at the King's recovery he was transferred to another regiment.

[3] T. Townsend.

Brother[1] at Mrs. Fitzherbert's,[2] and is so good as to call here before he goes.

This cough which I have now has confined me to my room every since last Monday was sevennight, and has for the time been more severe than any which I have ever had. I could not be permitted to lose any blood till yesterday, which I am surprised at, and sorry for too, for I think that if I had been blooded a week ago the effect would have been more than I find it to be yet. I must keep at home. Blisters are recommended, but as they are sometimes attended with painful complaints, so I cannot submit to them. In other respects I am perfectly well, and in spirits.

H.R.H. has been so good as to enquire after my health of the Duke, and I have desired him to say, that I find myself better, and am told that I may *go out* in a few days. I think it is most likely that I shall. I wish it were as likely that poor Corbet came in for something or other that would render his situation more comfortable to him.

My Lord tells me that he has had Zenks to dine with

[1] Frederick, Duke of York.

[2] Mrs. Fitzherbert (1756-1837). It was the occasion of much curiosity during her life and after if she were legally the wife of the Prince of Wales, afterwards George IV. The marriage took place in her own house, her brother and uncle being present ; a clergyman of the Church of England performed the ceremony. But by the Marriage Act of 1772 a marriage by a member of the Royal Family under twenty-five, without the King's consent, was invalid, and by the Act of Settlement a marriage by the heir-apparent to a Roman Catholic was also invalid. In 1787 the Prince, in order to obtain money from Parliament, without doubt gave Fox authority to deny the marriage in the House of Commons, though he pretended great indignation toward Fox to Mrs. Fitzherbert. On the Prince's marriage to the Princess Caroline, Mrs. Fitzherbert ceased for a time to live with him, but acting on the advice of her confessor, returned to him, and gave a breakfast to announce it to the fashionable world, where she was a favourite. About 1803 she broke off all connection with the Prince, retiring from the Court with an annuity of £6,000. George IV. wore her portrait until his death ; her good influence over him was recognised by George III. and the Royal Family, who always treated her with consideration.

him, which I shall undoubtedly quote as a precedent, whenever my friends *now* in Government shall think it right to bring forward in Parliament the Recovery of his Majesty's Reason.    I must own, my dear Lady C., that I think that you had all of you too much courage in allowing of that visit, and especially at dinner, amongst all the knives and forks.    I believe, if I had been there, I should have hemmed in all the children with the chairs, as a *chevaux de frise*, and placed myself before them with the poker in my hand.

Lord C. looks very well, and seems in great but modest glee.    I hope at least to have the comfort of seeing him gratified, and when I know how, I intend to write George a letter, who will believe, I am sure, that in that instance, if in no other, I shall lay aside party prejudices, and rejoice with him.

I had laid aside my paper, and intended to have wrote no more till somebody came to me to give me new information.    But I have had my apothecary at my bedside, who has been giving me an account of the examination of the physicians by the Privy Council.[1]    The physicians, one and all, declared his Majesty to be, at present, unfit for public business ; but when Mr. Burke, who was a leading man, and the most forward in asking questions, put this to them, whether there was any hope of his Majesty's recovering, they did not scruple to say that they had *more reason* to *hope* it than not.    Dr. Warren was the most unwilling to subscribe to this opinion, but did not refuse his assent to it.    It was, to be sure, the answer which Mr. Burke wished and expected.    He told me that the Party, as he heard, is very angry with Mr. Fox, and will not believe the indisposition, which confines him to his bed, not to be a feigned one.

This is my apothecary's news, but if it was the barber's only, I should tell it to you.    I wish to find it all true, but not a little also that Mr. F[ox] has displeased some

[1] The examination on oath of the five physicians in attendance on the King took place by direction of Pitt on December 3rd, the day before the meeting of Parliament.    Fifty-four members were present.

of his friends ; for if he has, and that should not be
Lord Carlisle, I shall have the better opinion of him.
Lord C. has held out to me, in his last letter, the language of a man of sense, of honour, and of feeling, but
the misfortune is that all he says, from the sincerity of
his mind and heart, will be adapted [adopted ?] by those
who have not one of his qualities, and yet are compelled
to talk as he does, to serve their own purposes.

As to Mr. Fox, although I am at variance with him,
and am afraid shall for ever be so, for reasons which I do
not choose now to urge, although I am determined never
to be connected with him by the least obligation, I am
free to confess that I am naturally disposed to love him,
and to do justice to every ray of what is commendable
in him ; and I will go so far as to protest, that, if he acts
upon this occasion with a decent regard to the K[ing],
and his just prerogatives, I will endeavour to erase out of
my mind all that he has done contrary to his duty, and
" would mount myself the rostrum " in his favour.   To
gain his pardon from the people would be now unnecessary, that is, with some of them ; with the best of them,
I know it would be impossible.

Lord North's speech I shall be very impatient to read,
for hear, I fear, that I shall not ; I see little probability
of my going out for some time.   I wish that I had gone
from Matson to Castle H.; I might perhaps be there now,
and have escaped this martyrdom.   You say nothing of
your coming here, and will not, I daresay, come the
sooner, for my impatience to see you and the children.
I must live upon that unexpected pleasure ; but whom I
shall collect to eat my minced pies on William's birthday,
I do not as yet know.

The business of Parliament does not begin till Monday ;
till then, it will be nothing but hearsay, speculation, &c.,
&c.   Some tell me that the present Ministry is determined to try the number of those who will support
them, and are not afraid of being overrun with Rats ;
*nous verrons.*   Lord Stafford[1] was to have come to me

---

[1] The Lord Gower of the preceding correspondence.

yesterday, when the Council was up, but it was too late.

Between the following and the preceding letter events had moved rapidly in France. The National Assembly had been formed to be changed into the Constituent Assembly, the tricolour had sprung into existence, and the Bastille fallen. The Declaration of the Rights of Man had been promulgated. But Selwyn's information upon the state of France was not very accurate.

[1788, *Dec.* 5 ?]—Postscript. Good God, Lady C., what have I done? Mie Mie wrote a letter yesterday to her mother; I was to put it in the same envelope with my own. They were only to thank her for hers, which the Comte d'Elci ¹ brought me from her, enquiring after Mie Mie's health. To-day I find Mie Mie's letter on my table. I shall send it by the next post, but I am afraid that I put into my envelope a sheet which was intended for Lord Carlisle. Pray ask him if he had two sheets, or what he had. I am in hopes that, *par distraction*, it was only a sheet of blank paper. Yet that I did not intend neither ; she shall have no *carte blanche* from me. I am miserable about this. What makes me hope that it was not part of my rhapsody to Lord C. is, that generally my sheets to him are barbouilled on all the sides, and I know there was nothing of that. *Tirez-moi de mon incertitude, si vous le pouvez.*

Lord Stafford has just been with me. He says that he had a letter from Windsor this morning. The K. passed a quieter night, but I do not find out that he is less to-day what we are obliged to call him now. It is a new event, and a new language never heard before in the Court. Mᵉ de Maintenon would say, "Heavens! Do I live to call Louis 14 an object of pity?" You remember that pretended letter of hers, which was said to be dropped out of Mᵉ de Torcy's pocket at the Hague. [Do I live]

¹ Angelo, Comte d'Elci, born in Florence in 1764, an Italian philologist and archæologist. He died in 1824.

to speak of my master at last as a lunatic [?]—Burke walking at large, and he in a strait waistcoat! Charles wrote a letter to the Prince the day he came. He wrote it about noon, and at one the next morning he received his R.H. answer. I wish Craufurd would pick it out of his pocket to shew me.

There may be another adjournment, as I am told. Business can be suspended a little longer. If supplies are wanted much in some places, they can be postponed in others. So the Cardinal de Rohan[1] is then chosen President of the States,[2] is that the phrase? But he is chosen President *toujours* of the notables,[3] or something. This I had last night from the Marquis de Hautefort.[4] What this Marquis and Grand d'Espagne has to do out of France at this time I have as yet to learn. I see that I am to have the introduction of him everywhere. He thinks me a man *d'une grande existence dans ce pais*. He says that I am *lié avec M. Pitt;* he wants me to present

[1] Louis-René-Edouard, Prince de Rohan (1734–1803). In 1760, soon after taking orders, he was nominated coadjutor to his uncle, Constantin de Rohan, Archbishop of Strasburg and Bishop of Canopus; in 1761 elected member of the Academy; in 1772 ambassador to Vienna on the question of the dismemberment of Poland; in 1777 made Grand Almoner of France; in 1778 Abbot of St. Vaast and cardinal; in 1779 succeeded his uncle as Archbishop of Strasburg, and became Abbot of Noirmoutiers and La Chaise. He led a gay, luxurious, and extravagant life rather than performed his clerical duties; he had political ambitions, but he was never able to overcome the predisposition against him with which Marie Antoinette had come to France. He was a dupe of Cagliostro, and of Mme. de Lamotte-Valois, the adventuress who, in 1782, drew him into the intrigue of the diamond necklace, for which he was sent to the Bastille, and which gave him the name of *le cardinal Collier;* he was acquitted in 1786, and in 1789 elected to the States-General; in 1791 he refused to take the oath to the Constitution, and went to Ettenheim in the German part of his province, where he died on the 17th of February, 1803.

[2] The States-General did not open until May 5, 1789.

[3] The Convocation of the Notables took place the 19th of December, 1788.

[4] Armand Charles Emmanuel, Comte de Hautefort, was born in 1741; he bore the title of Grand d'Espagne through his marriage in 1761 with the Comtesse de Hochenfels de Bavère Grand d'Espagne de la première classe.

him to him. He fancies that the P[rince] has a *couvert* here whenever he pleases. It is my singular fate for ever to pass for something which I am not, nor cannot be, nor desire to be—sometimes indeed for what I should be ashamed to be. But I am used to this. *On se trompe, on se détrompe, et on se trompe encore.* I do not find, *au bout du compte*, that it signifies anything. With one's friends one must be known, *tôt ou tard*, to be exactly what we are.

Richmond of to-day, with its villas and streets, a town of houses occupied by professional and business men who spend their life in London, is unlike the gay and lively resort of the last days of the eighteenth century. Then the *élite* of the fashionable society of England gathered on the hill and by the river as people now do on the Riviera or in Cairo. " Richmond is in the first request this summer," so wrote Walpole in the very year at which we have now arrived. "Mrs. Bouverie is settled there with a large Court. The Sheridans are there too, and the Bunburys. I go once or twice a week to George Selwyn late in the evening when he comes in from walking ; about as often to Mrs. Ellis here and to Lady Cecilia at Hampton." Once in Richmond men and women stayed there walking, talking, and calling on each other, sometimes driving into London, but enjoying it as a residence, not as a mere resort for an evening's pleasure. Selwyn communicated the news of Richmond to his country friends as one does in these days when at some German Spa. It may seem to us, to whom so many opportunities of enjoyment of all kinds and in all parts of the world are open, a tame kind of life to spend days and nights strolling about a London suburb, attending assemblies, playing at cards, with now and then a visit to town or a row on the river. But our ancestors were necessarily limited in their pleasures, and to them Richmond was a God-send, especially to men like Selwyn, or Queensberry, or Walpole, who delighted in social intercourse, and liked to enjoy what they called rustic life

with as much comfort as the age provided. Something of
this life we have learned from Walpole's and Miss Berry's
letters, but no truer picture of it can be found than in the
last letters of Selwyn. To the ordinary *habitués* of Richmond, however, there were in 1789 and 1790 added a
throng of French ladies and gentlemen. Driven from
their agreeable salons in Paris, they endeavoured to make
the best of life among their English friends at Richmond.
Exiled among a people whose language few of them could
understand, they received little of the hospitality which
had been so freely extended to English visitors in Paris.
It was the last and a sad scene in that remarkable intercourse between the most cultivated people of England
and France which is one characteristic of the society of
both nations in the eighteenth century. This *entente* was
destroyed by the French Revolution. Selwyn, who had
figured in this international society more than most men of
the age, lived to tell of its last days in the letters which he
wrote during the two final years of his life.

[1789, *Aug.* 21 ?] *Friday night, Richmond.*—I did not
come hither till to-day, because I was resolved to stay to
see the Duke [1] set out, which he did this morning for
Newmarket, from whence he goes with his doctor to
York. He said that he should not go to Castle Howard,
which I looked upon as certain as that the Princes will be
there. It would have been in vain to have held out to
him the temptation of seeing his goddaughter, and I
know that, if I had suggested it, he would have laughed
at me, which would have made me angry, who think
Gertrude [2] an object worth going at least sixteen miles
to see.

He was in very good spirits when he left London, and
in extraordinary good humour with me. But he would
not have me depend, he said, upon his going to Scotland,
although he has sent as many servants in different

---

[1] Of Queensberry.
[2] Third daughter of the Earl of Carlisle, married W. Sloane Stanley,
Esq.

equipages as if he intended to stay there a twelvemonth. It was quite unnecessary to prepare me against any kind of irresolution of his. After all, I hope that he will go to Castle Howard. I believe it is just five and thirty years since we were there together, and all I know is, that I did not think then that I should ever see it so well furnished as I have since, and I will maintain that Gertrude is not the least pretty *meuble* that is there.

I was so unsettled while I was in London that I did not even send to make enquiries about your brother or Lady Southerland. I could not have made their party if I had been sure of their being in town. Sir R. and Lady Payne are at Lambeth. They propose coming to dine here in a few days.

I dined with Crowle and the younger Mr. Fawkner yesterday at the Duke's, and asked them many questions about poor Delmé's affairs, and concerning Lady Betty. I hear that Lady Julia has been much affected with this accident. He had persuaded himself that he should die, although either Dr. Warren saw no immediate danger, or thought proper not to say so. The French, as I said before, have good reason to say that *il n'est permis qu'aux médecins de mentir*, and Delmé certainly justified the deception, if there was any ; but he had at last more fortitude or resolution as I hear than was expected. I hope that Lady Betty will be reconciled to her change of life ; there must have been one inevitably, and, perhaps, that not less disagreeable.

I am unhappy that I have not yet received any account of Caroline. Mr. Woodhouse has returned my visit. I did not conceive it to be proper that Mie Mie should wait upon Mrs. Bacon till an opportunity had been offered of her being presented to her, but I shall be desirous of bringing about that acquaintance. Mrs. Webb is now with us, which is a piece of furniture here, not without its use, and which I am in a habit of seeing with more satisfaction than perhaps Mie Mie, who begins to think naturally a *gouvernante* to have a *mauvais air*. I am not quite of that opinion *dans les circonstances actuelles*.

No more news as yet from France.    I expect to have a great deal of discourse on Tuesday with St. Foy, on the subject of this Revolution, which occupies my mind very much, although I have still a great deal of information to acquire.    It may be *peu de chose*, but, as yet, I know no more than that the House of Bourbon, with the *noblesse françoise*, their revenues and privileges, are in a manner annihilated by a *coup de main*, as it were, and after an existence of near a thousand years ; and if you are now walking in the streets of Paris, ever so quietly, but suspected or marked as one who will not subscribe to this, you are immediately *accroché à la Lanterne : tout cela m'est inconcevable*.    But we are I am sure at the beginning only of this *Roman*, instead of seeing the new Constitution so quietly established by the first of September, as I have been confidently assured that it will be.

Preparations were certainly making here for her Majesty the Queen of France's [1] reception, and I am assured that if the King had not gone as he did to the Hôtel de Ville, the Duke of Orléans [2] would immediately have been de-

[1] Marie Antionette.
[2] Louis Philippe Joseph, Duc d'Orléans (1747–1793).    As the Duc de Chartres he pretended to the philosophical opinions of the eighteenth century, but followed the dissolute customs of the Regency. Marie Antoinette never attempted to overcome or conceal her aversion to him, which helped to divide the Court.    On the death of his father in 1785 he came into the title of the Duc d'Orléans.    Interpolating the King at the famous royal sitting of the 19th of November, 1787, which he attended as a member of the Assembly of Notables, he was exiled to Villers Cotterets ; in four months he returned and bought the good will of the journals by money and of the populace by buying up provisions and feeding them at public tables ; he was nominated President of the National Assembly but refused the post ; he attempted to corrupt the French guards, and so serious were the charges brought against him that La Fayette demanded of the King that he should be sent from the country.    He went accordingly to England on a fictitious mission in October of 1789.    He returned in eight months to be received with acclamation by the Jacobins, who were, however, themselves irritated at the coolness by which he voted for the death of his cousin, Louis XVI., in 1792 ; he was present at the execution, which he beheld unmoved, driving from the scene in a carriage drawn by six horses to spend the night in revelry at Raincy, but the title Egalité, which the Commune of Paris had authorised him

clared Regent. There seems some sort of fatality in the scheme of forming (*sic*) a Regent, who, in neither of the two kingdoms, is *destiné à ne pas arrive[r] à bon port.*

But one word more of Delmé. I am told that if Lady Betty and Lady J[ulia] live together, they will not have less than two thousand a year to maintain their establishment, including what the Court of Chancery will allow for the guardianship of the children. That will be more comfortable at least than living in the constant dread of the consequences of a heedless dissipation.

It was conjectured that Lord C[arlisle] would bring Mr. Greenville in for Morpeth, which, if it be so, I shall be very glad to hear. Crowle says that the cook is one of the best servants of the kind that can be, and would go to Lord C. if he wanted one, for sixty pounds a year, *par préférence* to any other place with larger wages. I was desired to mention this; it may be to no purpose.

The King, as I hear, is not expected to be at Windsor till Michaelmas. I received a letter to-day in such a hand as you never beheld, from Sir Sampson Gideon, now Sir S. Eardley, a name I never heard of before, to dine with him to-morrow at his house in Kent. I was to call at his house in Arlington Street, and there to be informed of the road, and to be three hours and a half in going it. It was to meet Mr. *Pitt*, and to eat a *turtle : quelle chère !* The turtle I should have liked, but how Mr. Pitt is to be dressed I cannot tell. The temptation is great, I grant it, but I have had so much self-denial as to send my excuses. You will not believe it, perhaps, but a Minister, of any description, although served up in his great shell of power, and all his green fat about him, is to me a dish by no means relishing, and I never knew but one in

to assume for himself and his descendants, did not save him from the same fate. The Convention ordered the arrest of all the members of the Bourbon family, and he was guillotined the 6th of November, 1793. The Duc de Chartres visited England in 1779 and was intimate with the Prince of Wales ; on his return he introduced in France the English race meetings, jockeys, and dress. It was said that the Prince of Wales, on hearing of his conduct at the execution of the King, tore into pieces his portrait which he had left him.

my life I could pass an hour with pleasantly, which was
Lord Holland. I am certain that if Lord C[arlisle] had
been what he seemed to have had once an ambition for, I
should not have endured him, although I might perhaps
have supported his measures.

You desired me to write to you often. You see, dear
Lady Carlisle, *toute l'inclination que j'y porte, et que,
vraisem[bla]blement, si vous souhaitez d'avoir de mes lettres,
une certaine provision de telles fadaises ne vous manquera pas.*
But I must hear myself from Caroline, or nothing will
satisfy me ; as yet I have not her direction, and so bad is
my memory now, that this morning I could not even be
sure if Stackpoole Court was near Milford Haven, Liver-
pool, or Milbourn Port. I do not comprehend how I
could confound these three places, or be so *dépaisé* in
regard to the geography of this island.

[1789, *Aug.*] 27, *Thursday noon, Richmond.*—I have
received yours this morning, and a very fine morning it
is, and made still more agreeable to me by your letter,
which I have seated myself under my great tree to thank
you for. I have no doubt but every one who passes by
will perceive, if they turn their eyes this way, that I am
occupied with something which pleases me extremely. It
is a great part of my delight, and of Mie Mie's too, that
we shall see you so soon. . . . It would have been a great
satisfaction to me to have been able to have accommodated
Miss Gunning, and to have had her company with us at
C[astle] H[oward]. . . . I have had a letter from Lady
Caroline.[1] I have directed my letters to her at Stackpole
Court, Milford Haven. . . .

I received at the same time with hers a letter from
Lord Carlisle, who, as he says, finds it necessary to
recommend Gregg, for the remainder of this Parliament,
to the borough of Morpeth. I should have been glad
that the return could have been of the same person,
whoever he may be, who is designed to represent it at the

[1] Lady Caroline Howard was married to John Campbell, afterwards first Lord Cawdor, on July 28, 1789,

ensuing and general election. To be sure it seldom happens *que l'on meurt* in all respects *fort à propos*, and this death of poor Mr. Delmé is, as much as it regards Lord Carlisle, an evident proof of it.

Sir R. Payne and Lady Payne and Sir C. Bunbury intend dining here to-morrow.

Mr. Saintefoy, with Storer, dined here yesterday, but informed me of nothing new concerning France. We talked the matter over very fully, and it was very satisfactory to me, what I learned from Mr. Saintefoy upon the Revolution and the causes of it ; and now I think the constitution of that country, as it has happened in others, will be quite new modelled, and that the new adopted plain, after a time, will be so much established as that there will be, probably, no return, if ever, for ages, of the old Constitution, unless produced by the chapter of accidents, to which all human things are liable.

I should have gone to town to-morrow to have taken leave of your brother, but this intended visit from Sir R. and Lady Payne will prevent me. I was not in the least aware that during the week of the York Races your Ladyship would be alone, and am therefore much vexed that Mie Mie and I are not at C[astle] H. at this moment. It was indeed what came into her head, and very properly ; but the idea of running foul upon his R[oyal] H[ighness] (to use a sea term) was what prevented me from taking the measures which I should otherwise have taken. Lord C[arlisle] will leave C[astle] H., as I understand by his letter, on Saturday sevennight. I hope then to be at C[astle] H. by the time that he goes.

I am glad, for George's sake, that Lord H[olland] [1]

---

[1] Henry Richard Vassall Fox, third Baron Holland (1773–1840). The nephew of Charles Fox. He was imbued by his uncle with liberal opinions, which he upheld throughout his life. On the death of Fox in 1807 he became Lord Privy Seal in the Grenville Ministry. In 1830 he was Chancellor of the Duchy of Lancaster in the Reform Cabinet of Lord Grey. It was he and his wife, whom he married in 1797, who gave to Holland House a world-wide celebrity as a gathering place of eminent people. In Selwyn's lifetime he was only a youth.

has been with you, but you could not be surprised to find, in one of that family, a disposition to loquacity. He is, I believe, a very good boy, and his tutor is, they say, a very sensible man ; but he has a most hideous name, and if *you* do not know how to spell it, *I*, for my part, can with difficulty pronounce it, the sound of it being so near something else.

[1789,] *September* 3, *Thursday, Richmond.*—I am vexed to find, by the letter which I have had the pleasure to receive to-day, that I am expected to be at C[astle] H[oward] on Saturday, when I do not set out till Sunday, so that, as I told Lord C. in my last, which he should receive to-day, I shall not be there till Wednesday. I am dilatory and procrastinating in my nature, but am not apt to defer what, when done, will make me so happy as I shall be at C[astle] H., and should not have been so now, if I had been more early apprised of your wish to have our journey accelerated.

I am very glad that H.R.H. was pleased with C[astle] H[oward]. I am sure, that if he had not been so, he would have been *difficile à contenter*. But yet, it is a doubt with me, if he and I are equally delighted with the same objects. It is not that I expect others to love and admire your children as I do. There is a great deal in the composition of that ; but he might if he pleased have pleasures of the same nature, but he seems to have set so little value upon resources of that kind, that I am afraid we shall never see any of H.R.H.'s progeny, and that this country must live upon what is called the quick stock for some years to come. I wish that it had happened that he had dined at Castle H. to-day, and have celebrated Caroline's birthday, which Mie Mie and I shall do here in a less sumptuous manner.

I was yesterday morning at Mrs. Bacon's door, nay further, for the servant said that she was at home, and I was carried into the parlour, but there it ended ; Mrs. B. was dressing, and I could not see her. I left word with the servant that I was going into the North, where in a little time I should see Mr. Campbell,[1] and to receive her commands relative to him was the object of my visit. I must now leave this place without having made any progress in her acquaintance, or in that of her niece. All this you will, I know, put to Caroline's account, and indeed you may, for the talk of her was the pleasure which I had promised myself by both these visits.

So Lord C., I find, sets out to-day for N[aworth], and would not go to Wentworth. I cannot wonder at his preference. That you went is compliment enough, in my opinion. I shall ask George, when I see him, if he had any hand in penning the Address to His R[oyal] H[ighness], or in the answer. I shall desire also to know of him, if I am to approve of it. All I know of the times is what I am informed of by the World, which perhaps, like other worlds, is full of lies. It is equal to me ; I am very little interested in it, at present ; nay, if I was Argus, who by taking that title would make us believe that he saw and knew more, I should be only more satiated, and see more of what I dislike.

The French politics, as they move me less, suit me better ; but of these I begin to be tired, and shall for my amusement revert to more ancient times. The history of the Bourbons is become thread-bare, and their lustre too is extinguished, as suddenly as that of a farthing candle. This Revolution is by no means unprecedented, but being transacted in our own times, and so near our own doors, strikes us the more forcibly.

To-morrow we shall go to town, and *that*, and the *next* day will be taken up in our preparatives. It was not so formerly ; an expedition was fitted out at a much less expense, and in a shorter time. But a journey of above five hundred miles strikes us at present as a great undertaking. But after we shall have left Barnet, I know much of this will vanish, and I shall think of nothing but of my *gite*, and of all whom I shall see in a few days after. I will bring down the maps which you mention, and other things, if I knew which would be most acceptable to

---

[1] Afterwards married to Lady Caroline.

them, but as they will never tell me, I can but con-
jecture.

You do not say anything of the D[uke] of Y[ork];
perhaps he was not well enough to be of all the parties.
We have *here*, for our pride, and amusement, the third
brother,[1] who drives about in his phaeton, with his
companion, bespeaks plays, and seems to have taken
Richmond under his immediate patronage. A report has
been spread here that Mrs. F[itzherbert] has obtained
leave to come and lodge at the next door. I hope that
*that* will not be the case, for her own sake, as well as ours.

I thank William for his letter, although he tells me
little more than that he is my affectionate W. Howard.
He may be assured that he has from me at least an equal
return. Of Gertrude he says nothing, and yet, I am
confident, the P[rince] did not overlook her. My hearty
love to them all, and to Lady Caroline if you write
to her.

I read yesterday a little Latin poem upon a Mouse
Trap, with which I was most highly delighted; wrote
near a century ago, by a Mr. Holdsworth. It has been
much celebrated, but never fell into my hands before
yesterday. There is a great *éloge* upon the Cambrians,
but whether Mr. Campbell would be flattered with it
I am not sure. If I did not suppose it to be no more
a curiosity than was the Blossom of the Chestnut Tree,
with which I was so struck the beginning of the summer,
I should bring it with me. There is a translation of
it in English verse, that is little short of the original.
Dear Lady Carlisle, adieu. I never know when to leave
off when I am writing to you, nor how to express the
affection and esteem with which I am ever yours.

[1789,] *Oct.* 22, *Thursday, Matson.*—We arrived here
yesterday at four in the afternoon from Crome.[2] We
left there a very fine day, which grew worse every hour,
and before we got to the garden gate it was as bad

---

[1] William, Duke of Clarence.
[2] Croome in Worcestershire Lord Coventry's family seat.

and uncomfortable as possible. Mr. Bligh would have said *unprofitable*, and perhaps with truth, for I see no advantage in having come here, and shall be very glad to find no ill consequences from it. We found to receive us, Dr. Warner, who had been here almost a week, and another gentleman who was come to dine with me, and both of them so hoarse that they could not be heard. I was by no means elated with finding myself where I am, and it was well that, upon getting out of my coach, I had the honour of your Ladyship's letter, which was some consolation to me. But I find by it, what I have a long while dreaded, that Car's going away would be attended with great uneasiness to you. . . . It is well that you can meet it with so much reason and fortitude. I have, I know, the smallest portion of either that any man ever had.

This day has cleared up. I am as yet very well, and shall be very careful of myself, and I propose, as I told you, to set out from hence on Sunday sevennight, the first of the next month, and stay with George two days at Salt Hill. I am sure that I should not have the pleasure I have in meeting him, if there were not some intervals when I cannot see him, and I am convinced, that a life must [be] chequered to have it really a *plaisant* one. I am glad that he and W[illia]m were amused while they stayed in town. I expect to hear from them some account of it.

The new Bishop is at Gloucester, as I am told, with his family ; *c'est une foible ressource*, but it is one ; they are represented to me as very agreeable people. Other company we shall have none, I take for granted, and that Mie Mie, finding herself so much alone, will be glad to return to Richmond. . . . I am most excessively concerned for poor Lord Waldgrave.[1]

[1789,] *Nov. 6, Friday m[orning], Richmond.*—Lord C. will receive a letter from me this morning which will

---

[1] George, fourth Earl of Waldegrave (1751–1789). He married his cousin, Lady Elizabeth Laura Waldegrave, daughter of James, second earl, in 1782.

be sufficient to assure you that George is well. He is so indeed, *à tous égards*. I stayed with him all Wednesday, and yesterday about noon I left him, so that in reality his course of erudition had but one day's interruption from me. Mr. Roberts is *au comble de sa joie, et de sa gloire*, having gained the prize for a better copy of verses upon the Deluge than that of any of his competitors. They are to be printed, so I shall see what I can at present have no idea of, and that is, how he will find matter from that event to furnish a hundred or two of blank verses. I should think that no one, but one like our friend John St. J[ohn], who uses Helicon as habitually as others do a cold bath, is equal to it. I only hope, for my part, that the argument will not be illustrated by any *débordement* of the Thames near this house ; at present there is no appearance of it.

I stayed at Matson, I will not say as long as it was good, but before it became very bad, which I believe it did before we had left the place two hours. The storm was brewing in the vale, but upon the hills we bade it defiance. I am very glad to be at a place where I can be stationary for a considerable time ; and it is what is very requisite for my present state of health, which requires attention and regularity of living. If these are observed, I am as[su]red that after a time I shall be well, and that my lease for ten or twenty years seems as yet a good one. As for the *labour and sorrow* which his Majesty K[ing] D[avid] speaks of, I know of no age that is quite exempt from them, and have no fear of their being more severe in my caducity than they were in the flower of my age, when I had not more things to please me than I have now, although they might vary in their kind. When I see you and Lord C. with your children about you, and all of you in perfect health and spirits, my sensations of pleasure are greater than in the most joyous hours of my youth. It is no solitude, this place. We have got Onslows and Jeffreyes's, Mr. Walpole, &c., &c., and if Mr. Cambridge would permit it, I could be sometimes, as I wish to be, alone.

On Monday Mie Mie and I shall go to town for one night. I am to meet Mᵉ de Boufiers ¹ at Lady Lucan's. I think that if this next winter does not make a perfect Frenchman of me, I shall give it up. I hope, more, that it will afford Mie Mie also an opportunity of improving herself in a language which will be of more use to her, in all probability, than it can ever hereafter be to me. I am not disgusted with the language by the abhorrence which I have at present of the country. But these calamities, at times, happen in all climes, as well as in France. Man is a most savage animal when uncontrolled.

The last accounts brought from France fill me with more horror than any former ones. The King is to be moved only by the fear of some approaching danger to his person. The Queen is agitated by all the alarming and distressing thoughts imaginable. Her health is visibly altered ; she cries continually, and is, as Polinitz says of K[ing] James's Queen, *une Aréthuse*. Her danger has been imminent ; and the K[ing] left his capital, and her in it, as he was advised to do, *il eût été fait d'elle ;* she would have been, probably, dragged to the Hôtel de Ville, *et auroit fini ses jours en Grève.* She holds out her children, which are called *les enfans de la Reine exclusivement*, as beggars in the streets do theirs, to move compassion. "Behold, how low they have reduced a" Queen ! But as yet she is not ripe for tragedy, so John St. John may employ his muse upon other subjects for a time. To speak the truth, all these representations of the miseries of the French nation do not seem to me (very decent) proper subjects for our evening spectacles,

¹ Marie Charlotte Hippolyte de Saujon, Comtesse de Boufflers-Rouvel (1724–1800). One of those remarkable women who in Paris at the end of the eighteenth century united a love of intellect and literature with a pleasure in society. After being left a widow in 1764, she lived with the Prince de Conti. She was a friend of Hume and Rousseau, the rival of Mme. du Deffand. Her salon in the Temple was a meeting-place for a singular variety of persons, among whom she was known as Minerva the Wise. Her daughter-in-law, the Comtesse Emilie de Boufflers, was guillotined in 1794. She herself was imprisoned, but was released after the death of Robespierre.

and it is not, in my apprehension, quite decent that Mr. Hughes, Mr. Astley, or Mr. St. John should be making a profit by Iron Masques, and Toupets stuck upon Poles.

The D[uke] of Orléans's embassy here is universally considered as one devised for his own personal safety, and he is equally respected here and abroad. The subject of his credentials and object of negotiation had no more in them than to say that his most Xtian Majesty desired to know how his brother the K[ing] of England did. The answer to which was, very well, with thanks for his obliging enquiries. The King speaks to the D[uke] of O[rléans] civilly, *mais il en demeure là.* His behaviour to the Duc de Luxembourg [1] and to other Frenchmen of quality was more distinguished. He talked yesterday to M. de Luxembourg for an hour and 17 minutes. You know how exact we courtiers are upon these points.

Charles Fox was at Court, but was scarcely spoke to. *Il n'en fut pour cela plus rebuté.* He stayed in the apartments till five in the afternoon. Others of the Opposition were there. Lord North came to Court with his son-in-law, Mr. D.[2] *I* must wait for a future opportunity of paying my court. The Duke has finished his, I believe, for the present. I expected to have found him here or in London. He went again into Scotland last Friday, and will not be returned in a month, and this *sans qu'il m'en ait averti. Il faut avouer que notre Duc, à l'égard de tous les petits devoirs de la vie, est fort à son aise.* M^e de Cambis is also come ; *il en fourmille,* but all of them almost beggars ; some few, I hear, have letters of credit. Poor M^e de Boufflers, as Lady Lucan writes me word, is *dans un état pitoyable.* But for the French, *brisons là pour le présent.*

[1789, *Nov.* ?] 19, *Thursday night, Richmond.*—I left London to come here to-day to dinner, as I have told you that I should, but I did not come away till I had seen

---

[1] The Duc de Luxembourg and his family escaped with difficulty to England, 300,000 livres being set on his head. He arrived in London July 19, 1789.　　　　[2] Sylvester Douglas, Lord Glenbervie.

Miss Gunning,[1] who told me that she should write to your Ladyship either to-day or to-morrow. I found her *gaie*, *fraiche, contente*, and writing a letter, and when I began by saying, "So you persist then in leaving this very pretty room," she smiled. I think that she is perfectly satisfied with the option she has made, and I really think that she has reason to be so, *toutes choses bien considérées*. If I had been a woman, and could not have been my own mistress, I should have preferred subjection to a husband, whom I approved of, to a Queen (*sic*). We talked a great deal of the *ménage*, and I am to take my chair and have my *couvert* there when I please; and it is [a] stipulation that not a *petit pôt* is to be added on my account. She is to be married, I find, at the beginning of the new year, and she is to have immediately four children, three boys and one girl. I should on her account have liked it as well if she had begun *sur nouveaux frais*; but, it not being so, I think that the three boys and one girl is a better circumstance than if there had been more girls. He is really, as far as I can judge of him, a very worthy man, and I believe will make her a very good husband, and I have no doubt but that she will receive from his family as much regard and attention as any other woman would have had.

When I left St. James's, I went in search of M⁰ de Boufflers, and found her at Grenier's Hôtel, which looks to me more like an hospital than anything else. Such rooms, such a crowd of miserable wretches, escaped from plunder and massacre, and M⁰ de Boufflers among them with I do not know how many beggars in her suite, her *belle fille* (*qui n'est pas belle, par parenthèse*), the Comtesse Emilie, a maid with the little child in her arms, a boy, her grandson, called *Le Chevalier de Cinque minutes*, I cannot explain to you why; a pretty fair child, just inoculated who does not as yet know so much French as I do, but understood me, and was much pleased with my caresses. It was really altogether a piteous sight. When I saw her last, she was in a handsome *hôtel dans le quartier du Temple*

---

[1] Miss Gunning was married to the Hon. Stephen Digby on Jan. 6, 1790, see *ante* p. 235.

—a splendid supper—Pharaon ; I was placed between Monsr. Fayette and his wife. This Fayette [1] is her nephew, and has been the chief instrument of her misfortunes, and I hope, *par la suite*, of his own. I said *tout ce qui m'est venu en tête de plus consolant.*

I would, if I had had time, have gone from her to M$^e$ la Duchesse de Biron, but I went to Lady Lucan, with whom I have tried to *ménager* some *petit-petits soupers* for these poor distressed people. That must be, when Lord Lucan returns from Lord Spencer's, after the X'ning.

The Duke of Orléans, they tell me, goes all over the city to borrow immense sums, offering as a security his whole revenue. He cannot get a guinea, or deserves one. He is universally despised and detested. M$^e$ Buffon is said *de lui avoir fait le plus grand sacrifice, sans doute, le sacrifice de sa réputation et de son état. Que peut-on demander davantage ?*

There are parties among them, I find ; la Duchesse de Biron and M$^e$ de Cambis for the Etats Généraux ; M$^e$ de Boufflers [and] M. de Calonne [2] *pour le parti du Roi.* It was right to apprise me of all this, or I should, with my civilities, have made a thousand *qui pro quo's ;* but had I

---

[1] The Marquis de La Fayette (1757–1834). Assisted the Americans in the War of Independence. While in America he sent a challenge to Lord Carlisle, who refused to fight. He went home to aid the revolutionists in his own country. In 1789 he placed before the National Assembly a Declaration of Rights based on Jefferson's Declaration of Independence. It was he who introduced the tricolor. The Revolution assuming a character beyond constitutional control, he left Paris in 1790 for his estate until called to the head of the Army of Ardennes. After gaining the three first victories of the war, finding he could not persuade his soldiers to march to Paris to save the Constitution, he went to Liège, where he was seized by the Austrians. He was again active in the Revolution of 1830. He was greatly admired and beloved in America. In 1824, when in America by invitation of Congress, he was voted 200,000 dollars in money and a township of land.

[2] Charles Alexandre de Calonne (1734–1802) ; statesman, financier, and pamphleteer. On the 3rd of November, 1783, he was made Controller-General, but lost the post in 1787. "A man of incredible facility, facile action, facile elocution, facile thought. . . . in her Majesty's soirées, with the weight of a world lying on him, he is the delight of men and women " (Carlyle, " French Revolution," book iii. ch. ii.).

known that Lady Derby was in town, I should have gone to her, undoubtedly, *par préférence*, as I shall do, the very next time I go to London.   I am desired to dine there on Sunday with Lord Brudnell, but really the going, though but nine miles, *par des chemins si bourbeux*, and changing my room and bed at this time, is not to my mind.   I shall keep here quietly as much as I can, till I know of your being come to town, but when will that be?

If Lord Jersey [1] cannot keep himself steady neither on his legs or his horse, you may be confined at C[astle] H[oward] the whole winter, which is better than to be at Gainthrop with me, and Hodgsson, that is certain.   I did not hear but of one of his falls till yesterday, at Lord Ashburnham's.[2]   My respects to them both, I beg. Mie Mie sends hers to your Ladyship, with a thousand kind compliments besides.   Caroline will receive both from her and me a letter on her arrival at Stackpole Court, and I shall now make no scruple to write to her often, since I find, what I wished, that it is paying my court to Mr. C[ampbell] expressing my affection to her.

Poor William's watch I found in a sad condition.   I brought it to town, as he desired, and have lodged it safely with my watch-maker, against his coming home. Miss Digby, the Dean's [3] daughter, it is supposed, will be the new Maid of Honour.   Hotham has poor Lord Waldegrave's Regiment ; the chariot is not yet disposed of ; I will bet my money on Lord Winchelsea.

I wish that I could find out, if there were any thoughts of your brother's going Ambassador to France.   I have as yet no authority for it, but the papers.

The K[ing] was at the play last night, for the first time.   The acclamations, as I am told, were prodigious. Tears of joy were shed in abundance.   *Nous savons ce que c'est que la populace, et combien peu il en coute à leurs caprices, ou de pleurer, ou de massacrer, selon l'occasion.*

---

[1] George Bussey, fourth Earl of Jersey (1735–1805).
[2] John, second Earl of Ashburnham (1724–1812).
[3] William Digby, Dean of Clonfert (1766–1812).

We are at peace at home, I thank God, *pour le moment.*
I hope that it will continue, and that no Lord Stanhope,
or a Dr. Priestly, will think a change of Government
would make us happier.  John is now at the ackma [acme]
of Theatrical reputation, and we shall see his name on
every rubrick post, I suppose, of all the Booksellers
between St. James's and the Temple, with that of Con-
greve, Otway, &c., &c.

[1789, *Nov.* 21 ?] *Saturday night, Richmond.*—I finished
my short note of to-day with saying that I intended to
have wrote to you a longer letter, but I sent you all
which I had time to write before the post went out.  It
is, I think, a curious anecdote, and I know it to be a true
one ; I was surprised to find that the Duke had heard
nothing of it, but I suppose that his Highness the
D[uke] of O[rléans] does not find it a very pleasant
subject to discuss, and if the allegation be true, no one in
history can make a more horrid, and at the same time, a
more contemptible figure, for I must give him credit for
all which *might* have been, as well as for what was certainly
the consequence of his enterprise.  I hope that, for the
future, both he and his friend here will (to use Cardinal
Wolsey's expression) " fling away ambition.  By that sin
fell the angels.  How can man then hope to win by it ? "
And of all men, the least, *a Regent.*  If I had not been
interrupted by the Duke's coming soon after I received
the paper, I should have myself wrote a copy of it for
Caroline, because I must not have a Welch Lady left out
of the secret of affairs. . . .

The Duke[1] looks surprisingly well.  He came from
London on purpose to see us, and intended, I believe, to
have stayed, at least to dinner, but H[is] R[oyal] H[igh-
ness] interfered, as he often does with my pleasures ; so
the Duke dined at Carlton House—I do not say in such
an humble, comfortable society, as with us, but what he
likes better, *avec des princes, qui sont Princes, sans contredit,*

[1] Queensberry.

*mais rien audessus.  All in good time*, as M^c Piozzi [1] says frequently in her book, but what she means by it the Devil knows, nor do I care.  I only say, that her book, with all its absurdities, has amused me more than many others have done which have a much better reputation.

I heard the D. say nothing of his affairs in Scotland, of those in France, or indeed hardly of anything else, and I, for my part, am afraid of broaching any subject whatever, because upon all there is some string that jars, and to preserve a perfect unison, I think it best to wait than to seek occasions of offering my poor sentiments.  He is going again to Newmarket, to survey his works there I suppose, so that he holds out to us but an uncertain prospect of seeing him much here.  *Je l'attens à la remise*, as M^c de Sévigné says, and there, after the multiplicity of his rounds and courses, I might expect to see him, if the number of princes, foreign and domestic, were not so great.  *Dieu merci, je n'ai pas cette Princimanie*, but can find comfort in a much inferior region.

At Bushy are Mr. Williams, Mr. Storer, and Sir G. Cooper, and in their rides they call upon me, but besides the Harridans of this neighbourhood, the Greenwich's, the Langdales, &c., I have in the Onslows and Darrels an inexhaustible fund of small talk, and, what is best of all, I have made an intimacy, which will last at least for some months, with my own fireside, to which, perhaps, in the course of the next winter I may admit that very popular man, Mr. Thomas Jones, of whom I shall like, when I know him better, to talk with your Ladyship.

I am now going to share with Mrs. Webb a new entertainment, for I am made to expect a great deal from it. It is Dr. White's Bampton Lectures, which they say contain the most agreeable account imaginable of *our* Religion compared with *that* of Mahomet.  Mrs. W. reads them

---

[1] Mme. Piozzi, formerly Mrs. Thrale (1741–1821).  The reference is to " Her Observations and Reflections made in a Journey through France, Italy, and Germany," which was brought out in 1789.  She is best known as the friend of Dr. Johnson.

to go to Heaven, and I to go into companies where, when the conversation upon French Politics is at a stand, it engrosses the chief of what we have to say. I have a design upon Botany Bay and Cibber's Apology for his own life, which everybody has read, and which I should have read myself forty years ago, if I had not preferred the reading of men so much to that of books.

I expect you in London on Wednesday sevennight, and there and in Grosvenor Place will you find me, *en descéndant de votre carrosse.* I shall *then* begin to renew my attentions to the Boufflers, Birons, &c., and so prepare my thoughts and language for the ensuing winter ; but I shall not remove the household from hence till after Christmas. Till then, if you allow me only to pass two or three days in a week with you, I shall be, for the present, contented.

I am glad that this last mail from France brought nothing so horrible as what I was made to expect. Yet I am not at all at ease, in respect to that poor unfortunate family at the Louvre, which, I protest, I think not much more so than that of Calas.[1] Of all those whom I wish to have hanged, I will be so free as to own that I am more disposed in favour of the M. de la Fayette than of any other, because in him I do not see, what is almost universal in those who have pretensions to patriotism, an exclusive consideration of their own benefit, and meaning, at the bottom, no earthly good to any but to themselves and their own dependants. *M. Fayette est entreprenant, hardi, avec un certain point d'honneur, et avec cela, plus conséquent que le reste des Reformateurs, qui, après tout, est un engeance si détestable à mon avis, qu'un pais ne peut avoir un plus grand fléeau.* How often will that poor country regret the splendour of a Court, and that *Lit de Justice, sur lequel le Roi et ses sujets avoient coutume de dormir si tranquillement !* But when I think of ambition, it is not that of all kinds that I condemn. . . .

---

[1] Jean Calas (1698–1762), whose unhappy story was the subject or tragedies brought out in Paris in 1790 and 1791.

[1790 ?] *July* [*Aug* ?] 7, *Saturday, Isleworth.*—I hope
that this letter will reach you before you set out for
Cumberland, because I am impatient to tell you that the
*Perfection of Nature* is at this instant the Perfection of
Health. I came over here in my boat to write my letter
from a place where I am sure that your thoughts carry
you very often, and to make my letter from that local
circumstance more welcome to you. I brought over with
me two, almost the last, roses now in bloom, which I
could find in the Duke's garden ; one of them would
have been for you if you had been here, because I know
the complexion in roses which you prefer ; so I have
desired Lady Caroline to smell to it *sympathiquement.* I
found upon my table at Richm[on]d, when I came down,
as I expected, Lady Sutherland's letter *envelop[p]ée à la
françoise,* and in my next I will transcribe so many
extracts, as it shall be the same as if I sent you the letter ;
but I am not sure that sending the original itself would
not be illicit without a particular permission from her
Excellency. I am much obliged to her for it, and shall
do my best to obtain more, although France is a country
now which, if I could, I would obliterate from my mind.

Had this Revolution happened two thousand years ago,
I might have been amused with an account of it, wrote
by some good historian, or if it had happened but a few
years hence, I should not [have] felt about it as I do ; as
it is, the event is too near for me not to feel as I do. I
do not like to be obliged to renounce my esteem for any
individual, much less to think ill of such numbers. The
oppression suffered under the former Government, or
[and] the desire of giving to mankind the rights which
by nature they seem intituled to, are with me no excuse,
when a people sets out, in reforming, with acting in
direct opposition to all the principles which before they
thought respectable, and really were so, and, to become a
free people, commence by being freebooters. However,
as this savours too much of party zeal, I will have done
with it ; yet it is not relative to this country, which I
hope will be free from these calamities and abominations,

and so I need not fear expatiating sometimes upon the subject.

M<sup>e</sup> de Boufflers, *la Reine des Aristocrates réfugiés en Angleterre*, was to see us yesterday in the evening, and to invite Mie Mie and me to come sometimes to hear her daughter-in-law play upon the harp. I did not expect *melody in their heaviness*, but I shall certainly go, as the recitative part will be in French, and that you know is always some amusement to me.

The Duke, I hear, will be in London to-night, and so may come to Richmond to dine with us to-morrow. If he does, I shall be a little embarrassed between my two Dukes, for the Duke of Newcastle ¹ expects me to dine and to lie at his house at Wimbledon. If I can reconcile two such jarring attachments, I will ; if not, I believe I shall prefer my neighbour, as loving him very near as much as myself. Well, Mr. C[ampbell] and Lady C[aroline] are going out in their phaeton, so I shall now have done. . . .

[1790, *Aug.? (or Oct.?)*] *Saturday, Isleworth.—*. . . Mr. C[ampbell] called upon me yesterday. He came to see my two pictures, which I had cleaned by Comyns, and are very pretty, as Mr. C. allows, but he will not assent to Comyns's opinion that they are Cuyp's, although much in his style. Comyns values them at what they cost me, which was 50 gs. or thereabouts. Mie Mie has them in her dressing-room, and is vastly pleased with them. We all dine to-day at the Castle.² M<sup>e</sup> la Comtesse Balbi ³ chooses to give a dinner *there* to all her

¹ Thomas, third Duke of Newcastle (1752–1795).
² The Castle Inn in Hill Street, Richmond. It was for many years a fashionable resort as well as a noted posting house. Mrs. Forty, the wife of a subsequent proprietor, was the subject of Sheridan's toast at the Prince Regent's table—" Fair, Fat, and Forty."
³ Mme. la Comtesse de Balbi (1753–1832), celebrated for her connection with the Comte de Provençe, afterward Louis XVIII. At the epoch of the Revolution she retired to Coblentz with Monsieur. Leaving him she came to England, where she remained until the First

friends, the Mesdames Boufflers, the Comte de Boisgelin,[1]
M. d'Haveri (?), &c. The Duke, Mie Mie, and I are
invited, and the Duke intends to bring Mr. Grieve with
him, and as a Member *de la Chambre Basse* he will pass
muster, but he is most wretched at the lingo. They will
assemble in the evening at the Duke's, where I suppose
that there will be tweedle dum, and tweedle dee, for the
whole evening, till supper. George will not, after this,
call our house a hermitage ; if it is, it is a reform of a
merry Order, in which neither St. Francis or St. Bruno
have any share.

Lady Graham[2] has got her *Duché* very soon. A
report was spread here yesterday that Prince Augustus[3]
was dead, but it is contradicted in the papers of to-day.
Mr. C[ampbell] is gone to town, but he and Mr. Grevil
return to dinner.

I hope that Frederick liked my letter, and that in my
letter to Gertrude there was some bad French for her to
correct, and then I shall hear from her again. I hope
that William will be indulged in staying here a day or
two with his sister, and that George will not fly away on
his Pegasus to Oxford the instant he comes, although I
know that the Muses are impatient to see him, and will
set their caps at him the moment he comes. I hope that
you approve of my choice of what the colour of his gown
is to be. I think a light blue *celeste*, which Lord Stafford
had, would be detestable, and scarlet is too glaring. No ;
it must be a good deep green. I want to know the name
of his tutor. I hope that he will have a very good
collection of books in his own room, a sufficient allowance,
and a hamper of claret, *en cas de besoin*. I think, if there

Consul permitted the *émigrés* to return to their homes, but she was
soon discovered to be engaged in royalist intrigues and exiled ; her
endeavours to obtain the royal favour at the Restoration were vain.

[1] Louis de Boisgelin de Kerdu, Chevalier of Malta (1750–1816),
historian ; brother of the Cardinal.

[2] Caroline, daughter of the fourth Duke of Manchester, married,
in July, 1790, the Marquess of Graham, who succeeded his father as
third Duke of Montrose in September of that year.

[3] Augustus, Duke of Sussex, died 1843.

are to be no hounds or horses, we may compound for all the rest.    But these I believe the Dean will never suffer to be matriculated. . . .

I have some thought of going to pass a day in town, when Warner comes, and if I do I will certainly go there by Fulham, to see the Dean.    I have not heard one syllable about him a great while.    You know, perhaps, that Pyrome (?) is discharged, and *relégué à ses terres*. He [has] a *méchante langue*, and to keep himself in place he should cut it out.

[1790,] *Aug.* 12, *Thursday m[orning]*, 8 *o'clock, Richmond.*—I sit down now to write you with some satisfaction, because that I shall have to tell you, towards the end of my letter, that Caroline is perfectly well, but you must have patience ; I have not seen her to-day ; I shall finish my letter at Isleworth.    At present, I only know that about 12 o'clock last night she eat plumb cake and drank wine and water in my parlour—she, Mr. Campbell, and Mie Mie, and who besides I have not yet asked.    I was in bed when she came ; it was an *heure perduë*, but not lost upon me, for I was not asleep, nor could sleep till I heard that those two girls were come home safe.

From what, in the name of God ? you will say.    From seeing that *étourdi* Lord Barrymore [1] play the fool in three or four different characters upon our Richmond Theatre. Well, but what did that signify ?    Nothing to me ; let

[1] Richard Barry, seventh Earl of Barrymore (1769–1793).    Lord Barrymore was brilliant, eccentric, and dissipated, and in his short life he managed to spend £300,000 and encumber his estates.    He gambled, owned racehorses and rode them, played cricket, and hunted. He had a strong taste for the stage.    At Wargrave-on-Thames he had a private theatre adjoining his house, and liked to make up companies with a mixture of amateurs and professionals.    He is the prototype of many modern and aristocratic spendthrifts.    He was killed by an accident when he seemed about to be giving up his wild career for a more useful life.    He accepted a commission in the Berkshire Militia and threw himself into his work with characteristic zest.    When escorting some French prisoners near Dover, the gun which was in his carriage accidentally exploded and wounded him fatally.    (See " The Last Earls of Barrymore," by J. R. Robinson, London, 1894.)

him expose himself on as many stages as he pleases, and wherever the phaeton can transport him, but he comes here, and assembles as many people ten miles around as can squeeze into the Booth. I had every fear that Mrs. Webb's nerves or mine could suggest : heat in the first place ; I considered Car's situation ; an alarm, what difficulty there might be of egress ; but we provided, Mr. Campbell and I, against everything. Mrs. Vanheck, who has a most beautiful place at Roehampton, came and carried Mie Mie into her box. Places were separated in the pit ; at first Lady C[aroline] was to have been there with Mrs. Woodhouse, &c. ; but, I say, the egress was the point I wished for, and looked to. I got two places, by much interest and eloquence, in the hind row of the front box. A door opened into the lobby, and from the lobby you go directly into the street. So I shall hear, I suppose, to-day that all went *au mieux*.

I did not expect them to be clear of the House till near 12, so went into my room, and soon after to bed, but I slept well. For I had heard of them. They were all, I tell you, before 12 in my parlour, eating cake and chattering, and talking the whole farce over, *comme à la grille du couvent*. I can at present tell you no more, but I was impatient to begin my letter *à cette heure ; j'ai en quelque façon satisfait à mon envie*. I shall embark at eleven for Isleworth, and hope with a fair wind to land at Campbell-ford stairs in ten minutes after. From thence I will finish my letter. I shall there have the whole *en détail*. The Prince and the Duke of Q. were expected, but I heard from my servants nothing of them.

*Il fait un bien beau tems ; c'est quelque chose.* It has come late, and to make us only a short visit I suppose, and to tell us that we shall have a better autumn than we have had a summer ; no courtier cajoles one like a fine day. Yesterday was a fine day also, and I *completed*, as they call it, my seventy-first year. I dined at your sister's [1] ; Mr. Campbell and Car and Mie Mie were to

---

[1] Lady Louisa Leveson-Gower, married to Sir Archibald Macdonald in 1777. She died 1827.

have been of the party ; they had an apology to make, I had none.   71 is not an age to *Barrymoriser*.   There were only Mr. Woodcock and his wife.   I met on my return their Majesties, *que j'ai salués ;* and so ended my day.

[1790, *Aug.* 12,] *one o'clock, Richmond.*—I have been at Isleworth.   I found Car very well, and at her painting, with the Italico Anglico artiste of Mr. Campbell's, and Mr. Lewis.   Mr. C[ampbell] was gone to London. They were asked to dine to-day at Fulham Field, that is, I think, the name of the Attorney Gen[era]l's [1] place. I am not sure if she told me that they intended to go. Lord Barrymore danced the *pas Russe* with Delpini, and then performed Scaramouche in the *petite pièce*.   I asked how he danced ; Mr. Lewis said very ill.   How did he perform the other part ? execrably bad.   " Do you think," I said, "that he would have known how to snuff the candles ? "   " I rather think not," says Mr. Lewis.   Mie Mie is more satisfied with his talents ; she thought him an excellent *Escaramouche ; ce seroit quelque chose au moins.* But I am more disposed to think that Mr. Lewis is in the right, and I hope, for the young nobleman's own sake, that *toutes les fois qu'il s'avise de se donner en spectacle, et faire de pareilles folies, il aura manqué à sa vocation. Sa mère ne jouoit pas un beau rôle, mais elle y a mieux réussi.*

But enough at present of this.   No harm of any sort has come from it, but Mie Mie tells me that Mr. Campbell's anxiety the whole time was excessive.   After all, she was not in the places which I had provided for the greater security, but went into those which were originally intended for her.   The Prince was there, but not the Duke of York, or my friend the Duke of Q.

Now *à d'autres choses.*   I have in my last fright forgot one where there were better grounds for it.   The day I wrote to you last, as you know, I was at Isleworth. Coming from thence, and when I landed, the first thing

---

[1] Sir Archibald Macdonald, afterward Chief Baron of the Exchequer.

I heard was that people with guns were in pursuit of a mad dog, that he had run into the Duke's garden. Mie Mie came the first naturally into my thoughts ; she is there sometimes by herself reading. My impatience to get home, and uneasiness till I found that she was safe and in her room, *n'est pas à concevoir*. The dog bit several other dogs, a bluecoat boy, and two children, before he was destroyed. John St. John, who dined with me, had met him in a narrow lane, near Mrs. Boverie's, him and his pursuers. John had for his defence a stick, with a heavy handle. He struck him with this, and for the moment got clear of him ; *il l'a culbuté*. It is really dreadful ; for ten days to come we shall be in a terror, not knowing what dogs may have been bitten. Some now may have *le cerveau qui commence à se troubler*.

John [1] has a legacy from Lord Guilford [2] of £200 a year, the General [3] one of a thousand pounds ; Mr. Keene has a hundred. He has left in legacies about £16,000, as Mr. Williams tells me, but not much ready money besides. His estate was about 12 or 3,000 per annum. It is to be a Peer, I hear, who shall succeed him.

I will write no more to-day. I will send you the extract from Lady S[utherland's] [4] letter in my next. The President has told me this morning that Mr. Neckar [5] *à failli d'être pendu. Il voulut tirer son épingle du jeu ; il fut sur le point de partir ; on ne pousse pas la Liberté à ce point en France ; il n'avoit pas demandé permission à la Populace ; ainsi, sans autre forme de procès, on voulut le conduire du Contrôle à la Lanterne.* I am glad to hear that the brats are well. You set off, I understand, on Tuesday ; so this will find you in your *Château antique*

---

[1] John St. John.

[2] Francis North, Earl of Guildford (1704–1790), father of the statesman.

[3] Henry St. John.

[4] Wife of William, seventeenth and last Earl of Sutherland.

[5] Jacques Necker (1732–1804), the famous financier. He married Mdlle. Curchod, Gibbon's one attachment. Their only child became the celebrated Mme. de Staël. In 1790 he finally was forced to retire from office as Director-General of Finance.

*et romanesque. J'en respecte même les murailles; tout y a un air si respectable.*

I will write to my Lord in a few days, and when I hope to have seen the Dean, but from what his neighbour Mr. Woodcock told me yesterday, I shall have nothing very comfortable to tell him *touchant la santé de son bon précepteur, ni sur la mienne; elle exige un ménagement et une régime que je n'ai pas encore observée avec la rigueur nécessaire.*

Now I expect a troupe of French people whom I met in a boat, as I came this morning from Isleworth—le M. de Choiseul, M^e de Choiseul, &c. I have engaged myself to go with them to Mr. Ellis's, because it belonged to Mr. Pope. I said I must go home to finish *mes dépêches*, but I expect them every minute. *Je sers d'entreprète entre le M. de Choiseul et M^e sa femme.*

My love to George. I hope that *le Château de ses ancêtres a pour lui des charmes.* I read a great deal of the Howards in Pennant's[1] book. It is the only part that gives me pleasure; such an absurd superficial pretender to learning I never met with, and after all of what learning! Then he tries to copy Mr. Walpole's style in his Book of Antient Authors; *le tout est pitoyable.* Adieu, dear Lady Carlisle; *si vous pouvez supporter tout ce bavardage, c'est parceque vous aimez votre fille, qui en est en partie la cause.*

[1790,] *Aug.* 22, *Sunday, Richmond.*— . . . I have nothing [more] to tell you of Caroline, than that we saw her yesterday in the afternoon, *en passant*, that is, in her boat, which was full of the company she had had at dinner, and which, as Mie Mie told me, were the Greggs, but *ayant la vuë courte*, I could not distinguish, myself, who they were.

---

[1] Thomas Pennant (1726–1798), the naturalist and traveller, author of several "Tours" in the British Isles which have become classics. His energy in travelling and scientific spirit and capacity of observation made him too modern for Selwyn and his friends: Walpole said that Pennant picked up his knowledge as he rode.

My garden was as full as it could hold of foreigners
and their children—Warenzow's boy and girl, and the
Marquis de Cinque minutes, who, of all the infants I ever
saw, is the most completely spoiled for the present.  His
roars and screams, if he has not everything which he
wants, and in an instant, are enough to split your head.
His menace is, " *Maman, je veux être bien méchant ce soir,
je vous le promets.*"

The Duke was in the best humour the whole day I ever
saw him, who you know has been at times as *gâté* as the
other.  He said that my dinner was perfect, and so it was
*dans son genre*.  The ladies were much pleased with their
reception, and the Duke took such a fancy to them, and
to the place, that he believes that he shall be more here
than anywhere, and he went to town intending to send
down all preparatives for residence.  M⁰ de Bouflers
told me *que je m'étois menagé une très jolie rétraite*, and
indeed at this time it is particularly comfortable to me,
and the circumstance of Caroline having a house so near
is not by any means the least of its *agrémens*. . . .

*Monday.*—Yesterday was a fine day, but neither news
or event ; on the Thames *une bourgeoisie assez nombreuse*,
and in the Gardens.  I saw our friends at Isleworth in the
morning, before they went out in their phaeton.  They were
going to Lord Guilford's, and to-day dine at Mr. Ellis's.  I
believe that Madame de Roncherolles dines at Mr. Walpole's, for she has sent to me to carry her.  I do not dine
there myself, but shall go to fix with Mr. Walpole a day
for Caroline and Mr. C[ampbell] to see Strawberry Hall.
Her journey to Lady Egremont's is put off for a week.
To-morrow I go to Fulham, and from thence to London,
from whence I return on Wednesday.  Mie Mie and I
dine at Isleworth when I return.  Mr. Grevil is to be with
them this week.

Bunbury is returned from Portsmouth ; his news to me
were, that the emigration from France thither increases
every day, and that in the provinces, as these people say,
who are come last from France, the revolt increases, and
a desire for the old Constitution.  In Britany and Nor-

mandy the party is very formidable.　M. de Pontcarré,
President of the *Parlement de Rouen*, is in London ; so
there is another President for me, if I choose it.　The
young French people and their wives dined yesterday, as
they usually do, at the Castle. . . .

[1790, *Aug.* 23 ?] *Monday night,* 11 *o'clock, Richmond.*
—I wrote to you this morning, reserving to myself the
liberty of lengthening my letter, after I shall have seen
Caroline for the last time before her return from Cliveden,
where it was her intention to go to-morrow for a week or
ten days, *c'est selon*; but I must begin this appendix to-
night, late as it is.　I am still waiting till these French
Ladies come with Mie Mie from the play.　It is Mr.
Parson's benefit, and was expected to be very full.　The
evening is cold, that is something, but I must see Mie Mie
before she goes to bed.

We were to-day at dinner ten, besides the Duke ;
Madame de Boufflers, the Duke and Duchess of Devonshire, M. de Calonne, The Fish, Thomas,[1] Mie Mie and
myself.　I had liked (*sic*) to have forgot Lady E. Forster,
*que l'on n'oublie pas souvent, dans cette partie au moins*; but
now *on sonne déja*; *le reste donc sera pour demain, et pour
quand j'aurai été l'autre côte de la Rivière*; so, for the
present, I wish you a good night, my dear Lady Carlisle.

*Tuesday morning, Isleworth.*—Now, to begin my letter
properly, and in course, it would be to say "Good
morrow" to you, or, as they say in Ireland, "Good
morrow morning" to you, my dear Madam.

I hastened my coming here lest they should be gone,
but they do not set out till after dinner.　Caroline is well
enough to take a much longer journey than from hence
to Cliveden.　I came with a commission from the Duke
to invite them to dinner, to meet the Princess Chatterriski,
whom I suppose you know ; I find that she is no favourite
of Lady C[aroline], nor is her friend D'Oraison of mine,
but he comes to.　The Duke left me to go and invite

---

[1] Thomas Townshend.

the Boufflers, but whether they will come or not I do not know.

Calonne would have entertained yesterday. You never in your life saw any man so inveterate as he was against M. de la Fayette, and, to say the truth, he had reason, if all was true which he imputed to him, as I believe it was. But what diverted me the most was, that Fayette had seriously proposed to make him, Calonne, King of Madagascar. Surely there never was, since the Earl of Warwick's time, such a king-maker. I would to God that he had accepted of the diadem, but then perhaps he would not have dined with us yesterday. *Il en contait à Madame la Duchesse*, and sat at dinner between her and Lady E. Forster, *avec qui je faisois la conversation;* the Duke over against us on the other side of the table, *comme la Statue dans le Festin de Pierre*, never changing a muscle of his face. The Marquis was above, and there *M<sup>e</sup> la Duchesse lui donna à dîner.* I was determined upon an audience, and found *l'heure du berger.* He received me *avec un sourire le plus gracieux du monde*, and I was obliged to present my address of compliments. But I think that the Nurse is a bad *physiognimiste* if she did not see that what I said, and what I thought, were not *d'accord.* He is like the Duke if he is like anything, but a more uninteresting countenance I never saw—fair, white, *tâté, sans charactère.* In short, *on a beau faire, on a beau dire.* If *un enfant ne vous tient d'une manière ou d'autre*, I cannot admire it as I am expected to do ; and what a difference that makes will be seen two months hence. *Toutes mes affections parlent due même principe.* The Duchess offended me much by coming with a *couronne civique*, which is a chaplet of oak leaves. In England they are a symbol of loyalty. *Il n'en [est] pas de même en France.* I asked if she wore it before the Queen ; I was told yes. *Je ne comprens rien à cela.*

The whole behaviour of the Queen, in her present wretched, humiliated state, is *touchante et intéressante au dernier point. Elle ne rit, que quand elle ne songe pas à ses malheurs.* At other times she is, as Polinitz says of K[ing]

James's Queen, when he saw her after the Revolution, *une Aréthuse.* M. le M[arquis] de la Fayette comes to the Tuilleries, and although he be really no more or less than the jailer, he is received with graciousness.

But now, *pour les Evangiles du jour.* I had a letter from Warner this morning before I left Richmond, dated last Thursday night. Your brother's courier did not, however, leave Paris till the morning of Friday. Warner's words are these :—" The courier goes to carry the news of the Decree, of fitting out 25 ships of the line, and adhering to the Family Compact in the defensive Articles, which looks so like a war that it frightens us with the apprehension of being sent packing home to you, or rather without packing."

If the consequence of a war is your brother's return to this country, I do not think it a misfortune to him, and I wish no other may happen to us, than the expense at which we must be to support one campaign against these United Powers. Still I am of opinion that peace will follow immediately these preparations. But Calonne alarmed me yesterday, when he said, that he thought that the National Assembly would draw them into a war with us. He had not then received his dispatches. I shall hear a great deal of it to-day, true or false, from D'Oraison.

Mrs. Bartho is already gone to Lady Lewisham. Caroline stayed to dine in town, and they returned here about six. I think that Mr. C[ampbell] seems to-day not determined to stay so long at Cliveden as he thought to do. I shall wish them to return, be it only that I may have the more to say to you, and the better security for my letters being well accepted.

I hope that George was amused at the York races. I have seen this morning in Lizy's letter that he was there. Vixen is sitting for his picture, and this is all the news of Isleworth. I may have more to tell Lord C[arlisle] when I write to him, which I shall do by the next post. My love to them all, you know whom I mean.

What does Lord C. mean by calling himself alone?

*Peut-on être mieux qu'au sein de sa famille?* That was part of an *ariette* which M. de la Fayette's music played the day the K[ing] went to the Hôtel de Ville, as I have been informed by a pamphlet, wrote to abuse Mr. Neckar, and which is incomparably well wrote. I will get it for George if he desires it, and will promise to read it. I am afraid that he is too much of [a] *Démocrate*, but as a lover of justice, and of mankind, and of order and good government, he would not be so long, *s'il vouloit se rendre à mes raisons ; mais il croit que je n'en ai pas, et que je me retranche à dire des invectives, sans avoir des argumens pour soutenir mon système ; en cela il se trompe.* God bless him ; *je l'aime de tout mon cœur, et je l'estime aussi, qui est encore davantage.*

[1790,] *Sept. 4, Saturday m[orning], Richmond.*— . . . My larder is rich from Mr. C[ampbell's] *chassé.* I had some game the day after the first hostilities against the partridges commenced. . . . Our foreign connections here increase ; le Comte de Suffren and his family are going to establish themselves here in a house above the Bridge, and on the banks of the River. He came to the Duke's [1] yesterday, where we dined, and stayed with us the whole evening. He is an *aristocrate*, and a great sufferer by the troubles in France, but he is a very sober, moderate man, and intelligent. The Duke liked his company very much.

I am loaded now with pamphlets upon this great and extraordinary event; some entertain me, some not. I like much what I have just been reading, which is the opinion of the Abbé Maury,[2] delivered in the National Assembly, upon the *exécutif* and *législatif* power, in regard to declaring war, and concluding treaties of commerce and alliance. There is a great deal of good sense in it, and comes the nearest to my own opinion of what has passed. I suppose that Lord C has read it. I hope that George

[1] Queensberry.
[2] Jean Siffrein Maury, abbé, the eloquent supporter of the monarchical cause.

will read it too.  If I was sure that the speech was not
at Castle H. I would transcribe some passages out of it,
*à sa considération.*

I desire very much to be of his mind about everything,
but, if he is a Republican, I have done with him.  If he
will in his Republican system throw in a little royal
authority as ballast, we shall soon come to an agreement.
I wish him to come *neuf* to all those great and important
questions, and examine them *sans l'esprit de système*,
without prejudice and strong inclination to be of either
side, but to investigate the truth, and adopt it.  *Il est
fait pour raisonner ; il commence être d'un âge où le jugement
acquerera tous les jours de la maturité.*  My love to him, I
beg.

I think Lady Derby mends in appearance ; the Duke
and I go often to her.  I would cross the water and make
the Duchess a visit, but that I think it right to forbear
going in a carriage as long as I can ; and then, perhaps,
I may go with safety to London, from time to time to
see Caroline, when she removes thither. . . .

[1790,] *September* 7, *Tuesday,* 8 *o'clock, Richmond.*—
. . . I was surprised in the evening with a visit from Mr.
Campbell.  We were *au dessert,* that is, the party which
dined here after they returned from Egham. . . .  His
visit put out of my head, in a minute, all the pretty
French phrases which I was brewing. . . .  Mr. C. stayed
to converse with the Welch heiress, to talk with M^e de
Choiseul upon Greece and the Archipele, and of his
uncle's *voyage pittoresque,* and he spoke a great while in
Italian with M^e la Comtesse de Suffren.  I long to hear,
as I shall this morning, his opinion of the party.  I asked
them [a] few questions about their day's sport ; it was a
novelty with which I know that they would be pleased.

So M^e de Choiseul has obtained leave of her husband, I
believe without much difficulty, to stay here one day
more.  I shall, for my part, make no efforts to detain
them.  M^e de R. has explained to me sufficiently *en quoi
consiste la mauvaise conduite du Marquis.*  But young

people *ne regardent que le surface*. The Duke did not return ; I believe that he dined and lay at Oatlands. His horse had a violent fall ; but I heard of no other event. I suppose he may have lost by that accident.

I know as yet no more of Mr. C[ampbell's] motions than that he and Lady C. go to town this morning, but return to dinner. We shall dine with them, when these Races are over ; they finish to-morrow.

I sat yesterday morning a great while with the Fish's friend, M⁰ de Roncherolles. *Entre nous*, I like her much more than any of the whole set. She has neither *du brillant dans son esprit, ni une infinité de grace dans ses manières, je l'avoue, mais, elle est sans prétensions, et avec beaucoup de bon sens, même de la solidité, et elle est instruite suffisamment.* Mr. Walpole *ne lui donne pas la préférence.* He must have something *de l'esprit de l'Académie*, &c., something of a *charactère marqué. Je ne cherche rien de tout cela; je suis content du naturel, et de trouver une personne raisonnable, honnête, et de bonne conversation.* She is going to-day for a week or more to Lady Spencer's at St. Alban's. I am sure that it is not *there, que je trouverois cette simplicité qui me plaît.* But *this*, till it is time to embark for Isleworth, when I shall have something more interesting to talk of than the perfections of M⁰ de Roncherolles. . . .

[1790, Nov. ?] Thursday, Richmond.—You are so good, when you do not see me or hear of me, to be desirous of having some information of my state of health and existence. Now I must let you know that I have at this moment every distress, negative and positive, that I can have, *et les voici.* My negative one is, being for the moment in an impossibility of going to town to see you, Caroline, and the *bambino*, and that is enough, for it would be a great pleasure to me, as you must imagine. Then, I am, in a manner, here with one single servant. Pierre has left this house to go to his own, where he is very well looked after by his wife, and is [as] comfortably lodged as it is possible to be ; but he is, as Mr. Dundas tells me, in a very perilous situation, and yet, by excessive care, may recover.

He has been my doctor lately instead of his own, and given me, daily, powders which he said were the bark, and which I was to take. No such thing; they were powders of a different sort, which, it is fortunate, have done me no mischief. They were in the drawer, and so brought to me as bark. Dundas thought I neglected myself, and rejected the prescription. I maintained that I had missed taking the bark but one day. He knew the contrary from his shop book, and to-day only the mystery was cleared up.

My next grievance is, that *je péris de froid ; j'en suis pénétré au pied de la lettre*, and the reason is plain, but why I did not discover it myself is hardly to be conceived. I have no clothes ; my stockings are of a fine thin thread, half of them full of holes ; I have no flannel waistcoat, which everybody else wears ; in short, I have been shivering in the warmest room *sans sçavoir pourquoi*. But yesterday there was a committee at the Duke's upon my drapery, and to-day a tailor is sent for. I am to be flannelled and cottoned, and kept alive if possible ; but if that cannot be done, I must be embalmed, with my face, mummy like, only bare, to converse through my cerements.

Then, my other footman, the Bruiser, is that, and all things bad besides ; he is not an hour in the day at home, and is gaming at alehouses till 12 at night ; so the moment that I can get any servant that is tolerable to supply his place I shall send him out of the house, *sans autre forme de procès* ; but, till he is gone, my whole family lives in terror of him.

It is amazing to what a degree I am become helpless ; nothing can account for it but extreme dotage, or extreme infancy. I wish Barthow had left Lady Caroline, and was here only to dress me in warmer clothes, but she goes from here, I hear, to Lady Ailesford, so that I must not think of lying in and being nursed for some time. . . .

[1790,] *Dec. 8, Wednesday, Richmond.*—You have been

at C[astle] H[oward] ever since Monday sevennight, and
not one single word have you received from your humble
slave and beadsman. . . . Here is now come a snip-snap
letter of reproach from Lady Ossory for not having
answered her letter of compliments upon Lady C[aroline's]
delivery. I received yours on Sunday. That was no
post day, so I resolved to answer it in Berkley Square on
Monday. But I did not set out till three o'clock, lost all
the fine part of the morning, and did not get to town till
five in the afternoon—dragged for two hours, two whole
hours, through mud, and cold, and mist, till I was perish-
ing ; so that when I had eat some dinner I was fit for
nothing but to go to bed, and therefore did not go to
Berkley Square till yesterday at noon. . . . I saw
Caroline and her *bambino*. . . . The christening is to be,
as I understand, to-morrow. I hope in God that I shall
be well enough to assist, and name the child, and eat cake,
and go through all the functions of a good gossip. If I
am obliged to give up that which seems to have been my
vocation, *c'est fait de moi* ; I must declare myself good for
nothing. I carried yesterday the regalia. The cup has
been new boiled, and looks quite royal.

Sir L. Pepys was with me in the morning, and thought
my pulse very quiet, which could only have been from the
fatigue of the day before—*juste Dieu !* fatigue, of going
8 or 9 miles, my legs on the foreseat, and reposing my
head on Jones's shoulder. The Duke would make her
go, and everybody. He thinks that I am now the most
helpless creature in the world, when, from infirmity, I
want ten times more aid than I ever did. Sir Lucas
pronounced no immediate end of myself, but that I should
continue to bark, with hemlock. I'll do anything for some
time longer, but my patience will, I see, after a certain
time, be exhausted. As to poor Pierre, it is over with
him. Sir Lucas says the disorder is past all remedy. This
is a most distressful story to me, and how to supply his
place I do not know.

With this letter a correspondence, unique and delightful, extending over many years, ends. At its close we may well recall Lord Carlisle's words written fourteen years before, " I shall always be grateful to fortune," he said, ". . . for having linked me in so close a friendship with yourself, in spite of disparity of years and pursuits."

Selwyn returned to London shortly before Christmas, and died on the 25th of January, 1791. On this very day Walpole, with a touching simplicity and truth, wrote to Miss Berry, " I am on the point of losing, or have lost, my oldest acquaintance and friend, George Selwyn, who was yesterday at the extremity. These misfortunes, tho' they can be so but for a short time, are very sensible to the old ; but him I really loved not only for his infinite wit, but for a thousand good qualities."

THE END.

# INDEX

"Baptist," the, *see* Henry St. John
Barbot's Lottery, 88
Barker, Mr., 63, 117, 162
Barrington, Lord, 40 *note*, 42, 78
Barry, Mme. du, "Anecdotes of," 98
Barry, Richard, sixth Earl of Barrymore, 40 *note*
Barry, Richard, seventh Earl of Barrymore, 272 *note*
Barry, Mr., 131, 133, 274
Barrymore, Lady, 63
Barrymore, Lord, *see* Barry
Barth, Mrs., 280
Basilico, 139
Bath, 6, 14, 67 *note*, 68, 109
Beauchamp, Lord, 34 *note*, 76, 114
Beauclerk, Topham, 55 ; married to Lady Bolingbroke, 35
Beaufort, Duke of, 122
Beckford, Alderman, 51 *note*, 63, 187
Beckford, William, son of Alderman Beckford, author and collector, 187 *note*
Bedford, fourth Duke of, 6, 42 *note*, 171 *note*
Bedford, fifth Duke of, 183 *note*, 207, 233
Bedford, Duchess of, 43 *note*, 141, 152, 187, 205, 218
Bedford faction, 40 *note*
Bedford House, 149 *note* ; parties at, 150, 152
Belgiojoso, 154, 156, 170, 182
Berkeley, Lord, 217
Berry, Agnes, 54
Berry, Mary, 54
Bertie, Lord, 187
Bessborough, Lord, 92, 129
"Betty, Lady," *see* Howard, Lady Elizabeth
Biron, Duchesse de, 264
Biron, Admiral, *see* Byron
Biron, Mrs., 152
Biron, Duc de, 119 *note*
Blake, Miss, 39, 44, 47, 56, 62 *note*

Blake, Mr., 62
Blake, Mrs., 39
Blandford, Lord, 171
Blaquiere, Sir John, 80
Blenheim, 145
Bloomsbury Gang, 43
Bohn, Comte de, 151
Boisgelin, Comte de, 271 *note*
Bolingbroke, Lady, 34 *note*, 37, 39, 47
Bolingbroke, Lord "Bully," 35, 36 *note*, 39, 41, 52, 55, 58, 73, 103, 105, 106, 108, 206
Boon, Charles, 52
Boothby, Mrs., 78
Boothby, Sir Brooke, 63, 79 *note*, 117, 125, 143, 162, 172, 177, 204, 233
Boston, Lady, 128
Boston, Frederick, second Baron, 127 *note*
Bouverie, Mr., 171
Bouverie, Mrs., 249 *note*
Boufflers, Comtesse de, 261 *note*, 262, 263, 264 ; Queen of the émigrés, 270 ; at Richmond, 271, 277, 278, 279
Boufflers, Emilié, Comtesse de, 261 *note*, 263 ; at Richmond, 271
Brereton, Col., 36 *note*, 44
Bristol, Earl of, 111
Brodrick (Broderick), Colonel Henry, 147, 149, 174
Brooke, Earl of, 232
Brooks, Mr., 60, 103, 134, 136
Brooks's Club, politics and gambling at, 13, 181, 182 ; fortunes lost at, 18 ; card-room at, 20, 175 ; macaronis at, 44 ; Fox and Fitzpatrick at, 137, 139, 140, 141, 171 ; gossip at, 156 ; Selwyn at, 158 ; American question discussed at, 164 ; supper at, 170, 175 ; ill attended, 177 ; political discussion at, 188, 189 ; Weltzie's in opposition to, 190 ; Selwyn